THE
KILLING
ROOM

THE KiLLING ROOM

Richard Montanari

WILLIAM HEINEMANN: LONDON

Published by William Heinemann 2012

2 4 6 8 10 9 7 5 3 1

First published in Great Britain in 2012 by
William Heinemann
Random House, 20 Vauxhall Bridge Road,
London SW1V 2SA

www.randomhouse.co.uk

Addresses for companies within The Random House Group Limited can be
found at: www.randomhouse.co.uk/offices.htm

The Random House Group Limited Reg. No. 954009

A CIP catalogue record for this book
is available from the British Library

HB ISBN 9780434018932
TPB ISBN 9780434018949

The Random House Group Limited supports The Forest Stewardship Council
(FSC®), the leading international forest certification organisation. Our books
carrying the FSC label are printed on FSC® certified paper. FSC is the only forest
certification scheme endorsed by the leading environmental organisations, including
Greenpeace. Our paper procurement policy can be found at
www.randomhouse.co.uk/environment

Typeset in Janson Text by Palimpsest Book Production Limited,
Falkirk, Stirlingshire
Printed and bound by
CPI Group (UK) Ltd, Croydon, CR0 4YY

'*A hard heart shall fear evil at the last:*
and he that loveth danger shall perish in it'

– *ECCLESIASTICUS, 3:27*

For Nicoletta

WHEN YOU THINK ABOUT THAT NIGHT, IN THOSE MERCIFULLY rare moments when the weight of your sins becomes unbearable and your heart wants to hide from the light, the images rush by in a hellish roar, as if you had seen and heard it all from a passing train, as if you were just an observer to the horrors that took place in that dank, bloody basement, and not a participant in an act that left two people dead.

When you think about that night, you know the full debt of the living.

The church has only three other penitents at this young hour: an elderly man in a creased gray suit sitting in the first pew, his grocery bag waiting patiently in the aisle beside him; a couple in their early-twenties, both kneeling, eyes closed, hands clasped in supplication, the aura of grief and loss almost visible around them.

You've rehearsed the story so many times it has begun to resemble a fable, and you don't want to tell it that way. It was a brutal nightmare, and now that you know you are going to say the words aloud for the first time you feel something unmoor inside you.

You hold a rosary, not praying, rolling the beads instead as an affectation, something to do with your hands while waiting, something to keep your hands from trembling.

Thirty years.

How has thirty years passed in a single sunset?

You are late middle-aged now, your nest long empty, your friends dead or dying, the love of your life three cold winters in the ground.

Perhaps this will be the day of your confession, your absolution, a day that will return you to a time when all things were still possible, a time when you were a respected member of the Philadelphia Police Department, and the world had not yet become a living hell.

ONE

THE CHILDREN
OF DISOBEDIENCE

'And the smoke of the incense,
which came with the prayers of the saints,
ascended up before God out of the angel's hand.'

– *REVELATION, 8:4*

WHEN SHE WAS A YOUNG GIRL, BEFORE THE NIGHT EMBRACED HER WITH *its great black wings, and blood became her sacramental wine, she was, in every way, a child of light. To those who knew her in those years she seemed a studious girl, quiet and polite, given to watching clouds for hours on end, oblivious, as only the very young can be, to the crushing poverty that surrounded her, the chains that had enslaved her kind for five generations.*

She was six years old before she wore a pair of shoes she did not share. She was eight before she buttoned a dress someone had not stained before her.

For the longest time she lived inside the high stone walls of her mind, a place where there were no shadows, no demons.

In her thirteenth year, on a night when the candles fell cold and the moon was not to be found, she met the darkness for the first time. Not the darkness that follows day, descending upon the earth in a deep violet blush, but rather that which dwells within men, men who travel the hardpan roads, gathering to them the mad, the fallen, the corrupt of heart, their deeds the silt of backwater lore. On that night a seed was sown in her body, her spirit.

Now, these many years later, in this place of misery and wretchedness, in this house of seven churches, she knows she belongs.

There are no angels here.

The devil walks these streets. She knows him well – his face, his touch, his scent – because in her thirteenth year, when God turned his head, it was to the devil she was given.

SHE HAD WATCHED THE *young man for more than a week, having first spotted him on Broad Street near the Market East station, a gaunt figure etched on a granite wall. He was not an aggressive panhandler – indeed, his nearly skeletal body and spectral presence would not have presented much of a threat to anyone – but was instead a man reduced to mumbling incoherently to passersby, commuters rushing to and from the station. Twice he had been moved along by police officers, offering no resistance or response. His spirit, it seemed, had long ago been purloined by his addictions, the siren call of the streets.*

On most nights, after the evening rush hour, he would walk Market Street toward the Delaware River, toward Old City, stopping those who looked like an easy mark, cadging the occasional handful of coins, grubbing the infrequent cigarette.

She always followed him at a safe distance. Like most of his breed he went unnoticed, except to those like him, or those who would use him. On those rare occasions when he found a homeless shelter with room, he would stay the night, but would always take up position outside the Market East station by 6:30 a.m., beginning his cycle of despair and degradation all over again.

Once she followed him into a convenience store on Third Street, and watched as he pocketed high-sugar foods – honey buns, Ding Dongs, TastyKakes – all with one yellowed eye on the convex mirrors at the end of the aisle. She watched him wolf down the food in a nearby alley, only to throw it all up moments later.

On this day, when temperatures are predicted to drop below zero, she knows it is time.

BUNDLED IN FOUR THIN *sweaters and a pea coat ripped at both shoulder seams, the young man stands shivering in a doorway on Eighth Street near Walnut.*

She approaches him, stopping a few feet away, still mostly in shadow.

He looks up. In his watery eyes she sees herself, and knows the spirit is stirring.

'Spare change?' he asks.

It is as if she can hear the bones clattering in his chest.

He is in his twenties, but the skin around his eyes is purplish and sallow, the stubble on his face already gray. His hair is greasy beneath his watch cap. His fingernails are bitten raw. Blisters bubble on the back of his hands.

She remains in shadow, holds out a gloved hand. At first the young man is skeptical, but when she steps into the light, and he sees her eyes for the first time, he knows. He takes her hand as a hungry man would accept a crust of bread.

'Do you remember your promise?' she asks.

He hesitates before answering. They always do. In this moment she can all but hear the wheels turning, the fevered reasoning in his mind. In the end they remember, because this is the one vow they all know will one day be recalled. A single tear rivers down his scalded cheek.

'Yes.'

She glances down, notices a dark stain blossoming on the front of his trousers. He is wetting himself. She has seen this before, too. The release.

'Come with me,' she says. 'I will show you what you need to do.'

The young man steps forward on unsteady legs. She helps him. He seems to possess no weight at all, as if he were sculpted of steam.

At the mouth of the alley she stops, turns the young man to face her fully. 'He will need to hear your words. Your exact *words.'*

His lips begin to tremble. 'Can't I tell just you instead?'

'No,' she says. 'Your contract was with him, not me.'

The young man wipes his eyes with the back of his hand. 'Then he is real after all.'

'Oh, my, yes.' She points to the dark niche at the end of the alley. 'Would you meet him now?'

The young man shakes his head. 'No. I'm afraid.'

She meets his gaze in silence. A few moments pass.

'May I ask a question?'

'Of course,' she says.

He takes a deep breath, exhales. His breath is warm and vaporous and sour. 'What do I call you?'

There are many answers to this. At one time she would have been called Magdalene. At another, Babylon. At one time, indeed, Legion.

Instead of answering the question she takes his arm. She thinks about the approaching days, the end days, and what they are about to do. Ephesus, Smyrna, Pergamos. There is an order to it all. If there was no order she would surely go mad, and then she would live among the low people: the wicked, the dispossessed, the forsaken.

They dissolve into the city, followed by a long and solitary shadow. Around them the winter winds swirl, but she no longer feels the cold.

It has begun.

Seed, flesh, bone, dust.

Order.

TWO

T HE KID LOOKED DOOMED.

Detective Kevin Francis Byrne had seen it many times before – the blank stare, the knotted shoulders, the hands loosely held, ready to become fists at the slightest provocation. The tension, Byrne knew, was institutional, a twisted wire in the middle of the back that never uncoiled, never relented. Sadness haunted the eyes. Fear was carried on the shoulders.

For this kid, and the millions like him, there were enemies around every corner, dangers in every noise, whispers in the night that said:

What's mine is mine, what's yours is mine – you just don't know it yet.

The boy was eleven, but his eyes were an old man's eyes. He wore a dark blue hoodie, frayed at the cuffs, low-slung jeans, at least two fads out of date. His rust-colored Timberlands were scuffed and rutted, too large for his feet. Byrne noticed that the boots were tied with different type laces; rawhide on one boot, nylon on the other. He wondered if this was a fashion statement, or done out of necessity. The kid leaned against the dirty red brick wall, waiting, watching, another ghost haunting the city of Philadelphia.

As Byrne crossed Twelfth Street, bunching his collar to the raw February wind, he considered what he was about to do. He had recently signed up for a mentoring program called Philly Brothers, a group loosely patterned on Big Brothers Big Sisters. This was his first meeting with the boy.

In his time on the force Kevin Byrne had taken down some of the darkest souls ever to walk the streets of his city, but this encounter scared the hell out of him. And he knew why. This was more than just a man reaching out to an at-risk kid. Much more.

'Are you Gabriel?' Byrne asked. He had a picture of the boy in his jacket pocket, a school photo from two years earlier. He decided not to take it out. If he did it would probably only embarrass the kid.

As he got closer Byrne noticed that whatever tension was in the boy's shoulders ratcheted up a notch. The kid raised his eyes, but did not look into Byrne's eyes. He aimed his gaze, instead, to a place somewhere in the middle of Byrne's forehead. It was an old salesman's trick, and Byrne wondered where this kid had picked it up, or if he even knew he was doing it.

'They call me G-Flash,' the boy said softly, shifting his weight from one foot to the other, saying this as if it were common knowledge.

'All right. G-Flash it is,' Byrne said. 'My name is Kevin. I'm your Philly—'

'*Brother*,' the kid said with a scowl. He put his hands into the pockets of the hoodie, probably to ward off any kind of handshake. Byrne found his own hand suspended in space, halfway between himself and the kid, and suddenly didn't know what to do with it.

'I already *had* a brother,' the kid added, almost in a whisper.

Byrne rocked back on his heels, looked around, at the moment lost for words. 'You made it here okay on the bus?' he finally asked.

The kid smirked. 'The bus go where the bus go. I was just on it, right? Not like I'm driving it.'

Before Byrne could respond, a PPD sector car, parked in front of Maggiano's, a half-block away, fired up its lights and siren, taking off on a call. The only two people standing near the doors of Reading Terminal Market who didn't look up were Byrne and the kid. Sirens were a big part of both their lives.

Byrne glanced at his watch, even though he knew exactly what time it was. 'So, do you want to get some lunch?'

The kid shrugged.

'What do you like to eat?' Byrne asked.

Another shrug. Byrne had to do a quick remodeling of his own attitude. Usually, when he encountered this kind of wall, it was with a suspect. In those instances his inclination was to kick the wall, as well as the suspect, to the ground. This was different.

'Chinese, KFC, hoagies?' Byrne continued.

The kid looked back over his shoulder, his level of boredom nearing the red line. 'They a'ight, I guess.'

'What about roast pork?' Byrne asked. 'You like roast pork?'

Byrne saw the slightest upturn of one corner of the kid's mouth. Nothing close to a smile. God forbid. The kid liked roast pork.

'C'mon,' Byrne said, reaching for the door handle. 'They have the best roast pork sandwiches in the city in here.'

'I ain't got no money.'

'That's all right. My treat.'

The kid kicked at an imaginary pebble. 'I don't want you buying me *nothin*.'

Byrne held the door open for a few seconds, letting two women in. Then two more. This was getting awkward. 'Tell you what, I'll buy us lunch today. If we like each other – and there's no guarantee of that, believe me, I don't like too many people – then the next time we get together you can buy *me* lunch. If not, I'll send you a bill for half.'

The kid almost smiled again. To cover it, he looked up Filbert Street, making Byrne work. The moment drew out, but Byrne was ready for it this time. The kid had no idea who he was dealing with. Kevin Byrne had spent the past twenty years of his life as a homicide detective, at least half of that on stakeouts. He could outlast a cement block.

'A'ight,' the kid finally said. 'Whatever. Cold out here anyway.'

And with that Gabriel 'G-Flash' Hightower rolled through the door, into Reading Terminal Market.

Detective Kevin Byrne followed.

*

As BYRNE AND THE kid waited in line at DiNic's neither of them spoke. Despite the cacophony of sounds – the half-dozen languages, the rattle of plates, the *swish* of slicing machines, the steel spatulas scraping across grills – the silence between Gabriel and himself was profound. Byrne had no idea what to say. His own daughter Colleen, who was now in her first year at Gallaudet University, had grown up with so many advantages this kid had not. If you could call having a father like Kevin Byrne an advantage. Still, despite being deaf from birth, Colleen had flourished.

The kid standing next to him, hands still in his pockets, steely glare in place, had grown up in hell.

Byrne knew that Gabriel's father had never been in the picture, and that his mother had died when the boy was three. Tanya Wilkins was a prostitute and a drug addict, and had frozen to death one frigid January night, passed out in an alley in Grays Ferry. Gabriel's only brother, Terrell, committed suicide two years ago.

Since then, Gabriel rattled from one foster home to another. He'd had a few minor scrapes with the law, mostly shoplifting, but there was no doubt which way he was headed.

When they got to the counter Byrne ordered them a full sandwich each. The sandwiches from DiNic's were so big that Byrne had only finished one by himself on a handful of occasions, but he ordered them one each anyway, instantly regretting it, acknowledging that he was trying to show off.

The kid's eyes got wide when he saw that the huge sandwich was all for him – not to mention the additional bag of chips and a soda – but he went back to his pre-teen too cool for school posturing just as quickly.

They found a table, sat down, spread out, dug in.

As they ate in silence, Byrne tried to think of some kind of conversation with which to engage the kid. He imagined sports would be a safe topic. Both the Flyers and the Sixers were playing. Instead, he remained silent.

Ten minutes later he looked at Gabriel, who was already more than half done. Byrne had to wonder when the last time was the kid had eaten.

'Good sandwich, huh?' he asked.

The kid shrugged. Byrne figured he was at that stage. Byrne had been a shrugger at around thirteen or fourteen, everything posed to him a conundrum, every question an interrogation. Instead of exposing his ignorance on a subject, like most young teenagers and pre-teens, he'd simply feign indifference with a shrug. Times were different now. Eleven, it seemed, was the new fourteen. Hell, eleven was probably the new *eighteen*.

As they finished their sandwiches Gabriel pushed up the sleeves on his hoodie. Despite Byrne's best intentions he scanned the kid's arms, hands, neck, looking for tattoos or burn marks or wounds that might have meant an initiation into a gang. If ever there was a kid ripe for recruitment, it was Gabriel Hightower.

Byrne saw nothing. He couldn't decide if this meant the kid didn't need someone like him in his life, or just the opposite: that this was a pivotal time, a time when Gabriel might need him the most.

WHEN THEY FINISHED THEY sat in a fresh silence, one that preceded the end of their visit. Byrne looked down at the table, and there saw a small, beautifully folded paper boat. Gabriel had idly crafted it out of the paper in which the sandwiches were wrapped.

'Can I take a look at that?' Byrne asked.

The kid nudged it closer with a forefinger.

Byrne picked it up. The folds were precise and elegant. It was clearly not the first time Gabriel had made something like this. 'This is pretty cool.'

'Called origami,' Gabriel said. 'Chinese or something.'

'You have a real talent,' Byrne said. 'I mean, this is *really* good.'

One more shrug. Byrne wondered what the world record was.

WHEN THEY STEPPED OUT onto the street the lunchtime crowd had thinned. Byrne had the rest of the day off, and was going to suggest doing something else – a trip to the mall maybe, or a tour of the Roundhouse – but he figured the kid had probably had enough of him for a first date.

'Come on,' Byrne said. 'I'll give you a ride home.'

The kid took a half-step away. 'I got bus money.'

'I'm going that way anyway,' Byrne lied. 'It's really no big deal.'

The kid started rooting around in his pocket for coins.

'I don't drive a police car, you know,' Byrne said. 'It's just a shitty old Taurus with bad shocks and a worse radio.'

The kid smiled at the word *shitty*. Byrne took out his keys.

'Come on. Save the bus money.'

Byrne grabbed the lead, walked across the street, willing himself not to turn around to see if Gabriel was following.

About a block up Filbert he caught sight of a small shadow coming up next to him.

THE GROUP HOME WHERE Gabriel Hightower lived was on Indiana Avenue between Third and Fourth Streets, deep into a blighted area of North Philly called the Badlands. Byrne took Third Street north and, during the entire ride, neither of them said a word. When Byrne turned onto Indiana Gabriel said, 'This is cool right here.'

The group home was nearly a block away.

'I'll take you all the way. It's not a problem.'

The kid didn't say anything. Byrne acquiesced and pulled over. They were now a half block from one of the most infamous drug corners in the city. It didn't take Byrne long to spot two young men scouting the area for 5-0. He caught the eye of one hard-looking kid of about eighteen, trying his best to look inconspicuous. Byrne threw the look back until the kid looked away. The spotter took out a cell and sauntered in the other direction. Byrne had clearly been made. He put the Taurus in park, kept the engine running.

'Okay, G-Flash,' he said. As he said this he looked over, saw Gabriel roll his eyes, shake his head. Byrne understood. The only thing worse than hanging out with an old white guy – and an old white *cop* to boot – was having that old white guy say your street name out loud.

'Just call me Gabriel, okay?'

'You got it,' Byrne said. They went quiet. Byrne got the feeling that, if he didn't say something soon, they would sit there for the rest of the day. 'Well, we're supposed to give this three times, see what's what. You think you might want to hang out again?'

Instead of answering, Gabriel stared at his hands.

Byrne decided to give the kid an exit line, make it easy on him. 'Tell you what. I'll give you a call in the next few weeks, and we can see where we are then. No pressure one way or the other. Deal?'

Byrne stuck out his hand. He put it right in front of Gabriel, so the kid was either going to shake hands, or disrespect Byrne big time. The kid hesitated for a few moments, then put his hand in Byrne's. It wasn't really a handshake, but more the *idea* of a handshake. After a second or two Gabriel tossed up his hood, opened the door, and got out. Before he closed the door he turned back, looked at Byrne with his young old eyes, and said: 'John's is good, too.'

Byrne had no idea what the boy was talking about. *Who is John?* Then it registered. He was talking about John's Roast Pork.

'John's? You mean over on Snyder?'

The kid nodded.

'That's true,' Byrne said. 'John's *is* good. We can go there some time if you want.'

Gabriel started to close the car door, stopped, thought for a moment. He leaned in, as if to share some kind of secret. Byrne found that he was holding his breath. He leaned forward, too.

'I know you know about me,' Gabriel said.

'Know what about you?'

'*Man.*' Gabriel shook his head. 'White people always got a piece of paper when they talk to me. Social workers, counselors, teachers, people who work for the county. Foster-home people. They all look at that piece of paper, *then* they talk to me. Gotta be *something* on there, right?'

'Yeah,' Byrne said, keeping his smile in check. 'I guess I know a little bit.'

'Well, there's one thing you gotta know, something that ain't on that piece of paper.'

'What's that?'

'He didn't bang.'

'What do you mean?' Byrne asked. '*Who* didn't bang?'

Gabriel looked up and down the street, behind, watching his back. 'My brother Terrell,' he said. 'Terrell didn't bang like they say.'

A few seconds later Gabriel closed the car door and quickly cut across a snow-covered vacant lot, gracefully skirting a discarded refrigerator and a small pile of demolished concrete blocks. Soon, all Byrne could see was the top of the boy's faded hoodie, and then Gabriel Hightower was gone.

BYRNE MADE HIMSELF A microwave meal for dinner – some sort of too-sweet chicken and limp snow pea pods – then, finding himself restless, went out. He stopped by the American Pub in the Centre Square Building, across from City Hall. He always felt completely dislocated on his days off. Whenever he pulled seven or eight tours in a row, including the inevitable overtime the job of being a homicide detective in Philadelphia demanded, he often found himself daydreaming of what he would do on his day off. Sleep in, catch up on the DVDs he found himself renting but never watching, actually *doing* laundry. When it came time to do these things he always found himself twitchy, wondering about lab results, ballistic reports, whether some witness had come forward in a current case, anxious to get back into the harness, compelled to be in motion, to pursue.

He was loath to admit it, but his job was his life. If you opened a vein, Kevin Byrne would run blue.

He left the pub around 11.30. At the corner of Pine and Fifth Streets, instead of heading home, he headed north.

BYRNE HAD CALLED THE office earlier in the evening and gotten a few more details on exactly what had happened to Terrell Hightower.

After Tanya Wilkins's death, Gabriel and his brother – both of whom had been adopted by Tanya's third husband, Randall Hightower, himself killed in a high-speed chase with the PPD – were put into two different foster homes. By all accounts, Terrell Hightower was a good student at Central High, a tense, fidgety kid who came up at a time when there was no such thing as ADD, at least not in the inner city, a time when kids who tapped their feet or banged their pencils on their desks or acted out in any way, were sent to the office for being a disruptive influence.

When he was fifteen, Terrell found an outlet for all that nervous energy. His outlet was track and field. With hardly a single season of training under his belt he became a holy terror in the 100- and 200-meter events, taking all-city in his sophomore year and leading his team to the state finals as a junior. Scouts came from as far away as UCLA.

One night, while Terrell was sweeping up at his part-time job at an auto body shop on Frankford, two men entered. They fired six bullets into the shop's owner, James DuBois, two into Terrell's stomach. DuBois was DOA; Terrell was rushed to Jefferson Hospital where, within four hours, he was listed in stable condition.

Nothing of value was stolen.

Police investigated the case, but neighbors, as expected, saw nothing, heard nothing. Another phantom killer in the city of Philadelphia. Word on the street was that a North Philly drug dealer named DeRon Wilson had done it as a payback to Terrell because Terrell had disrespected Wilson by not joining the gang.

A week later Terrell Hightower was released from Jefferson Hospital in a wheelchair. He went back to school, but his heart was no longer in his studies, as his legs were no longer able to carry him to victory on the track. He eventually walked again, with a cane, but his dreams of an athletic scholarship vaporized. After high school Terrell worked briefly as a mechanic in Camden, but the jobs didn't last. He went from there to minimum-wage jobs, to disability, to the pipe.

Ten minutes into the day that would be his nineteenth birthday Terrell Hightower put the barrel of a 9mm pistol against the soft palate in his mouth and pulled the trigger. Around his neck were two dozen ribbons he had won on the tracks of southeastern Pennsylvania.

It was with these images in mind that Kevin Byrne pulled over near the corner of Third and Indiana. He knew he could be seen from any number of vantage points, had already been spotted. He wanted to be seen.

Byrne reached into the glove compartment, took out a cold Colt .38 revolver. He checked the cylinder, snapped it back, thinking:

In this city, any city, you are the hunter, or you are food.

Byrne put the weapon on the seat next to him, six words stalking the corners of his mind:

Terrell didn't bang like they say.

THREE

AS AN ICY DRAFT KNIFES ACROSS THE BASEMENT, THE YOUNG MAN SITS RIGIDLY on a wooden chair. He is naked: Adam banished to this bleak and frigid garden. There are myriad whispers here, the last pleadings of the faithless.

He has been here one full day.

She looks at him, sees the bones beneath his skin. This is a moment for which she has waited all her days. In her fingertips now lives an ancient magic, a power that gives her dominion over the thieves, the fornicators, the usurers.

'It is time,' she says.

The young man begins to cry.

'You must tell him what you said. Word for word. I want you to think carefully. It is very important.'

'I . . . I don't remember,' he says.

She steps forward, lifts his chin, looks into his eyes. 'Do you want me to tell you what you said?'

The young man nods. 'Yes.'

'You said: 'I would do anything not to get AIDS. I would even sell my soul to the devil.'

The young man does not respond to this. No response was expected. He glances at the opening into the other room. 'I can't look at him. When it happens, I can't look at him.'

She removes her coat, folds it gently onto the altar cloth on the floor.

'*Your name has meaning in the Bible,*' *she says.* '*Did you know that?*'
He shakes his head. '*No.*'

'*Your name means "God is my judge."*' *She reaches into her bag, removes the hypodermic, prepares it.* '*According to the Word, Daniel was brought to Babylon. It is said he could interpret dreams.*'

Seconds later, as the first drop of blood falls, as it did that terrible day on Calvary, she knows that the screams of the children of disobedience will soon fill the city.

All contracts are due.

The devil has returned to Philadelphia.

FOUR

GET IT TOGETHER, JESS. IF YOU DON'T, YOU'RE GOING TO DIE RIGHT HERE,
right now.

Detective Jessica Balzano looked up. The mass of humanity that
stood no more than ten feet away from her had the purest form of
evil in its eyes she had ever seen. And she had seen a lot. In her time
in the Philadelphia Police Department she had squared off with all
types of miscreants, deviants, criminals and gangsters, had gone toe
to toe with men almost double her weight. She had always come out
on top.

How? A combination of things. Flexibility, speed, excellent peripheral vision, an innate ability to sense the next move. These things had
served her well on the streets, in uniform, and in the Homicide Unit.

But not today. If she didn't get her shit together, and get it together
quickly, she was dead.

The bell rang. 'Let's go,' Joe said. 'Give me two hard minutes.'

Jessica was in the ring at the Joe Hand Boxing Gym on North
Third, stepping into the third round of a three-round sparring session.
She was in training for an upcoming exhibition bout for the Police
Athletic League annual boxing tournament.

Her opponent this day was a young woman named Valentine
Rhames, a nineteen year old who boxed out of the Rock Ministry
Boxing Club on Kensington Avenue.

Jessica was no expert, but she figured girls named Valentine weren't supposed to have fourteen inch biceps and shoulders like Sasquatch. Not to mention fists the size of canned hams. The kid was built like *Ving* Rhames.

The upcoming event was for charity, and nobody was supposed to get hurt, but as the sound of the bell ringing in round three began to fade, and Valentine stormed across the ring, it appeared that the young woman had not gotten the memo.

Jessica sidestepped the onslaught with ease, and even though her headgear cut down on her peripheral vision, she was able to land a glancing right hand to the side of Valentine's head. An illegal blow, technically speaking, but Jessica intended to worry about that at some point in the future.

Two minutes later the bell rang again. Jessica was drenched in sweat, hurting all over. Her opponent bounced across the ring, fresh as a daisy, put her arms around Jessica. Valentine Rhames stepped back, and delivered the knockout blow.

'Thanks for the workout, ma'am.'

Ma'am.

Jessica wanted to drop the kid like a cheap prom dress, but remembered she'd just had the opportunity to do so and failed miserably.

JESSICA AND VINCENT BALZANO spent the first eight years of their marriage with one child, and for a long time Jessica had all but believed that this single blessing would be their only one.

For three years they tried mightily to conceive, consulting with their family physician many times, reading just about every book on the subject, stopping just short of visiting a fertility specialist.

Then, last year, a miracle happened. A two-year-old boy named Carlos came into their lives. They adopted him and life began anew.

To Jessica's amazement, having a second child did not double the responsibility of being a mother. Somehow that responsibility increased four fold. Somehow it was four times more work, took four times the planning, attention, caution. Jessica still thought about having another baby, but the past year had made her second guess herself in this area.

She had grown up in a small family – by South Philly Italian Catholic standards anyway – with just herself and her brother Michael, so a boy and a girl, a few years apart, was just fine.

Still, she wanted to have another child.

A year earlier they moved from Lexington Park, in the northeast section of the city, back to South Philadelphia, just a few blocks from where Jessica was raised. The advantages were many – they were just a block from Sophie's school, Sacred Heart of Jesus, and not far from the Italian Market. There was bread from Sarcone's, *sfogliatelle* and cannoli from Termini's, cheese from DiBruno's.

This morning, as Jessica put the cereal bowls on the table, her husband Vincent came breezing through the kitchen. In a flash he had his coffee poured into his travel mug, a power bar in hand, his coat on. He gave Jessica a kiss on the cheek, said 'Love you, babe', and was out the door.

Jessica sipped her coffee, looked out the window. As she watched her husband cross the street, and get into his prized, restored TransAm, she considered just how much buckshot was loaded in that *love you, babe*. On the surface, it meant he loved her, and she could never hear those words enough. But the rest of the load meant: for this little show of affection *you* get to make breakfast, dress both kids, make their lunches, close up the house, get them to school and pre-school, then get to work on time, doing a job that is at least as hard – the case could be made that it was harder – as mine.

Love you, babe.

Vincent Balzano was good. *Really* good. It was one of the reasons he was one of the most feared and respected detectives working out of the Narcotics Field Unit North. Vincent could turn a witness into a suspect without the person ever knowing they were giving it up. Jessica knew all his tricks, and Vincent mostly got over with his Italian charm and swarthy good looks because she let him.

With breakfast more or less eaten, Jessica did a tornado cleanup of the kitchen, piling everything in the sink for later, wiping down the countertops. Sophie and Carlos sat at the table. They had a few minutes before they had to leave.

'Okay,' Sophie said to her little brother. 'Do you remember how to play?'

Carlos nodded. At three years old he was just learning to comb and part his hair, a vanity he fiercely guarded. Today, though, the part in his hair made the Schuylkill River look straight by comparison.

'Okay.' Sophie made a fist with her right hand, held it in front of her. 'This is the rock.'

Carlos mimicked his sister, clenching a small fist. 'Rock.'

Sophie flattened her hand, palm down. 'This is paper.'

'Paper.' Carlos put his hand out palm up, then corrected himself, turning it palm down.

Sophie made a *V* with her index and middle finger. 'And this is scissors.'

Again, Carlos followed the instructions. 'Scissors.'

'Okay. Do you remember what beats what?'

Carlos nodded.

'Ready?' Sophie asked.

'Ready.'

Sophie put her hand behind her back. Carlos followed suit. Sophie said, 'One, two, *three*.'

As Sophie pulled her fist from behind her back, and said 'rock,' Carlos threw out his hand – index finger and thumb extended – and yelled, 'Gun!'

Sophie rolled her eyes, looked at her mother, back at her brother. 'There *is* no gun, Carlos.'

'No?'

'No. The game is called *rock, paper, scissors*.'

Carlos giggled. 'Okay.'

Sophie looked again at Jessica. Jessica just shrugged.

'Boys,' Sophie said.

THE ROUNDHOUSE, THE POLICE administration building at the corner of Eighth and Race Streets, was humming when Jessica walked in at just after 8 a.m. Thank God the humming in her ears had stopped. It would begin again, she imagined, when she next stepped into the ring, sometime in the next few days. She didn't want to admit it, but she just didn't bounce back like she did in her twenties.

Still, she had stood her ground with a buff nineteen year old, and came out of it with just a bruise or two. And sore hands. And, if truth be told, it kind of hurt on the right side when she took a deep breath. Other than that . . .

Maybe she *was* getting too old for this.

THE HOMICIDE UNIT WAS ninety detectives strong, working three tours. Although the murder rate in Philadelphia had dropped in the past few years, the violence had not. New trauma centers in urban areas had eased the number of fatalities, and victims who may have died in the past were now reaching emergency care more quickly. But, as the old saying went: a homicide is just an aggravated assault gone wrong.

Somehow, with the three cases Jessica and Byrne had pending, St Michael – the patron saint of police – had smiled upon them, and they had three suspects in custody, with preliminary hearings spread out over the next two weeks.

For this one glorious moment, their plate was clean.

In most professions, that was a good thing. An empty outbox makes for a clear conscience on payday. In homicide work it meant that you were back up on the wheel. It meant that any minute someone in the City of Brotherly Love was going to pick up a gun or a knife or a bludgeon and visit violence on another human being, and it would then become your job to sort it all out, making sure the guilty party was apprehended and brought to justice, and that the loved ones of the victim were notified, their grief assuaged, their anger and rage corralled.

With this in mind Jessica sat at a computer terminal. One of her cases was a double homicide in Juniata Park, and witness statements put a second man at the scene, gun in hand, although ballistics could only ID one weapon. With only a rough description of the second suspect, Jessica decided to begin with known associates of the man they had in custody. She scrolled though mug shots, six at a time. No one looked promising.

After a few fruitless minutes the phone on the desk rang. Jessica looked longingly at her Spinach Florentine breakfast wrap from Così, the one she probably shouldn't be eating, but somehow couldn't resist. She hadn't even got in a single bite.

If this call was a new case, it would be hers. She picked up the phone, punched the button.

'Homicide. Balzano.'

At first it sounded like white noise, albeit white noise at the lower end of the spectrum, like the setting on sound conditioning machines that simulate rainstorms.

Jessica waited. And waited. Nothing.

'This is Homicide, Detective Balzano.'

'One God,' the caller said.

The words were spoken in a soft whisper. The volume was so low that it was impossible to tell if it was a man or a woman speaking.

'Excuse me?' Jessica asked. 'Could you speak up a bit?'

'Seven churches.'

It sounded like the caller said *seven churches*. 'I'm afraid I don't understand. Are you calling about a case?'

For a few seconds the caller said nothing. Jessica was just about to hang up when she heard:

'You will find the first of the dead at Amber and Cumberland.'

Dead. *First* of the dead. This got Jessica's attention.

She took out her notebook, started writing. 'Amber and Cumberland, you say?' Technically, this meant *East* Cumberland Street, but hardly anybody called it that. This told Jessica she was probably talking to a native Philadelphian. But not necessarily.

'Beneath the dove,' the caller whispered.

'Okay. The dove. Got it. We'll check it out. In the meantime, why don't I –'

'We will not speak again.'

The line went dead.

Jessica held the phone for a few seconds, trying to digest what she'd just heard. Crank call? Maybe yes, maybe no. The nutcases usually called 911. This was on a direct line.

First of the dead.

Jessica put the phone back in its cradle, her day suddenly changed.

The purview of the PPD Homicide Unit was to investigate every suspicious non-hospital, non-hospice death. Sometimes the jobs turned out to be suicides, sometimes they turned out to be hoaxes. Jessica had been on many of each.

She debated for a moment whether to take this to Dana Westbrook, the day work supervisor. After all, it wasn't a citizen call to 911 that started this, it was a direct call to the Homicide Unit.

She had no choice. As she walked toward Sergeant Westbrook's office, the siren call of her Così breakfast wrap grew cold, as did the sandwich itself.

'AND YOU COULDN'T TELL if it was a man or woman?'

'No,' Jessica said. 'The voice was just a whisper.'

'What did the caller say again?'

Dana Westbrook was in her early-fifties, fit and toned and agile. Although she was easily four inches shorter than Jessica's five-eight, she was by no means petite. And God help you if you crossed her, or shirked your duty.

Women in law enforcement worldwide knew that when you were in uniform you had to work twice as hard as men. It was a fact of life. At the command level it was double even that. Jessica did not envy Dana Westbrook's rank, just as she knew she would never try for the position. Detective work was hard enough.

Jessica flipped a page in her notebook. 'Whoever it was said *One God*, then something about *seven churches*.'

'Seven churches?'

'Yeah.'

'Any idea what that means?'

'Not a clue.'

Westbrook thought for a moment, tapping her pen. 'Does that intersection mean anything to you? Anything that might be relevant to an open case?'

The thought had, of course, crossed Jessica's mind. She hadn't brought it up because she really didn't want to follow up on this. 'Doesn't ring a bell, Sarge.'

'And what was the other thing? The "first of the dead"?'

'"First of the dead." Then, "We will not speak again."'

'*Will not*? Not *won't*?'

'Will not.'

'Precise,' Westbrook said. 'Not a contraction. Interesting.'

Shit, Jessica thought. She connected the dots, tried to look at it from her boss's point of view. All things considered, it looked like Detective Jessica Balzano was going on this call whether she liked it or not.

Westbrook looked out the window for a few moments. She twirled her pen. Jessica recognized it as a technique used by cheerleaders. She'd never have the courage to ask Dana Westbrook – tough, ex-Marine, veteran of Desert Storm Dana Westbrook – whether or not she'd ever been a cheerleader.

'Check it out,' Westbrook said. 'If it's nothing, you get a nice visit to Kensington. I hear it's beautiful this time of year.'

Jessica smiled, ever the cheerful and loyal centurion. 'You got it, Sarge.'

Ten minutes later Jessica walked out of the office, grabbed her coat and car keys, along with a two-way radio out of the charging station. On the way she stopped by the secretary's desk, wrote the location down on a separate page from her notebook – along with the bit about the dove – tore it out, handed it to the secretary. 'Let's get a sector car started to this address,' she said. 'Might be something, might be nothing.'

On the way to the elevator she ran into Byrne.

As THEY DROVE TO Kensington, Jessica filled her partner in on the details of the phone call.

'Sound like a suicide reach out?' Byrne asked.

'Could be. But why call homicide? Why not call the suicide hotline?'

'Now where's the drama in that?'

This was true. 'On the other hand it was a direct-line call.'

'Not good.'

'Not good.'

The direct-line numbers into the Homicide Unit were not published anywhere – not in a brochure, not in a directory, certainly not in any phone book. If someone had any of the direct line phone numbers of the homicide unit they most likely got them from a business card. All other calls were routed from police radio.

'And you didn't recognize the voice?' Byrne asked.

'No. But I didn't hear much of it. It was pretty much a whisper.'

'And what was the line about the dead? "First of the dead"?'

'Yeah.'

'Also not good.'

'Who the hell says "of the dead"?'

It was a rhetorical question. Neither detective really wanted to find out.

'Did the caller say your name?' Byrne asked.

Jessica had to think about this. She really couldn't remember. Unlike calls that come in to 911, direct calls to homicide were not automatically recorded and logged, so there was no audio record. 'No. I don't think so.'

'Did you hear anything in the background? TV? Radio? Music of any kind?'

'No,' Jessica said. 'But to be honest, I wasn't paying all that much attention. The call came out of the blue.'

Byrne went quiet for a while, processing it all.

'Hey, I forgot to ask. Did you ever do that Philly Brothers thing?' Jessica asked.

Byrne did not answer immediately. Jessica had known the man a long time, and knew that whatever she was about to hear was only going to be part of the story. She also knew she would get the entire story when Byrne was ready to tell her.

'Yeah,' he said. 'I did.'

'And?'

'And it went okay, I guess. Kid's eleven. It's like talking to an alien.'

'What's his story?'

'Father was a ghost, mother walked the streets, died of an overdose. Gabriel's older brother swallowed a gun.'

'Jesus.'

'Tell me about it.'

'The kid's a walking gang recruitment poster.'

'No tats or scars,' Byrne said. 'None I could see anyway.'

'You think he's at risk?'

'They're *all* at risk these days. Hard to tell with him, though. He seems pretty smart, but that's just an impression. I don't think he said fifty words the whole time I was with him.'

'You guys going to get together again?'

Another hesitation. Another half-story coming up. 'I brought it up, but all I got was his thousand-yard stare. I'm going to call him though, give it a shot.'

They stopped at the light at Eighth and Spring Garden. A cold blast of wind buffeted the car. Jessica kicked up the heat a notch.

'On the other hand, I'm probably not his ideal Philly Brother, you know?' Byrne added. 'Big middle-aged white cop. I don't think he's going to bring me in for show and tell any time soon.'

'What are you talking about? You're a total catch.'

'Right.'

'You are. In fact, I heard that *Philadelphia Magazine* is going to do another one of its "Philadelphia's Sexiest Bachelor" issues. I'm going to submit your name.'

Byrne smiled. 'No, you're not.'

'Oh, yes I am.'

'Make sure you tell them I live in a three-room apartment and keep my socks and underwear in a file cabinet.'

'Babes will line up around the block for that. I'm seeing crowd control issues.'

'And don't forget to mention that I once mixed up a can of Pledge with my Arid Extra Dry.'

Jessica laughed. 'I thought you smelled kind of lemony fresh that day.'

KENSINGTON WAS A NEIGHBORHOOD in the lower northeast section of the city. It was at one time a bustling shipbuilding district, before giving way to manufacturing and mill work. When the mills began to close, Kensington fell on hard times, becoming one of the most depressed areas of the city, an era of decay and desolation from which it was still struggling to emerge.

Because Amber Street was one-way, Jessica and Byrne drove down to York first, then cut back. As they neared the address Jessica saw a sector car parked on Amber, its lights flashing. On a street like this, the longer the bar flashed, the more likely it would be to draw people out of their houses. Right now they didn't need a crowd. In fact, unless the perpetrator stood at the front in an orange jumpsuit with a sign around his neck confessing to the crime, they *never* needed a crowd.

The patrol officer was an Hispanic woman in her twenties.

Before getting out of the car Jessica studied the scene. The address was a freestanding, two-story, red-sandstone building. Buildings such as these were common in Kensington, structures rehabbed and repurposed over the years. While many had been torn down over the past three decades, as Kensington and neighboring Harrowgate, West Kensington, and Fishtown attempted to gentrify, many remained, sandwiched between blocks of rowhouses and commercial buildings.

The two front windows of this building were barred. To the right was an alleyway. Above the entrance was a low bell tower.

Jessica and Byrne exited the car, crossed the street. They clipped their badges onto their coats. Before they reached the curb Byrne got Jessica's attention. He nodded at the high wall of the old warehouse next to their address. On it someone had painted a mural with a large gray dove perched on an olive branch.

You'll find the first of the dead at Amber and Cumberland. Beneath the dove.

The young patrol officer paced nervously near her car. As they got closer Jessica could see the officer's eyes. Something was very wrong. The officer looked like she had seen a monster. Her nametag identified her as P/O A. MARTINEZ.

'Good morning,' Byrne said.

''Morning, sir.'

'What can you tell me?'

Officer Martinez took a deep breath. When she exhaled the air came out in short, frosty blasts. She pointed at the building behind her, explained how she had taken the call, searched the alleyway, found nothing. She said she'd then remembered the 'beneath the dove' detail she'd gotten from dispatch. It was then she noticed the mural on the wall, and that the door to the building was ajar.

'I entered the premises, found a white male, twenties, in the basement. Whole lotta blood, sir. Whole *lotta* blood.'

Jessica and Byrne looked at each other. It wasn't a prank call after all.

'DOA?' Byrne asked.

'Yes, sir.'

'Did you check vitals?'

The officer looked everywhere but Byrne's eyes. In other words, *no*. Martinez knew she had to answer, and do so truthfully. She did. 'No, sir. But he's –'

'So you're not sure he's dead?'

Another pause. 'No, sir. But there's –'

'Did you call for backup, clear the building?'

Martinez cleared her throat. 'I cleared the basement.'

'By yourself?'

The look on Martinez's face said that she was ready to turn in her badge, even if this *wasn't* a firing offense. It appeared that whatever she had seen inside this old stone building was worth throwing away her time at the academy. Jessica had seen the look many times. She imagined *she* had looked this way to more than a few detectives during her rookie year. It was a look that said: *I didn't sign on for this.*

Byrne put a comforting hand on the young woman's shoulder. 'Where exactly is the body?'

Martinez pulled it together. 'Down the stairs, hard right, under the steps.'

Byrne pointed to the door. 'Is this where you gained entry?'

Martinez nodded.

'Did you announce yourself?'

'Yes, sir.'

Byrne looked at the building, back. 'Call for two more units,' he said. He pointed at the sector car. 'And kill the lights.'

If Martinez looked embarrassed before, she looked mortified now. 'Yes, sir.'

P/O A. Martinez took a few steps away, keyed her shoulder microphone, officially a veteran first-responder to what was probably her first homicide. She opened the car door, reached in, turned off the flashing bar lights.

Jessica glanced at the building. She was not looking forward to entering, considering how this young patrol officer had reacted. But this *was* what she had signed on for, and she was going inside, whether she liked it or not.

THE SECOND SECTOR CAR arrived a few minutes later. These officers were veteran patrolmen with whom Jessica and Byrne had worked before. Byrne instructed them to clear the first and second floors of the structure, along with the tower. It may have been a typically small, converted commercial space – probably no more than 2,000 square feet total – but there were lots of places to hide, and they had no idea what they were walking into.

After the two officers cleared the first floor, and moved on to the second floor and tower, Jessica and Byrne walked up the crumbling cement steps, entered the building. As they did Jessica ran her Maglite along the doorjamb. The wood around the deadbolt was freshly splintered. This had probably been the initial point of entry.

Inside was a large square room with a crudely constructed and braced partition in the center. What had once been large windows on either side had long ago been bricked in. What natural light there was came from a pair of small windows placed high on the back wall. On the face of the false wall in the center of the room was a faded painting of a crucifix, with clouds in an unnaturally blue sky above, along with a heavenly golden light radiating from the bottom.

A pair of old wooden chairs stood in the center of the space, facing each other. Next to them was an overturned milk crate, dotted with spent matches and balls of charred aluminum foil.

The rest of the room was empty of furniture and fixtures, but littered with damp magazines, newspapers, fast-food trash. In the corner was an old portable TV on its side, the glass screen shattered, knobs dangling.

'Second floor and tower's clear,' one of the patrolmen said, descending the stairs. 'You want us down there?'

'No,' Byrne said. 'Take the front and the rear.'

'You got it.'

The two officers would now take up position at the front and back doors. The responding officer – P/O A. Martinez – would be in charge of the crime-scene log, a duty that consisted of signing and time-coding the arrival and departure of all personnel, including detectives, crime-scene techs, and investigators from the medical examiner's office, all of whom would be en route as soon as the primary detectives made the call.

The third sector car, which had just arrived, would work on keeping the gathering onlookers as far from the crime scene building as possible.

With the rest of the building clear, it was time to head downstairs. Jessica and Byrne met at the top of the stairs leading to the cellar, exchanged a glance they had come to know well – the one that said they were about to enter a room wherein anything could happen.

Was this going to be a job? Jessica wondered. *Was this going to be one that stayed with her for years?* The truth was, you never knew. In this profession a phone rang and you stepped into a maelstrom, an ancient storm that began the moment Cain raised his hand to Abel.

The two detectives clicked on their Maglites. Jessica opened the door. She would be the first to go down. It was something she and Byrne had wordlessly worked out long ago. Jessica had never wanted any special treatment because of her gender, had even rushed toward the door in admittedly foolhardy attempts to display her courage, at least back in the early days. Also, because she was the daughter of one of the most decorated officers in the history of the PPD, she felt the extra burden to not only prove herself on her own terms, but to never give the impression she was being favored.

It had been this way for years, and today was no different. This was her job, her door.

She ran her flashlight down the steps. The darkness below seemed to devour the light. She took a deep breath, put her hand on the rail.

And that's when they heard the scream.

J ESSICA THOUGHT: *THE BASEMENT*. YOU NEVER GET USED TO THE basement.

She stopped, her hand on the grip of her weapon. Byrne took up position on the other side of the door.

If it was cold outside, it was numbingly frigid here. Their breath formed icy clouds in front of them. Despite the chill, Jessica could feel a latticework of warm sweat trickle down her back.

She eased onto the top tread. The steps below were dark and forbidding. The old wood groaned under her weight. Even from the top of the stairs Jessica could smell the unmistakable metallic tang of blood.

'Philly PD!' she yelled. 'Who's down there?'

Nothing.

Jessica drew her weapon, held it at her side, edged downward. She heard Byrne behind her, his weight now on the top step.

Jessica followed her flashlight's beam down the stairs, looking for broken or missing boards. On one tread was a child's plastic toy – a duck with one foot missing, a dirty string wrapped around its head. Two steps below was a ball of dry, shredded newspaper, probably once home to a family of mice.

A few seconds later Jessica made it to the second last step. She ran her Maglite around the room. The ceiling was low, dense with cobwebs and spider webs. The smell of mold and urine was overpowering.

Down the stairs, hard right, under the steps.

Jessica heard the voice coming from beneath the staircase, although *voice* was not entirely accurate. What she heard did not sound human. It was a depleted sound that seemed to crawl along the damp floor.

Byrne put a hand on Jessica's left shoulder, silently telling her that he would flank left when they got to the bottom of the stairs.

Jessica crouched down, swept her flashlight across the floor. Scattered food trash, dried chicken and rib bones, picked clean. In one corner were the remnants of a rusted bicycle, the chain, wheels and pedals gone. Another corner held a collection of old fluorescent tube lights.

Whole lotta blood.

Jessica reached the bottom step. She held up a hand, then pointed to the right. With a silent count of three, she stepped onto the cold cement floor, rolled to the right, leveled her weapon in an attack stance, finger along the trigger guard of her Glock.

A man was sitting under the steps. Or what was left of a man. He was seated in a wooden chair, hands behind his back, his head and chest awash with fresh blood. At his feet were a pair of rats that stood up to the beam of the flashlight, staring back with tiny, defiant black eyes.

The man was nude, his chest crisscrossed with barbed wire. Some of the barbs were rusted and cut deep welts into his flesh from his neck to his waist. Steam emanated from his wounds as the warm blood met the frigid February air.

But while the barbs cut into his chest and arms, it was the wire wrapped around the man's neck that was doing the mortal damage. Jessica could see one razor sharp polished point, bright silver in color, digging into the skin near the carotid artery.

The man was still alive. The patrol officer should have checked his vitals, but Jessica could understand why the young woman did not want to.

Byrne moved to Jessica's left, keeping his flashlight and weapon trained on the man. Jessica turned, scanned the rest of the room. There were no other doors, no niches or alcoves large enough to hold another person. The basement was clear.

Except for the all but destroyed human in front of them.

Jessica stepped away for a moment, took out her two-way, and in a low voice contacted dispatch, requesting an EMS unit. The man was still alive, but not for long.

Jessica kept her weapon angled low, moved to the right. She could now see that the man's hands were bound with wire behind his back. The wire was connected to the loop around his neck. If the man's head dropped forward, he would sever his jugular vein.

They had to keep him awake and alert.

'Sir,' Jessica began. 'My name is Jessica Balzano. I'm with the Philadelphia Police Department. We're going to get you out of here. Medical assistance is on the way.'

The man tried to speak. 'He . . .'

'He what?' Jessica asked softly. 'Who are you talking about?' Perhaps the man was trying to tell them who did this to him. Jessica noticed that with each labored breath the man took the barbed wire tightened further around his chest and abdomen, rusted tines digging deeper into his flesh.

The man did not answer. Instead, he began to cry.

'Sir,' Jessica said, holstering her weapon, holding her hands out to the sides, showing no threat. 'I want you to know that we have paramedics on the way. We have people coming who are going to get you free. People who will treat your wounds. You're going to be fine.'

The man started to violently shake his head. Blood flicked across the room. Both Jessica and Byrne stepped back. When the man stopped moving Jessica could see that the one polished barb had now cut into his neck.

'Stop!' Jessica yelled. 'Please do not move, sir!'

The man's head slumped forward, his eyes closed. Jessica looked at her watch. She listened for the siren of the EMS unit. She heard nothing. This man was going to bleed out right in front of them and there was nothing they could do about it. Jessica wanted to keep him talking, to keep him from going into shock, but the sound of his voice and the amount of blood he generated with each word frightened her.

The man's head fell further forward. The blood had begun to pool at his feet. The two rats had now become five.

'Detectives?'

The voice came from the top of the stairs. Jessica had never been happier to hear another human voice in her life. The ambulance unit had arrived. 'Down here!' She yelled. 'Hurry!'

The first paramedic came down the steps, rounded the corner, saw the victim. He was in his early-thirties, short but powerfully built. His nametag read E. GONSALVES.

'*Madre de Dios,*' he said softly. '*Santa Maria.*' He made the sign of the cross, pulled out a pair of latex gloves, snapped them on, just as his partner made it to the bottom of the steps. She was a tall, lanky white woman in her mid-thirties. Her tag IDed her as F. CHRISTIAN.

'Do you have anything to cut the wires off with?' Jessica asked.

'No,' Gonsalves said. He got on his portable unit and called for a PFD ladder truck. Jessica wondered if they could respond in time.

Christian ran up the stairs. A full minute later she came down with a portable EKG unit, followed by a pair of PFD firefighters.

One of the firefighters had in his hand a large pair of bolt cutters.

Jessica and Byrne both put on gloves. They stepped in to hold the victim steady. Within seconds their hands were slicked with the man's blood. The firefighter cut one side, then the other, freeing the man's wrists. Together Jessica and Byrne gently eased the victim's head back. Although the pressure of the wire around his neck had lessened, there was still a barb slicing ever more deeply into the area at the man's carotid. Despite their efforts, within seconds it cut deeply into the artery. Blood jetted across the room.

'*Shit!*' Jessica yelled.

Gonsalves made the call. At this moment it was his scene. He peeled the wire from the victim's neck, and the three of them eased the man back onto the Reeves. The Reeves spine board was for patients with spine and neck injuries, designed to minimize movement during transport.

Gonsalves opened a large gauze pad and pressed it to the now-spouting wound.

'Give us room,' he said.

Jessica and Byrne, along with the two PFD, backed away as Christian took a hypodermic needle from the bag, filled it.

In seconds the first gauze pad was soaked. Gonsalves ripped open a second and third, put pressure on the wound. 'Come on, man,' he said softly.

The techs were veteran paramedics. Like Jessica and Byrne they had seen a few things. They had treated gunshot wounds, knife wounds, beatings with weapons ranging from fists to claw hammers to Louisville Sluggers. If there was a way for one human being to damage another, they had likely seen it. But there was a feeling in this room that they had all entered special waters, a place reserved for a mind devoid of passion, or even anger.

While Gonsalves tried to stanch the bleeding, his partner started a pair of IV drips, then gently worked the bolt cutters under the wire that wrapped the man's chest. Christian carefully snipped the steel. The man's torso instantly expanded, sucking in air, which immediately burst out through his nose and mouth, bringing blood and saliva with it.

Gonsalves leaned in, wiped the blood from the man's face, put his ear to the man's mouth. The victim mumbled something. Gonsalves leaned back. While Christian readied fresh gauze pads, Gonsalves began to pump the man's chest.

'Come on, man,' he said. 'Don't you fucking code on me.'

Gonsalves hooked the victim to the EKG machine, stared at the reading. They were losing him. They had to get him to the nearest trauma center.

'Breathe man, breathe,' Gonsalves said. 'I lose nobody today. It's my birthday today, man. I lose *nobody* on my birthday.'

As blood spread into a large pool on the dirty cement floor, the two paramedics worked feverishly to stabilize the patient. A full minute later Christian took a pulse reading. Her eyes went distant. She looked up, directly at Jessica, and shook her head.

The man was dead.

'Mother*fucker*,' Gonsalves yelled. 'God *damn* it.' He stood up, turned full circle, then crouched back down, trying again to resuscitate the victim. Everyone knew it was futile, especially Gonsalves, but no one tried to stop him.

When Gonsalves was spent, he knelt for a few moments more, perhaps in prayer, then got up and walked to the corner of the small, cramped basement. The air was redolent with the smell of blood and feces.

It was over.

Gonsalves looked at Jessica, tears limning his eyes. He wiped them away, tried to compose himself. 'My birthday.'

Jessica knew that these paramedics and firefighters were witnesses to far more of these moments than homicide detectives. They were the ones who did God's work. For the most part Jessica's job began long after this moment, sometimes months or years later. The frontline against violence and its aftermath were the patrol officers, the fire-fighters, the paramedics. Jessica was glad she was long out of uniform. She had nothing but admiration and sympathy for the first responders in her city. She couldn't imagine a harder job. Even trauma surgeons had it easier. They got to work in sterile environments with state-of-the-art equipment, not to mention the certainty that whoever had committed the atrocity before them was not lurking around the corner, gun or knife or bludgeon in hand.

Jessica looked at the victim. His arms were straight out to his sides, his feet together, almost Christ-like. Then she noticed the small white book on the floor to the right of the victim.

Had it been in his hands?

Jessica knelt down, shone her light on the book. It was covered in blood, both fresh and dried. Through the blood she could read the title.

MY MISSAL

Later she would think about this instant – kneeling in a frigid basement in Kensington, a destroyed human being on the cold stone floor in front of her – as the moment it all began.

Gonsalves snapped out of it, looked for something to kick, but soon realized he was in the middle of a crime scene, most likely a homicide scene. He ran up the stairs, out onto the street. Jessica could hear his plaints from the basement. She imagined most of Kensington could hear him as well.

Forty minutes later, after Tom Weyrich, an investigator from the medical examiner's office, made the official pronouncement at the scene, the Crime Scene Unit took their photographs and videos, and Jessica and Byrne began to search the basement in earnest. CSU had set up their field lighting, running in an electrical line from a generator on the first floor. If the room had looked daunting in the beam of the Maglites, it looked worse in the pitiless glare of the halogens.

The room was about twenty-five by thirty-five feet, mirroring the layout of the room above, with three poles holding up support beams. Hanging from the ceiling were rusted straps and clamps which at one time secured copper water lines that had long ago been scavenged for cash. Anything and everything of value had been stolen – furnace, water heater, sheet metal ductwork, even the silver-coated insulation used to wrap the pipes and plenum.

In one corner was a stained and water-damaged bathroom vanity. Its fixtures and sink were missing, but the unit itself was still bolted to the concrete wall and cement floor, but not for a lack of effort in attempting to dislodge it. Looking at the dented and chipped wood where the fixture met the wall, Jessica was sure someone had tried mightily to pry it from its place, without success. She slipped on a fresh latex glove and gently opened one of the doors under the sink. The cabinet was empty.

With the help of bottled water and a hundred paper towels, Jessica managed to get most of the victim's blood from her arms and hands. She had discreetly washed up in the back of the PFD truck on scene, disinfected as many exposed areas of her body as she could, and slipped on a fresh sweater and jacket she always kept in a gym bag in the trunk of the departmental sedan. She felt one percent better.

Jessica noticed Gonsalves standing across the street, leaning against a half-wall, smoking a cigarette. As she approached him she noticed two things. One, that he was wearing a crucifix on a chain around his neck. She had not noticed it earlier. The other thing she noticed was that his hands were shaking.

'I'm sorry,' Jessica said, immediately recognizing how inadequate it sounded. Gonsalves nodded a thank you. 'What's your first name?' she asked.

The man looked up. His eyes were wet and bloodshot and, at the moment, looked much older than his years. 'Ernesto,' he said. 'Ernie.'

'You did what you could in there, Ernie.'

Gonsalves shook his head. 'Not enough.'

A few moments passed. Jessica knew that this man had seen at least as much carnage as she had, that he was going to bounce back from this, but for some reason she couldn't just walk away. Gonsalves finally broke the silence.

'He talked.'

Jessica looked at the man. 'Who talked? The victim?'

'Just before he coded. He said something to me.'

Jessica wondered why Ernesto Gonsalves had waited to tell her this. She didn't press him on it. Instead, she waited for him to gather his thoughts.

'I hear a lot, you know?' he said. 'I mean, I've heard a *lot* of last words from people. I once had a guy tell me to erase the hard drives on his home computer. Gave me the keys to his house and everything. His *keys*, man. Said he would go to hell if I didn't do it. Two bullets in his gut and he's worried about his hard drive. You believe that shit?'

Jessica just listened.

'There was this other guy this one time. Up in Chestnut Hill, right? Big guy, maybe six-two, two-fifty. Well-dressed, though. Tailored. Valentino suit. I check the labels sometimes.' Gonsalves gave her a sheepish look. Jessica returned a smile.

'This guy, he confessed to embezzling a shitload of money from the bank he worked in, told me where it was at, told me to give it to charity.' Gonsalves shook his head. '*Cash*, man. He trusted me to do the right thing with his *cash*. Never met me, didn't know me from *Adam*, right?' Gonsalves flicked away ash. 'They teach you how to carry a bed board up the steps, how to do a tracheotomy, how to use a defibrillator, all of that. But they don't tell you what to do with all these words in your head. People look at me like I'm a priest, you know? *Shit*, man. I mean, who knows what it looks like in those last few seconds? Maybe *everybody* looks like a priest.'

Gonsalves hit his cigarette hard, continued.

'But *this* guy . . .'

Jessica waited a few seconds. She was losing him. She prodded. 'What did he say?'

Ernesto Gonsalves tossed his cigarette into the gutter. His hand then went to the chain around his neck. He found the crucifix, began to run his fingers over it. Jessica, who had been wearing the same fourteen-carat gold crucifix around her neck since she was thirteen, a present from her father, often did the same thing. It sometimes eased the more difficult things she had to say in her life.

'Two words, detective. Two words.' Gonsalves wiped at his eyes. 'He didn't say *tell my wife I love her*, or *give my babies a hug from their daddy*. Nothing like that. He lived all that time, and his life came down to two words.'

'What two words?'

Gonsalves looked at Jessica, the pain of all the city's dead in his eyes, and said:

'*He lives.*'

B Y NOON A SECOND TEAM OF HOMICIDE DETECTIVES WERE ON THE scene. They would help with the neighborhood interviews.

The past year had brought a number of retirements in the Homicide Unit, plus a few detectives had moved into other squads. In all there were eight new detectives in the unit, including two more women. Jessica was grateful for this in more ways than one. Although she loved her job, and her partner, the presence of another two women in the duty room was a nice counterbalance to the heightened levels of testosterone that seemed to drive the unit. An added bonus was that it kept a lot of the male detectives on their toes. With one female detective it was easier to tell the sexist joke, or make the derogatory remark. With three in the room, it was easy to get flanked. Add to this the fact that the day watch commander was also a woman, and the place was getting downright dainty.

Could lace curtains in the duty room be far behind?

The second team was comprised of Detective Joshua Bontrager, who had grown up Amish in rural Berks County, and Maria Caruso. Maria was in her late-twenties – young for homicide, but Jessica wasn't much older when she joined the unit. Maria was very attractive, with dark chocolate eyes and a clear olive complexion. She was a good officer, had worked with Jessica and Byrne a few years earlier on a case involving a mad magician and his murderous plan for the city of Philadelphia. Time would tell if she was right for homicide.

As Bontrager walked across Amber Street, Jessica watched him. His progress through the PPD had been nothing short of amazing. The first time she had seen him, when he was brought up from the Traffic Unit to work a case, he had been a fish out of water, a country boy suddenly thrust into one of the toughest jobs, in one of the toughest areas, in the city. Now he walked with an old school homicide detective's swagger. Recently Jessica caught a whiff of some pretty expensive cologne when Josh passed her in the office. The joke around the squad for the next few days had something to do with Josh wearing *Eau de Cowlogne*.

Josh took it like a good sport.

Jessica briefed detectives Bontrager and Caruso on the case. She took out her iPhone, showed them some of the photographs she had taken of the scene, and the victim.

'Oh, my goodness,' Bontrager said.

For Josh, this was the equivalent of a profane tirade by any other cop in the city. Maybe the world.

'Any witnesses?' Maria asked.

'Just starting the canvass,' Jessica said.

Maria took out her notebook and pen. 'What time did that call come in?'

'Had to be eight-fifteen or so,' Jessica said.

Maria wrote it down.

'What did the caller say again?' Bontrager asked.

Jessica repeated the phone call verbatim.

'That's what the caller said?' Bontrager asked. '*One God, seven churches?*'

'Yeah,' Jessica said. 'Mean anything to you?'

Bontrager thought for a few moments. Considering his childhood and background, Josh Bontrager was kind of the go-to guy around the unit when it came to all things Christian and Biblical. 'Not off the top. Let me think about it.'

'Sure.'

Bontrager pointed over his shoulder. 'We'll head up Cumberland.'

Jessica nodded. She and Byrne would work Amber Street.

Josh Bontrager stepped out of the way to let Maria Caruso go ahead of him. Part of the reason, Jessica surmised, was that Bontrager was by nature a gentleman. The other reason was that Detective Maria Caruso was given to wearing tight slacks and fitted jackets, as she was today. Josh Bontrager was single and unattached. Amish or not, he had to enjoy the view.

AN HOUR LATER THE four detectives met back in front of the crime scene building, no wiser for their efforts. As expected, mass amnesia. No one had seen or heard anything.

Bontrager pointed to the PPD camera on the corner. 'We're gonna head back to the house, check the footage.'

Jessica held up her cell phone. 'Keep me posted.'

As BYRNE PREPARED TO leave for the Roundhouse to begin the paper-work, Jessica waved him over. She was standing by a lamppost directly in front of the crime-scene building.

'What is it?' Byrne asked.

Jessica pointed to the lamppost. There was a symbol in the shape of an *X* painted on it at about eye level for Jessica. Byrne looked closely. It was not spray-painted graffiti. It was dark umber in color. Byrne glanced at Jessica, then got the attention of a CSU officer. The crime scene had just gotten larger. The *X* looked like it may have been drawn in blood.

Byrne pointed to the side door of the building. 'I think I'm going to walk it again.'

Jessica knew what he meant. As good as they were as a team, she had long ago learned to give her partner time and space on a new homicide. Kevin Byrne had his own methods.

DUE TO THE AMOUNT of blood and other bodily fluids, when they wheeled out the body, the paramedics did not zip the victim into a body bag, for fear that it might compromise crucial scientific evidence.

A crowd had formed across the street, and at the sight of this savaged man on the gurney, many turned away.

With Byrne inside the crime-scene building, Jessica scanned the small, milling crowd. There were twenty or so people gathered, shivering in the cold. The show was just too good, it seemed, for them to worry about frostbite or pneumonia. The gathering was a mix of neighborhood residents, mostly grandmothers and children too young for school. Jessica noticed a woman across the street, seemingly mesmerized by the pageant in front of her. The woman was in her thirties, well-dressed. She caught Jessica's eye, and immediately made her way around the corner.

Jessica followed.

JESSICA CAUGHT UP TO the woman about a half-block away, got her attention. She was about to get into her car.

'Is there something you wanted to say, ma'am?' Jessica asked.

The woman looked at the ground for a few moments, closed her car door. 'I'm not sure,' she said. Although she was probably not yet forty, her hair was a beautiful, shimmering silver, blunt cut, down to her shoulders. The look was quite striking, Jessica thought.

'Can I get your name?' she asked.

The woman glanced up, resigned. She was going on the record. 'Mara,' she said. 'Mara Reuben.'

'Do you live in the neighborhood ?'

'No, no,' she said. '*God*, no. That's my mother's house. I've been trying to get her to move for fifteen years, but she won't have it.'

'Is your mother home right now?'

'No. She's in the hospital. I stop by here twice a day to pick up the mail, get the flyers and newspapers off the stoop, check on things. Her house has been broken into twice in just this past month, and I figured that a build-up of stuff by the front door is a sure tip-off that no one is home.'

Jessica studied the woman. She had long ago learned that you can tell a lot about a person by their grooming habits and clothing. Many times, with women, their accessories told you the most. This woman wore a stylish pair of drop earrings, a tennis bracelet, a single sapphire ring, third finger right hand.

'Can I ask what happened over there?' she asked.

'Right now it looks like there was a homicide in that building,' Jessica said.

The woman covered her mouth. 'That's terrible.'

'Ma'am, if you think you saw something, no matter how insignificant, it might be very helpful. Everything you tell me will be confidential.'

The woman took a few seconds. 'Okay. Well. In that case, maybe I do have something you might find useful.'

Jessica flipped to a fresh page in her notebook.

'I came down here last night, around ten o'clock, just to check on things,' the woman said. 'I picked up the newspaper, unlocked the door – there are three dead bolts, so it takes awhile – then stepped inside. I did a quick check of the windows and the back door, and around ten minutes later I was ready to leave. I stepped out and accidentally dropped my keys next to the steps, and had to walk around. As I was picking them up, I thought I heard someone talking across the street.'

'You heard a conversation?'

'No, not really a conversation. I saw a man standing over there. In front of that closed-up building.'

'A man,' Jessica said. 'One man.'

'Yes.'

'And he was talking?'

'Yes.'

'To whom?'

'Well, to himself, I guess.'

'Was he on a cell phone?'

'I don't think so. I mean, he didn't have a phone up to his ear. He might have had on one of those earphone headset thingies, but I didn't see it.'

'Did you get a good look at him?'

'Not really,' the woman said. 'I couldn't see too clearly. It was dark.'

'And this was about ten after ten last night?'

'Yes. I'm usually down here every night at that time. Just to check on things.'

'Can you describe anything about the man you saw?'

'Well, like I said, it was dark, but I'm pretty sure he was wearing a long black coat, and he had on a hood.'

'A hood?' Jessica asked. 'Like a hoodie? A hooded sweatshirt?'

'No, more like a pointed hood.'

Jessica wrote down: *pointed hood?*

'About how tall was he?' she asked.

'Not sure. On the tall side though.'

'By tall side, what do you mean?'

'I saw you talking to that man in front of the building. How tall is he?'

'About six-three,' Jessica replied.

'Maybe six feet then. Perhaps a little less.'

'Do you recall what he was doing?'

The woman shrugged. 'He wasn't doing anything, really. Just standing there talking to himself.'

Jessica glanced down the street. There was no bus stop. Whatever the man was doing, he wasn't waiting for SEPTA.

'Can you characterize the sound of his voice?' Jessica asked.

'I'm not sure what you mean.'

'Was he whispering, shouting, mumbling?'

'He wasn't shouting, that's for sure. It sounded more like – this is going to sound weird.'

Jessica just waited.

'It sounded more like a prayer. Like an old chant or something.'

'A chant?'

Mara Reuben closed her eyes for a moment, as if she were listening to the sound, as if reliving the moment. 'Yes. It had that rhythm, you know? Like in the old Latin mass. Are you Catholic?'

'I was raised Roman Catholic, yes.'

'It sounded like it might have been Latin he was speaking,' she continued. 'I can't be certain, though.'

'Are you sure he came out of that building?'

'Well, I was until you asked me that. I couldn't swear to it. Sorry.'

'That's okay. We want you to be sure. Is there anything else you can remember?'

'No,' the woman said. 'Nothing I can think of right now. To be honest, I didn't think anything of it at the time. You know better than I do that Philly has its share of characters. I just locked the locks, got in my car, and drove away.'

'Okay. This has been very helpful. If you –'

The woman held up a finger. 'Wait. I *do* remember something else. When I drove away I looked in the rearview mirror, and it looked like he was touching the post. I do remember that.'

'The lamppost in front of the building?'

'Yes.'

Jessica made a note to expedite the lab test on the substance they found on the lamppost, as well as the latent prints, if any. This woman might have seen the man painting the *X* on it.

'And you say you're down here every night at ten?' Jessica asked.

'Yes.'

'May I ask what brought you back down here this morning?'

'Well, like I said, I'm pretty paranoid, my mother having had two break-ins this month. I was just going to drive by, then I saw all the police cars and I freaked.'

'That's understandable.' Jessica handed the woman a card. 'If you think of anything else, no matter how trivial it might seem, please call me.'

'I will.'

'And if it's any consolation,' Jessica added, 'your mother's house should be okay for the next few days. There are going to be police all over the place around here for awhile.'

The woman offered a faint smile. 'Yeah, well, I'm still going to use this to get her to move in with me.'

There was no response to this. There were good areas and bad areas of the city. Jessica had investigated homicides in penthouses and flophouses. Nowhere was safe from violence.

Ten minutes later Jessica stood on the corner, across from the crime scene. She tried to imagine the street when it was empty, as it had been at ten o'clock the previous night. She tried to imagine a man standing there, clad in a long black coat and a pointed hood, speaking aloud.

In Latin.

She glanced at the police pole camera on the corner. If they were going to get lucky on this one – and, considering how they'd struck out completely on the neighborhood interviews, they were going to need luck – the camera would be operational, and they would have an image.

SEVEN

BYRNE KNEW THE MOMENT HE WALKED INTO THE BUILDING. THE feeling settled first on the surface of his skin, a damp sensation of dread that seemed to bleed from these walls, stone that had stood witness to a hundred years of secrets, and before that the history of the land from which it had been quarried. Byrne all but heard the hooves on wet sod, the fading heartbeats of the fallen.

Here, in this place where the stone had long ago been keyed and weighted, this place where murder was done, the walls protected its ghosts.

The Boy in the Red Coat.

Byrne had not thought of the boy in many months, a long time considering his history with the case. The Boy in the Red Coat was one of the more famous, and lurid, unsolved crimes in Philadelphia's history. Byrne had gotten a call from the pastor of St Gedeon's, the South Philadelphia church of his youth. When he arrived the church was empty save for a dead boy in the last pew, a child clad in a bright red jacket.

Byrne secured the scene, waited for the divisional detectives. That was where and when his official involvement with the case ended. In the years since, many detectives, including Byrne himself, had looked at the files, tried to track down fresh leads. The case remained open. But Byrne had never forgotten the sensation of walking into that huge, empty cathedral that day, seeing the dead child.

It was the same feeling he had walking into the dank basement on this day, seeing the young man so barbarously wired to the chair, his body bathed in scarlet.

In his time as a homicide detective Byrne had borne witness to every imaginable violence, every conceivable way for one human to cause the death of another. Since he'd had his own near-fatal experience many years earlier – an incident where he was pronounced dead, only to come back to life a full minute later – he had been both blessed and cursed with this vision, this *sight*. It wasn't as if he could see into the future, or the past, or had any sixth sense that made him special. He felt special by no means. It was, instead, more of a sense of presence, a sense of *being*, an incarnation of the men and women who had occupied these rooms before him. Many times he walked into a crime scene, a place fresh from the murderer's touch, and felt as if he walked in the killer's skin for a fleeting instant. It was an ugly, sickening sensation, to feel even for a moment a soul devoid of compassion, a heart bereft of sorrow.

Many times, late into a night of bad dreams, Byrne had wished this ability would go away. Just as often he wished it would develop, becoming more clear and profound, something he could channel. It never happened. It had always been – and, he suspected, would always be – something that came and went. Something that had its own power and agenda.

Ever since the visions began Byrne believed he would one day walk onto a scene and know that it was the beginning of the end, that he was about to engage in a great battle, a stand between good and evil.

This was that day. He didn't know how he knew it, but he knew it.

It was finally happening.

IN THE VESTIBULE OF the old building was a narrow door to the left, slightly ajar, its hinges rusted, its jambs out of square. Byrne shouldered the door. It opened just enough for him to squeeze through.

He mounted the winding stone staircase to the bell tower. When he made it to the top he stepped inside. The bell itself was long gone; the two small windows were covered with thin slats of wood lath.

Byrne pulled a few of the slats free. The parched wood came loose with very little effort. The gray light coming through the opening gave him a better view from the landing.

He closed his eyes, felt the feeling wash over him, the knowledge that –

– *this evil has just awakened and the mother and child mother and child mother and child the –*

– mother and child.

Byrne opened his eyes, looked out the window. He saw Jessica on the street, talking to one of the CSU officers. Next to Jessica stood Maria Caruso and Josh Bontrager. Behind them stood thirty or so people gathered to bear witness to what had happened today, many of them women –

– *having given birth to a child who would one day grow to be a man who would expiate the sins of his father by becoming his own father, a man who would walk the dark corners of the night and –*

– do murder.

Byrne thought of Jessica, of her daughter and newly adopted son. He thought of his ex-wife Donna and their daughter Colleen. He thought of Colleen, who would one day soon find love and have a child of her own. He thought about Tanya Wilkins and her sons Gabriel and Terrell. He thought of all the women who hoped for the best for their sons and daughters. He thought of that day long ago when he walked into a church and saw the small figure in the back pew, that blood red coat, the smell of death, a scent he would forever carry in his soul.

Mother and child, Kevin Byrne thought.

Mother and child.

EIGHT

B Y THE TIME THEY RETURNED TO THE ROUNDHOUSE THE VICTIM HAD
been transported to the morgue. There he would be fingerprinted,
which was protocol for a John Doe. Prints were rarely, if ever, lifted
at the scene. Once the prints were taken they would be sent to the
latent print section, where they would be run through IAFIS, the
Integrated Automated Fingerprint Identification System, a program
run and maintained by the FBI. If the victim had ever been arrested,
or worked for a government agency, his prints would be on file.

While Jessica waited she did the initial paperwork, including filling
out the body chart, the standard Police Department form that had
four outlines of the human body drawn on it, front and back, left and
right side. It also had space for the fundamental details of the crime
scene. Whenever someone came onto an existing case, this was the
first document they consulted.

But this body chart was a bit more difficult than usual. It was not
easy to diagram the wounds on the body. The fatal wound – the
laceration that had probably been responsible for the victim bleeding
out – was the one barb that looked to have been specifically sharpened
for that purpose. They would know a lot more about that when the
victim was autopsied the next morning.

While all this was pending Jessica called a friend of hers at L & I.
The Licenses and Inspections Department was the agency dedicated

to, among other things, enforcement and regulation of the city's code requirements regarding public safety, including building, plumbing, electrical, mechanical, fire, property maintenance, business, and zoning regulations.

After being on hold for more than five minutes she hung up, deciding to just go there and get what she needed. She crossed the duty room to where Byrne sat at a terminal, running the names of some of the witnesses they had spoken to.

'I'm going to run over to L & I and get a history on that building,' Jessica said.

In a city like Philadelphia, with a 300-year history, there was always a battle being fought between progress and preservation. The crime-scene building from that morning had easily been more than a hundred years old. There was nothing particularly interesting or attractive about it, and it clearly had been used for a number of purposes over the years. A visit to the zoning archives would give them a handle on who, if anyone, owned the building now, and what it had been used for in the past.

Jessica slipped on her coat, looked at her watch. 'Who's on at the morgue today?'

Byrne picked up the phone, made a call to the latent print division. During day work – the shift that was on duty between 8 a.m. and 4 p.m. – the print unit kept a technician at the morgue to take exemplars from unidentified victims. It was the least glamorous duty in the unit – if indeed there *was* a glamorous section to the latent print unit – and sometimes there was a backlog. Every homicide detective wanted their John or Jane Doe prints yesterday, but sometimes the bodies had to go into the refrigeration rooms pending the process, which made a lousy job even worse.

Byrne hung up the phone. 'Judy's on.'

Jessica smiled. 'Lucky us.'

Judy Brannon was in her late-thirties, single, and looking. She was also fearless. Jessica had once visited the morgue on a high-profile case, with the intention of walking the prints through the system. She watched Judy Brannon trying to get prints from a cold corpse when all of a sudden, in the middle of the process, the dead man's hand contracted, closing around Judy's wrist. Jessica had jumped a foot when it happened – not to mention enduring two sleepless nights as a result – but Judy had remained completely calm throughout.

In addition to her valiant work, and rather Rubenesque figure, Judy Brannon had a mad crush on Kevin Byrne.

'Bring me back something sweet,' Jessica said to Byrne as he walked out the door, heading to the morgue.

'Besides myself?' he asked.

'Not that sweet.'

THE ZONING RECORDS FOR the city of Philadelphia were located at the concourse level of the Licenses and Inspections offices at 15th and JFK. The area dedicated to studying the archives was a warren of drab gray cubicles.

While she waited, Jessica considered that, because this was part of a homicide investigation, she could have had her commissioner call the commissioner of L & I, thereby greasing the wheels. She decided that sometimes it was easier to save the chit, and wait in line. She flashed her badge and a smile, and before too long an L & I employee led her over to a terminal, and showed her how to access the information she wanted.

The process was a little confusing at first, but Jessica soon found the data on the crime-scene building. She began to read the history of the address, which went back more than 150 years.

Working front to back, she waded through documents such as zoning and use permits, prerequisite approvals, limited cooking permits (the building had once been used to house a restaurant it seemed), plot plans, electrical permits, and other documents. Although she found out that the property was abandoned, due to non-payment of taxes, she decided to check records all the way back to the building's original owners.

After twenty minutes or so of dry, municipal data, one name popped out, and changed everything.

'You've gotta be freakin' *kidding* me,' she said, loud enough to draw attention from the handful of people at the other terminals. She looked up, offered a silent *sorry* to all of them.

Jessica printed off her findings, grabbed her coat, and all but ran back to her car.

WHEN JESSICA RETURNED TO the Roundhouse, Byrne was waiting for her. She didn't even have to ask. He proffered a white bakery bag – always a good sign.

God, she was going to become a cow. She decided she would put these empty calories into the bank of time she owed the treadmill, as opposed to the other bank she owed the elliptical trainer. She figured she was up to somewhere around four and a half months straight on the treadmill, at a four-mile-per-hour pace. If she ran all the way to Baltimore, and halfway back, she'd be paid up.

She finished the Danish, took the computer printout from her portfolio.

'You ready for this?' Jessica asked.

'I love conversations that begin that way.'

Jessica handed Byrne the printout she made at L & I.

'This is the ownership history of that building?' Byrne asked.

'Yeah. Skip down to the bottom of the second page. The rest of it is pretty boring.'

Byrne flipped a page, scanned the next one. It listed the previous owners of the property.

'Check out the owner in 1853,' Jessica said.

'Holy shit.'

'Well put.'

Byrne read it again. 'John Nepomucene Neumann?'

'Himself.'

'As in Bishop Neumann?'

'Well, *Saint* John Nepomucene Neumann now, but yeah.'

Jessica had asked the clerk in zoning about ownership. It turned out that, for many years, property owned by the Catholic church listed the bishop of the diocese as the owner. As a Catholic Jessica probably should have known this, but it was far from the only thing about her faith on which she was clueless.

'So, this means that the property was at one time a Catholic church,' Byrne said.

'It does. It was originally called St Adelaide's. After St Adelaide's merged with a larger parish the building was sold to the Methodists, and I guess they couldn't make a go of it either. As you can see, it's been a lot of things since.'

'It still had that Catholic vibe though, didn't it?'

'Oh, yeah.'

Jessica knew that 'vibe' meant one thing to Byrne, and another to her. When she saw her partner go back into St Adelaide's, on his own, she knew that he needed time inside by himself. She had long ago learned to accept and respect Kevin Byrne's gifts. They didn't talk about them too much, but the knowledge was always there, always between them. Jessica figured one day Byrne may spill his guts to her about it. Doubtful, but maybe.

'And no one is on the books for the property now?'

Jessica shook her head. 'No one has paid taxes on it in ten years. I checked the last owners. Long out of business. In the wind.'

Philadelphia had the unfortunate distinction of having more real estate tax deadbeats than any other big city in the United States, with more than 100,000 properties in default. There were tens of thousands of empty buildings and vacant lots in North Philadelphia, Fairhill, and Nicetown/Tioga alone.

Byrne filed the zoning documents in the binder, considered some of the exterior photographs of the building that was once St Adelaide's. 'The X on the pole,' he said. 'It means something.'

'It has to,' Jessica said. 'Let's get on ViCAP today. Plug all this in.'

Started by the FBI in 1985, ViCAP – the Violent Criminal Apprehension Program – was a national registry of violent crimes: homicides, sexual assaults, missing persons, and unidentified remains. Case information submitted to ViCAP was available to authorized law-enforcement agencies around the world, and allowed investigators to compare their evidence to all other cases in the database and identify similarities.

Jessica crooked a thumb over her shoulder, in the general direction of the morgue on University Avenue. 'So, how'd we do, Romeo?'

'Have I failed yet?'

'It's the lemon Pledge. I'm telling you.'

'Judy said she would red line the fingerprints,' Byrne said. 'It's in the works.'

'Guys?' came a voice from behind them.

Jessica and Byrne turned. Josh Bontrager was in the doorway to the duty room.

'What's up, Josh?' Jessica asked.

'There's something you should see.'

THE VIDEO MONITORING UNIT was on the first floor of the Roundhouse. The huge space was arranged in three tiers with long curved tables on each level. Each table had a number of wired terminals into which a technician could plug a laptop, and from there monitor any of the hundreds of police cameras that were deployed around the city.

At the front of the room was an enormous monitor, measuring ten feet diagonally. At any given time, any image from any camera in the city could be displayed on this.

When Jessica and Byrne walked in with Josh Bontrager there were four technicians at work. Bontrager led Jessica and Byrne over to a monitor at the far end of the top tier. On the laptop was a high-angle night shot of a street corner. A now-familiar street corner.

'This footage is from that pole cam?' Byrne asked.

Bontrager sat down at the terminal. 'Yeah. As you can see, it covers the entrance to the alley next to the building, over to just left of the front door.'

'How far back can we go on this cam?' Byrne asked.

'This cam dumps every two weeks, so we have footage of our victim and someone else entering the building. Or at least their shadows.'

Bontrager hit a few keys on the keyboard. The image on the small screen was dark, but Jessica was able to pick out some details. There was a light-colored van parked directly in front of the church. The space in front of the van was empty. Every so often someone would pass by, walking either up or down Amber Street. Jessica constantly checked the time code. At the 10:05:44 p.m. mark Bontrager stopped the recording.

'Okay, here we're going to see two individuals enter from frame right. At least it looks like two individuals. No way of knowing what's out of frame.' Bontrager tapped the screen, lower right. 'As you'll see, they hesitate, then go down that alley. Which, as you know, is a dead end.'

'They don't walk in front of the camera?' Byrne asked.

Bontrager shook his head. 'Just our victim, and just for a second.'

The recording inched forward. For a moment, the streetlamp caught the figure on the left in profile. Although Jessica wouldn't swear to it in court, it looked a lot like their victim. But it did not look as if he were being coerced or forced down the alley. Despite the moment's hesitation, he looked like a willing participant. A second later there were only shadows on the alley wall, one of them wearing a pointed hood. Then they were gone.

'And we never get another angle?' Byrne asked.

'Unfortunately no. The cam was set up to catch activity on the corner. We're lucky to have this much.'

'Can you run that back?' Jessica asked.

Bontrager rewound the recording, replayed it. He isolated the frame where the victim was most discernible.

Jessica checked the date code. It was a week and a half old. 'Wait. You're saying he was in that basement for *ten days*?'

'It looks like it,' Bontrager said. 'I ran the recording forward, and no one goes in or out of that alley, except for that person in the hood, and then we only see the shadow.' He pointed to the time code in the corner. 'And always at the same time every night.'

'Always around ten?' Jessica asked.

'Always around ten.'

Jessica shuddered at the idea of being strapped to a chair for ten days, gagged and bound by barbed wire, in virtual darkness.

Bontrager fast-forwarded through the recording for the next ten days. Every night, around 10 p.m., a figure would go up that alley, then emerge a few minutes later. It was impossible to see anything other than the shape of the pointed hood.

'And this brings us to last night,' Bontrager said.

He hit the key. A few seconds later the figure entered the frame, stood for a moment, raising both hands, as if in benediction, then reached out and touched the lamp post, marking it in a slashing motion. This was the 'X' they had found.

A moment later the figure walked off, frame right. Jessica looked at the time code. It was 10:10:54.

'Is there any way to see this more clearly?' she asked.

'Well, not more clearly, but bigger,' Bontrager said.

He backed up the recording to the point when the hooded figure finished marking the pole. He hit a few more keys, and threw the image onto the huge monitor at the front of the room. He hit a button, and the recording began to progress one frame at a time. Bontrager got up, walked down the tiers, positioned himself next to the huge monitor.

Onscreen, the hooded figure stood, hands raised. They could now see that the figure's hands were white, but that may have been gloves.

'I don't suppose we could get this in any more detail,' Byrne said.

'No,' Bontrager said. 'I asked the techs. This was recorded at night, with low-level light. What we're seeing here is about it.'

'Can they get us a printout of this frame?' Byrne asked.

'*That* they can do,' Bontrager replied. He looked at his watch. 'Maria and I are going to recanvass. It's possible that someone might have had an angle from the other side of Amber Street.'

While Byrne studied the image on the huge monitor, Bontrager walked back to the table, gathered his belongings. He lingered for a moment.

'What is it, Josh?' Jessica asked.

'She's really pretty.' He turned, looked at Jessica, reddening by the second. 'I said that out loud, didn't I?'

Jessica smiled. 'I'm afraid so. You're talking about Maria?'

Bontrager nodded, swallowed hard.

'Yes, she is,' Jessica said.

Bontrager lowered his voice. 'Do you know if she's, you know, *seeing* anyone?'

Jessica knew that Maria Caruso had an on-again, off-again relationship with a lieutenant in the 23rd District. It was mostly off-again these days, if Jessica wasn't mistaken. 'I don't think she is, Josh.'

'I wonder what would happen if I asked her out.'

'Worlds would definitely collide,' Jessica said. 'The heavens would fall, the seas would dry up. I don't think we'd even get cable anymore.'

'Okay, okay,' Bontrager said. 'Seriously. Do you think she would go out with me?'

'Why wouldn't she?'

'Do you want the long list or the short list?'

Jessica had to smile. Josh Bontrager was terminally shy.

'I think it's time to bust a move, detective. No time like the present, right?'

Bontrager thought for a moment. 'You're right. Maybe I will.' He slipped on his coat. 'Thanks, Jess.'

He put his shoulders back and left the room, a spring in his step. A few minutes later a uniformed officer stepped in. 'Detective Byrne?'

Byrne turned from the monitor. 'Yes?'

The officer held up a pair of documents. 'You just got this from latents.'

Byrne crossed the room, thanked the officer, read the sheets. He came back to where Jessica was standing.

'Looks like we have an ID,' Byrne said. 'Our victim's name is Daniel E. Palumbo.'

'He was in the system,' Jessica said.

'He was.'

Jessica, recalling the needle marks on the victim's arms, figured he had been processed at some point in his life. She looked back at the monitor, at the façade of the abandoned church. She now had a name to go with the horror that took place in that basement.

'You ready for this?' Byrne asked.

'Now, see, that's just payback for before.'

'He was a cop.'

Jessica was stunned. *More* than stunned. '*What?*'

Byrne tapped the paper in his hands. 'He was a patrol officer for eighteen months.'

'Here in Philly?'

'Here in Philly.'

'Wait a minute,' Jessica said. 'He was only on the job for eighteen months? He was just a kid.'

'Yeah.'

'Why'd he retire?'

'No idea,' Byrne said. 'But I'm *really* interested in finding that out. Aren't you?'

'Oh yeah.'

JESSICA AND BYRNE RETURNED to the homicide duty room. Once there, Jessica sat down, rolled her chair over to a computer terminal, and entered the name in the database. In seconds she got a hit. She compared the photo on the computer monitor to the one she had taken of the victim at the scene. In her photograph the victim's face was so covered in blood and cuts, it hardly looked human. Still, prints never lie, and according to Judy's expert work, the prints were an eight-point match.

Daniel Palumbo had been twenty-three years old. He grew up in South Philadelphia, and became a police officer three years ago.

Jessica looked again at the two photographs. The man they found bleeding out in a church basement now had a name: Daniel Elias Palumbo. *Patrol Officer* Daniel Elias Palumbo. They had a minimum amount of information about him.

He had been arrested and convicted of possession of a controlled substance a few months after quitting the force, but had gotten off with time served and community service.

They had a date of birth. They had a brief life story. Now they had a date of death.

'We have a last known?' Byrne asked.

'Yeah, we do.' Jessica grabbed her coat and keys. 'His mother's house. She still lives on Latona Street.'

A s they rode to South Philly Jessica scrolled through the pictures on her iPhone. She looked at the photos taken at the St Adelaide's crime scene.

The first three were of the basement room in which the victim was found. The condition of the room was horrific, but nothing compared to the condition of the body. She knew that there were all manner of religious sects that practiced self-flagellation and self-mutilation as part of their ceremony, but she had a hard time believing their victim had wrapped himself in barb wire. Even if he had, he definitely had help tying his hands behind his back.

My Missal. Had the book belonged to the victim? It looked like a child's edition. If it was, why was this grown man carrying it? Did it belong to him? Did it belong to the killer?

Jessica also considered the *X* on the lamppost. If it was rendered in the blood of the victim they might be able to pull prints off the post, although the rusted surface of the metal might make that difficult.

They stopped for a light. 'What do you think?' Jessica asked.

'I think I need another day off already.'

'Do you think this was a ritual killing?'

'Well, the ritual killings we've investigated in the past have been just that, right? Killings. This guy was alive when we got there. I think he was left that way on purpose. For ten days.'

'But why that place?'

Byrne turned onto Latona Street. 'Good question. Maybe he used the place to shoot up. There was plenty of paraphernalia on the first floor.'

'You're not thinking this was a drug hit, are you?'

Byrne shook his head. 'I doubt it.'

Jessica agreed. This wasn't really a drug dealer's style. They usually went for an efficient, cost-effective double tap to the back of the head. Although there *were* serious sadists in that business. Both Jessica and Byrne had investigated drug-related homicides that had been committed with hatchets, shovels, machetes, and sundry other weapons.

While the murder did not seem like a drug killing at the moment, if Jessica had learned anything in her time in the unit, it was that you couldn't rule anything out in the first few hours of an investigation.

'What about the cop angle?' she asked. 'I'm wondering if this could be a holdover from his days on the street.'

'Could be that,' Byrne said. 'Could very well be that.'

THE PALUMBO ADDRESS WAS a well-kept, white-washed two-story rowhouse on Latona Street, between Eighteenth and Nineteenth. Entrance was via a black-wrought iron security door, flanked by a mailbox to the right, address above. Under the front window was an empty flower box, painted brown, partially wrapped in blue plastic sheeting. Two basement windows were clad in vented glass block.

Byrne rang the doorbell. After a few moments the door opened.

The woman standing before them was in her late-fifties or early-sixties. She had moist blue eyes that drooped slightly at the corners, and wore a light green waitress uniform with the name LORRIE stitched on the left side. She had the weary countenance of someone who had worked on her feet her entire adult life. In her hands was a well-laundered pink dishtowel.

Jessica and Byrne produced their badges and ID.

'Are you Loretta Palumbo?' Jessica asked.

'Yes,' the woman said, a bit cautiously, as if she had done this many times before. She squinted against the sudden blast of cold air. 'I am.'

'Ma'am, my name is Detective Balzano, this is my partner, Detective Byrne. We're with the Philadelphia Police Department.'

The look on the woman's face said that she knew. Not that she was aware that her son was dead, or any of the circumstances surrounding his murder, but just that she *knew*. It was a look that all but proclaimed that she had been waiting for this visit every day for a very long time.

'You're not with the Drug Unit,' she said.

'No, ma'am,' Byrne said. 'May we come in?'

The woman hesitated, then stepped to the side. 'I'm sorry. Please.'

The front room was very tidy and well-kept. The floral brocade sofa and chair against the sidewall were old, but covered in clear plastic. There were crystal ashtrays on every table, all brightly polished. On the walls were a half-dozen framed renderings of Jesus and the Virgin Mary. On the mantel over the bricked-in fireplace was a picture of Danny Palumbo in uniform, wearing his patrolman's cap, dress blues. It was hard for Jessica to reconcile this handsome young man with the person she had seen bleed out in that frigid basement.

What had happened to him?

'Is there anyone else here right now?' Byrne asked.

'No. I'm here all by myself.'

'Ma'am, do you have a son named Daniel?'

'Yes,' she said. 'Danny is my son.'

'When was the last –'

'He's dead, isn't he?'

The question floated in the dry, overheated air for a moment. 'Yes, ma'am,' Byrne said. 'I'm afraid so.'

The woman's gaze slowly moved from Byrne to Jessica, as if Jessica might have a different opinion, as if Jessica might disagree with Byrne and tell her that there might have been some kind of a mistake. Jessica had seen the look before, many times. Unlike the incidence of disease, there were no second opinions in homicide.

'We're very sorry for your loss,' Byrne said.

The woman crossed the kitchen, reached into a cupboard, pulled out a cup. It was not a coffee mug, but rather a child's brightly colored plastic tumbler. Jessica noticed that it was decorated with characters from the Flintstones. The woman didn't pour anything into it – no coffee, no soda, no juice. She just held it. Jessica wanted desperately to look at her partner, but stopped herself.

'What . . . what happened?' the woman asked. 'Was it the drugs?'

Jessica knew the convenient answer would be to say *yes*. *Yes, he died of an overdose*. It would make the job so much easier if they could blame all of this on a weakness, not the cracked mind of a killer.

'No,' Byrne said. 'We think he was murdered.'

The woman steadied herself with the arm of the sofa. 'Why?'

'We're not sure yet, ma'am,' Byrne said. 'We're just beginning our investigation. And we could use your help. I know this is a terrible shock. Do you feel up to answering a few of our questions?'

'Yes,' she said. 'I think so.'

Byrne took out his notebook and pen. 'When did you last see Danny?'

The woman thought for a few moments. 'I saw him two weeks ago. Maybe longer than that.'

'Do you remember the day of the week?'

The woman's stare was blank. Jessica had seen this many times also, the way sudden grief could steal even the smallest details from your memory. It was a form of shock.

'It's okay if you can't remember right now,' Byrne said. 'We can get to it later.'

Loretta Palumbo nodded.

'Did Danny live here?'

'No, not for years,' she said. 'It's just that sometimes he would stay here when he . . .'

When he got sick, Jessica thought. When he needed money. She looked around the room. There was no television, no DVD player, no stereo. Jessica wondered if those things had gone up Danny Palumbo's arm.

'I wouldn't let him do his drugs in this house,' Loretta said. 'I just couldn't.'

The woman's legs got a little shaky. Byrne crossed the room, eased her into a chair. He pointed to the plastic cup in her hands. 'Can we get you some water, ma'am?'

Loretta Palumbo pulled a tissue from a square box on the coffee table, dabbed her eyes. 'No, thank you.'

Byrne nodded to Jessica, who took out her notebook. Byrne put his away, sat on the couch. 'When Danny was here, the last time you saw him, how did he seem? Did he seem particularly troubled?'

Loretta stared at the framed photographs on the end table. One of them showed a much younger Loretta Palumbo leaning against the trunk of a 1980s compact car, a baby in her arms. 'He was always troubled,' she said. 'Even as a baby. Always restless, never could stay in one spot too long. One time he got out of his playpen and crawled almost to the corner.'

Byrne let the woman talk.

'When his father died, Danny was only ten years old. He came to me after the funeral holding my husband's toolbox. His father was quite handy around the house, you know.'

'When Danny stayed here, did he have his own room?' Byrne asked.

'Of course,' she said.

'May we take a look at it? There may be something in there that might help us.'

'It's upstairs,' Loretta said. 'On the left.'

Byrne nodded to Jessica, telling her that he would sit with the woman while she searched the victim's room.

JESSICA TOOK THE STAIRS two treads at a time, suddenly feeling claustrophobic in this cramped rowhouse, suddenly wanting to move on. Notification was never an easy thing – indeed, it was the worst part of her job – but for some reason she was having a harder than usual time with this one. It was all such a waste.

She opened the door to the bedroom on the left. The first thing that struck her was how spartan the room was. Against the wall with the window that looked out the front of the rowhouse there was a single bed, tightly made up with a light blue blanket, hospital corners. Next to the bed was a worn nightstand and lamp. At the foot of the bed was a dresser; next to it a low bookcase with what looked like five years' worth of crossword magazines, the kind that feature number-seek puzzles. That was it. No paintings or photographs on the walls, no throw rugs, no decorations of any kind. Jessica had enough experience with drug-related homicides to know that Danny Palumbo did not maintain a space this clean and spare.

She crossed the room, opened the drawers on the dresser. Inside she found a few old T shirts, a pair of jeans. She checked the pockets. All empty. In the bottom drawer she found Danny Palumbo's certificate from the police academy. It was unframed. Beyond this, there was no other clothing or accessories that indicated a police officer had ever occupied this room.

Jessica crossed the room to the sole closet, opened the door. The space was empty. There weren't even hangers on the rod, or anything stacked on the pair of shelves. Mounted on the inside of the closet door was an inexpensive full-length mirror. Jessica looked at her own warped reflection for a moment, thinking back to the day she had graduated from the academy, how proud her father had been. She wondered if Loretta Palumbo had felt the same way. She was sure of it. She *wanted* to be sure of it.

Jessica closed the door and, just to be thorough, got down on her knees and looked under the bed and the dresser. The only thing she found was a pair of worn green corduroy slippers under the bed. She looked inside, found nothing. She arranged them precisely as she had found them, matching their position to the dust-formed silhouettes.

She got up, walked back to the door, stepped into the hall. She was just about to close the door when something on the ceiling caught her eye. She glanced up.

There, in front of the doors and the windows, burned into the plastered ceiling, were marks in the shape of a cross.

WHEN JESSICA RETURNED TO the front room she found Byrne and the woman standing near the door.

'Do you know any of Danny's acquaintances?' Byrne asked. 'Someone we might talk to regarding his whereabouts for the past few weeks?'

Loretta Palumbo thought about this. Whatever crossed her mind brought a look of distaste to her face. 'He did bring a friend over a few times.'

'Do you remember this friend's name?'

'He was dirty. I didn't like him,' she said. 'I think Danny called him Boise, or something like that.'

'Boise? Like the city in Idaho?' Jessica asked.

'I don't know.'

Jessica made the note.

'He had the HIV, you know,' Loretta Palumbo added. 'They said he had the full AIDS a year ago, that maybe he didn't have too long to live, but then he got better.'

Jessica looked at Byrne. This meant two things, at least in the immediate sense. One, it opened up the possibility of this being some sort of hate crime, in addition to the motive having something to do with the time Danny Palumbo had been in uniform. Second, and more importantly, was that Jessica and Byrne had both been exposed to Danny Palumbo's blood. They had been wearing gloves when they touched him, and they both disinfected at the scene, so they were 99% safe. Still, you never knew.

'Your son was HIV-positive?' Byrne asked.

Loretta Palumbo nodded.

'I know this next question is going to seem very personal, but it is something we have to ask,' Byrne said. 'Was Danny gay?'

'No. He got it from the . . . you know . . .'

'He got it from sharing a needle.'

She didn't answer. She didn't need to.

'Mrs Palumbo, do you have a cell phone?' Byrne asked.

'A cell phone?'

'Yes, ma'am.'

'No. I just have the regular.' She pointed to the cordless phone on the wall near the kitchen door.

'I left my phone in the car,' Byrne said. 'Would you mind if I used your phone? It's a local call, and I won't be on long.'

'Not at all,' she said. 'Please.'

Byrne crossed the room, picked up the phone, dialed. After a few seconds he hung up. 'No answer.'

As Byrne buttoned his coat, preparing to leave, he gestured to the walls, to the framed renderings of Christ. 'I see you're a God-fearing woman.'

Loretta Palumbo stood a little straighter. 'The Lord is my salvation.'

'Was Danny a religious young man?'

'He was. He was baptized, he was confirmed. He went to Catechism.'

'Did he also make his first Holy Communion?'

'Oh, yes.' Loretta walked over to one of the end tables, populated with a dozen framed photographs. She lifted one from the back. In it an eight-year-old Daniel Palumbo sat posed for a professional photographer, wearing a long-sleeved shirt and thin white tie. 'He was a very devout boy.'

'Do you know if Danny owned a little white prayer book?'

'A prayer book?'

'Yes, ma'am. A book called *My Missal*?'

They had considered showing the woman the photograph they had of the book, the picture taken at the crime scene. Considering that it was covered in blood, they had decided it was not a good idea.

'I don't know,' she replied. 'He read the Bible all the time when he was small. I don't know about now.'

Byrne took out his card case, thumbed a business card. 'Ma'am, once again, on behalf of the city of Philadelphia, we're very sorry for your loss. We may have some more questions for you.' He handed the card to the woman. 'And we're going to need a member of the immediate family to make a positive identification.'

Loretta nodded. 'There's just me now. No one else.'

Byrne took her hand, held it for a moment. 'I'll let you know when we need you to be there. I'll come and get you. You won't be alone. And rest assured that the entire police department feels this loss. Danny was, and will always be, one of us.'

The woman stepped forward, put her arms around Byrne. From where Jessica stood, it didn't look like something this woman did often. It appeared that now that her son and husband were dead, it might be the last time she would have someone to embrace.

Byrne seemed to sense this too, and gently put his big hands on the woman's back. He let her break away first.

When she did, Byrne squared himself in front of her. 'You call me if you need anything. Anything at all.'

'God bless you,' she said.

'Thank you, ma'am,' Byrne said. 'Thank you.'

THEY WALKED BACK TO the car in silence. It was still bitterly cold, but at least the wind had died down. As they reached the curb, waiting for traffic to pass, a cloud sifted by the sun, bathing the street in a watery winter light.

'So, that was his baby cup that she took out of the cupboard, wasn't it?' Jessica asked.

'Yeah. It probably was.'

'He was twenty-three years old. She still has his little sippy cup. His Flintstones cup. It was the first thing she thought of.'

'Yeah.'

'Jesus, Kevin.'

There was no longer any traffic, but they didn't cross. Neither of them wanted to get back into a police car at the moment.

'You know, when I first came to the unit, I thought notifications were going to get easier over time,' Jessica said. 'They don't, do they?'

'No. Every one takes a little something from you.'

'And you never get it back.'

'No,' Byrne said. 'You don't.'

Jessica recalled coming home from the hospital when her mother died. She was only five years old at the time, but she remembered it as if it were yesterday. She recalled sitting in the small living room of their Catharine Street rowhouse with her father and brother, no one speaking. The mail came, the neighbors stopped by with food, cars passed. Other than that the only noise was when the furnace kicked on, and Jessica recalled being grateful for the sound, any sound, that would replace that roaring silence of anguish.

Sometimes, when she visited her father – who still lived in that house in which Jessica had grown up, who still had the same couches and tables and chairs – the silence returned, as did the reminder that there was still a hole in her heart, a hole that nothing would fill, no matter how long she lived.

Loretta Palumbo was just beginning the process.

WHEN THEY GOT INTO the car Jessica told Byrne what she had seen in Danny Palumbo's bedroom.

'And the crosses looked *burned* in?' Byrne asked.

'Yeah. Like someone took a soldering iron and made crosses in the plaster.'

'Not drawn.'

'No,' Jessica said. 'Burned.'

'And they were just in front of the doors and the windows? Not in the middle of the room? Not on the floors or furniture? Nowhere else?'

'Just on the ceiling,' Jessica said. 'Above the doors and windows. Like maybe Danny was trying to keep something out.'

'Or in.'

Yeah, Jessica thought. *Or in.*

Byrne looked back at the Palumbo rowhouse. 'Do you think it was Loretta Palumbo who called you this morning?'

'I don't know.'

Byrne took his cell phone out of his pocket; hit the button that took the phone from silent to ring tone. He hit a few more buttons. And Jessica understood. Byrne had called himself to get Loretta Palumbo's number. If they requested a log of calls into homicide from that morning, they would be able to rule in or out whether or not the call came from this address. It was a lot easier, and faster, than getting a warrant to get a list of calls from Loretta Palumbo's house phone.

Byrne put his phone away.

As Jessica buckled in she turned to look back at the rowhouse. Before Byrne pulled away Jessica glanced up at the second-floor window. There she saw a shadow behind the sheer curtains. It was Loretta Palumbo. She was in her dead son's room.

TEN

THE SMELL WAS OVERPOWERING. AT FIRST SHANE THOUGHT IT WAS A delectable brew of spoiled fish and rotting lemons, with a backstory of wet coffee grounds, but soon he detected the unmistakable top note of used kitty litter.

There was nothing quite like that blend of pine-flavored clay and cat shit to open the sinuses, he thought. In fact, he had gotten so good – had acquired quite the nose, as oenophiles say – that he could instantly tell the difference between clumping and conventional litter at the very first whiff.

Not that the subject would come up that often in his small circle of friends dining at Le Bec Fin or Striped Bass.

In between the fish and the kitty he smelled banana peel, vinegar, something that had to be months-old tomato sauce, and it occurred to him – not for the first time by any means – that a good deal of his ability to read people was based on his aptitude in reading their garbage.

People *are* their garbage.

Tonight he had rubbed a little Vick's VapoRub under his nostrils so the smells were not that bad, all things considered. Standing in an alcove behind an upscale rowhouse in Society Hill, he knew he had to get in and out quickly. Dry heaving in the middle of Delancey Street was not part of the plan.

As always, he sifted through the paper products first. Paper was his grail. First up was a wad of catalogs stuck together by God knows what: *Restoration Hardware, Crate & Barrel, Pottery Barn, L. L. Bean, Land's End*. All the usual yuppie suspects. He gently peeled them apart. You never knew what people were going to use as bookmarks inside books or catalogs. He once found a very intimate letter inside a copy of *Field & Stream*, a missive left there – unsent and undelivered – by a married middle-aged man, addressed to a young girl who worked as a waitress at this man's neighborhood Denny's.

This night he found nothing inside the magazines. He checked the address labels. All the same, all belonging to the homeowner. No information or direction was to be gleaned in a dissimilar address.

Next was a similarly clumped stack of magazines: *Mac World, Architectural Digest, Tropical Fish Monthly*.

Mac user and fish aficionado, Shane thought, registering the two bits of data in his finely compartmentalized brain.

An *afishianado*.

Pay attention, Shane.

He riffled through these mags. *Nada*. The only loose material the periodicals contained were those blow-in cards the magazines annoyed you with to get you to subscribe. Shane had never used a blow-in card, based solely on principle.

The next paper products were a series of opened #10 and corresponding #6 return envelopes. These were mostly those not-so-cleverly disguised pitches for reduced credit-card APR rates that arrived in envelopes with no return address, designed to sucker the recipient into thinking it was some sort of invoice or bill.

IMPORTANT ACCOUNT INFORMATION ENCLOSED! barked an announcement on the front of the envelope. Shane found almost all of these torn neatly in half, although some people, after perhaps the fourth or fifth ruse, took the time to tear them into confetti-sized pieces.

Beneath the paper layer were smaller plastic trash bags. These were from the bathroom, kitchen, home office. As gross as most of this was, the smaller bags used in the bathroom posed other problems. Shane had once sliced a finger on a double-edge razor. Since that incident he always carried a small bottle of antibacterial foam in his pocket.

The small bags in front of him now were from the kitchen, packed with crushed Diet Coke cans, cardboard coffee containers bearing the Starbucks logo, as well as a number of meal-sized Styrofoam containers. Inside these containers were nothing more than half-eaten sandwiches and salads, along a small pile of cigarette butts. He noted that half the butts had lipstick on the filters.

Mac. Tropical fish.

A girlfriend? Lover? *Prostitute?*

He looked at his watch. He still had time.

The last of the trash was a pile of crumpled bags from the Whole Foods on South Street, and a pair of large potato chip bags. The last bag he picked up had contents that rattled. There was something plastic inside. Shane eased open the top, and saw them.

Jackpot.

There, at the bottom of the empty super-size bag of Lay's Potato Chips, were four empty pill vials.

Heart racing, Shane carefully picked out the vials, shaking each one to make certain they were empty. They were.

'And what have we here?' he quietly asked the night.

He angled the first vial's label into the beam of his pen flashlight. The prescription was for a drug called Mirtazapine. Shane had never heard of it. The others were Diazepam, Benazepril, and Zolpidem.

Shane fished out his smart phone, got on the Net. He entered the names of the drugs. Mirtazapine was used in the treatment of depression. The Benazepril was used to treat high blood pressure. The others – Diazepam and Zolpidem – Shane knew all too well. They were the generic names of Valium and Ambien, respectively.

Let's see, he thought. *High blood pressure, depression, anxiety, and insomnia.*

Not only was the man on the edge, all his medications were generic.

Cheap prick.

As Shane began to refill the garbage bag, he thought about how people didn't realize that, if someone went through their trash, it was the same as having them go through their house. Better, actually, from Shane's point of view. In your house you could hide things, keep visitors from going into certain rooms, lock closets and cabinets, put things in a safe. When you threw things into a garbage can, rarely did you consider the order of it all.

Shane was so accomplished at this, that he could – and many times had – determine a timeline for a person's week. Monday on the bottom, Tuesday layered on top that, all the way to trash day. At home he had a database detailing every trash pickup in every neighborhood in Philadelphia. He was, in many ways, an archaeologist, wasn't he?

He looked at his watch again. Now he was late.

Shane pulled together the four corners of the plastic sheet, gathered the middle sections, and stuffed it all back into the large Hefty bag. Somehow, it didn't all fit. It never did. It was one of the great mysteries of life. It was like when you bought a portable television or some other kind of oddly shaped appliance. You could never get the pieces and cables and user manuals and adapters back into the box if you had to return it. Shane figured that manufacturers depended on this. He often wondered how many people kept some crappy item because they were too embarrassed to admit they couldn't fit the thing back into the box.

Which was one of the reasons he carried a variety of plastic garbage bags with him at all times. If you had to re-trash a pile of garbage, for whatever reason – and yes, if *re-gift* was a word, *re-trash* was a word – you wanted to match the brand and size and color so as not to arouse suspicion. If there was an extra bag, so what? People never remembered how many bags they put out. But if they found a blue bag amidst their basic black – there was a flag. Shane always carried three colors and five sizes.

He got all the garbage back inside the bags, tidied up the area. He looked at the photograph on his phone, the one he had taken on arrival, nudged two of the bags closer to the rear of the house.

Perfect.

He was just about to leave, newly acquired swag in hand – that being the four empty pill vials – when his phone vibrated. It was a text message. Three letters:

WTF

'I'm coming,' Shane said. '*Bitch.*'

SHANE DROVE TO NORTH Philly. He parked, got out, climbed into the backseat of his car, eyed the area, taking it all in. As he took off his sweatshirt and undershirt he glanced at the rowhouses on the east side of the street. Typical North Philly clapboards. There was a bodega of sorts on the corner, a closed sandwich shop. Nothing terribly cinematic.

He rummaged through his gym bag, found the Wet Wipes. He pulled two of them out, wiped under his arms. As he did this he scanned the other side of the street. On that side was a wig store and a nail salon, next to them a tavern. Oh, yes. He framed the tavern sign with his hands, and had a moment of Spielbergian inspiration.

Perfect.

He slipped on a dress shirt – like garbage bags, he always carried a fresh supply with him, highly starched and neatly folded in the backseat – then reached for the hanger bearing his collection of neckties. He then got out of the car, tucked in his shirt, knotted his tie. There was nobody faster on earth at tying a necktie without the aid of a mirror.

Note to self: Pitch a reality around something like this.

Shane circled to the back of his car, lifted the trunk lid, unzipped the garment bag inside. He slipped on a blazer, along with a cashmere overcoat.

He began his vocal exercises – *red leather yellow leather red leather yellow leather* – took a deep breath, checked himself in the tinted rear window, channeling the late great Roy Scheider (who himself had channeled the late great Bob Fosse) and said:

'*Show* time.'

WHEN SHANE ROUNDED THE corner Cyndy was already there, stamping her feet against the cold, blowing into her gloved hands. He was only a few minutes late, but you didn't want to piss off Cyndy Jovovich.

Shane liked working with Cyndy, who was nicknamed Mortal Cyn, due to her fearlessness when moving in on a dead body with her camera. At just over six feet tall, weighing in at a solid 190, Cyndy Jovovich could bench press Shane Adams, then throw him like a shot-put. More than once she had run point on a story. Shane, of course, preferred to fight his own battles, but he was no dummy. Cyndy Jovovich could deck a professional hockey player with one whistling right hand.

'Fucking diva,' she said. 'I've been here for ages.'

'No, you haven't.'

Cyn was the hottest shooter at the station. For some reason, most of the television photographers Shane had worked with, regardless of market, had been women. He preferred it, actually. Of all those women, Cyndy Jovovich was the best.

Unfortunately, she knew it.

They were doing a follow-up to a story that had aired a week earlier, a story about a Philadelphia city councilman who had been under investigation on charges of corruption and kickbacks. The ruling had come down that afternoon – exonerating the four-term councilman of any wrong doings. The councilman had declined to comment on air, so they decided to do a standup across the street from his modest law offices, which were located on the second floor of the building that housed the tavern.

Shane took Cyn aside and showed her what he was thinking. She shook her head, put the camera on the tripod, framed it, locked it down. 'You are *so* bad.'

'And still you won't fuck me.'

'Not if you were the last dick in the Delaware Valley.'

Shane laughed. The best part of riding with Mortal Cyn was that she was openly gay, Shane was openly straight, so there was never any sexual tension between them. There was, and hopefully always would be, a lot of sexual banter.

Cyn flipped on the light, and silently counted him down.

Exactly thirty-one seconds later, wrapping up:

'This is Shane Adams, Action News.'

In this follow-up piece about the councilman (who everyone in the city of Philadelphia believed was guilty of taking kickbacks), they had framed the shot of Shane's stand-up carefully to include a portion of the neon sign for the Crooked Toad Tavern on the corner. The way they composed the shot, with the tavern's sign at the right side of the screen, cut out most of it, leaving a single truncated word over Shane's left shoulder while he was talking. A word written in bright yellow letters:

CROOK

Shane watched the playback on the camera's LCD screen.
Perfect.
God, he loved his job.

AT HOME, SHANE SHOWERED and ran an electric razor over his face. He followed with toner and moisturizer. Next to the bathroom mirror he always kept a life-size color photograph of his face, taken on the first of every month. He had these pictures going back nearly ten years. He had a file of more than one hundred of them. In this way he charted the changes to his face, which was his life. He'd never had any plastic surgery, not even a dermabrasion or single shot of Botox, but now that he was getting older he was already pricing various procedures.

Still in his robe, he sat at his iMac, launched his database application, clicked onto the file he needed. He then launched iPhoto, maneuvered over to the corresponding folder.

He had first noticed her coming out of her rowhouse on Fitzwater Street about six months ago, and had watched her a few times since. She was tall and leggy, had deep auburn hair (Clairol Dark Spice Natural Reddish Brown). She was well dressed (Nordstrom and Bluefly), and had what appeared to be an Imelda Marcos-sized shoe collection (mostly Zappos, with a *lot* of returns).

Shane had systematically gone through her trash every other week for the past three months, meticulously recording the details he might need, inputting it all into his ever-growing database.

For instance, he knew she subscribed to *Wine Spectator* and, according to three separate receipts from a Center City chi-chi eatery, had ordered a Barolo. She was also a fan of novelist Sue Miller, having recently bought a copy of *The Good Mother* at amazon.com. Three of her recent emails – which she for some reason printed out and subsequently discarded – had recommended the book to friends.

She also ordered Mexican food from a delivery service, favoring tapas on Tuesday and frijoles on Friday nights.

Note to self: Write a Broadway lyric around this.

Shane closed his eyes, visualized the upcoming encounter. He had learned this technique from a shrink he had been forced to see as a result of a run in with the PPD the first week he had been on the job in Philadelphia. The court had thought he might be unstable.

Little did they know.

Twenty minutes later he dressed in a Zegna sport coat, Seven For All Mankind jeans, along with an inexpensive white shirt from J. Crew, locked the two deadbolts on his door, and left the building.

AFTER STOPPING AT THE Barnes & Noble at Rittenhouse Square, and making his purchase, Shane entered the lobby bar at Le Meridien at just after nine. There was only one seat open at the bar. A Sixers game was on the plasma.

He saw her at her favorite banquette with her overweight work friend – older woman, mid-forties, wearing a navy blue, off-the-rack Chico's pantsuit. Shane knew this woman to be Arlene. He had found a Christmas and birthday card from her in the trash.

Shane took up a position a few seats down from them. He slipped in a pair of earbuds, but did not start any music on his iPod. He needed to be able to hear. He opened his brand new copy of *The Good Mother*, began to read. Out of the corner of his eye he saw the woman look over, then look a second time a few seconds later, the way people do when they think they know someone, but they're not sure in which world to place them. School, work, social, casual. Ever since Shane had become an on-air personality in Philly it had started. This worked in his favor, as well as against, in seemingly equal measure.

Tonight it was golden.

'Excuse me,' she said. As she said this, she reached over and touched his arm. He glanced at her wine glass. It was almost empty.

Perfect.

Shane looked up, made eye contact. He felt a shiver of excitement. He imagined that it was the same feeling that prosecutors get when they trap a witness in a lie, or that of a marlin fisherman when he feels that unmistakable pull on the line.

He took the earbuds out, smiled. 'Hi.'

'Hi,' she said. Her full name was Danica Evelyn Dooley. Twenty-six, five-nine, 120 give or take. Mostly give lately. She'd been putting away a few bags of Pepperidge Farm Milano cookies a week. She worked at Progressive Insurance, drove a Ford Focus, had two brothers named William and Thaddeus. She liked Versace *Crystal Noir* perfume. She was wearing it tonight. 'I know you from somewhere.'

Shane smiled even more broadly. 'Oh, I don't think so,' he said. 'I'd certainly remember you.'

She blushed. 'My name is Danica. This is my friend –'

Arlene, Shane wanted to blurt out, just to keep things moving. He did not.

' – Arlene,' Danica said.

'My name is Shane.' He reached out, shook hands with both women, lingering a split second longer with Danica's hand. The gesture was not lost on anyone. 'Delighted to meet you both.'

Not entirely true.

Danica pointed at Shane's book. 'I can't believe you're reading that. I just finished it. It has to be one of my favorite books of all time.'

Shane put his earbuds away, committing to the conversation, then held up the new paperback. 'Well, I'm on my third read,' he said. 'Had to buy a new copy. I lent mine out, never got it back.' He had read all the amazon.com reviews of the book before leaving the house, of course, and with his nearly eidetic memory, remembered them word for word. If pressed, he could more than hold his own in a book discussion with Danica. 'Every time I read it I find something new.'

The waiter approached the table. 'What can I get you, sir?'

Shane looked at the wine list, even though he didn't have to. He had this memorized, too. 'I think I'll have a glass of the Barolo.'

'This is amazing,' Danica said. 'Barolo is my favorite.'

'Anything else for the ladies?' the waiter asked.

Danica and her friend made instant eye contact, the way friends do at a moment like this, and Arlene got the message. She looked at her watch.

'Nothing for me, thanks,' she said. 'I've got to get going.'

The waiter turned to Danica. She tapped the rim of her wineglass. 'I'll have the same.'

Perfect.

Danica and Arlene made their goodbyes. Shane politely shook the other woman's hand. When she was gone, he took up position on the other side of the table, opposite Danica Dooley. She really was beautiful. A symmetrical face, soft features, a minimal amount of makeup and jewelry.

When the waiter left, they clinked glasses, sniffed, swirled, sipped. A few seconds later Shane found Danica staring at him, smiling. '*Now* I know who you are,' she said. 'You're on the *news*.'

'Yes.'

She fluffed her hair, smoothed a cheek. She seemed a little star-struck, or maybe it was the second glass of Barolo. Shane preferred star-struck.

Danica pointed to the wine and the copy of *The Good Mother*.

'I can't believe we have exactly the same tastes.'

You have no idea, Shane thought.

He left Danica's apartment around 3 a.m. When he got home he showered again, prepared everything he needed for the morning, a day that was going to begin in just three hours.

Before crawling into bed, he opened the database, put the red *X* in the field next to Danica's name, looked at the next few entries on the list. It was a list that had grown to seventy entries.

Shane fell asleep to the sound of the intermittent crackling of the police scanner he kept next to his bed. He had gone to sleep this way for many years. Although Shane might be loath to admit it to anyone outside the business, he could no longer sleep without it.

Soon he drifted off, the sound of swirling water filling his dreams, as it had every night since he was five years old, the sound of the baptismal waters engulfing him, filling his mind.

Before I formed you in the womb, I knew you. Before you were born, I set you apart, came the phantasm of his mother's voice.

On the good nights the sound of the waters lulled him to sleep.

On the bad nights he drowned.

ELEVEN

I N THE DAYS FOLLOWING THE DISCOVERY OF DANIEL PALUMBO'S BODY in the basement of the North Philadelphia building that once housed St Adelaide's, the Homicide Unit interviewed more than three dozen people who either knew Palumbo, or had been in the neighborhood at the time.

Ultimately, they learned nothing about Danny Palumbo's movements the day he either voluntarily went, or was led, to the abandoned church where ten days later he would die.

The medical examiner performed an autopsy on the victim, and the official cause of death was ruled exsanguination, meaning Palumbo had bled to death. A toxicology report was also filed, and concluded that, in addition to small traces of heroin and Ativan, an anti-anxiety drug, there was also trace of a drug called Pavulon.

Jessica had run into the drug Pavulon once before. It was a neuro-muscular blocking agent, essentially a paralytic. It was used for general anesthesia during surgery as an aid to intubation or ventilation. In higher doses it would completely paralyze the muscles, though have no pain-numbing effect.

Jessica considered Danny Palumbo in that chair, unable to move, the barbed wire wrapped around his body and neck. When he finally *could* move, his head fell forward from fatigue, and the sharpened barb cut into his carotid.

As to the crime scene, there were enough partial prints in that building to keep the latent print division busy for months, and that was not going to happen. In a building that old, the number of people who had passed through the space, touching those surfaces most likely to retain full prints – doors and jambs, handrails, window panes – numbered in the hundreds. In time, dust and soot formed a layer on everything, reducing the viability of the surfaces to yield clean, identifiable prints.

A half-dozen partial exemplars had been run, yielding no hits. The only good prints belonged to the victim, fingerprints in blood on the back of the wooden chair in which he was bound.

There were no eyewitnesses, and no other blood types were found on the victim or at the scene. They had not found anyone in the PCIC system named Boise.

The barbed wire used to wrap Danny Palumbo's body – essentially, the murder weapon, their only lead at this point – was unremarkable in every way. The firearms unit determined that the wire was anywhere from five to fifteen years old. It was made of galvanized mild steel, a type used primarily in agriculture, and would not, if left unaltered, be sharp enough to accomplish what their killer so clearly wanted to accomplish. That was why one of the barbs had been honed to a razor-sharp tip and carefully placed against Daniel Palumbo's carotid artery.

Finding where the barbed wire was acquired was nearly impossible. If a length of concertina wire had been stolen from a Philadelphia business, and reported to police, they would have something to go on. Because the wire used to wrap the victim was agricultural, it left only a million acres of Pennsylvania farmland to investigate.

Ligature marks were found on the victim's cheeks, as were cotton fibers, indicating Danny Palumbo had probably been gagged the whole time.

CSU found trace evidence of metal filings on Danny's right shoulder.

On the final night of Danny Palumbo's life, had the hooded figure they had seen on the street returned, and shaved down that barb to make it sharper? Had that person backed off on the paralytic drug so that Danny Palumbo could move his head, and thereby deliver the fatal wound?

The thought gave Jessica a chill.

But, if this were the case, why had the killer left Danny in there for ten days? Why not just do it and have done with it? Was the amount of time significant?

It had to be.

Jessica had put in a call to the Archdiocese of Philadelphia, and received a rather terse fax in reply, stating the obvious and expected: that since the building had not housed a Catholic church in more than seventy years, they had no information relevant to the recent crime. The fax referred Jessica and the PPD to Licenses and Inspections, which, of course, was where Jessica's inquiries began.

The Crime Scene Unit had collected its physical evidence and removed the tape. A secure padlock had been put on the door and, for all intents and purposes, to anyone walking or driving by, nothing bad had ever happened at that address.

THE CRIME LAB WAS a state-of-the-art facility at Eighth and Poplar Streets, often shorthanded as the FSB – Forensic Science Bureau. It housed many of the department's scientific divisions, including the fingerprint lab, the drug lab, the Firearms Unit, the DNA lab, and the document section.

The head of the document section was a man named Sergeant Helmut Rohmer. Jessica and Byrne had worked with Rohmer – who preferred to be called Hell – on a number of cases.

A giant of a man at six-four, Hell was a sight to behold, with his spiky white-blond hair and huge, but gentle hands. Since getting married to another one of the techs at the lab, a young criminalist named Irina Kohl, he had put on an extra twenty or so pounds. Despite the extra girth, it seemed that married life agreed with him. He was a bit calmer than he had been, but no less thorough. At least he was eating well.

Hell Rohmer was also known for his collection of black T shirts, although he was probably up to the Big and Tall 3X size by now. Today's gem read:

SILENCE IS GOLDEN.
DUCT TAPE IS SILVER.

They got their chitchat out of the way.

'I've good news and bad news,' Hell said. It appeared that he was about to continue, when he suddenly stopped. For a few long moments he stared into space.

'What is it, Hell?' Jessica asked.

'It just occurred to me that I've never said that before.'

'What, ever?'

'*Ever*,' Hell said. 'And it also occurred to me that it always bugs the shit out of me when anyone says it to me. So I don't think I'll ever say it again.'

Silence.

'Hell?'

'Right, okay,' he said. 'Well, I'm not going to say "which do you want first" now, am I?'

'Can I pick?' Jessica asked.

'Of course.'

'I'll take the good news.'

Hell sprang into action. 'Okay. I have a fix on the little prayer book. It took a number of methods to dry it out, seeing as it was soaked in blood, but that's why I get dental and two weeks a year in Biloxi.'

Jessica glanced at Byrne. They decided not to ask.

'There were a few pages I could not separate without destroying them – yet – but I think we have a pretty good start.'

He pinned a half-dozen photographs on the wall.

'The text is pretty standard issue. It has excerpts from the King James version, with selections from *Genesis, Hebrews, Matthew, Numbers,* and *Revelation*. There was no red ribbon like you used to get in books like these. Remember those?'

Jessica did. She said so.

'I always liked those,' Hell said. 'Anyway, there *was* a red ribbon once, but it was torn out.' He tapped a close-up photograph of the top of the book where the stub of the red ribbon was once attached. 'Savages.'

Jessica almost smiled. The case was a brutal homicide where a man was wrapped in barb wire for ten days, and Hell Rohmer had harsh words for someone who ripped a ribbon out of a missal. Lab rats were a breed apart.

'The print section had it before I did, and they dusted the exterior cover,' Hell continued. 'It has a pebbled surface, so no dice there. However, the inside of the book cover is a smooth plastic, so that holds some promise, print-wise. They'll get this back in the afternoon.'

Hell then opened a drawer, reached in, pulled out a manila envelope. 'And now the *pièce de* whatever it is.'

'There's more good news?' Jessica asked.

'I kind of grouped the good news together into one big sundae,' Hell said. 'I hope that's okay.'

'Sundaes are good.'

'Cool.'

Hell reached into the envelope, held up a small plastic evidence bag. He put it under his lighted, swing-arm magnifier. 'I found a hair between one of the pages. Root and all. Not sure if it belonged to the vic or not. Either way, if we ever get the order to run DNA, there's plenty here to work with.'

'Awesome,' Jessica said. She knew there was only so much a microscopic examination of a follicle of hair could determine – race, gender, sometimes approximate age. Everything else came from DNA testing.

'Well done, big man,' Byrne added.

Hell beamed. He loved being called 'big man,' especially by a guy like Kevin Byrne, who was pretty big himself.

As Hell basked in the glow of his accomplishments, the moment lingered.

'And what about, you know, the *other* stuff?' Jessica asked, trying to avoid the phrase 'bad news.'

'Oh, yeah. That.'

Hell pinned up another photograph, an enlarged image of the missal's copyright page.

'These missals were printed in a small town in West Texas, by a company called Mighty Word, Inc. Unfortunately, the book was printed in 1958, and the company has been out of business since 1961. There is no way to trace where or when this was purchased, unless you guys do some serious digging and can find someone who once worked there, or if they got bought out by another company and the records still exist.' Hell shrugged his massive shoulders. 'I'm afraid that stuff is out of my wheelhouse.'

'Can we take that page with us?' Byrne asked.

'Captain, my captain.' Hell produced a pair of printouts.

On the way out Jessica turned, looked back. Hell stood, hands on his hips, proudly looking at the photos, Pablo Picasso in front of a half-completed *Guernica*.

THE SERVICE FOR DANNY Palumbo was held at All Souls Cemetery in Chester County. In all, there were twenty or so officers from the PPD. After the interment ceremony, Jessica and Byrne stood near the entrance to the parking lot. A young officer approached them. His nametag identified him as G. Hyland. He was in his early-twenties – trim, blond, muscular.

Byrne had put in a call to the commander of Danny Palumbo's old district. As a favor the commander had freed Officer Hyland from duty for as long as they needed him.

'Greg Hyland,' the young man said.

'Good to meet you,' Byrne said. 'Kevin Byrne. My partner, Jessica Balzano.'

They all shook hands.

'Just trying to get a handle on what happened,' Byrne said. They had the official version of why Daniel Palumbo had quit the force. They were hoping to get the real reasons now. 'We appreciate your time.'

Hyland nodded.

'You came up with Danny?'

'Yes, sir,' Hyland said. 'Same class at the academy.'

'What can you tell us about why he quit?'

'It was probably a number of things,' Hyland said. 'But there was one thing that was probably the tipping point for Danny.'

Jessica and Byrne just listened. The pained expression on Hyland's face spoke of the friendship the young man had once shared with Danny Palumbo, a fellow officer

'We were working day-work,' Hyland said. 'Summertime. Hot as hell. There was a BOLO on a guy who had been seen touching girls around the parking lot behind Holy Spirit.'

'Over on Hartranft?' Byrne asked.

'Yes, sir. We made it a point to check on the school more than usual, making a few extra passes. This one morning we came around the corner, saw this guy kneeling down in front of this little girl. The girl looked really scared. The guy fit the general description so we parked, got out. Danny approached the guy, asked him to move away from the girl, asked for ID. The guy stood up, all squirrelly, like he was ready to bolt. Danny put a hand on him, and that's when the guy took a swing. He punched Danny in the shoulder . . . no damage really. Nonetheless we took him to the ground, booked him, made out the report, got back on the street.'

Hyland turned his cap a few times in his hands.

'Two days later the real perp gets caught in the act. Had a little girl with her pants down behind those apartments on Eighteenth. That night our guy, who didn't make bail on the assault on a police officer charge, hangs himself in his cell. Turns out he was a little challenged – developmentally challenged – and used to play with a lot of the kids in the playground.'

A true nightmare for a cop, Jessica thought. One of the worst.

'Danny took it hard,' Hyland said. 'He was never the same after that. It wasn't his fault, of course, but that didn't seem to matter. Media hounded the guy – especially this one piece-of-shit reporter who wouldn't get off his case. Danny started drinking, showing up late for his tour. Eventually he just quit. Then he got popped for possession. All downhill from there.'

'Did you know he was using?' Byrne asked.

'I never saw him using.'

Jessica knew, like Byrne and Greg Hyland knew, that the question asked had not been answered. But that was okay. For now.

Hyland continued. 'You want to know if he was using when he was a cop? Here's what I know. Danny wouldn't have disgraced the uniform that way. He was a good man. He was a good officer.'

'Did you stay in touch after he left the force?' Jessica asked.

Hyland looked at the ground, perhaps a bit ashamed. 'Not as much as I could have. Not as much as I *should* have. You know how it is. Life takes over. The job takes over.'

'When was the last time you saw him?'

'Maybe six months ago. He was standing on the corner of Broad and C. B. Moore. I passed him in my sector car, had to do a double take. I barely recognized him. I pulled over, sat there for maybe five minutes, thought about going up and talking to him, but I didn't. I think it would have done more harm than good. I think he would have been humiliated.' Hyland slipped his patrolman's cap back on, squared it. 'I wish I had now. Maybe I could have done something.'

'You do what you think is right at the time,' Byrne said. 'We all do.'

Hyland shrugged, remained silent.

Byrne stuck out his hand. 'Thanks for talking to us, Officer.'

'Not at all.' Hyland shook Byrne's hand, looked at Jessica, touched a finger to the brim of his cap. 'Ma'am.'

'Have a safe tour,' Byrne added.

'You, too.'

As they watched P/O Hyland return to his car, Jessica thought about what a fine line there was between making the right call and the wrong call, how police officers were expected to be perfect in their judgment every time out. Lives were always at stake.

As they headed to the car, Jessica spotted Loretta Palumbo in the parking lot. She was standing by herself. She looked lost. Jessica got Byrne's attention. They walked across the lot. As they approached, Loretta looked up. At first it appeared that she did not recognize them, then recollection lit her face.

'Oh. Hi,' she said. 'Thank you for coming.'

This woman looked five years older than the one Jessica had met only a few days earlier, despite her hastily applied makeup. Jessica could tell that Loretta Palumbo was a woman who generally eschewed vanities like lipstick and blush. She wore an old camel hair calf-length coat, sixties or seventies vintage, perhaps her mother's. Jessica noticed there was a button missing.

You wear your best to a family member's funeral, Jessica thought. Especially the funeral of a child. The thought that this was Loretta Palumbo's best coat broke Jessica's heart a little more. This woman deserved better.

When everyone was out of earshot Byrne said, 'I'm sorry to say there has been no progress in the investigation.'

Loretta Palumbo nodded. She put her hand on the door handle of her car, hesitated, took her hand back. 'You don't expect to bury your children,' she said. 'My husband was ten years older than me, you know. He had a bad heart. But Danny . . . You shouldn't have to bury your son.'

Jessica felt another flush of sorrow. She thought about Sophie and Carlos, and was suddenly filled with an unnamable dread about their future. Parents burying their children happened all too often in a city like Philadelphia. 'No, ma'am,' was all Jessica could think of to say.

Loretta Palumbo looked out over the cemetery, at the just-turned earth of her son's plot.

The wind suddenly picked up, slicing across the grounds. Neither Jessica nor Byrne was going to cut this meeting short. They would give this woman all the time she needed.

'His father's suit,' Loretta said softly. 'The blue one.' She smoothed the front of her coat, pulled her gloves a little tighter to her wrists.

They stood this way for a long time.

'Did you ever talk to Danny's friend?' Loretta finally asked.

'His friend?' Jessica replied.

'He didn't come today. I thought maybe he would.'

The question brought the two detectives back to the moment. 'You mean the man you mentioned? The man named Boise?' Byrne asked.

'Yes.'

'No, ma'am. We weren't able to locate him.'

Loretta Palumbo bunched her collar around her neck, warding off the wind. 'Danny told me once that they used to get meals down at St John's.'

'St John's Hospice?' Jessica asked. 'Over on Race?'

The woman nodded. 'Do you know it?'

Jessica knew it well. It was just a few blocks from the Roundhouse. 'Yes.'

'It's a soup kitchen, you know.'

It wasn't a question. Jessica heard the shame and sadness and defeat in the woman's voice. This proud woman had her *own* kitchen, one in which her son was always welcome. Before Jessica could respond, Loretta Palumbo continued.

'You might find him there,' she said. 'Unless . . .'

She did not have to finish the sentence. Both Jessica and Byrne knew what she meant.

Unless he's dead, too.

TWELVE

Located on Race Street, between Twelfth and Thirteenth, Saint John's Hospice was established in the early-1960s as a ministry to address the needs of the Center City homeless. Next door was the Good Shepherd mission, a live-in program for medically fragile men.

Called 'Father John's' on the streets, St John's Hospice provided food, clothing, shelter, and in winter was often the only lifeline to Center City homeless men in need. And while most homeless men were penniless, some did have money coming in – military benefits, pension benefits, welfare benefits – so St John's also operated as a mail drop.

When Jessica and Byrne parked on the corner of Twelfth and Race Streets there were men lined up halfway down the block, reaching almost to the corner of Thirteenth Street, perhaps fifty in all. They were of all races, sizes, and builds, different in many ways, but they all carried the same weight on their shoulders, the same yoke of despair. They huddled close to each other to deflect the biting wind, cupping cigarettes in hands. In the time it took for Jessica and Byrne to get out of the car and lock it, three more men queued up.

Jessica slipped on her gloves, considering that there were two different ways to go about finding out if any of these men were, or knew of, a man named Boise. They could split up, with Jessica taking one end of the line, Byrne taking the other, interviewing each man separately, gathering and collating a ton of information that would probably be completely useless and, to an almost certainty, incoherent.

The other way was the preferred way, even though it was a bit less scientific, and a lot less by the book.

'Hey, Boise!' Byrne yelled.

A few of the men in line looked over, but Jessica noticed that only one of them nervously looked around, signaling that he might be the guy they were looking for. Oily hair, ratty jacket, stained Levi's, somewhere in his twenties, although with the homeless it was always wise to deduct ten to twenty percent, considering what life on the streets did to one's appearance. When the man saw Jessica and Byrne standing across the street he instantly made them as cops. He stamped from one foot to the other, eyes shifting from the man in front of him to the entrance to the mission, and back. He butted his cigarette against the wall, pocketed it.

Jessica caught Byrne's eye, and directed his gaze to the jumpy guy at the back of the line. Byrne slowly worked his way around a parked delivery truck. When he emerged at the other side, now standing about twenty feet from the man in line, the man noticed. When Byrne stepped off the curb, the man turned and bolted down Race Street, full stride, rounded the corner onto Thirteenth. As Byrne took after the man, Jessica cut up North Carmac Street.

In the end, it was a good thing she was chasing after two men with virtually no aerobic conditioning. She came around the corner and saw Byrne at the end of a dead end alley. The man was there too, leaning against the wall, as was Byrne. Both were out of breath. The guy looked like a junkie, so his being out of shape was understandable.

Jessica approached, gave Byrne her when-are-you-gonna-start-hitting-the-gym look, but remained silent on that matter.

When the two men had somewhat recovered, Jessica sidled up to the homeless man, asked, 'How ya doing?'

'Never better.'

'Why did you run?'

The man stood up straight, caught the last of his breath, or all that he was going to catch. 'I'm a health nut,' he said. 'I like to get my ten miles in before lunch.'

Jessica believed the nut part. Byrne stared at the man until he realized he had to answer the question.

'Why did I run? *Look* at me. I'm like a chew toy to you guys.'

He had a point. 'What's your name?' Jessica asked.

The man shook his head. 'Look, officer, I don't want no trouble.'

'Did you kill someone?' Jessica asked.

The man recoiled. 'Kill someone? I didn't do *nothin'*.'

'Then you're not in any trouble,' Jessica said. 'What's your name?'

The man stared at the ground, remained silent.

'Trust me on this, these are the easy questions,' Jessica said. 'I keep the hard ones down at the Roundhouse. Right next to the holding cells in the basement. I have the feeling you know the place I'm talking about. Question is, ever see a guy like you after seventy-two hours in the box? Like *Dawn of the* fucking *Dead*.'

The man continued to look at his feet, which Jessica noticed were clad in two different brands of old running shoes. One Reebok. One Nike.

'My name's Boyce,' he said. 'Thomas L. Boyce.'

Jessica glanced at Byrne. *That's* why there was no 'Boise' in PCIC. His nickname was *Boycie*.

'Do you know a man named Daniel Palumbo?' Jessica asked.

Boyce looked up, a light in his eyes. Maybe this wasn't about him. 'Danny? Yeah, I know Danny. Good dude, man. But I ain't seen him in a while. What did he do now?'

'Mr Palumbo is dead.'

The light went out. '*Dead?*'

'I'm afraid so,' Jessica said. 'Was he a friend of yours?'

'Friend?'

Jessica was getting impatient with Mr Thomas L. Boyce. And she knew that if she was getting impatient, Byrne was about to blow. 'Do I need to speak louder?'

'No. I can hear okay. I'm just, you know, a little freaked out. Danny's dead? Can't believe it.'

'How did you know Danny Palumbo?'

Another pause. 'Let's just say we have mutual acquaintances.'

'Let's just say a lot more than that.' Jessica said. 'Did you know Mr Palumbo when he was a police officer?'

Boyce looked pummeled. 'What are you talking about? Danny was a *cop*?'

'He used to be, yes.'

'Wow.'

Jessica believed Boyce had not known this. 'When was the last time you saw him?'

'Two weeks. Right around there.'

'Can you be more specific?'

'I lost my BlackBerry, okay? Things kinda blend together for me.'

'*Where* did you last see him?'

'Around, you know? On the street.'

Jessica just stared.

'Okay. We scored. Then we hit this gallery over on Venango. But that's the last I saw of him. Swear to God.'

'Did Mr Palumbo have any kind of problems with a dealer?' Jessica asked. 'Someone who might have wanted to do him harm? Maybe someone he owed money to?'

'We don't get a lot of shit on credit, if you know what I mean. It's pretty much cash on the barrel head for me and guys like Danny.'

'What about other people on the street? Is there someone Danny had trouble with?'

'Not really. Danny pretty much kept to himself. I mean, if he got pushed around he would push back, but he didn't go looking for trouble. Not Danny. He was a floater.' Boyce looked down the alley, back at them. 'He gave me something.'

'What do you mean?' Jessica asked.

'Last time I seen him, Danny gave me something.' Boyce pointed to the bulging plastic bag on the ground at his feet. 'Do you want to see it?'

'Yes,' Jessica said.

Boyce knelt down, opened the plastic bag, which was really three plastic bags, one inside the other. The bags had been twisted and knotted so many times they had begun to rip. After moving some things around inside, Boyce slowly dug to the bottom. He finally pulled out a grease-stained burgundy nylon knapsack. One of the straps was torn, and had been rather inexpertly mended with a bright orange thread. Boyce put the knapsack on the ground, then tied the plastic bags together again. He picked up the knapsack, but did not unzip it.

'This bag belonged to Mr Palumbo?' Jessica asked.

'Yeah.'

'And why is it in your possession?'

Boyce went twitchy, perhaps anticipating something bad, something he hadn't considered. Like a robbery charge. 'He told me he wanted me to, you know, *watch* it for a while.'

'Did he say why?'

'He didn't. I just figured he was going somewhere where his stuff might be, you know, at risk.'

Jessica looked at the battered and stained bag. She couldn't imagine it or its contents warranting any heightened measures of security. But one man's treasure, right? 'Did he say where he was going?'

'No.'

'Did he say when he might be coming back for this?'

'No. He didn't say.'

'Did he ever ask you to watch his things before?'

Boyce shrugged. 'Can't say that he did. I mean, not a whole lot of people trust people out here, you know? Danny and me were tight and all, so I guess he thought his stuff was safe with me.'

'Did you open the bag since he gave it to you?'

'*What*? No, man. It ain't my stuff. I got no business going in there.'

Jessica didn't fully buy into the code of the street, but for some reason she believed Thomas Boyce.

'We're going to need to take this with us,' she said.

'Yeah,' Boyce said. 'Sure. I mean, I figured.'

He handed the bag to Jessica, who took it with a gloved hand, held it by the end of one of the straps.

'Do you remember what Danny said to you?' Byrne asked. 'The very last thing he said?'

Boyce thought about this for a few moments. 'When he was walking away, up Tenth Street, he turned and yelled something to me. I was a little high at the time, and I remember it was kind of weird. But that was Danny, you know. He was always on about the devil this, the devil that.'

'The devil?'

'Yeah. He was a believer.'

'He believed in the devil?'

'Well, you believe in God, you believe in the devil, right?'

'What about you, Mr Boyce?' Byrne asked. 'Do you believe in the devil?'

Boyce laughed, but it was a nervous sound. 'Shit, man. I got plenty of my *own* demons, right? I don't need someone else's, church or no.'

'We may need to talk to you again,' Jessica said. 'Where can we get hold of you?'

'Have your people call my people. We'll do lunch.' Boyce shook his head. 'I'm *homeless*, man.'

'Do you stay at shelters a lot?'

'When there's a bed. There ain't always a bed. Plus, them places are dangerous. You might want to mention that to the mayor the next time you see him.'

Jessica knew that a lot of homeless men did not like going to shelters, which they considered, rightfully so, to be risky. Especially the city-operated shelters. Not to mention that most shelters wanted their men to get into some kind of recovery program. The combination of these two things made most homeless men prefer to be out on the street. But some nights, code-blue nights – when the temperatures dropped below freezing – there wasn't much choice.

'I'll tell him next time we play tennis,' Jessica said. Boyce smiled. It wasn't pretty. She handed the man her notebook and pen. 'Write down the places you stay.'

Boyce hesitated, then took the pad and pen. 'Sometimes I stay at St Francis Inn,' he said.

Jessica knew the place. Located in Kensington, it was run by Franciscans on a fully volunteer basis. They also operated a thrift store and an urban center.

Boyce wrote down the name and general addresses of three shelters in North Philly. Jessica looked at the list. Surprisingly, the man's penmanship was legible, almost elegant.

While Jessica put her notebook away, Byrne took out his camera phone.

'Mr Boyce,' Byrne said.

Boyce turned to face Byrne. Byrne took the man's picture.

'Oh, now, that's *got* to be some kind of violation of my civil rights,' Boyce said.

Jessica took out a business card, handed it to him. 'Have your attorney contact me. In the meantime, if you think of something else, or you remember what Danny said to you on the last day you saw him, please give me a call.'

Boyce took the card, looked into Jessica's eyes. He fashioned what he probably figured was a charming expression. 'Do you think there might be like a reward or something?'

Jessica was suddenly downwind from Thomas Boyce. She wanted to move on. 'There may be something in it for you. But that offer is only good for a few days.'

This, of course, was not true. There was no statute of limitations on homicide, and a tip that came in ten or twenty years after a murder would be followed up on. Boyce did not need to know this.

The man perked at the possibility of a cash stipend. 'I'll ask around. I have an erudite and learned circle of acquaintances. You never know.'

'You never know,' Jessica echoed.

With that, Thomas L. Boyce picked up his plastic swag bag, backed away from Jessica and Byrne a few paces – just to make sure it was okay to leave – then turned and walked up the alley.

'You meet the most interesting people on this job,' Jessica said.

When Boyce was gone, Jessica and Byrne returned to the car. The line into St John's had disappeared, reduced to just a few men in the small courtyard. The rest were now inside.

Jessica unzipped the knapsack, and gently deposited the contents onto the hood of the Taurus. What she and Byrne saw were the sad remnants of a discarded life – a dirty pair of Levi's, a ball of sweaters and T shirts. It all had that monkey-house smell of body odor and disinfectant. There was a gray-bristle toothbrush with a broken handle, a small bar of soap wrapped in a paper towel, a few pamphlets for local shelters and free clinics. What they did not find was a reason that put Daniel Palumbo in the basement of that church. While Jessica went through the pockets of the Levi's – all empty – she glanced at Byrne. He was standing at the back of the car, his distant stare in place. Of course, with Byrne, it was probably an inward glance.

Byrne took out his phone, dialed, put it on speaker. Soon there was a click.

'Hey, Kevin,' Bontrager said over the speaker.

'Where are you, Josh?' Byrne asked.

'I'm over at St Adelaide's. We're just wrapping up.'

'You've searched the whole place?'

'Everywhere.'

'Did you go up in that bell tower?'

'Yeah,' Bontrager said. 'Nothing up there.'

'Could you check it again?'

Pause. No detective liked to be told they had not done a thorough job, but Josh Bontrager held Byrne in such high esteem, he wasn't about to question why. 'Okay,' he said. 'What am I looking for?'

'Not sure,' Byrne said.

'On my way.'

Through the tinny speaker on the cell phone they could hear Josh Bontrager walking across the small church, up the steps. They heard the creak of the door as he pushed it open. 'Okay,' he said. 'I'm in the bell tower.'

'What do you see?'

Another pause. 'There's really nothing here. There's some straw and sticks on the floor. I'm thinking it was an old bird's nest.'

'Anything else?'

'Nothing I can see. Sorry.'

Byrne closed his eyes for a moment. He opened them. 'Are there any gang tags on the walls, any carvings?'

'No tags,' Bontrager said. 'Let me check for carvings.'

Another minute or so passed.

'No. Nothing *I* can see anyway. The walls are pretty dirty. Nothing recent. Do you want CSU to take a bunch of photos up here?'

'Not yet. What about loose stones?' Byrne asked. 'Are any of the stones loose?'

'Let me check,' Bontrager said. 'I'm going to put the phone down for a second.'

They heard him put it down, heard him moving around the small space. After a full minute he came back on. 'No loose stones.'

Byrne walked a few paces, turned back. 'Check right near the top. Check the stones along the soffit.'

'I'm going to have to climb on the sill,' Bontrager said. 'If you hear a scream fading into the distance, that's me falling out the window.'

Both Jessica and Byrne smiled at this.

They once again heard Bontrager put down the phone, heard the sounds of exertion as he climbed on the sill. There was another thirty seconds of virtual silence. Then:

'Oh, *hello.*'

Jessica glanced at Byrne. He was transfixed. Bontrager came back on the line.

'Guys? There *is* a loose stone.'

'Did you pull it out?'

'Yes.'

'Was there something behind it?' Byrne asked.

'Yes,' Bontrager said, his voice now alive with the excitement of discovery. 'You guys better get down here. I think this means something.'

'We're on the way,' Byrne said.

Jessica, wondering what she had just witnessed, picked up the knapsack, walked to the back of the Taurus, put it in the trunk. It hardly took up any room. Everything that Daniel Palumbo had accrued in his life fit in one tiny corner of the trunk of a midsize car.

As Jessica got behind the wheel, and they headed toward the church, she was suddenly overcome by a debilitating sadness. All she could think about was Loretta Palumbo holding that plastic cup, the cup her son used when his life was new and full of promise.

THE SCENE OUTSIDE ST Adelaide's looked nothing like it had four days earlier. If you didn't recognize the departmental sedans parked out front, and didn't notice the new doorjamb and padlock installed on the door, you would have no way of knowing anything had recently happened there. Certainly not cold-blooded murder.

When they stepped inside, Josh Bontrager was leaning against the far wall. The room was powdered with the black dust used by CSU for latent prints.

'What do we have, Josh?' Byrne asked.

'Take a look at this.' Bontrager proffered a small clear evidence bag. Inside the bag was a portion of an old prayer card.

These were small rectangular cards handed out by Catholics during funeral wakes, visitations, memorial services. Sometimes they were given out as 'thank you' cards after the funeral or memorial service, or sent to those unable to attend. The card Bontrager had found was old from the look of it, perhaps a 1950s or 1960s vintage. Jessica had a small boxful in her house from the various family members and friends who had passed. There was very little chance that she would look at her collection of prayer cards again, but there was no chance she could ever throw them out. It just wasn't done.

Jessica flipped the bag over. The torn card was from a funeral held on 20 January 1966 at St Damian's Church.

Jessica handed the card to Byrne. He examined it closely.

'This was behind the stone?' Byrne asked.

'Yeah.'

'How was it positioned?'

'It was leaning against the back. Up against the stone façade on the outer wall of the tower.'

Byrne didn't have to ask if Bontrager had handled it carefully by the edges. Josh was a pro.

'St Damian's,' Byrne said. 'Do you know it?'

'No,' both Jessica and Bontrager replied.

'I took some pictures of the area around the stone,' Bontrager added. 'It looks to have been recently pried loose. CSU is up there now.'

Byrne thought for a few more moments. 'What exactly did the caller say again?' he asked Jessica.

'*One God, seven churches.*'

'Churches.'

'Yeah.'

Byrne held up the prayer card. 'I think we should take a ride over to St Damian's,' he said. 'Just to say we did.'

As Byrne got on his cell phone to get the location of the church, Jessica put the evidence bag containing the card on the floor, knelt down, took out the camera, took a close-up photograph of the new find. She handed the evidence bag to Bontrager. 'Let's see if we can get the lab to hump this.'

'You got it,' Bontrager said.

As Jessica and Byrne returned to the car, Jessica had to wonder what, if anything, they were going to find at the second church.

THIRTEEN

S t Damian's was a small church on Eighteenth Street near Diamond. The church proper was constructed of soot-blackened sandstone, with a tall Palladian entrance arch. Above the door was a carved pediment. A small stone cross jutted from the peaked gable.

On either side of the church were narrow, three-story, red-brick structures, most likely containing the rectory, as well as administrative offices.

A low wrought-iron fence guarded the entrance, but it appeared the gate had long ago been stolen. Jessica could only imagine that it now graced the entrance to someone's home in North Philly. She had always imagined that the surest route to hell was to steal something from a church. Once, when she was about seven or eight, she had taken an umbrella from the vestibule at St Paul's. She brought it back the next day, and after somewhere around 400 Hail Marys was certain she would dwell in fire for all eternity.

In all, St Damian's looked to be a typical, struggling Philly neighborhood parish. Except for one glaring fact.

'It's closed,' Jessica said.

A small sign next to the door confirmed what seemed apparent. The parish had merged with another, larger parish, located three blocks away.

Jessica and Byrne walked around to the back of the rectory, peered into the windows. The glass was grimy and nearly opaque with soot and exhaust.

At the rear entrance was a gate that led to a square courtyard. Jessica pushed open the gate. In the small area were a few trash bags, a pair of bald tires.

'Kevin.'

Jessica pointed to the broken window in one panel of the door. She looked more closely. There was no glass on the outside, so it had the signs of a break in. She shone her Maglite in the window. The glazing had been puttied and reputtied many times, so this did not appear to be the first time someone had broken into the property.

Jessica looked inside. The shattered glass on the floor did not have dust on it. The break-in was recent.

THE NARROW PASSAGEWAY LED to the rear of the nave, the main part of the church. On the right was the sacristy, long ago defiled by tres-passers. As they stepped into the church, Jessica instinctively reached to the side, expecting to dip her fingers into the holy water font. There was none there.

Ahead, the nave was virtually empty. There was black plastic taped over the windows. The stained-glass panes had either been transferred elsewhere, stolen, or broken. Some daylight leaked in, but the interior was dark. Jessica and Byrne both used their Maglites.

As she moved toward the front of the church Jessica saw that most of the pews had been removed, as had most of the statuary. One small statue of the Virgin Mary lay on its side to the right of the altar.

A few pigeons, frightened by their presence, took wing into the eaves.

There was dust and grime and bird droppings on every surface. The air was suffused with dry rot and the sickly sweet smell of long dead flowers.

'I'm going to check downstairs,' Byrne said.

'Okay.'

When Jessica reached the vestibule, which let in a little bit of light from the street, she saw that the ambry – the niche used to house the three oils – was intact.

Jessica turned, looked down the aisle that had once led to the altar. She thought for a moment what it must have been like when this church was new, about families in the neighborhood coming here on Saturday afternoon for confession, on Sunday mornings for mass. She thought about the baptisms, marriages, and funerals. She thought about how small churches were truly the pillars of a neighborhood, and how sad that this once proud place of worship now stood abandoned.

Mostly she thought about her own childhood, how St Paul's was the center of her life. She had attended kindergarten through eighth grade there, had made her first Holy Communion and confirmation there. She had gotten married by the same priest who had baptized her, Father Rocco Basconi.

'Jess.'

Jessica looked toward the stairs leading to the basement. She saw the beam of Byrne's flashlight playing against the doorjamb. She crossed the church, stood at the top of the stairs, looked toward the cellar.

Byrne stood there, his tall frame silhouetted against the stone backdrop. As Jessica descended the steps she felt a new chill, even deeper than the cold of the unheated church.

When she reached the last step Jessica pointed her flashlight at the opposite wall. The basement was entirely empty, save for an object on the floor, perhaps directly underneath where the altar was on the main floor.

'What is it, Kevin?'

Byrne didn't answer. Jessica saw the muscles cord on his neck. She had seen it happen many times before, and it never bode well. Byrne took out his cell phone, stepped toward the stairway.

Her flesh rising in goose bumps, Jessica glanced at the box on the floor. It was not a box after all. It was, instead, an old washing tub, oval in shape, about twenty inches across. It reminded her of the brushed aluminum tubs in which her grandmother would let her and her brother Michael sit on the hottest days of August, the South Philly equivalent of an above-ground pool.

This tub was covered with a worn and laundered burlap cloth. Jessica snapped on a latex glove, gently peeled back the burlap.

What she saw took her legs from under her.

There, inside the tub, suspended in a crystalline block of ice, was a newborn baby.

TWO

IN NOMINE PATRIS

*'His eyes were as a flame of fire,
and on his head were many crowns'*

– REVELATION, 19:12

I T IS SATURDAY AFTERNOON, AND THE CHURCH IS FILLING WITH PEOPLE coming to confession. You watch them file in and take their seats.

Across the aisle is a family of five: mother, father, two young girls of eight and nine, a boy of four. They are well-dressed, well-groomed, well-behaved. They are not arrayed in their Sunday finest, but are still dressed appropriately, still respectful of this place. You had long ago thought this custom had passed.

The little boy studies you. You smile at him from across the aisle, across the years, and think back to a time in your life when you came to church to admit your sins, to seek the grace of penance.

I took the Lord's name in vain three times.

I dishonored my mother twice.

I stole a candy bar.

What about now? What would happen if you walked into that small confessional, closed the door behind you, lowered yourself onto the kneeler, and waited for the panel to slide over? What would you say to your confessor?

Do you remember your Act of Contrition?

Would you tell the truth? *All* of it?

It has been so many years since you confessed your sins that you would certainly have to group your transgressions together, like a shepherd gathering his flock.

What is the punishment for taking a life? Even with the grace of forgiveness, it cannot be forgotten. Each night the darkness gets deeper.

Suddenly, you do not remember that night thirty years ago, that frigid February night that changed your life forever. How can this be? You've replayed it over and over again in your mind, your heart. You've thought about your fellow officers, how you might have conducted yourself differently, how you might have avoided the nightmare of what happened.

How has it all slipped away?

You have to relive it. You have to breathe in the frigid air, the scent of blood filling your senses, the taste of it dripping warm and coppery on the back of your tongue.

As you wait to tell the story, you take yourself back to that moment, that split second when the door closed behind you, the moment you drew your service weapon and waited for the shadow to fall.

FOURTEEN

A LONG THE CORNICE OF A HILL OVERLOOKING A DEEP GREEN VALLEY, three miles south of Bruceton, West Virginia, sat a golden pavilion, a beacon of light in the sweltering summer evening. Mosquitoes and fireflies danced and swirled around the structure in a graceful ballet, making the large, luminous tent look as if it were itself moving to the rhythm of the joyous music coming from within.

But it wasn't the music that drew the girl near.

It was the cross.

The back-lighted cross inside the tent painted a soft cruciform on the ceiling of canvas so that anyone seated inside could look above their heads and know that their souls were rising toward salvation.

For twelve-year-old Mary Elizabeth Longstreet it was magic. She knew that the revival – the Holy Thunder Caravan it was called – was going to be in town for only three more days. In that time she knew she had to work up the nerve to cross this field and enter the tent, or she would never forgive herself.

Although she had been baptized Mary – named for the Blessed Mother herself – everyone called her Ruby, due to her beautiful auburn hair, hair that would seem to catch fire in the late-summer months, turning a rich and vibrant red.

Ruby Longstreet was the middle child of five, a waif-like girl with inquisitive blue eyes and a shy smile. She had two brothers and two sisters. They lived in Jefferson County, West Virginia, not far from the Maryland line.

From the time she could talk Ruby could recite the Word. At two she said grace at her family table, a rough plank slab which rarely bore anything more than boiled potatoes or, on Sunday, a piece of boiled lamb shank.

For most of her childhood she kept a dog-eared copy of the King James Bible on a cloth on the floor next to the bed she shared with her sisters Esther and Ruth. In the night, when she could not sleep, she would read the Word by moonlight, and it would give her comfort, easing the hunger she had in her belly, the longing of her spirit.

As she and her sisters grew toward adolescence, their father would come into their room and sit at the edge of the bed, smelling of motor oil and sour mash, each night drawing closer. Elijah Longstreet was a coarse man, ill-mannered and quick to anger.

On the night he came for Esther, Ruby pretended to be asleep. She kept her eyes open, watching the shadows rise and fall on the wall, her ears filled with her sister's muffled pleas, the smell of liquor and body odor filling her world.

A month later Esther went away. For days Ruby would walk to the end of their long, dusty driveway and watch for her sister. Esther did not return.

Has she gone to the Lord? Ruby wondered. She had no idea, and she dared not ask.

On the night her father came for Ruby he sat on the edge of the bed for the longest time. That previous winter Elijah Longstreet had lost half his weight, so much of it that by the time he came for Ruby he was skin and bones. But still he came. The need the devil had planted in his soul was powerful.

Before he could mount Ruby he began to cough so violently that not only the bed, but the entire room seemed to shake. Ruby had never forgotten that sound, that sodden animal grating.

By dawn, his daughter untaken, Elijah Longstreet was dead at the foot of the bed, Ruby's Bible clutched in his hands, the index finger of his right hand stuck between the pages of *Revelation*, a pool of foul blood and bile around his head.

Everyone knew what Elijah Longstreet had been doing in Ruby's room, but it was never spoken of. On the day he was buried, in the small family plot behind the outbuilding, Ruby's mother watched from the parlor window, but did not set foot on the gravesite.

That day was six months before the caravan came to the valley, and in the intervening months Ruby Longstreet had sprung up, if not out. She was tall for her age, and had begun to bud, but she still had about her a little girl's awkwardness, all elbows and knees and shoulder blades.

Finally, on the last night of the revival, Ruby crossed the field, toward the tent, the sound of 'Give Me Oil in My Lamp' – a song Ruby knew by heart – filling the summer night, echoing off the surrounding hills.

As she approached the tent she was noticed by two men leaning against an old, fender-wired pickup. One of them looked at Ruby the way she had seen her daddy look at her, all wet-lipped and fake smiley. The other one, the older man, just nodded toward the opening. Ruby could smell the roadhouse whiskey all the way across the road.

Ruby gathered her courage, her heart fit to burst with fear and excitement. The sound of joyous singing was thunderous. She parted the flaps, stepped inside, and saw the Preacher for the very first time.

THE PREACHER STOOD BEFORE the crowd of a hundred, divine and young and handsome in his white linen suit and lemon yellow shirt. He was willow-slender and graceful, and moved mink-like around the area at the front of the church, just below the cross. He projected a lightning force, an energy that came across even when he was just standing still. Ruby imagined it was the Holy Ghost that filled him, pure and simple. Behind the Preacher's head the bright light over the makeshift pulpit created a golden aurora.

Ruby knew all about the Preacher, knew of his hardscrabble past, not that different from her own. She knew these things because the Preacher had written a book about his life – *I Am the Spirit* – and Ruby read it so many times that the words were now starting to fade from the page. She once dropped the book into a rain puddle and ran home, drying it before the fire, ironing each page flat with her aunt Hazel's dry iron.

In his life, in the days before the light, even the Preacher knew darkness. A backwoods boy, a son of Appalachia born in Letcher County, Kentucky, he had survived the devil in two fathers, and a mother whose mind was taken by Satan himself.

When the Preacher was still a boy his stepsister Charlotte was murdered. Many believed it was this terrible tragedy that put him on the path to salvation.

THE HOLY THUNDER CARAVAN traveled all over, passing through northern Kentucky, southern Ohio, southwestern Pennsylvania. The Preacher also appeared on the radio. When Ruby knew that his program was going to be on she would park herself at the table and listen, letting his beautiful voice fill her with the Spirit.

This night Ruby took a chair at the back of the gathering, and listened to the congregation raise their voice in praise, heard the music soar to the heavens. She did not have the courage to join in, but just being this close to the Preacher filled her with a happiness she had never known.

The next day the caravan moved on. Ruby cried for days. She walked six miles to the small library every Saturday looking for news in out-of-town papers. Once she was rewarded with a notice that the Preacher and his Holy Thunder Caravan would be stopping in nearby Brandonville.

Ruby went to work taking in washing, sweeping out stalls, anything she could to make money. In the end she saved eleven dollars, enough for a round trip on the Greyhound.

THIS TIME THE PREACHER spoke about the evils of the flesh. When he called those who had not been saved by the Word to come forward, Ruby found herself on her feet, hands raised in testimony.

When the Preacher finally came to her he touched her forehead. The feeling began in her toes, a sensation of warmth and serenity she had never before experienced. The world soon became a bright white light and there was no doubt – no doubt at all – that it was the Spirit rising within her.

The next thing Ruby knew she was lying on a cot behind the tent, a cold cloth on her forehead. The woman sitting next to her was big and jolly. She wore old grease-stained overalls and smelled of hand-rolled cigarettes and orange candy.

'Am I in heaven?' Ruby asked.

The woman laughed. 'No, little darling, you're still in West Virginia. It's been called a lot of things, but heaven sure as hell ain't one of them.'

Ruby knew that evangelists were travelers, just as she knew that there had always been wanderlust in her own shoes.

That night she went home, did her chores. At dawn she took her school dress and her good dress, her few other possessions, and left.

She never went home again.

WHEN RUBY RETURNED TO the campgrounds, the tent was dark. She entered, saw a solitary figure standing at the pulpit. It was himself. Ruby would always remember how the Preacher looked – tall and regal and divinely sent – silhouetted against the cream-colored canvas of the tent in the moonlight.

The Preacher saw her and smiled. Ruby felt as if she might faint again, but she put her hand on the edge of a chair, and after a few moments she felt fine. The Preacher came around, pulled out a chair, and welcomed her.

And thus Mary Elizabeth Longstreet became a member of the Holy Thunder Caravan.

RUBY SPENT THAT SUMMER traveling with the caravan, roaming across southern Ohio and northern West Virginia, to towns like Grand Run, Friendly, Sistersville, and Paden City. The Preacher liked to move along the banks of the Ohio River which, in the summer months, made it convenient to baptize folks.

At first there were just seven people in the entourage. You wouldn't think by just looking at the tent and the hundred or so chairs that there was so much work involved in planning, moving, setting up, taking down, packing.

Ruby was not a big girl, but she was much stronger than she appeared. Many times she matched the two older boys who helped out.

At each stop the Preacher would set them up at a small motel or a campsite, then go into the town to spread the word. When possible he would get himself interviewed on the local radio station. He could always get the Holy Thunder Caravan mentioned on the religious pages of the local newspapers for free, but it wasn't until he took a small ad in the entertainment section that the bigger crowds began to show up.

Some nights the Preacher would summon Ruby to his room. There he would sit in front of the mirror while Ruby brushed his beautiful golden hair. One of the few things Ruby carried that was of any value was her grandmother's hairbrush. The brush had a gold-tone stamped metal handle, along with a base inset bearing a hand-embroidered floral petit point sample. Night after night Ruby would brush the Preacher's hair – never fewer than one hundred strokes – while he regaled her with stories from the Good Book.

Over the next few months, while she toured with the caravan, Ruby spent much of her time with the twins, Abigail and Peter. The twins, who had been taken in by the Preacher when their parents were killed in an automobile accident near Elkins, were just toddlers at the time, and had been touched by the Lord in a way that made them special.

On many nights, when the tent had been struck and packed away, when the chairs and booths had been loaded into the truck, and the caravan was ready to depart at dawn light, Ruby would read to Abigail and Peter.

Their favorite story was from *1 Samuel*, 17, the story of David and Goliath.

*

WHEN RUBY WAS THIRTEEN, her womanhood bursting, everything changed.

One evening, on a hot July night, just outside Moundsville, the Preacher took her hand and said, 'Come with me, child.'

They went to his RV, a grand place where Ruby had never been. Inside were soft golden sofas, a television, and the ceiling was painted with a bright blue sky.

At the back of the main part of the RV, hanging from a hook, was a pink dress, store-bought and beautiful. The preacher told her it was hers, and that she should put it on.

They had supper, just the two of them, at a fold-down dining table. Ruby was so nervous she had to remind herself to chew her food. She had wine for the first time in her life.

When they were finished, and Ruby had cleared the plates, they sat across from each other on the sofas.

'You know, the Lord has very big plans for you, Mary Elizabeth.'

'He does?'

The Preacher waited a few moments, as was his way, then rose. This night he wore black, right down to his tie. He moved like a cat across the small space. He sat on the sofa next to her, took her hand in his. This close, she could see the small flecks of gold in his eyes. She felt light-headed at his nearness.

'There will come a time – not for many years, God willing – when I will no longer be able to bring the Word to the people,' he said.

'Why not?' Ruby managed. She fidgeted on her cushion, the store-bought dress a little too tight.

The Preacher smiled, and Ruby felt her knees begin to knock. She did her best to stop them.

'Although I am young now, it will not always be so.'

She knew what he meant, but she could not imagine him any other way than he was at that moment. 'Let us drink the Lord's bounty,' he said, handing her a crystal goblet. He took his own, and they touched the rims together, making a sound not unlike the pealing of a bell on a great, shining chapel on a hill.

She lifted the glass to her lips and drank. At first she found this new wine to be bitter, but the more she had, the less bitter it became.

The Preacher read to her from the Scriptures well into the night, and as he did they continued to drink the bitter wine.

IN THE DREAM THAT was not a dream, the Preacher stood at the foot of the bed. He was now dressed in red, and wore a Roman collar.

'Mary,' he said softly.

In the dream that was not a dream Ruby was naked. She felt the humid night breeze through the window. She could smell the honeysuckle and summer hyacinth.

In the dream that was not a dream the Preacher entered her. The pain was terrible, and in the dimness of the bedroom she saw his eyes, felt the heat of his breath, and for a moment she looked inside him, and there saw deep and terrible chasms of fire.

RUBY AWOKE IN HER own sleeping bag, inside one of the trucks. She sat up, her head hurting and spinning, her body aching, a wicked thirst inside her. She frantically tried to find her new dress.

It was gone.

THE NEXT STOP WAS near a small town in southwestern Ohio called Hannibal. They set up the tent in a field overlooking a lake. It was late-summer and the mosquitoes were out in full force. The Preacher sent two boys into town to tack up the flyers.

By 6 o'clock the people began to arrive. It wasn't a large crowd, but this was only the first night. The Preacher always stayed three days in a new town in order for the word to spread, and it always did.

There were a total of nine people in the caravan in those days.

The Preacher learned that, when they were in small towns, poor towns, by the second night he had gotten what money he could get from the people. It was then that the Preacher instituted his *From Thy Bounty* nights, encouraging the people to bring food as offering, instead of money. He would hold an abbreviated service, and donations of money would of course be accepted, but mostly people would come with home-baked breads, smoked meats, jams and preserves, and home-made pies.

They always ate well after that.

WHEN THE CARAVAN REACHED New Martinsville they were joined by a man named Carson Tatum. Carson was in his mid-fifties, a kindly widower with more money than faith. Carson Tatum had sold his small chain of hardware stores at a tidy profit, it was said, and dedicated his life to the Word as revealed by the Preacher.

The Preacher needed a driver to haul the ever-increasing amount of gear, and a bargain was struck. The gatherings had grown from an average of fifty or so people to well over two hundred, expanding as word of the Preacher's healing powers spread.

Carson, who had never had children of his own, took immediately to Ruby, and they became fast friends. Many times she would ride in the front seat of his F-150, and he would delight her with stories of his time as a merchant marine, making stops in faraway places like Singapore, Shanghai, and Karachi.

A FEW MONTHS LATER they stayed at a rundown motel outside Youngstown, Ohio. The entourage had grown to eleven people by then.

Ruby had not been feeling well, and another girl, a year or so younger, had taken over the care of Abigail and Peter.

The new girl was blond and pretty, but withdrawn, and had about her many of the ways Ruby had had when she first joined the caravan. She revered the Preacher, could barely look his way when he spoke to her.

Ruby's illness began with a sour stomach every morning, which many times led to her vomiting. More than once she could not make it to the Porto Sans that were always set up near the tent for the people who attended the meetings.

IN HER THIRD MONTH Ruby began to show, and despite her efforts to hide the presence inside her, she knew what was happening. She came to the Preacher's RV one night to tell him the wondrous news, but she was turned away.

Before she went back to bed she saw the new girl, Bethany, playing with Abigail. They were playing a game of hide and seek among the tangle of rusted Fords and pickups.

Bethany was wearing Ruby's pink dress.

On the way back to the tent, tears streaming down her face, Ruby thought she heard a growling sound nearby, a low keening coming from just beyond the edge of the forest. As she approached the wood, she saw two black dogs, big males by the cast of their shadows.

As she stepped into the tent Ruby saw the dogs lope forward, heads lowered, then lay down on either side, their heedful black eyes like shiny marbles in the growing dusk.

TWO WEEKS LATER, OUTSIDE Coshocton, Ruby helped set up chairs. When she was finished, she stepped outside the tent for a cup of water, and caught sight of something moving at the edge of the field. When she stopped and looked closely, the sight made her heart jump. It was the two black dogs she had seen in Youngstown, nearly seventy miles away. They had followed the caravan.

When the dogs approached, tails between their legs, Ruby felt something stir inside her.

FIVE MONTHS LATER, IN early spring, on the evening of Holy Saturday, the Preacher put them all up at a motel in Morristown, Pennsylvania. Ruby had her own room.

In the middle of that restless, sleepless night, the baby said it was time to be born. Ruby barely made it to the door of her room before her water broke. She opened the door, hoping she could make it to the next room where Carson Tatum was sleeping.

What she saw in the parking lot stole her breath.

The caravan, and everyone in it, was gone.

*

RUBY AWAKENED IN A clean room. She would soon learn it was a family clinic in Waynesburg, Pennsylvania. When the doctor came to speak to her, she found she had no voice. They brought the baby boy to her. He was beautiful.

After a week, she bundled the boy, took his medicines, and lit out. The first three nights they slept on the side of the road.

The dogs were never far away. Sometimes they would bring food to them, food they had found in the Dumpsters and back lots of diners.

It was warm enough so that Ruby did not yet have to worry about the boy catching his death of cold. In those next months they moved at night, taking refuge in daylight.

Before long they would come to know the darkness.

BY THE TIME THE boy was three, Ruby had flowered. They had been taken in by people they met along the roads. For nearly two years she and the boy were the boarders of a man and woman who ran a general store in southwestern Pennsylvania. One of her employers along the way was a small community college in Ohio, and Ruby, sleeping only a few hours a night, would wander the stacks of books in the library. She spent a good deal of time gathering food scraps from the cafeteria, but most of her free time she would spend in the library, reading everything she could. She discovered early that she had a facility for memory. She read to the boy from the time he was six months old.

A YEAR LATER SHE saw the man at a diner in Romansville, Pennsylvania. Ruby and the boy were staying at a bed and breakfast where Ruby was performing housekeeping chores in exchange for room and board.

He had gotten heavier, the flesh of his neck grown flabby. His shoulders had acquired a weight that only time and sadness could build. But there was no mistaking him. When Ruby and the boy approached the booth, Carson Tatum looked up. For a moment he looked as if he had seen ghosts. Then his face softened, and he was Carson again.

They got their pleasantries out of the way.

'Let me look at you,' he said. 'You are a sight, Ruby Longstreet.' He reached out and touched the boy's shoulder. 'And your boy is quite the man.'

'He is my joy,' Ruby said. 'Is the caravan nearby?'

Carson nodded. 'Just over in Parkesburg,' he said. 'It's just down to the Preacher and three others now.'

Three others, Ruby thought. She said nothing.

Carson stirred his coffee for the longest time, even though there wasn't but an inch in the cup, and probably cold at that. 'It was wrong what he done,' Carson finally said. 'Just wrong.'

Ruby had no reply to this. None that she would say.

Carson looked over his shoulder, then back at Ruby. 'The Preacher has thrown in with a traveling midway. It's the only way he can draw people anymore. I want you and the boy to come this afternoon.' He reached into his pocket, took out a pair of billets, along with a tight spool of red ride tickets. 'You come about three o'clock. I'm going to have something for you.'

'Something from the Preacher?'

'Yes, ma'am.'

Ruby chose her words with care. 'There's something else I need you to get from him,' she said. 'If he's still got it. Can you do that for me?'

Carson Tatum just smiled.

THE CARNIVAL WAS SMALL, worn out. It smelled of axle grease and spun sugar and despair. Whatever it had once been, it was no longer. In fact, it was not much of a midway at all. There was a small Ferris wheel, a carousel with painted horses, a track with only four little cars, along with the usual games of chance. There were a half-dozen food stands offering elephant ears, funnel cakes, caramel apples. Fireworks were promised.

Ruby had been here before. She knew this the moment she stepped onto the field, and the knowledge electrified her senses.

She had been here in her dreams.

Ruby took the boy by the hand, gave the man at the front booth their tickets. She looked to the edge of the field and, as expected, saw the black dogs. She had long ago stopped trying to tell which dogs were which. Ruby figured they were probably on their fourth or fifth litter. But there were always two. And they were always near.

At three o'clock she saw Carson standing by the carousel. Ruby and the boy walked over. Carson took them behind one of the stands.

'Big news. He's about to pack it in,' Carson said of the Preacher. 'I just heard that he is going to go to –'

Philadelphia, Ruby thought.

'– Philadelphia,' Carson said. 'He lived there at one time, you know.'

Ruby knew. She had read the Preacher's book. When the Preacher's mama left Jubal Hannah, and moved to North Philadelphia, the Preacher was only four.

Ruby knew the past, just as she could see the future in her dreams. She saw her son grown tall and strong and wise. She saw him silhouetted against the waters of the Delaware River, at long last free from the devil within him.

'Preacher said he's gonna start a mission up to Philadelphia,' Carson continued. 'A storefront church of sorts. Maybe a second-hand store.'

This was in her dreams, too.

'Did you get what I asked?' Ruby asked.

'Yes, missy. I sure did.'

Carson looked around, reached into his coat, took out a thick paper bag. He handed it to Ruby.

'Let him think it was me,' Carson said.

Ruby hefted the sack. It was much heavier than she thought it was going to be. 'What else is *in* here?'

When Ruby peeked inside she almost fainted. In addition to what she asked Carson to get for her there was a fat wad of money.

'There should be forty thousand there,' Carson said. 'You take it and go make a life.'

Ruby forced down her sense of shock, hugged Carson long and hard and tearfully, watched him walk away. He had developed a limp on the right side. An affliction, she imagined, from all the heavy lifting he had done for the Preacher.

When Ruby paid her two spool tickets for the carousel, and she and the boy stepped on the platform, she saw Abigail and Peter for the first time in years. How big they had grown. Her heart ached with their nearness. She wanted to throw her arms around them like she had when they were small. She couldn't.

A few minutes later she saw the Preacher. Despite his troubles and the intervening years he still looked beautiful. Ruby reckoned she would have seen him this way no matter what he did to her.

He did not see her.

The Preacher put Abigail and Peter on horses. It all seemed to happen in slow motion, as Ruby imagined it had for Saint John.

THE PREACHER CHOSE A white horse for Peter, a red one for Abigail. The two children were fraternal twins, but now they looked a great deal alike, as if they were identical.

Ruby then saw the Preacher put a small boy on a black horse. Ruby did not have to wonder whose child this was. The boy looked just like the teenaged girl standing by the cotton candy stand, the thin, nerve-jangled girl named Bethany, the girl who had come after Ruby. Ruby wondered how many girls there had been since.

RUBY HELPED HER BOY onto the horse directly across from where the Preacher stood. This horse was old, unpainted. Its eyes were a faded gray, but most surely had one time been a coal black, as black as the dogs that were always near.

The carousel began to turn; the throaty old calliope played its song. Ruby looked at her boy, imagined him years from then, saw in her mind's eye a time when he would be powerful, unstoppable.

The Preacher, just a few feet away, had no premonition, even though the signs were clear and unambiguous.

Weren't they?

Or maybe the signs *would* have been clear if the Preacher had truly been anointed. For Ruby, the moment was preordained, and spoken of in the Word.

And I saw, and behold, a white horse.

Peter began to laugh as the carousel picked up speed, his white horse moving up and down to the rhythm.

I heard the second living creature say, 'Come!' And out came another horse, bright red.

Little Abigail, so much like her brother, began to laugh, too. She held tight to her red horse.

I heard the third living creature say, 'Come!' And I saw, and behold, a black horse.

The boy on the black horse was scared. The Preacher held him with his free hand.

Faster and faster they went, the sound of the pipe organ filling Ruby's mind like a sermon. She looked at her boy. He seemed to know where he was, what it all meant. Ruby clutched the money close to her, and knew they would leave this night, never to return, just as she knew they would all meet again, in the city of two rivers. In Philadelphia.

And there would be a reckoning.

As Ruby held tight to the pole, she ran her hands over the smooth, unpainted surface of the carousel horse. She imagined, as she always had, that this horse had at one time been a lustrous roan. Now it seemed to be translucent. She could almost hear its heartbeat within.

I heard the voice of the fourth living creature say, 'Come!' And I saw a pale horse, and its rider's name was Death, and Hades followed him.

IN THE MONTHS FOLLOWING that day the boy became very ill with tuberculosis, almost unknown in the modern world, but all too common among Ruby's kind. She sat with him, night after night, a cloth over her mouth, the boy's terrible rasping filling her nights.

One night, just outside the clinic in Doylestown, in the third month of the boy's affliction, the two black dogs came and sat next to her. All night she patted their heads. In that night she had terrible dreams, dreams of men wrapped in barb wire, old men filled with stones. When she awoke to a white, healing light, the dogs were gone.

She went rushing into the clinic, mad with worry. They told her that, somehow, her boy had been healed.

They said it was a miracle.

RUBY GREW TO BECOME a slender, beautiful young woman, and her charms were not lost on any man. She learned to use her wiles, borrowing many of the techniques of persuasion she had learned from the Preacher himself. She invested the money Carson Tatum had given her wisely, saving every penny she could, reading every book she could borrow.

One day she read in the newspapers of how the Preacher had proven himself to be the devil's minion, how he had become a man who took souls unto himself, a man who did murder to avenge the loss of his stepsister Charlotte.

When Ruby learned of these dark deeds she knew the end days had begun.

ON THE DAY OF the third church, Ruby – who had long since been known by another name, who had long ago forsaken her red hair – went to a street in North Philadelphia.

And Hades followed him.

They stood on the corner, across from the cathedral, watching. The people of the city milled around them, each parson to his tabernacle, each sinner to his deeds.

Mother and child, Ruby thought.

There are seven churches in all.

FIFTEEN

J ESSICA STARED AT THE PHONE, WILLING IT TO RING. THIS HAD NEVER
worked in the past, but that did not stop her from the practice.

Long after the baby's body had been removed from the basement
and the church had been sealed as a crime scene, long after the CSU
officers had collected their evidence, Jessica and Byrne had stayed
behind, not a single word passing between them for what seemed an
eternity.

The two detectives 'walked the scene,' recreating, in their view,
what might have happened. They examined the point of entry, envi-
sioned the route the killer had taken. Jessica knew this was a different
exercise for her partner than it was for her. She had never known
anyone more compassionate than Kevin Byrne, but she knew that *he*
knew what the experience of finding a dead – murdered was the right
word – newborn baby must mean to her, to any mother.

After thirty minutes of silence, the solitude of the old stone church
became oppressive.

'Talk me out of thinking this is a homicide,' Jessica finally said.

'I wish I could, Jess.'

'Tell me a story about how some mother was giving her little baby
girl a bath, something terrible happened to the mother, and the baby
just accidentally drowned in that tub.'

Byrne said nothing.

'Tell me it was just an accident, and the mother – let's assume she's some religious nut job, just for the sake of argument – took the baby, her *beloved* baby, down to this church and tried to baptize the child, and something went terribly wrong.'

Jessica walked the aisle, up the three steps to where the altar once was, back down, over to the steps leading to the basement.

'I need to think this was not a deliberate act, Kevin. I need to think this is not part of some plan, and that we're never going to see this again. Ever.'

Byrne didn't say anything. Jessica hadn't really expected him to.

In front of the church, on the lamppost, they found another *X*.

EVENTUALLY THEY WENT OFF duty that day, Byrne to his life, Jessica to hers. Jessica hugged her children a dozen times that night, sat up all night in the hallway between their two rooms, checking on them every ten minutes, finally falling asleep a half-hour before the alarm clock rang.

Two days later the hot rage that had burned inside became something else, a feeling she'd had only a few times as a police officer. She had taken every case she'd ever been assigned as a homicide detective seriously, and had the utmost respect for the dead, even if the victim was a despicable person. Every detective Jessica knew felt the same way. But there were cases that put you to bed, woke you up, ate with you, and walked with you. There were cases that took showers with you, went shopping with you, and sat with you in a movie theater. You never escaped their scrutiny, until they were closed.

This was one of those cases.

She knew that there was a process – not to mention a backlog – that was in place when it came to forensics. Blood typing, fingerprint identification, hair and fiber, DNA testing. These things took time.

Jessica knew all this and it still didn't stop her from calling the lab every hour on the hour. She had not slept twenty minutes straight since leaving that church.

Those tiny fingers and toes. Every time the image crossed her mind she felt the anger and fury begin to surge.

It was far from the first dead body she had ever seen, of course. It was far from the first dead *infant* she had ever seen. You work homicide in a place like Philadelphia and there is no confirmation of man's inhumanity that shocks or surprises.

It was the *way* they had found the baby. The flawless preservation in that frozen block of ice. It was as if the baby would remain a child eternally, forever stalled mid-breath, eyes open. Perfect, crystal blue eyes.

The media had gotten hold of the case and was running a headline constantly:

WHO IS BABY GIRL DOE?

Both the broadcast and print outlets were running a silhouette of a Gerber baby style cut-out with the standard question mark over the face.

Preliminary forensics had come in from the two crime scenes. The evidence on the lampposts in front of the two churches was not blood. It was, instead, a composite of substances including a starchy compound, soil, and tannin.

Beneath the body, frozen into the ice, was another copy of *My Missal*, identical to the book found at St Adelaide's. The book was currently being processed, although the possibility of collecting forensic evidence from something that long in water was slight.

The ME's office had told them that it would be three or four days before an autopsy could be performed on the infant, or physical evidence could be gathered from the small body. When Jessica protested, she was told that any attempt to warm the body by other means would simply destroy the evidence. The infant's body was currently in a chilled room at the medical examiner's office on University Avenue.

Jessica thought about Daniel Palumbo's dying words.

He lives.

Who lives?

So far, no one had come forth to claim the baby, despite the story being splashed all over the newspapers and television. For Jessica, this was as horrifying as anything connected to the case.

Was it possible that there was a mother somewhere in the city of Philadelphia who didn't know that her infant child was missing?

Soon the lab results would start to roll in, and they could begin to piece this all together. So Jessica watched the phone. And waited.

BYRNE HAD THE AFTERNOON off, and by one o'clock Jessica was crawling out of her skin. She had to hit the streets and *make* something happen.

She went through the pamphlets and papers they had found in Danny Palumbo's backpack, courtesy of Thomas Boyce. A few of the papers were torn from legal pads. One had a series of times of the day, along with what might have been street addresses.

She input some of the addresses onto major thoroughfares, came up with nothing. None were long enough to be phone numbers.

Were these meal times at shelters?

She got a list of shelters, and none of the addresses matched. Then it hit her. AA or NA meetings. She looked up Philadelphia AA chapters, and the locations and times matched perfectly. They could start attending these meetings, but the whole point of AA was anonymity, and even in the course of a homicide investigation, it was unlikely they would find anyone who would go on the record about one of their attendees. If, indeed, Danny had even attended these meetings. They'd do this if they had to, but it probably would be a waste of time.

On the back of that page was a series of numbers, seven lines deep. This made even less sense. Jessica filed the paper away, chalking it up to a man with a disturbed mind, sadly at the end of his life.

Jessica turned her attention to the as yet unidentified baby. She could not imagine a mother not coming forward. It either meant the woman could not do so, or was unaware that the baby was gone. But that would mean the baby was left in the care of someone else who didn't know or care that it was missing.

Jessica moved forward with the premise that the baby's mother was poor and/or on drugs. If that were the case, the woman probably wouldn't have a personal physician. It meant she would have sought out prenatal and postnatal care either at emergency rooms, or free clinics.

Jessica decided to start with free clinics. There weren't that many in Philadelphia. She would begin in North Philadelphia, then West

Philadelphia. Hopefully, Byrne would be back to help her with South Philly. She printed off a list, and got on the road. Anything was better than staring at a phone.

BY MID-AFTERNOON SHE HAD visited four community clinics, spoken to a half-dozen doctors and administrators, all of whom were aware of the Baby Doe story. None of them had treated a white female infant, aged two months, in or around the timeline that surrounded the murder. More than ninety percent of the children at these North Philadelphia clinics were Hispanic or African-American.

The last North Philly free clinic was the St Julius Clinic on Lehigh near Twelfth, run by the parish. By the time Jessica walked in she was bone weary, hungry, and starting to feel that all of this was a very long shot. But it was a shot she had to take.

THE ST JULIUS FREE Clinic was a three-story converted rowhouse. On one side was a second hand store, on the other was a funeral home. Jessica stepped inside. The waiting room was small and cramped, with warped vinyl tiles on the floor, posters of Philadelphia landmarks on the wall. Two young Hispanic women, very pregnant, sat next to each other. Jessica pegged them at no more than seventeen. Across from them sat a young black kid holding a blood-soaked kitchen towel to his forehead.

To a lot of the people in this neighborhood, and this part of the city, this *was* health care.

While Catholic hospitals were run by religious orders – St Mary was run by the Franciscans – the archdiocese itself did not run or operate any hospitals or clinics in Philadelphia. The few that were in existence were run by local parishes.

Jessica approached the young woman at the front counter, showed her ID, and asked to speak to someone in charge. She was told that that would be a man named Ted Cochrane, but he had three patients that were in triage, the worst of which was probably a rupturing appendix, and they were waiting for EMS. It might be a while.

After ten minutes or so, during which the appendectomy candidate was picked up and transported to nearby Temple University Hospital, a man emerged from the back room, spoke to the young woman behind the desk. The woman gestured to Jessica. The man signed a few papers, came around the desk.

'I'm Ted Cochrane,' he said. 'How can I help you?'

Jessica made him to be about twenty-two. Tall and well-built, dark hair and eyes. It didn't seem likely, based on his youthful appearance, but Jessica asked anyway. 'Are you a doctor?'

Cochrane smiled. 'Not yet. I'm an LPN. I'm heading to med school this fall.'

'Is there somewhere we can talk privately?'

'Sure.' He got the young woman's attention, pointed to a back room. The receptionist nodded. Cochrane led Jessica to a small examination room off the main hallway. It looked like every other examination room she had ever been in, but shabbier, more exhausted. On the wall was the ever-present hand sanitizer tube. Cochrane pulled a small ball of disinfectant foam, ran it over his hands, partially closed the door behind them.

'What can I do for you, detective?'

'Well, maybe you can start with what you do here at the clinic.'

'We patch and repair, mostly. Lots of bumps and bruises, 'flu shots, sore throats. We're pretty much first line. There is usually a doctor here six hours a day, but the MD on today's sheet got called into Temple for an emergency surgery.'

Jessica noted the crucifix on the wall. 'How much religion do people get here?'

'As much or as little as they want. None at all, if that's what they want. We are partially funded by the parish, but belief in Christ is by no means a prerequisite to medical care.'

'Like AA?'

'Like AA,' Cochrane said. 'Our evangelism is really just that wall of pamphlets in the waiting room. We don't proselytize.'

'Are you a Catholic?'

Cochrane smiled. 'No, born and raised Methodist.'

'Do you do pediatrics here?'

'We do just about everything here. Pre-natal, post-natal, pediatrics, all the way up to and including geriatric medicine.'

'What about mental-health services?'

'Absolutely. Family counseling, substance abuse counseling, group therapy, some Cognitive Behavioral Therapy.'

'You have the staff for this?'

He smiled again. 'No, far from it. We are blessed to get a lot of *pro bono* work through the Catholic hospitals. The Archdiocese has been very good about turning the emotional and professional screws on its faithful.'

'Have you treated any young infants in the past few weeks?'

'Oh, my, yes. At least five or six.'

'Any white female babies?'

Cochrane considered the question. 'Is this about the baby on the news? Baby Doe?'

'I need you to keep this inquiry confidential, but yes.'

Cochrane nodded. 'I had some down time yesterday, and I started going through records from the last few weeks. As you might expect, most of the children we treat here are minorities. But we did see a Caucasian female infant recently. Her information will be in the database.'

'Why do you think this is related?'

Now it was Cochrane's turn. 'I need this to be confidential, as well.'

'Of course.'

'The mother of this baby, Adria Rollins is her name, has some mental health issues. When she visited she came with her great-grandfather, who is pretty frail. That's why the flag went up when I saw the news story. I thought the child might be at risk.'

'Do you have contact information for the mother?'

'Maybe, maybe not. We do our best here, but half the time the addresses we get are fake.'

'Could you take a look?'

Cochrane hesitated. Jessica was losing him.

'I wouldn't ask if this wasn't very important,' she said. 'I know how crucial it is to keep medical records confidential, but this may well be related to a homicide – perhaps two homicides – and I promise I will treat the information with discretion.'

It was touch and go for a second, but Cochrane soon relented. He sat down at the terminal, hit a few keys, then a few more.

'Here it is,' he said. 'The address on her record is of her great-grandfather's apartment. It looks like he is her legal guardian.'

Jessica wrote down the address. It wasn't that far away.

The woman from the front desk poked her head in the room. 'I'm sorry to interrupt, but we need the room.'

Jessica and Cochrane stepped into the narrow hallway. The woman led in a man who appeared to have scraped half the skin off the back of his left hand. The nurse closed the curtain.

'If I recall correctly, we have a few pictures of the Rollins baby,' Cochrane said. 'We sometimes take photographs of children when we suspect abuse.'

'Are you saying this baby was abused?'

'It's possible. I can show you the pictures.'

'I would appreciate it.'

Cochrane went into the back room for what seemed like fifteen long minutes. In that time four more people came into the clinic. Nobody made eye contact with anybody else, perhaps out of some sense of shame. They all seemed to wait patiently, reading coverless five-year-old copies of *Sports Illustrated* or *Essence*.

Finally Cochrane emerged, a manila file folder in hand. He took Jessica to the side, extracted two photos from the folder. One was a close-up of the back of an infant's leg.

'This is Ceci,' Cochrane said. The photograph showed a deep purple bruise, just at the top of the right calf. 'That's her nickname, of course. Her full name is Cecilia.'

'This is Adria Rollins's baby?'

'Yes.'

Jessica studied the photograph. 'And this bruise is the result of abuse?'

'Hard to tell,' Cochrane said. 'If a baby comes back with other evidence, we'll have this record, then we make the call to Children's Services. As I'm sure you know, unless the abuse is flagrant – which this is not – there has to be a pattern of abuse before a case can be made.'

With this Cochrane took out the other photograph, turned it over.

The plummeting feeling in Jessica's stomach was instant, and debilitating. It took every ounce of her strength, and every moment of her training, not to break down in tears. The photograph in front of her was of the baby they had found frozen to death in that shuttered church.

There was no doubt in her mind.

She now had a name to go with the face that she was sure would live in a dark corner of her mind for a very long time, long after this case was closed.

The dead little girl's name was Cecilia.

SIXTEEN

THEY SAT AT A TABLE AT THE SUBWAY ON FRANKFORD AVENUE, NEAR Cottman. It was between the lunch and dinner hours, and the regulars had not yet descended on the place. At this hour, the restaurant was nearly empty.

Byrne found himself covertly checking his pager every few minutes, hoping he wasn't being obvious about it. The cases weighed heavily on his mind, but there was a team on it, and he knew if something broke he would get a phone call. He had his phone on vibrate, but it was on. When he decided to become Gabriel Hightower's Philly Brother he knew there were going to be times like this, times when he should be chasing shadows instead of taking the days off he had coming. On the other hand, they had no hot leads at the moment, and the dead stay dead.

Gabriel was alive.

'What did you think of the movie?' Byrne asked. Gabriel had lobbied for every R-rated film on the roster, regardless of subject matter. In the end, Byrne picked a PG-13 action film, hoping that the action, and the sex, were muted. They were, as were much of the plot, characterization, and wit.

Gabriel shrugged. This time, Byrne noticed, it was only a one-shoulder shrug. Maybe they were making progress.

'It was okay,' Gabriel said.

'Just okay? Is that better than *a'ight?*'

Gabriel smiled, his first bona fide grin. 'I liked the part where that old guy wasted that kid. That was cold, man.'

They sat in silence for a few moments, sipping their sodas through straws. Gabriel made bubbles. A pair of teenaged girls sat at the next table. Gabriel tried to make eyes without making eyes. Byrne remembered that stage very well.

'So, you never told me how you got that nickname G-Flash,' Byrne said. 'Are you a photographer or something?'

Another smile. 'Nah, it's because I'm *fast*, man.'

'Are you now.'

'For real. But my brother, Terrell, he was *real* fast. Like lightning fast. He got medals and everything.' Gabriel began to fold and unfold the wax paper his sandwich came in. Byrne just listened. 'I remember this one time, when I was just little, maybe five or six or something, we had this dog. Real ratty-lookin' thing. Called it Bitley.'

Byrne smiled. 'Bitley? Where'd the dog get a name like that?'

Another one-shoulder shrug. This time the left. 'Wasn't my idea. Came with the dog, I guess.'

'Okay.'

'But this dog was *fast*. When he got out the door, he would be all the way up the street to the Boulevard before you knew it, right? Come home in a hour all dirty and shit.'

Gabriel looked up, realizing he swore. Byrne took no notice.

'So this one time . . . time when Terrell was training for the state finals? He's in the front, and I come out and leave the door open by accident? Bitley come outta the house like a bullet, man. Well, Terrell he ran after it, and *caught* it. Can you believe that? Outran a *dog*, man.' Gabriel finished his Coke with a loud flourish, rattled the ice. 'You gotta be *fast* to do that.'

There was a lot Byrne wanted to ask the kid about his brother, about life. For now he was content to listen. The kid was talking, and that was a good thing.

After a few more moments of silence, Gabriel asked, 'So how come you became a cop?'

Byrne had a very long, convoluted answer to this, so he had to think of a short version. 'Well, it was a different time when I came up. I guess I looked at it as a way to do something for the city, you know? Do something to make it a better place.'

Byrne realized this sounded like a recruitment pamphlet, but when Gabriel just nodded, he realized it was probably adequate for the time being.

'What about you?' Byrne asked. 'Ever think about what you want to do for a living someday?'

'Sometimes.'

'What do you think you might want to do?'

'I don't know. Architect or something. I like to draw. I like to build things.'

'An architect, huh?' Byrne said, thinking to himself how expensive the tuitions for that were. The kid didn't have much of a shot at it. Maybe with a full scholarship it would happen. 'That's great.'

Byrne heard the door open, turned to look. A pair of young priests entered the restaurant. Byrne glanced over at Gabriel. He sat a little straighter. Byrne thought it odd. He decided to ask, in a roundabout way.

'So are the folks at the foster home religious?'

'Nah,' Gabriel said. 'Not really.'

'What about you?'

'A little bit. I remember Terrell used to pray before every track meet. He prayed to St Sebastian.'

'Why St Sebastian?'

'Said he was the saint of athletes or something.'

You learn something new every day, Byrne thought. 'You're Catholic?'

'My real mom was,' Gabriel said. 'I don't remember her too good, though. I was just little when she passed. I don't know *what* I am.'

Byrne had been in his late-thirties when his mother died. He still missed her every day. He wondered what his teenaged years would have been like without her. Would he be a different man today? There was little doubt of that.

'How 'bout you? You Catholic?' Gabriel asked.

'*Oh*, yeah. I went to Catholic school and everything.'

Gabriel nodded. At his age, where you went to school meant everything. Along with what sneaks you wore, what labels were sewn into your clothes, and which cell phone you used. It pretty much told the world everything they needed to know about you.

'Do you go to church?' Gabriel asked.

Now it was Byrne's turn to shrug. He suddenly felt as if he had to defend himself. Maybe he did. Maybe he *should* have to defend himself, not that he had a valid argument in his arsenal. 'Not as often as I'd like.'

Gabriel smiled. 'Somethin' *stopping* you?'

Damn, Byrne thought. Nothing gets by this kid. 'You're right. Nothing's stopping me.' Byrne balled up the wax paper on the table, tossed it expertly into a nearby can. 'Tell you what, I'll go if you go.'

'Okay.'

The kid put out a fist to bump. They *were* making progress.

This time Byrne dropped Gabriel at the foster home. Pulled right up out front, large as life. Byrne got out, walked around the car. He knew he was being watched. There were two runners on the corner. He turned and looked at the apartment building across the street. He saw a shadow in the window on the third floor. By the time Byrne opened the door for Gabriel he saw the kid on the corner move out of his sight, taking out his cell phone. If there was one thing an unmarked detective sedan was in this part of the city, it was a clearly marked police car.

Byrne and Gabriel walked up the steps to the front door.

'So, I'll call you in the next couple days or something?' Byrne asked.

'Cool.'

By the time Byrne got back down to the street he saw one of the thugs from the corner standing behind his car. The kid was trying to look casual, invisible. But Byrne could see that he had his cell phone in hand, and that the front of the phone was pointed at the rear end of the department-issue Taurus. The kid was trying to take a picture of Byrne's license plate.

'Something I can help you with?'

The kid seemed surprised at Byrne's speed at getting down the steps and across the sidewalk. Before he could stop himself, the kid flicked a glance to the third-floor window across the street, then back at Byrne.

'Just crossing the street, man,' the kid said.

'You mean *jay* walking across the street. Now that's illegal. You wouldn't want to break the law, would you?'

Byrne pulled back the hem of his coat, revealing the badge on his belt. He knew the kid already knew he was a cop, but it never hurt to show your hand. The kid tried to hold Byrne's gaze, but gave up after a second. He backed onto the curb slowly, then turned and strolled to the corner. Before getting back in the car, Byrne checked the window across the street. The shade was now down.

Byrne then glanced at the foster home. Gabriel was in the front-room window. He had seen the whole exchange. Byrne lifted a hand to wave. To Byrne's relief, Gabriel waved back.

Byrne slipped into the car, waited to pull out into traffic. He looked down at the passenger seat. There he saw a small white object, and had to smile.

It was an origami eagle.

BYRNE DROVE TO ST Damian's, parked across the street. The building was still a crime scene, still ringed with bright yellow tape.

I will give thee a crown of life.

These words had come to him the day they found the prayer card at St Adelaide's. How had he known the crown referred to the bell tower? How had he known to send Josh to look there?

The truth was, he had not. Not with any certainty. It was a feeling he'd had, and it had been right.

But no feeling like this had come to him about St Damian's. Not yet. For some reason he could not shake the notion that there was another clue inside this old stone church, a calling card telling them where to look next. He would come back to this place soon, he thought. Or maybe he would *find* himself here.

By the time Byrne reached Eighth Street, his pager vibrated for the fourth time. It was Jessica. He flipped his phone, speed-dialed her number. She answered in half a ring.

'What's up?' Byrne asked.

'We found the baby's mother.'

'How did you track her down?'

Jessica filled him in on her visit to the clinic.

'Where are you?' Byrne asked.

'Twelfth and Lehigh.'

'I'll pick you up.'

As Byrne approached the corner of Twelfth and Lehigh he saw that Jessica was pacing. She only paced when she was upset. For Jessica it was like opening a steam valve. Byrne pulled over, Jessica got in.

Byrne pointed to the ramshackle building.

'That's the clinic?' he asked.

'Yeah,' Jessica said. She told him about Ted Cochrane, and the rest of the details she had learned at the clinic.

'This LPN treated the baby?'

'He said that they suspected some kind of abuse, but they couldn't be sure.'

'What kind of abuse?'

'The baby had a bruise on the back of one of her legs. It was hard to tell from the photograph.'

As they drove toward Fifth Street Jessica found that she had tightened her hands into fists. It had not gone unnoticed to Byrne. He put a hand on her forearm for a moment. She knew what he was trying to communicate. You go into an interview with anger and you come out with nothing.

'When I got the mother's name I called it in,' Jessica said, trying to calm down. 'Maria ran it.'

'The mother's got a sheet?'

'No criminal record. But she has been institutionalized a few times for mental disorders.'

'How bad?'

'One time it was for more than a month.'

'In other words . . .'

'Yeah,' Jessica said. 'Bad.'

'Why do you think it's our baby?'

Jessica reached into her portfolio, took out the color photograph Ted Cochrane had given her. At a red light Byrne took it, studied it.

'That's her, isn't it?' Jessica asked.

'Yeah,' Byrne said. 'That's her.'

SEVENTEEN

THE APARTMENT BUILDING WAS A LOW-RISE, BROWN-BRICK BUILDING on Fifth Street. Jessica and Byrne parked the car, entered. There was no security door through which they needed to be buzzed in. Jessica noted that many of the mailboxes in the lobby were pried and dented. An old Dymo label identified the Rollins apartment as number Six.

As THEY ROUNDED THE corner on the second floor, heading to the last apartment on the left, they smelled it. It was unmistakable. The stench of death filled the hallway.

'I'll get the super,' Byrne said.

Jessica bunched the collar of her coat over her nose and mouth and eased herself to the door of apartment number six. She knocked, listened. Nothing. She knocked again, announced herself.

No one came to the door.

Jessica again put her ear against the door and listened. From inside, faintly, she heard music. It was a child's song, one that she remembered from her own childhood. Because it was so faint she could not quite put a name to it, even though it was familiar. She doubted that it was the radio. The sound was scratchy, like an old record from another era.

Other than this sound she heard nothing – no voices, no television, no footsteps moving around the apartment. She eased her hand onto the doorknob, gave it a slight turn. The door was locked. There were no deadbolts on the door, just the old skeleton-type key hole.

She glanced down the hallway. She was alone. Keeping the collar of her coat over her mouth and nose, she got down onto one knee and looked through the keyhole. She couldn't see much, but putting her face this close to the small opening gave her a much stronger smell of decomposing flesh.

There was a dead body in this apartment.

A few seconds later Byrne came down the hallway with an older man whom Jessica assumed was the superintendent of the building. He wore a heavy coat and pilled woolen mittens. On his head was a filthy ball cap.

Jessica walked halfway down the hall to meet them.

'Edward Turchek, this is my partner, Detective Balzano.'

The man grunted a greeting.

'Can you tell us who lives in apartment number six?' Jessica asked.

'Just old Duke Rollins,' Turchek said.

'Alone?'

He shook his head. 'Sometimes his granddaughter lives with him. When she's not . . . you know.'

'No, we don't know,' Jessica said. 'Why don't you tell us?'

'Well, it's just that she's a little bit . . . you know.' The man made a twirling motion by the temple on the right side of his head, the universal hand gesture meaning crazy.

'This is Adria you're talking about? Adria Rollins?'

'Yeah,' Turchek said. 'That's her name. Adria.'

'And you're saying she has some mental health issues?' Jessica asked.

The man snorted a laugh. No one joined him. He cleared his throat. 'Yeah. You could say that.'

'And you say she is the man's granddaughter? Not his *great*-granddaughter?' Jessica asked.

'Granddaughter, great-granddaughter, I don't know. Duke is pretty old.'

'Have any of the neighbors complained about the smell?'

Turchek pulled a face. 'What smell?'

Jessica looked at Byrne, back. 'When was the last time you saw anyone go in or out of this apartment?'

'Not for a while, I guess. I pretty much mind my own business here.'

Jessica looked up at the peeling paint on the walls, the cracked and taped window at the end of the hall, the bootlegged electric and cable TV wires stapled to the ceiling, the uneven floorboards in the hallway.

I bet you do, Jessica thought.

'Do you know if Mr Rollins or Adria are home now?' Jessica asked.

'No idea,' the man said. 'Did you knock?'

Jessica's eyes burned a hole in the man's forehead until he looked away.

'We're going to need to get into this apartment,' she said. 'Do you have a master key?'

The man ran a hand over his stubbled chin. 'I don't know if I'm allowed to do that.'

Byrne took a step toward the man, backing him to the wall.

'I'm looking a half-dozen building code violations, and that's just the shit I can see from here,' Byrne said. 'Now, just based on the odor you don't seem to be able to smell, we can take down that door. That's plenty of probable cause. If you want to spend the rest of the day repairing the damage, then deal with L & I, who I'm going to contact right now, you are welcome to it. Your call.'

'I got the key right here,' the man said. But he didn't move.

When Byrne stepped to the side the man all but ran down to the end of the hall. He put the key in the lock, turned it. He opened the door a few inches, slipped to the side.

Jessica and Byrne stepped up to the doorway. Jessica knocked again, this time on the jamb. No footsteps. Just the children's song, which had started over again.

Byrne pushed the door. 'Philadelphia Police!' he said.

No answer.

Ahead of them, against the far wall, was an old cranberry red sofa.

On it were three or four dirty gray bed sheets, a pair of flat bed pillows with large grease stains in the center. In front of the sofa was a chipped maple coffee table with stacked plastic trays from a few dozen microwave dinners. To the left was a 1970s vintage console television, tuned to a game show, sound all the way down.

Still, from somewhere in the apartment, the children's song played. Now that she was inside, Jessica identified the song as 'A Smile and a Ribbon', an old children's song from the 1950s that she used to play. The sound seemed to be coming from a bedroom at the end of the hall.

Jessica turned to see the superintendent standing in the doorway. He had no reaction to the condition of the apartment, and still seemed unable to smell the appalling stench of decomposing flesh.

'We'll let you know if we need anything else,' Jessica said.

The man looked up, shrugged, and walked down the hall.

To the left of the living room was the doorway to the kitchen. The overhead ceiling light was on and through the doorway Jessica could see the pile of dirty pans and dishes overflowing in the sink. The pans were at least fifty years old, and reminded Jessica of her grandmother's cookware. With Byrne just behind her, she eased through the doorway and peered inside. The electric stove was on, all four burners radiating bright red. It was freezing in the apartment, so Jessica figured the stove was on for heat. It barely warmed the one corner of the tiny kitchen.

They walked across the living room, down the hallway. The first door on the left was the bathroom. There was no door. Jessica peered inside, and in the grim gray light coming through the translucent window she saw the bleak state of the room. There were piled rags and towels in the corner, an unflushed toilet, no shower curtain. The tub had not been washed in years.

The two doors at the end of the hallway were clearly the bedrooms. The horrible smell was coming from the bedroom on the left; the music from the bedroom on the right.

Jessica flanked the door on the right, while Byrne knocked on the door on the left.

'Philly PD,' he said. 'We're coming in.'

He looked at Jessica. Their eyes met. On a silent three Byrne reached out, eased the doorknob to the left. He threw the door open, stepped to the side.

Nobody came through.

In the room was a single bed by the windows, which were covered by an old army blanket. There were magazines, newspapers, fast-food trash, and dirty clothing everywhere. On the bed, under the sheets, was an old man. Based on the smell of decaying flesh he had been dead more than a week. The sheet over him was stained with urine and feces. Byrne stepped in, holding his tie over his nose and mouth. He flipped open the closet door. A pair of worn and shiny suits from the 1950s hung there. Beneath, a pair of dress shoes bearing a thick layer of dust.

Byrne closed the door, stepped out of the room. The two detectives addressed the other door. The song started again. The repetition was maddening. Jessica got on her two-way, called for backup and an EMS unit. They looked at each other again. It was time.

'Philadelphia Police!' Jessica said. 'We're coming in.'

Byrne turned the doorknob, slowly opened the door. Jessica put her hand on the grip of her weapon and peered around the jamb. What she saw would live in her mind forever.

The room was a jumble of boxes and brightly colored children's furniture. There seemed to be a dozen old and broken bassinets, cribs, high chairs, and small plastic tables. One of the cribs sat near the window, which was wide open, which helped to explain why the apartment was freezing.

The music came from an old red-and-white portable record player in the center of the room.

In the clutter Jessica did not see the figure sitting in the chair for a few seconds. But when the young woman coughed, both detectives spun around and nearly drew their weapons.

There, in the corner, sitting on a threadbare almond-colored upholstered chair, was a young woman, no more than nineteen. She was thin and gaunt, and wore three bathrobes, all institutional – polka-dotted, floral, pastel. In her lap was a large doll. The doll, which was missing an arm, had knotted and haphazardly cut orange hair. The young woman was calmly combing the doll's hair with a large, tarnished silver serving fork. She looked up at them.

'Is it dinnertime?' she asked.

While Jessica crossed the room, Byrne skirted the broken furniture, cleared the closet. It was empty.

'Are you Adria?' Jessica asked.

'Yes!' she said. 'Adria! That's me!'

'My name is Jessica. We're going to get you help.'

Adria nodded, smiled. 'Help!' she exclaimed. She hugged the doll. 'Pretty baby.' She put the doll back on her lap, continued to comb its hair.

Byrne crossed the room. The crib beneath the window was the cleanest thing in the room. It had a neat stack of newborn Pampers next to it.

Taking all of this in, Jessica knew the truth. Adria Rollins was not guilty of anything. The baby had been taken right from this room.

The force of Jessica's emotional reaction rocked her. She got Byrne's attention. When he saw her eyes he understood.

'Go check on EMS. I've got this,' he said.

Jessica ran out of the apartment, down the hall. She found she could barely breathe. Her heart felt ready to pound from her chest.

And still, faintly, she heard the words of the song as it played.

By the time Jessica reached the lobby the tears came. She did nothing to stop them.

EIGHTEEN

N THE WORLD OF BROADCAST TELEVISION NEWS THERE WAS ONE GOD, and His name was Nielsen. Stations lived and died by Nielsen ratings and, for reporters, you were judged not by your clothes or your face or your hair, not by your silky smooth delivery, your engaging and topical segues to sports and weather – although these things, more often than not, got you the on-air job to begin with, especially if you were a woman – but rather by one all-important number.

Your market.

Markets were determined by the number of television households in an area, and the deeper the penetration, the higher the market number, the higher the station could adjust its ad dollars.

At the yearly conventions most conversations were buoyed by the understanding (usually unspoken) of what market you were in. The top three tiers in the US were all but chiseled in stone, those being New York, Los Angeles, and Chicago. Philadelphia consistently ranked number four.

To say you were an on-air personality in one of these major markets carried a lot of weight because, in the strata of the Nielsen ratings, which ranked more than 200 markets, it was a constant challenge and struggle to reach bigger and bigger markets. If you were in a feeder market – so-called because it was a smaller market that fed a larger market – all you thought about was how you could eat your way up the food chain. Any reporter who claimed anything to the contrary was full of shit.

I decided to stay in my home town of Weehauken so I could be near my family.

I've gotten comfortable in this sized market. It's about the people.

Bullshit, Shane thought. The truth is you've been sending out your reel for six straight years and even Wheeling turned you down. You've put on fifteen pounds, your crow's feet are taking over your face, you've whitened your teeth, and it still ain't happening. Save your boosterism for those idiotic station promos that show you flipping pancakes, hugging three-legged poodles, and wearing a hat shaped like a fucking radish.

In terms of the nation, these rankings were easy. But that's just where the bloodshed began. The real battle, the in close knife fighting, was for ratings *within* a market.

Philadelphia, of course, had three network affiliates on the air, ABC, NBC, and CBS, in addition to the Fox affiliate and the stations for WB, PBS, and UPN.

Although a bit before his time, Shane knew that the game changer, as far as broadcast news went, was *Entertainment Tonight* and its hybrid of news and entertainment to which straight news had to respond. Instead of covering a dozen stories in a half hour, local news now was compelled to cover thirty or more. And fast. In this day and age, more than ever, the headline *was* the story.

When it came time to pick a professional name, Shane gave it a lot of thought. It was not a decision to be made lightly. He studied the names of the giants in the business.

Most had two-syllable last names. Murrow. Cronkite. Huntley. Brinkley. Brokaw. Jennings. Rather.

Shane was his choice for a first name. A little bit of the outlaw, a little bit of the hero, though just about no one under the age of fifty was familiar with the Alan Ladd film, unless you were a film buff.

The last name was harder. It had to be two syllables, had to convey trust, had to roll off the tongue, and look good on the lower third of the TV screen. He considered a lot of names, but arrived at Adams. When he'd chosen it, he'd had no idea he would end up in a top ten market – no less a market than Philadelphia, where the name of a founding father would be perfect – but he figured a name like Shane Adams would carry him anywhere.

So far, so good.

And while the pioneers of broadcasting were iconic, there was one name that mattered, a man after whom Shane had patterned his career, if not his life – except for the part about being raised a Vanderbilt – the man whose face adorned the only poster in Shane's tiny apartment.

Anderson Cooper.

Whenever Shane was faced with a decision, he asked himself: WWACD.

What Would Anderson Cooper Do?

When Cooper's book *Dispatches from the Edge* was released, Shane scoured the trades, hoping for a book signing tour, and was rewarded. He stood in line at the Borders on South Broad Street, waiting nervously. Every so often he'd sneak a peek at Cooper who was dressed casually in denim, his silver hair glowing under the fluorescents. Shane had practiced what he might say when he got up to the table, but instead of anything witty, urbane, or clever, he just said. 'Hi. I'm a fan.'

Cooper smiled. He said: 'I saw your report last night. Good work.'

Shane was flabbergasted. He floated on those words for the next week or so. Who was he kidding? He was *still* floating on those words.

What Shane revered most about the journalist was Cooper's phrasing. Shane had studied with two voice coaches and an acting coach, trying to get the perfect TV voice. It was called *standard stage*, a mélange of upper-crust, Mayflower New England and midwestern housewife. Heightened language, some called it. A style of speaking with which you pronounce . . . each . . . syllable. Complete and unaccented.

It wasn't *kah-fee* or *koh-fee*.

It was *coffee*.

Shane had spent thousands of hours reading newspaper articles aloud, ridding his inflection of any trace of his accent.

But as good as he got, there was always someone younger coming up behind him. And that person was usually female.

The new threat at Shane's station was Dawn Reilly. Twenty-six, petite and perky, Dawn was the new face. Or, more accurately, the new boobs. She had just moved up market from the CBS affiliate in Cleveland (currently ranked #18).

From the moment they met sparks had flown. Dawn was every bit as ambitious as Shane, but she had arrows in her quiver Shane had not. Although he couldn't prove it – not yet anyway – he knew she was sleeping with the quite-married news director, and therefore getting the plum assignments. He had twice shadowed her to the clubs on a Friday night, and twice gone through her trash. He had nothing tangible, nothing he could use.

Yet.

SHANE LOOKED AT THE footage from outside St Damian's. The place was right out of a gothic horror novel. Cyn had gotten some low angle stuff, the spire of the church against dark, moving clouds.

Last night I dreamed I went to Manderley again . . .

Shane had to laugh. He loved old movies, especially Hitchcock, especially *Rebecca*. He'd seen the film at least ten times with his mother. He often thought that one day, in his dotage, after retiring from CNN with a den full of Emmy Awards, he would like to write a gothic novel.

He brought himself back to the moment, turned to the short piece that had appeared in that morning's *Inquirer*. His eye flew down the page, absorbing the details. He had long ago stopped believing anything he read anywhere was fact. Today's media was all about *first*, not *accurate*. It was accurate until it was disproven, then an apology was issued and life went on.

Shane sensed someone nearby, turned around. Cyn was standing behind him. He pointed at the screen.

'This is great stuff, Cyn.'

'I know,' she said. 'And I'm not buying you lunch.'

'So, this church was abandoned?'

They had tried, unsuccessfully, as had every other station in town, to get inside St Damian's, but were turned away. It was still an active crime scene.

'Not abandoned,' Cyn said. 'I don't think the archdiocese just walks away from a building, unless they sell it. It was closed. The parish merged with another parish.'

Shane had put in three calls to the archdiocese, and each time had been told that there was not, nor would there be, any comment.

'So someone broke in and just left that baby?' he asked.

'Looks like it.'

'And it froze to death?'

'Looks like it,' Cyn said. 'And it's a *her*, not an *it*.'

Whatever, Shane thought.

'Do we know if there was any trauma? Like if the baby was strangled or anything?'

'You are one twisted fucker, you know that?'

'That's why you love me.'

'I haven't heard or read anything about that. So far, it's just a baby who was found frozen inside an old aluminum washtub. That might have to be enough for you.'

Bullshit, Shane thought. *Nothing was ever enough.*

Thinking about the story, Shane got the feeling, almost sexual in nature, of where this story might lead. He knew this had all the makings of a lurid, scandalous tale, which was his lifeblood. Something that might turn into a ratings winner. Something that might get him a few on-set pieces, which were the kind of stories that vaulted you from roving beat reporter to one who got to sit next to the anchors. Not that you wanted to. He'd yet to meet an anchor who wasn't a world class narcissistic asshole.

You had your Church involvement (in Philly, anything involving the Catholic Church had the potential to explode), you had the possibility of some sort of ritual killing, and you had a dead baby. Talk about a hat trick! He could see the graphics now: pentagrams, crosses, baby shoes.

Blood.

He had to stop, or he'd give himself an erection.

'Any of the other stations on this?' Shane asked.

Cyn gestured to the monitors across the room. 'No one's breaking in with it.'

'Where's Dawn?'

Cyn looked under the news director's desk. 'I don't see her at her usual lunch spot.'

Shane laughed, then started the B-roll footage Cyn had shot. In it, a man and a woman got out of a PPD detective car, and walked down the alley next to the church. Shane ran it back and forth a few times. He only saw the cops from the side momentarily, then from the back as they disappeared down the alley.

'Do you know these detectives?'

'Oh, yeah,' Cyn said. 'They've been involved in some pretty high profile cases since I've been here. Kevin Byrne and Jessica Balzano.'

'Are they accessible?' Shane wanted to ask whether or not *Jessica Balzano* was accessible, but Cyn would have seen right through that.

'As accessible as any of them,' Cyn said.

Shane knew what she meant. It was rare that a detective, especially a homicide detective, would talk to the media about an ongoing case. Unless, of course, they needed the media's help in finding a suspect. Then they were all sweetness and light. It was truly a love/hate relationship, as well as symbiotic. Shane always thought of it in terms of rust needing oxygen.

'But Kevin Byrne is a hard case,' Cyn added.

'How so?'

'Well, he really plays it all pretty close to the vest. Even things he'd be allowed to talk about, he just keeps walking. If you press him he always just refers you to the media relations officer.'

'Yeah, well, he's never been exposed to my highly persuasive charms.'

Cyn barked a laugh. 'Did you see how *big* this fucking guy is? Your persuasive charms might end up putting you in a bed with an IV drip.'

We'll see about that, Shane thought.

While Cyn went off to dump the footage and get started editing, Shane sat down at a computer terminal, got online and began to look up background on the two detectives. For any number of reasons it was always wise to learn as many of the names as you could if you wanted to work the crime beat. Detectives, prosecutors, judges, defense attorneys. You never knew what you would need in the future.

What Cyn had said – that these two detectives had been involved in high profile cases – was the understatement of the year.

Shane started with Jessica Balzano and discovered that *Philadelphia Magazine* had done a profile on her a few years earlier. He learned that she was a South Philly girl, that she was married to a narcotics detective named Vincent, that they had a daughter named Sophie. He learned that her father, Peter Giovanni, was a much-decorated officer in the PPD, retiring with the rank of lieutenant.

Kevin Byrne was a little tougher. Shane learned that he had been involved in the Rosary Killer case – Shane had been working in Zanesville at the time, and the story had gone wide enough for him to have learned about it – and that the detective had been nearly mortally wounded in that case.

Shane wrote down the names, even though he didn't have to. He remembered every person he ever met.

He then got onto the white pages database, and tried to look them up. There was no listing for a Jessica Balzano, or Vincent Balzano. There were a few hits for Kevin Byrne, but Shane doubted any of them were the detective. This made sense, of course. Why would a detective have a listing? It was bad enough that the psychos out there knew where they worked, why let them know where they lived?

Of course, this never stopped Shane Adams from trying.

He did an image search on Jessica Balzano, and all of them were the accompanying photo from the *Philadelphia Magazine* piece. In it, she stood in the foreground of the Roundhouse. Her lustrous brunette hair was long, a little windswept. She had dark eyes, a smooth complexion, full lips. She was slender, but not skinny, not by any means. It mentioned in the article that she had boxed, and in this photograph she looked very toned. She was beautiful.

Shane wondered what she was like. He wondered if she ever cheated on her husband. He wondered what she ate, drank, drove.

He had every intention of finding out answers to all these questions.

He had the feeling this case, this *story*, was going to be big. Dead babies and the Catholic Church. It didn't get better than that. Forget the whole abortion issue, this was a murdered child. And Shane Adams was at the tip of the sword on this one.

He opened his laptop, put in the password to open the encrypted folder, opened the database file. He started two new entries:

Jessica Balzano
Kevin Byrne

J ESSICA AND BYRNE STOOD IN SILENCE LONG AFTER THE EMS van had left with the old man's remains, long after the two DHS workers had taken Adria Rollins to the psychiatric unit at Temple.

Whatever promise it had begun with, the day was on a downward turn now. They would not be questioning Adria Rollins, not anytime soon anyway. The real question was why Adria – who clearly had a long history of mental illness – was allowed to keep custody of her newborn baby.

Apparently the great-grandfather had been ambulatory and lucid two months earlier, and those people tasked with the decision figured he was able to take care of both Adria and the baby.

Regardless, whatever the explanation was, whatever the answers to these questions might be, it was for another agency, another set of investigators, not homicide.

A quick search of the Rollins apartment yielded little. The utilities, for what they were worth, were included in the rent, so there were no electric or gas bills. There was no telephone.

In the old man's room they had found some news clippings from the *Inquirer*, stories about a much younger Duke Rollins when he had returned from World War II.

What they wanted to find they had not located. They did not find a birth certificate for Cecilia Rollins, which would tell them who the father was and open a new conduit in the investigation.

They already had calls in to all the appropriate agencies, but considering the speed at which these bureaucracies worked, it could be weeks before they learned anything along these lines.

They had also knocked on every door in the apartment building. Half of their attempts yielded no answer. The other half yielded nothing fruitful.

Jessica and Byrne had walked the alleyway behind the building. Their theory – and it was the only one to run with at the moment – was that someone had climbed the fire escape, entered Adria's room, and taken little Cecilia out of her crib.

Unfortunately, the building behind the apartment building was a shuttered warehouse. There were no other apartment windows facing Adria's room, no one to question.

They would have to return in the next few days, talk to people on the street, discover their routines, catalog them, ask if they had seen anything suspicious in that alley in the past few weeks.

It was an exercise in futility and frustration.

THE PRESENCE OF THE Catholic Church in Philadelphia was as old as the city itself. Not long after William Penn founded the city, the first Catholic mass was celebrated in 1733, at Old St Joseph's Church. In the eighteenth century, Philadelphia was one of the only cities in the English-speaking world where Catholics could practice their faith in the open.

The residence of the Archbishop, who was the titular head of the Archdiocese of Philadelphia, was located in the northwestern part of the city.

Dana Westbrook had put in the request, through the DA's office, and an appointment was made with the media relations director for the archdiocese.

It was in the best interest of the Church to meet with investigators. The murders were all over the media. A dead man and a dead baby found in two different Catholic Churches was big news. The tabloids were already running stories about exorcisms and ritual killings. Considering all the scandals the Catholic Church had had to endure over the past decade, it made good PR sense for the archdiocese to get out in front of anything that might hurt their reputation.

THEY WERE MET AT the door by a stout woman in her sixties. Although she wore street clothing Jessica knew she was a nun. Twelve years of Catholic school education clued you into who was and who was not part of the Church.

After a few pleasantries she led them to a study off the main entrance hall. The room in which they were to meet the spokesperson was oak-paneled, formal, lined with books. In the center was a round table, highly polished, ringed by six velvet-seated chairs.

A few minutes later the door opened.

Father Michael Raphael was much younger than either Jessica or Byrne expected. In his twenties, athletic looking and handsome, he carried about him an air of boyish vulnerability, as well as the outward confidence needed by the point man for such a powerful organization as the Archdiocese of Philadelphia. The archdiocese covered not only Philadelphia, but Bucks, Montgomery, Chester, and Delaware counties as well. Its reach, and influence, was great.

Jessica didn't know that much about the priesthood, but she did know that for Michael Raphael to have been ordained at this young age, he'd had to have entered the seminary with a bachelor's degree. His age and position were surprising on many levels. Priests fresh out of the seminary were usually assigned to smaller parishes, or to menial tasks in the larger ones. This duty, being the public relations officer for the Archdiocese of Philadelphia, was a plum position.

And while his good looks were beguiling, it was his eyes that held you – dark, penetrating eyes that seemed to look right through you.

'I'm Michael Raphael,' he said. 'Welcome.'

'Nice to meet you, Father,' Jessica said. It seemed odd for her to be calling someone around ten years her junior 'Father,' but old habits died hard. Especially those drilled into you by a Catholic school education.

They all shook hands.

Raphael gestured to two chairs at the table. 'Please,' he said. 'Make yourselves comfortable.' He then indicated a beautiful antique serving cart near the tall windows. 'May I offer you tea or coffee?'

Both Jessica and Byrne declined. Raphael poured himself a black coffee, took a seat opposite them. They exchanged small talk about the long, brutal winter, the plight of the Sixers and Flyers.

'I have to say that we were expecting someone older,' Byrne finally said.

Raphael smiled. 'I get that a lot. Alas, this will stop a lot sooner than I would like.'

'I don't hear much eastern Pennsylvania in your voice,' Byrne said. 'You're not a Philly boy?'

'Very astute, detective. As much as I would like to claim the City of Brotherly Love as my hometown, I cannot. I'm from Ohio. Southeastern Ohio to be more precise, just across the West Virginia border.'

'I thought so,' Byrne said. 'Browns or Bengals?'

'Browns, I'm afraid. We Franciscans are a long-suffering order.'

Small talk finished, Byrne got down to business. 'Have you been briefed at all about why we're here?'

Both Jessica and Byrne took this as a given. They'd had to put together a bullet list of things they wanted to discuss before being granted a meeting.

Raphael nodded, sipped his coffee. 'I have,' he said. 'As you might expect, the archdiocese is quite concerned. We're here to assist in any way we can.'

'We appreciate it,' Byrne said. He continued, giving the priest basic details and timelines regarding the murders of Daniel Palumbo and Cecilia Rollins.

Raphael listened, expressionless.

'While the buildings were vacant, it is likely that whoever is doing this is committing these crimes in a Catholic church for a reason,' Byrne said.

The unspoken part of what he was saying was that there might be a connection between the killer and the Church itself. Whenever a church closed, there were bound to be disgruntled parishioners, not to mention priests, nuns, lay workers.

At one time, in a small section of North Philly, there had been a Catholic church every few blocks, churches with primarily parishioners of the same ethnicity – Italian, Polish, German, Lithuanian, and 'general' parishes, as they were known. In Philadelphia the Irish parishes were called 'general' parishes because, at one time, if you were Catholic and spoke English, and you lived in Philadelphia, you were probably Irish.

Byrne picked up his notebook, flipped a few pages. 'Can you tell us, briefly, the process by which the archdiocese closes a church?'

Raphael thought for a moment. 'This is not something undertaken lightly, of course. It's a process that can take many months, sometimes years, often accompanied by a great deal of heated discussion and debate. A neighborhood parish is, for many people, the center of their community. It is where babies are baptized, the young are confirmed, marriages begun, lives honored at funerals.'

When Raphael said the word 'babies' Jessica's mind flashed on the image of little Cecilia frozen into the old washtub. She felt the rage rise within her. She battled it back.

'As I'm sure you're aware, there have been many church closings over the past fifteen to twenty years,' Raphael said. 'When enroll-ment in the parochial schools drops, the revenue begins to dwindle. The sad truth, at least for the city parishes, is that most Catholics have moved into the suburbs. The exodus really began after the Second World War, but accelerated in the seventies, eighties and nineties.'

Raphael turned his cup in its saucer, continued. 'When a parish shrinks it is usually stuck with a hundred-year-old building, which is a monster to keep up, and there simply aren't enough people to sustain it. So the building is closed or consolidated with another parish.'

'What happens to the churches themselves?' Byrne asked.

'Some are torn down. Some are sold to other denominations. Not often, but it happens. A classic example was St Stephen's on North Broad Street. It was sold to the Baptists, and they are having a hard time keeping it up.'

'So, you hold the final mass at a church, then what?'

'Well, the first thing we do is remove all the objects that are either sacred or valuable. The stained glass, the marble railings, the tabernacle. There are a few repositories for sacred items, the largest being in Corpus Christi, Texas.' Raphael smiled. 'We don't want to have things ending up as curios in karaoke bars.'

Jessica had once gone to a friend's wedding reception in upstate New York, held at a large meeting hall. At her table were candlesticks with IHS on them, a Christogram widely used to depict the first Greek letters of Jesus's name.

'Secondly – and this happens with a lot of the older churches – we have to deal with the fact that the founding pastors were buried beneath them. Of course, they have to be moved. Keep in mind that, once a parish is canonically founded, anywhere in the world, they must receive permission from Rome to close. It is mostly *pro forma*, but still required.'

'Is there a ceremony?' Byrne asked.

'A ceremony?'

'When a church closes. Is there some sort of ceremony? A taking back of the blessing?'

'You mean deconsecration?'

'Yes.'

'Nothing formal, at least that I know of. Although something like that is a bit outside my wheelhouse. A consecration is a blessing. The opposite would be a curse.'

Byrne said nothing.

'Every rite is to bring the Lord's blessing to something, detective,' Raphael added. 'Not take it away.'

Raphael rose, poured himself more coffee, looked out the window, toward the skyline. The question about deconsecration seemed to have rattled him.

'Can you get us a list of churches that have been closed?' Byrne asked.

Raphael turned back to them. The expression that crossed his face at that moment was one of sadness and concern. It was obvious why the Philadelphia Police Department wanted a detailed list. These churches – these *closed* churches – were seen as potential killing grounds.

'Of course,' Raphael said. 'I can have these collated and sent over by tomorrow morning.'

As they prepared to leave, Jessica looked around, at the majesty and grandeur of the office. She then studied Father Raphael for a few moments.

'May I ask how you came to this position at such a young age?' she asked.

Raphael smiled. Jessica found it disarming.

'I'm very fortunate to have a great memory for dates and figures, as well as an insatiable appetite for world history. I did my under-graduate studies in just over two years, and entered the seminary when I was twenty.'

'Where did you do your undergraduate work?'

'At Bethany College.'

'Bethany is in West Virginia?'

'Yes. I had a double major – communications and, of course, reli-gious studies.'

'Were you a deacon?'

Raphael smiled again. 'It was waived in my case.'

Michael Raphael's ascent was impressive. If ever there was an organization where traditions moved forward at a glacial pace, it was the Catholic Church. Most of the other men doing Michael Raphael's job were in their forties or fifties.

They made their goodbyes.

As Jessica and Byrne got into the car, both detectives absorbing what they had learned, neither having any idea how the information would help their investigations, Jessica looked up, saw Father Michael Raphael standing in the window, watching them. For a moment, the reflections of clouds made him appear diaphanous.

A consecration is a blessing, Jessica thought.

The opposite would be a curse.

TWENTY

J ESSICA PULLED UP IN FRONT BYRNE'S APARTMENT BUILDING. IT WAS only 6 p.m., but it was already dark.

'You hungry?' Byrne asked.

'I'm okay. Vince is cooking for the kids. I'll eat later.'

'Coffee?'

Jessica glanced at her watch. 'Sure,' she said. 'I don't think I'm going to get a lot of sleep tonight anyway.'

'Drop me by my car,' Byrne said. 'I have a few boxes I want to bring up.'

JESSICA TOOK THE STEPS to the second floor, walked down the hallway to the last apartment. Byrne's door was ajar. She pushed it open, entered, closed the door behind her.

Byrne was in the small kitchen, making coffee. The apartment looked exactly the same as it had the last time Jessica had been there, maybe five months earlier, right down to the same magazines in the same places.

'Love what you've done with the place,' she said.

'It's a process.'

Byrne walked into the living room with two mugs of coffee. He handed one to Jessica. She blew on it, sipped. It was good. 'What's all this?' she asked, gesturing at the small dining room, which had boxes stacked floor to ceiling.

'I moved all my crap out of storage,' Byrne said. 'I was paying two hundred a month to keep a bunch a junk I don't need anymore. I donated most of it. This is the stuff I couldn't part with. I've got five more boxes in my car.'

On top of one of the boxes on the dining-room table was a framed eight by ten photograph, a picture of a younger Kevin Byrne standing next to a heavyset black man. They were in front of Downey's on Front Street. Jessica picked it up.

'Did you know Marcus Haines?' Byrne asked.

Jessica had heard the name, but never met the man. She knew that his picture was on the wall in the lobby of the Roundhouse, the wall dedicated to fallen officers. 'No,' Jessica said. 'Never had the honor.'

Byrne took the picture from her. 'Marcus was a piece of work, Jess. A true character. Great cop, lousy at everything else. Married three times, three alimonies, always looking for an angle to make a buck. At the end of the month he was always in the hole.'

'He was in homicide?'

'Yeah. When my old partner Jimmy had his first heart attack, he was out for six months. I partnered with Marcus for a while. We worked a few cases, closed a few cases, knocked *back* a few cases of Jameson.'

'Why do I feel a story coming on?'

Byrne smiled, sipped his coffee. 'If you insist.' He leaned against the wall. 'So, one August night we get this call, a domestic gone bad. DOA was the boyfriend, and it looked like the girlfriend was good for it.

'We get there, and the job is laid out by the numbers. It's like there was a tag on everything. Body, killer, weapon. Everything but motive, but that wasn't a mystery. The woman is sitting on the couch, the boyfriend is on the floor, brains on the wall. The responding officers said the gun was on the floor at the woman's feet. Open and shut, right?'

'Sounds like it.'

'I take it all in, and I look a little more closely at the woman on the couch, and she is stunningly beautiful. Coffee-colored skin, amber eyes. Couldn't have been more than twenty-four, twenty-five. But all of that was beneath a layer of crack. It was clear she was on the pipe, and she looked all beat to shit.'

Byrne propped the photograph on the windowsill.

'Marcus walks in, and all of a sudden it's like he's seen a ghost. Mumbling, walking in circles, clicking his pen. He takes me into the kitchen, lowers his voice, says, 'Kevin. I know her, man. I *know* her.' He goes on to tell me that he's been seeing this girl, that he met her on a job a year earlier when the girl's mother was shot in West Philly, and he walked her through it all, held her hand at the trial, and one thing led to another. He asks me what I can do for her, seeing as how I caught the case.'

Jessica considered the options. There were only a few, none of them good. 'What *could* you do?'

'Yeah, well, I had no idea. I walked back into the room, looked at her on the couch, and immediately saw the next two decades of her life, how she would look after twenty years in Muncy.'

'What did you do?'

'I interviewed her. She said that her boyfriend would usually come home drunk, beat on her, night after night. Went on for almost a year. She showed me her left arm where he broke it. Never healed right. She said she told him a week earlier, in no uncertain terms, that if he ever did it again she was going to get a gun and kill him. She said he laughed at her, said when he came home that night, he started to push her around, and she just pulled a .38, drew down and popped him. Single shot, center mass. One dead asshole to go.'

'But she wasn't assaulted that night.'

'No,' Byrne said. 'There wasn't a mark on her. She could have walked away, but she didn't. And you know how a jury was going to see it.

'So I look out the window, and I see CSU and the ME's office show up. I tell Marcus to go down there and stall them. I also told him to call paramedics. When he leaves I go back over to where the girl is sitting, and I ask her to tell me what happened one more time. *Very* carefully.'

Jessica knew what Byrne meant. Sometimes the good people, the citizens, needed a little help remembering.

'Right at that moment she completely shuts down, so I told *her* how it went down. I told her that her boyfriend came home, roaring drunk. He started pushing her around. She told him to stop. He hit her in the face, and that's when she picked up the gun. Then *he* picked up a baseball bat, came at her again, and that's when she fired.'

'What did she say?'

'At first she didn't say anything. I think she was still a bit in shock. I told her that she had to decide if that's what really happened, because any second there were going to be a dozen people in her apartment and then there would be no going back.' Byrne picked up the photograph again. 'After what seemed like a full minute, she looked up at me and said, "Ain't got no bat."

'When I told her I would take care of that, she looked straight at me, and it all fell into place. She glanced at the body on the floor, then back at me. I knew what she meant. I crossed the room, crouched down. The dead man was wearing a ring on his right hand. I got down, pulled off the ring, put it on the same finger on my hand, walked back to where she stood. She nodded, then closed her eyes.'

Jessica knew what was coming next. It wasn't going to be pretty.

'I hit her, Jess. I meant to pull it, but I didn't. She went down. A few seconds later I slipped the boyfriend's ring back on his hand. I knew that CSU would be able to match the mark on her face with the ring, and that they would also find trace evidence of the girl's skin on it. I also knew that I could spin the two rookies who responded if it came to that. There had been no pictures taken at that point. I'd get a bat into evidence.'

Jessica had a thousand questions, but she just listened. Byrne had to play this out.

'By the time paramedics showed up, the girl had come around. As they were wheeling her out, she looked up, directly at me. The left side of her face was completely swollen. Our eyes met, and I couldn't tell if she remembered what we talked about. If she didn't remember, or she suddenly decided she still loved this dead fucker, she might bring charges against *me*. But when they wheeled her by me she reached out a finger, and ran it along the back of my hand. And I knew. I knew it was going to be all right. For her, anyway. I wasn't so sure about me.'

'What do you mean?'

Byrne looked up, out the window, at the traffic crawling up the street. A light snow had begun to fall. Byrne didn't respond. Jessica waited a while, moved on.

'What happened to Marcus?' Jessica knew Marcus Haines was on the wall at the Roundhouse, so this story was not going to have a happy ending.

'A month later Jimmy came back, and I didn't work with Marcus again. Not on the line anyway. Marcus went to the Fugitive Squad. I ran into him one night at Bonk's. He was hitting the Jameson hard. Told me the affair with the girl was over. Three weeks after that I got loaned out to Fugitive to serve a warrant on a couple of bad actors.

'Marcus took the door – my door. He didn't make it three feet before they opened up. He took the first two in the vest, but the third was a head shot. Clean hit. Died on his feet. Never got off a single shot.' Byrne took a deep breath, exhaled slowly. 'Those rounds were meant for me, Jess.'

Jessica gave the gravity of the moment a respectful pause. 'What about the young woman?'

'She gave her statement, the DA looked it over, never brought charges. Went down as a justifiable.'

Byrne ran his finger over the surface of the photograph.

'There's more, isn't there?' Jessica asked.

Byrne said nothing for a few seconds. 'What I did was wrong.'

'No, what you did was right. At that moment, it wasn't about procedure. It was about right and wrong. We all have to make those calls.'

'I know. But when I hit her, I *really* hit her. It all came out of me. I hit her hard because she was stupid, because she was on the pipe, because she hooked up with loser after loser, because she was beautiful, because I can't change a fucking thing about this city, no matter how hard I try.'

Jessica knew she had to say something. She couldn't just leave it like this. She tried to bring the conversation around to the present.

'We'll get this guy, Kevin. We'll get him off the streets, and it *will* make a difference.'

Byrne reached into his pocket, took out a single key. 'Here.'

Jessica took the key from him. 'What's this?'

'It's the key to this apartment. It occurred to me that the only other person with a key is Colleen, and she doesn't even live in this city anymore. I want you to have it.'

Jessica was more than a little moved by this. She hoped it didn't show. 'I promise not to drop it in any high-crime areas.'

'I appreciate it.'

Jessica slipped the new key onto her key chain, pulled on her coat, opened the door, turned. 'You sure you're okay?'

'Top of the world.'

'Right,' Jessica said. 'How come all Irish cops quote Jimmy Cagney?'

Byrne smiled, but it was sad.

'Call me if you need me,' Jessica said.

Byrne didn't respond. Jessica hadn't expected him to.

When she stepped through the doorway, she turned one last time. Byrne was still at the window, the old photograph in hand, looking out at the silent, snow-covered street.

TWENTY-ONE

THE OLD MAN STANDS AT THE BACK OF THE AUDITORIUM. IT IS A LARGE, rectangular room, decorated with bright streamers and multicolored bunting, with folding chairs aligned row by row, eighty in all. There is a small stage with risers at the front. The event is a chorale of first- and second-grade children singing songs that welcome spring, which is just a month or so away.

In the audience are scores of proud parents and grandparents, flip cameras in hand. Onstage thirty or so children are singing: 'If You're Happy and You Know It.'

She watches the man from the other side of the room – his eyes, his hands, the cant of his shoulders. He has the countenance of a kindly uncle, but she knows better. She knows what he is.

At the end of the song she walks across the room, sidles up next to him. He does not notice her.

'Hi,' she says.

The man turns to her, a bit startled. He quickly looks her up and down, tiny predator's eyes assessing threat. He finds none. He fashions a smile. 'Hello.'

She gestures toward the stage. 'They are so precious when they are this age, aren't they?'

The old man smiles again. 'That they are.' He looks more closely at her, this time with a flicker of remembrance. 'Have we met before?'

They always ask. She shakes her head. 'Where you've been I cannot go.'

The man looks at her quizzically. Before he can respond, she continues. 'Is one of them your grandchild?'

The hesitation says so much. It says the truth.

'No. I just come here to watch them. It makes me feel young again.'

'You do more than watch though, don't you?'

The man slowly closes his eyes. A moment later, when he opens them, he looks at her, and knows.

They are silent for a long time, the joyous singing of the children a backdrop to their transaction, one this man has awaited with dread for years.

'I knew this day would come,' the man says. 'He is real after all.'

'Oh, he is real,' she echoes. 'Did you doubt him?'

'One lives in hope. Ever since I was a child, not much older than these children, I have believed in him, have known he walks with me.'

She points out the window, to the old church across the street. 'He is waiting for you.'

'In the church?'

'Yes. And now is the time.'

The man glances back at the stage, knowing that this will be the last time. 'I'm not ready.'

'There will be no more negotiations.'

He turns to face her fully. 'Is this the only way?'

The pedophile knows the answer to this. There is no need to respond. She does not.

A few minutes later they leave the auditorium. They cross the street, walk down the alley next to the church. The door is already open for them. They enter, descend the stairs into the basement.

'I feel him,' the man says.

She gestures to a small room, directly beneath the sacristy. 'Remove your clothing.'

The man looks up, his eyes no longer those of the predator, but rather that of cornered prey. 'This is something I must do?'

'Is it not how you came into the world?'

Slowly, piece by piece, he removes his clothes. He folds them neatly, lays them on the floor, next to the pile of white stones.

She gestures for the man to sit. Naked, he eases himself to the frigid stone floor. He makes the sign of the cross. Soon, a single tear runs down his cheek. 'I grew up in a very religious house,' he says. 'If we didn't say our prayers we would be beaten.'

She says nothing. This is all known to her. They all have a devout background. It is why they know, in the end, there is only one penance.

'May I make an Act of Contrition?' he asks.

'Yes.'

The old man clasps his hands. 'O my God, I am heartily sorry . . .'

She waits for him to finish. When he does she asks the question. 'Do you remember what you said?'

'Yes.'

'I want you to tell me. Word for word.'

The man closes his eyes for a moment, perhaps remembering, perhaps taking a moment for a second silent Act of Contrition. 'I said, "If you keep me out of prison, I will do anything. I will even make a pact with the devil."'

'The devil.'

'Yes.'

'When you made this deal, did you think it would never come due?'

The man remains silent. For him, and all his sins of the flesh, the story is told.

A moment later, without another word, he opens his mouth and swallows the first stone.

TWENTY-TWO

B YRNE WAS HUNGRY, BUT HE DID NOT FEEL LIKE EATING. HE WANTED a drink, but he did not feel like drinking. When he felt this way, he always drove down to the river. This time he parked in the lot of an old warehouse in Port Richmond.

What was the connection between Danny Palumbo and Cecilia Rollins? Byrne thought. *Was Danny the baby's father?* Byrne and Jessica had discussed this and dismissed it. Danny Palumbo could not have killed the little girl. When the baby was placed in that tub in the basement of St Damian's, Danny Palumbo was strapped to that chair.

Or was he? They didn't have a precise time of death on the baby. They might never have this data.

Byrne had called Loretta Palumbo, and she said she'd never heard Danny mention a girl named Adria.

The two victims were from different parts of the city, different worlds. Were they both selected at random?

No. These killings were not random.

Byrne looked down the street. Sometimes it seemed like the blight didn't end. He had seen good neighborhoods go bad, burn to the ground, then rebuild, only to go bad again. Block after block; mile after mile. And, if that were the case, what was he doing with his life if he knew it would never end?

They were all gone, all the old school cops. Jimmy Purify, Byrne's rabbi when he first came to the unit, was in the ground more than five years now. The retirements of Nick Palladino, Ike Buchanan, Rocky Wade and Sal Aspite over in Major Crimes. And then there was Marcus Haines.

The future belonged to detectives like Jessica, Josh Bontrager, and Maria Caruso.

Maria reminded Byrne a lot of Jessica when Jessica first came up. He remembered the day he walked into the duty room and saw Jessica standing there for the first time, the South Philly in her stance, her attitude. At the time she seemed too young to be doing the job, but Byrne realized then, as he did now, that this was just arrogance on his part. He wasn't all that much older than Jessica or Maria Caruso when he had come up. The two of them, as it turned out, knew a lot more about the job than he did.

Homicide work was about instinct, the ability to divine motive in a desert of evidence, a wasteland of bullshit. Jessica was as good as, or better than, anyone he had ever met at this. The good cops could walk into a room full of citizens and pick out the one bad actor every time.

An unnerving thought suddenly occurred to him. *Was he the oldest detective still on the Line Squad?* He probably was. There were a couple of guys on the Fugitive Squad and in SIU that had a few years on him, but as far as the Line Squad went – the unit that handled the new homicide cases as they came in – Detective Kevin Francis Byrne was The Sphinx.

Great.

He opened the glove compartment, was happy to find a pint of Old Forester in there. He opened it, took a long pull.

Two churches. Two *closed* churches.

Byrne shut his eyes, lay his head back on the head rest. It was impossible to shake the image of that child in the wash tub. He thought about the strength, the *commitment*, it must have taken to do something like that. Every human instinct must fight the urge to carry out such an act.

Byrne took out his phone, dialed. The woman answered, and Byrne asked for Gabriel. A few seconds later the boy came on the line.

'Hey, Gabriel. How's it going?'

Pause. 'I'm okay.'

He wasn't. 'Something wrong?' No answer. 'Listen, the reason I'm calling is that I might be able to wrangle a pair of courtside tickets. Sixers and Lakers. This guy I know owes me big time. What do you say?'

Silence. Something *was* wrong. Byrne glanced at the screen on the phone. Yes, they were still connected.

'Gabriel?'

'I . . . I don't know.'

'Okay, man, now I *know* something is up. Why don't you tell me? Maybe I can help.'

'Maybe we shouldn't hang out no more.'

The words stung. 'What do you mean? Why not?'

'I don't know.'

'I thought we had fun. Didn't we have fun?'

'Yeah,' Gabriel said. 'It's just . . .'

Byrne waited for the next words. There were divides between them – race, class, heritage – that might not ever be bridged. Byrne had known this going in. It had not stopped him.

'It's just what?' he asked.

'It's just not . . . a good idea.'

And suddenly Byrne knew. 'Gabriel, I'm going to ask you something, and I want you to tell me the truth. Okay?'

Silence.

'Gabriel?'

'Okay.'

Byrne had to get the words right, or he would lose the boy forever. And that could not happen.

'Has someone told you not to see me?' Byrne asked. 'And I don't mean someone from social services, or someone from Philly Brothers, I mean someone from the neighborhood.'

Gabriel didn't answer.

'Listen to me. If someone told you that you should not hang out with me, if someone threatened you, you have to tell me. We'll deal with it.'

Byrne flashed on the first time he had dropped Gabriel off, on the thugs on the corner. He also flashed on the second time, when he braced the punk standing behind his car. He thought of Gabriel's brother Terrell, and the notes on the activity sheet about Terrell's suicide. The *name* on the activity sheet. DeRon Wilson. It all fell into place.

'Someone told you to stay away from me, right?' Byrne asked.

After a long, silent eternity, Gabriel said, softly, 'Yeah.'

Byrne gripped the steering wheel. He felt as if he could rip it from the column. 'Were you threatened?'

'No. I don't know. Not really.'

'Okay, okay,' Byrne said. 'Here's what we'll do. I don't want you to say his name. *I'll* say his name, and you just tell me if I'm right. Okay?'

Nothing.

'Gabriel, is it this guy DeRon Wilson? Is it DeRon Wilson who told you to stay away from me?'

No response.

Byrne had his answer.

TWENTY-THREE

B YRNE PARKED ON THE CORNER OF THIRD AND WESTMORELAND. According to information he had gotten from a friend of his named Joe Miciak, a detective in North, Wilson maintained three apartments. Word was, on this night, that he could be found at this one.

Byrne looked at the sheet on the seat next to him. He had breezed into the office, run DeRon Wilson's name. Besides being a person of interest in Terrell Hightower's shooting, he had two counts of possession with intent, five counts of misdemeanor assault, lewd vagrancy, shoplifting, possession and passing of counterfeit currency. And that was just the first page.

Byrne entered the building, took the back steps. The walls were covered in tags, the stair platforms were stacked knee-high in plastic bags and loose debris. The smell was all but toxic.

He pushed open the door to the second floor. Byrne noted that more than half the doors had jimmy marks along the jambs, splintered wood that indicated a break-in. Some of the apartments had padlocks on the outside. Sounds filled the hallway – hip hop, game shows, radio ads, arguments, barking dogs.

DeRon Wilson's was the last apartment on the right. Byrne opened the window at the end of the hall, checked to see if there was a fire escape. There was, so he left the window open. If Wilson decided to jump out, at least Byrne wouldn't have to break the window to chase him.

Byrne stepped up to the door, knocked. He heard the volume of the television lower, footsteps padding to the door. He saw the peep-hole go from light to dark, then light. Nothing. He knocked again.

'Philly PD,' he said.

Byrne was just about to knock a third time when he heard the bolts turn. A girl opened the door. She was light-skinned, pretty, no more than seventeen. She wore a short silk kimono.

Byrne showed his ID. 'I'm looking for DeRon Wilson.'

'Don't know him.'

She went to close the door, but Byrne got a foot inside the jamb. 'Miss, it's very important that I speak to him.'

'I *said*, I don't *know* him.'

Again she tried to slam the door, but this time Byrne got a shoulder into it. He heard doors open in the hallway behind him. He glanced inside the apartment. The walls were covered in a vinyl, wood-grain wallpaper. A 60-inch plasma TV against the far wall showed an old music video. The floor was littered with brightly colored toddler toys.

Before the girl said another word a man came out of one of the bedrooms.

'It's cool, baby,' the man said.

DeRon Wilson stepped into the living room. Even though Byrne had the man's stats, DeRon was a lot smaller than Byrne had antici-pated – chiseled hard, late-twenties, standing about 5'4''. He couldn't have weighed more than 125. A real bantam, in all respects. In his most recent mug shot he had short dreads, but now his head was shaved. He was covered in tats. He wore a white wife-beater T, jumbo shorts, slung low. Byrne looked at his hands, the pull on his belt. If he had a gun, it was not tucked into his shorts.

'PPD always welcome here,' Wilson added. Heavy-eyed, he prof-fered a smile.

'Are you DeRon Wilson?'

Wilson stepped fully into the doorway. The girl disappeared into the bedroom. Byrne backed up, giving the man space. All part of the power play.

'What can I do for Philly's finest?' Wilson asked.

'You can start by answering my question,' Byrne said. 'Are you DeRon Wilson?'

'Everybody knows me.'

'I'm going to take that as a yes,' Byrne said. 'Do you know a boy named Gabriel Hightower?'

Wilson smiled. Three golds in the grill. 'I know lots of boys.'

More doors opened. Byrne turned to see a half-dozen people in the hallway. They all had cell phones in hand.

'Do you know him?' Byrne repeated.

'I might. But why I gotta tell you?'

'Mr Wilson, could we step inside? This will only take a few moments of your time.'

Wilson did not back up, did not invite Byrne inside. Instead, he moved further into the hallway, making Byrne retreat a few more steps.

Wilson put a finger into Byrne's chest. 'I think you need to get out my *face*.'

Byrne looked down at Wilson's finger, swept the hem of his coat back and unsnapped his holster. 'You need to take a step back.'

'I don't need to do a *damn* thing.'

'Lower your voice and calm down,' Byrne said.

'I'm calm, motherfucker. I'm JB fuckin' Smoove. What *you* need to do is to get the *fuck* out my house.'

At this Wilson put his hand into the pocket of his shorts. Byrne couldn't take the chance. Before Wilson could pull out his hand Byrne exploded across the hallway and threw one of his massive shoulders into Wilson's chest, all but putting the man through the wall. The drywall split, raining gypsum dust onto the floor. It was as loud as a shotgun blast.

From his not-too-intimidating perch on the floor, Wilson shook it off, yelled, 'I'm gonna *own* you for this, motherfucker.'

Byrne grabbed Wilson by the front of the shirt and yanked him to his feet.

'You're gonna *own* me?' Byrne drew his Glock, put it to the center of Wilson's forehead. 'I might as well buy the whole loaf then, right? How many do you want? Let's negotiate. Give me a fucking number.'

DeRon Wilson closed his eyes, waited for the pain.

'This is how it's going to be,' Byrne said. 'You come near that kid again, you even look his way, and I will make it my *personal* fucking mission in life to make sure you never sleep again. You feel me?'

Wilson remained silent. Byrne pushed the weapon harder into the man's forehead.

'Answer me or I will drop you where you stand.'

Wilson opened his eyes and said, 'Yes.'

Byrne took a few moments, backed off. DeRon Wilson sagged to the floor.

Byrne held his weapon at his side and slowly walked down the hallway, accompanied by shouts of 'police brutality' and the like.

A few minutes later, as Byrne walked out the front door of the apartment building, he turned to look at the second floor. Every window was filled with a tenant, leaning out, each with a camera cell phone in hand.

| TWENTY-FOUR |

SHANE HAD FOLLOWED KEVIN BYRNE AT A DISCREET DISTANCE, watched as he left his apartment in South Philly, then to the Roundhouse, then down to the river in Port Richmond. He watched him sit in the parking lot for what seemed like an hour.

Shane had felt himself drifting off, until he heard the screech of tires, and looked up to see Byrne's car fishtailing out of the lot. He headed up Allegheny.

As he tailed the detective, Shane checked his rearview mirror and side mirrors every few seconds. He saw no one else from another TV station, at least anyone in a car with the station logo on the side. Shane had learned long ago that, if you were going to work in a television market – especially a top ten market – the first thing to find out was what kind of cars the police department used, then get that same make and color. More than once he had been able to park among a group of departmental vehicles unnoticed. If you didn't check the plates, you would think they all belonged to the police. He had gotten inside the tape on many occasions this way.

When Byrne took a right on D Street, Shane got caught at a light, and lost him.

He banged a fist on the steering wheel, pulled over a block away from where he had last seen Byrne's car, turned up the volume on the scanner. Something was happening. Something was definitely happening. Byrne had taken off like a bat out of hell.

Shane thought about calling the TV station, getting a shooter, but he didn't need Cyn or anyone on this. He had his own rig in the trunk, and there was no better one-man-bander in Philly.

He found himself right in front of a coin laundry, so he rolled back about thirty feet, taking himself out of the electric glow of the fluorescent lights. He berated himself for staying too far away, for not being better at shadowing a subject.

Did this have something to do with the ritual killing of the baby?

Shane had to laugh. He was already categorizing what happened to the baby and the other victim as a ritual killing.

He listened to his scanner. Nothing that sounded relevant. The police band in Philadelphia was rarely silent for long. Shane was just about to go into the trunk when he saw a shadow coming up on him. Fast. He spun around.

The kid was on top of him before he knew it. Black kid, thirteen or so, dark hoodie. He had a small face, tiny, fold-down ears. He rode a mountain bike that looked new.

Shane did a quick inventory of his possessions. He always kept a hundred-dollar bill in his wallet. He liked to think it was for emergencies – which it was – but he wanted to think the urgent situation would come in the form of a midnight tryst with a beautiful woman, and he needed it to pay cash for a bottle of champagne.

'Hey,' Shane said. 'What's up?'

The kid looked away, around, back. 'You that guy on TV?'

Shane felt a cold wave of relief. 'Yeah. Shane Adams.'

The kid nodded. 'Yeah, yeah,' he said. He chucked a thumb at the apartment complex. 'I saw what happened.'

'What do you mean?'

'I was there.'

Shane had to play along, like he knew all the details. 'You saw that, huh?'

'Yeah.'

He wasn't being mugged after all. 'You saw all of it?'

The kid nodded again. 'Saw po-po beating on DeRon.'

Shane had to take a shot here. 'You mean DeRon Jefferson?'

The kid rolled his eyes. 'DeRon *Wilson*.'

'Oh, yeah. Right, right.'

'I got it all. *All* of it.'

Shane's pulse began to spike. *Got* all of it. Was he hearing what he *thought* he was hearing? 'So, are you saying you have video of what happened?'

'Yeah,' he said. 'I got it.'

'Can I see it?'

The kid recoiled. 'I'll sell it to you.'

'Well, I have to see it first. If it's something I think I might be able to use, we'll talk.'

The kid sized him up again. After a few long seconds he reached into his baggy jeans, fished out a cell phone. He opened it, scrolled down. Before starting the video he looked up. 'How much could I get?'

'That all depends on the footage.'

The kid made a face. He had no idea what *footage* was. Cell phone video wasn't measured in feet.

'The video,' Shane said. 'It all depends on what you have on the video.'

Another face. 'I *said*, I got it *all*, man.'

Shane glanced at the kid's phone. It wasn't an iPhone 4, or any of the higher end Android smart phones, so the footage wasn't going to be that good, quality-wise. No 720p here. Still, in the past few years, stations had broadcast absolutely terrible quality video, if the subject matter was compelling. Many times when it was not. If it came down to broadcasting sub-VHS quality video or getting scooped, there was no argument at all. Visuals were everything.

The kid moved slowly. Shane wanted to say something, but he realized he was in the kid's world, not his own. He couldn't visualize Anderson Cooper in some back alley in Tikrit rushing some Iraqi kid with cell-phone footage. He waited.

Finally the kid held up the phone and pressed the button.

At first the video was just a blurry image, moving along dirty carpeting. Then there was shouting. The words were unintelligible, but that could be cleaned up. Shane instinctively glanced at his watch. Plenty of time. He looked back at the camera phone, and now saw the image of a long, sparsely lit hallway. A few of the doors were open. People stepped out of them. The camera moved down the hall, shaky as hell, but that just added to the immediacy.

Then he saw Kevin Byrne brace a man against the drywall so hard that the drywall cracked. Shane found he was holding his breath.

'That's DeRon, right?'

'Um-hmm,' the kid replied.

Shane then saw Byrne pull out a gun and put it to the man's forehead. Shane did his very best not to make a sound. At that instant he thought about his acting classes, and what this moment called for. It called for an action, and that action was indifference. Hardest thing he had ever done.

When the video cut to black Shane took a deep, yoga breath, said, 'I don't know man. The lighting's pretty bad.'

Shane didn't expect the kid to discuss lumens, but he did expect a response. The kid didn't say anything.

'Ain't exactly hi-def, you know what I mean?' Shane added.

Cold silence from the kid.

'Tell you what. I'll give you twenty for it.'

The kid snorted. It seemed Shane's offer was beneath contempt. Which, of course, it was. Shane, on the other hand, expected a counter offer. The kid turned to leave.

'Hang on.'

The kid stopped, but still kept his bike headed in the other direction.

'I could maybe go fifty,' Shane said, and immediately realized that he had only the hundred-dollar bill in his wallet, and maybe six singles in his pocket. Did he expect the kid to have change? He looked down the street, saw an all-night deli. Maybe he could crack the C-note there. 'But that's coming out of my pocket. My station doesn't pay for this shit. *Ever.*'

The kid just shook his head.

Fucking thief.

'Okay,' Shane said. 'A hundred is the best I can do. Anything more than that, and I have to do paperwork. Take it or leave it. The video ain't all that, believe me.'

The kid stared at him for an uncomfortable amount of time. Maybe this was a mugging after all. Maybe the kid just showed him the footage to keep him around until his friends showed up. The kid then looked over at Shane's car.

'That your whip?' he asked.

Shane was glad that his bag – including the Panasonic camera, digital still camera, and lenses – was in the trunk, and not visible through the passenger side window. 'Yeah.'

The kid smirked. Shane soon realized why the kid had asked. The car was a piece of shit. If he had been driving a BMW or a Lexus, the kid would have either held out for more, or walked. Or worse.

Shane had him. Saved by a shitty car.

'Let me see the money.'

Shane fished out his wallet, peeled out the long creased C-note. He unfolded it, but didn't hand it over. 'How do I get the footage? Can you email it to me right now?'

The kid handed him the cell phone.

Shane was dumbfounded. 'What, are you just *giving* this to me?'

The kid dug into his pocket, pulled out four or five other phones in a rainbow of colors.

Shane shook his head, handed him the bill. The kid held it up to the light streaming from the coin laundry's windows. Then, apparently having confirmed that the bill was genuine US currency, turned his bike around, started pedaling, and disappeared into the darkness.

Shane stood there for a moment, a bit paralyzed by what had just happened. He soon snapped out of it, glanced at his watch. He had time to get this to the station, edit the video, and get it on at eleven. He sprinted to the driver's side, unlocked the car, got in, and sped off.

Fifteen minutes later, when he made the turn onto Broad Street, his heart still racing, he pulled to the curb. He picked up the kid's phone, and soon made sense of the menu. He navigated to the footage. In the confines of the car, the phone's tinny speaker was too loud. He dialed it back.

He watched the footage. It was beautiful. No, it was beyond

beautiful. He saw no other reporter or shooter in the hallway, or even in the neighborhood for that matter.

What did he have in his hand?

He had a white Philadelphia police detective threatening an unarmed black man with a gun. Not just threatening. He had the gun up to the man's *forehead*.

Not quite the Rodney King footage, but damned close. And he got it for a hundred bucks.

Shane pulled back into the traffic, already thinking of how soon he would be sending his reel to CNN.

TWENTY-FIVE

BYRNE SAT AT THE BAR IN THE QUIET MAN PUB ON THE LOWER LEVEL of Finnigan's Wake complex, named for the famous John Ford film starring John Wayne and Maureen O'Hara.

He wanted to be all right with what he had done, but wasn't. He had lost his cool. Pure and simple. The fact that he had a relatively short fuse was no secret, but the point of it all was to never let it control your behavior. He had felt the rage building all day. When he heard the fear in Gabriel's voice it had all come out.

Good work, Kevin.

When Margaret, one of the best bartenders in the city of Philadelphia, saw Byrne sit down, she knew it was a Bushmills night. There was a glass in front of him before he'd gotten his coat off.

Halfway through his first drink, he allowed himself to think about what had really happened in that dilapidated hallway, the real message he'd received when he laid hands on DeRon Wilson, the feeling of –

– cold stone walls, the expression of The Boy in the Red Coat as he looks up in silence –

– the coming confrontation.

Byrne drained his glass. Before he could call for the next drink a shadow spilled across the bar next to him. There were four open stools to his right, so it was not someone looking for a spot.

'Crazy days, huh?' a female voice said.

Byrne turned to look. The woman was in her early-thirties, dark-haired, pretty. She wore a black turtleneck sweater, tight jeans. Around her neck was a delicate silver chain. Byrne had the feeling they had met before. He couldn't place her.

'Well, we live in interesting times,' he said. It sounded like the right response. He *hoped* it was, considering how pretty this woman was.

She smiled, and Byrne realized she was a little older than he had originally thought. He placed her in her mid to late-thirties.

'We didn't get to meet properly the other day,' she said. 'I'm Faith.'

The other day? How could he not remember this woman?

And it hit him. She was F. CHRISTIAN. She was the female paramedic who had come to the scene at St Adelaide's. On that day she'd had her hair in a ponytail, had no makeup on, and wore glasses. Not to mention a bulky parka. He had hardly noticed her that day, but that was not unusual, considering the circumstances.

'Kevin Byrne.'

'I know,' she said. They shook hands. 'Mind if I join you?'

'Not at all.' Byrne moved his coat to the stool on his left. Faith slipped onto the stool, and Byrne caught her full profile. She was beyond attractive. She had a ring on her right-hand ring finger in the shape of a cross.

'Wait a minute,' Byrne said. 'Your name is Faith Christian?'

She smiled, rolled her eyes at what had to be the ten-thousandth time she'd heard this. 'Don't ask.'

'See, now I have to know,' he said.

'We just met. We'll probably get to it.'

'You think?'

'We'll see.'

'In that case, what are you drinking?' Byrne asked.

She smiled again, gave it a moment's thought. 'I think I'll have an Old Fashioned tonight.'

Margaret, standing a few feet away, topping a Guinness, nodded her head. She'd heard. Margaret heard everything.

'You know, I've never met a woman who ordered an Old Fashioned before,' Byrne said. 'It's so Joan Crawford.'

Faith smiled. 'You know, it's odd. I don't really have a drink.'

'Then you're not from Philadelphia, I take it.'

'No. Not originally.'

'See, it's a city ordinance here.'

'Well, I've been working on one since college, but I'm pretty fickle that way. I started watching that show *Mad Men*, and the main character drinks them. I thought I'd give it a try.'

'Classy drink.'

'Yeah, well, I need all the help I can get.'

Hardly, Byrne thought. He glanced over Faith's shoulder, at the door that led to the stairway and the first floor. A few minutes before Faith showed up Byrne thought he had seen someone standing there, and now he could see he wasn't mistaken. Whoever it was stood in shadow. Byrne always felt safe at Finnigan's Wake, but he had long ago acquired the habit of never sitting with his back to the door. Any door.

'So, how long have you worked as a paramedic?' Byrne asked.

'About eight years,' she said. Margaret delivered the Old Fashioned. Faith sipped, nodded her approval. 'I can't believe it's been that long, but here I am.'

'Is it something you always wanted to do?'

She ran the swizzle stick around the glass. 'Not really. I thought about nursing school – I still think about nursing school. But you know how it is. Life intervenes, mortgages happen, car payments are due, your dreams run out of gas.'

Byrne flicked another glance to the doorway. The shadow was still there. Unmistakably a man, on the tall side. Byrne had the feeling they were being watched, and he was *rarely* wrong about that feeling.

'What about you?' Faith asked. 'Did you always want to be a cop?'

'Yeah. I don't remember ever wanting to be anything else.'

'Not even a fireman?'

'Please. E*specially* a fireman.'

The friendly rivalry – and sometimes not so friendly rivalry – between police and firefighters was alive and well in Philly.

'I know a lot of guys at the 10th Battalion,' Faith said. 'I'm telling them you said that.'

'Bring it on.'

Faith smiled, took another sip. They spent the next twenty minutes talking about the city, their jobs, their favorites. Another round of drinks came and went. They finally got around to the important things.

'So, do you have any kids?' Faith asked.

Byrne nodded. 'One daughter. Colleen. She's away at college. Somehow.'

'What do you mean?'

'I mean about two months ago I was putting together a Big Wheel for her third birthday.'

Byrne went on to tell Faith about Colleen, about what her deafness meant to her, how she had never treated it as a disability, and how that had always been an inspiration to him.

'What about you?' he asked. 'Do you have any kids?'

Faith seemed to hesitate before answering, but maybe it was Byrne's imagination. Or maybe it was the Bushmills. 'I do,' she said. 'I have a son.'

Byrne looked at her for a few moments. When she didn't add anything he got the feeling it was making her uncomfortable. He decided to make light of it.

'So, is your son having trouble in kindergarten or something?'

Faith laughed, wagged a finger at him. 'You are good.'

'It's a gift.'

'He's a *lot* older than that, my friend.' With this she playfully slugged Byrne on the shoulder. It stung. Faith was stronger than she looked, but then again she had to be. She had to lift dead weight every day. 'I *wish* he was still in kindergarten.'

They sipped from their glasses. Byrne glanced back at the door. The shadow was still there. He took out his phone.

'Excuse me one second,' he said.

'Sure.'

He sent a text to the bar manager, Mickey. Mickey would send two of the mountainous guys that worked the doors at Finnigan's Wake to see what was what with the mysterious figure in the shadows of the lower-level landing.

A minute later Mickey texted him back to tell him that by the time the boys got down there, whoever had been lurking was gone.

Paranoia, Kevin.

'Everything okay? Faith asked.

Byrne put his phone away. 'Never better.'

'You are such a good liar. I like that in a man.'

Byrne smiled, drained his Bushmills. 'You know, you keep talking like that, you're never going to get me into bed.'

Faith smiled, put a hand on his leg. 'Yes, I will.'

'Oh, yeah? What makes you so sure?'

She leaned in, kissed him gently on the lips. 'I've had much tougher cases.'

'Have you now?'

Their eyes met, and it all came down to that second. You are connecting, or you're not.

They did.

Byrne stood, dropped a pair of twenties on the bar. Margaret, at the other end, knocked the bar twice, smiled.

As Byrne and Faith walked down Green Street, toward their cars, Byrne couldn't shake the feeling they were being observed. He was sure of it, but he had no idea why.

'I like your place,' she said.

'I'm glad you're not wearing your glasses.'

She looked beautiful in the soft candlelight. The first time they'd made love it had been manic – clothes everywhere, barely making it to the bed. The second time was slower, sweeter, as if they'd known each other for years.

Byrne pointed at the candle. 'You always bring your own candles with you?'

She had reached into her bag when they arrived, taken out a large, scented pillar candle, put it on the nightstand, lighted it.

'I'm getting into aromatherapy. This is clary sage and nectarine. Do you like it?'

'I do.'

She turned in his bed, pulled the sheet around her, rested her head on his chest. Byrne tried to remember the last time he'd been in this position. It had been a while.

'You know, our jobs are not all that different in a lot of ways,' she said. 'What I mean is, we see a lot. Does it ever get to you?'

'I'm not sure what you mean.'

'I mean, do you ever want to just walk away from it. Say enough is enough?'

Byrne didn't know any detective with twenty-five years in who didn't think about retiring, sometimes on a daily basis. 'I've been doing this job a long time,' he said. 'Longer than most. At least in homicide. I've learned to move on.'

'Always?'

There was no point in lying, in trying to be the macho cop. 'Not always. In all this time there have been a few cases that have stuck with me. So, yeah. Sometimes it gets to me.'

'Open cases?'

'Open cases,' Byrne said. 'Every so often I pull out the activity sheets, make a few notes. I read over the evidence, check the witness statements, hoping that I'll see something that I never saw before.' Byrne wanted to tell her more, much more, about how he sometimes picked up a piece of evidence and got a feeling about the killer. But they'd just met. He didn't need to scare her off.

'Do you think it's real?' she asked.

'Do I think what is real?'

'Evil.'

'That's a tough one. If you're asking whether or not I think a person can be born bad, the answer is yes. I didn't always, but I do now.'

They fell silent. Byrne drifted in and out of sleep. He'd gotten about four hours a night for the past week. Add the Bushmills, and it was no wonder he was fatigued. He felt himself floating, floating. He opened his eyes, looked at the clock. It wasn't yet eleven. Somehow he thought it was morning. He felt the bed next to him, but Faith wasn't there.

He looked up and saw her standing at the foot of his bed. She wore a red coat. Next to her stood a tall young man in a pointed hood. Byrne knew it was the same man who had been watching them in Finnigan's Wake, the same man they had seen in the surveillance video across from St Adelaide's. Byrne tried to get out of bed, but his hands and feet were tied to the bed posts.

'You were right, detective,' she said.

'Right?'

'Evil is flesh.'

Byrne woke in a sweat. He turned, sat up, his heart pounding in his chest. Faith was gone. On the pillow was a note. He flipped on the light, read it. In the note she said she was on midnight to eight. She left her phone number.

BYRNE SLIPPED ON A pair of jeans, walked to the kitchen, shaking off the nightmare, still in the grip of broken sleep. He flipped on the TV, poured himself a short one. Then poured the rest of a tall one. He checked the TV screen.

It was a recap of the day's news. He found the lead story very interesting. The caption pretty much said it all.

VIDEO OF PHILLY COP GOES VIRAL

It was a grainy hand-held video, the kind you saw showing up more and more often these days, a video of him bracing DeRon Wilson.

'This is Shane Adams reporting.'

Byrne turned off the TV, walked over to the fridge, opened it. The feeling of dread that had been building inside him since the moment he had walked into St Adelaide's was growing by the minute. He opened a beer, swallowed most of it.

He looked out the window, at the glow of Center City and beyond. He then sat at his small dinette table, turned on his phone. He looked at the screen. There were thirty-nine messages. He turned it off, walked back to the bedroom, smoothed the sheets and blanket, wondering if he'd get back to sleep this night. He doubted it. The room still smelled of sex, of Faith Christian, of sage and nectarine. He sat on the edge of the bed, picked up the candle, blew it out.

I will come to thee quickly, and will remove thy candlestick.

The words were almost shouted in his head.

THERE WERE NO SECTOR cars deployed at St Damian's any longer; the yellow tape had been removed. It was no longer an active crime scene. The window pane that had been broken to gain entry had been covered over by plywood.

Byrne had anticipated this. He brought with him a large iron crow bar. The plywood square came off with ease, and within seconds he was inside.

Like St Adelaide's, the interior was covered in black fingerprint dust which, at this hour, served to make the space even darker, seemed to absorb the beam of Byrne's flashlight.

I will come to thee quickly, and will remove thy candlestick.

He moved to a section to the right of where the altar once stood. It was an area devoted to the lighting of memorial votive candles. Although the three-tiered table was still there, the glass candleholders were boxed up beneath. Byrne pulled the boxes out. Most of the candle-holders were broken. Byrne could see that a number of the glasses were imprinted with a cross. Some of the larger shards of glass had been dusted for prints, but not bagged.

Byrne snapped on a glove, aligned the glass holders on the old oaken table. They were identical. Some still had paraffin clinging to the sides. Even with the flashlight and naked eye, Byrne could see dozens of fingerprints. A glass surface – a glass surface coated with wax residue – was just about the perfect surface to leave a textbook exemplar of a fingerprint.

Byrne looked at the three dozen glasses, examined them, then saw something he had not noticed before. One of the glasses was a deep amber color, not red. He picked up the amber glass. The cross on the front was slightly different as well.

He turned it over. There, on the bottom, was a small metal plate that read:

PROPERTY OF ST REGINA

It sounded as if he had awakened her. Entirely likely, seeing as it was 1.30 in the morning.

'Jess. Have you ever heard of St Regina's?'

'St Regina's?'

'Yeah. The church.'

Byrne heard a liquid rustling of sheets, the flick of a lamp. 'I hope you don't think I have every church in Philly memorized,' Jessica said. 'Hang on.'

It seemed like minutes before she picked up the phone again.

'I found it,' she said. 'It's in Rhawnhurst.'

'Get it onto radio,' Byrne said. 'I want everybody and his mother down there now.'

Byrne didn't wait for a reply.

TWENTY-SIX

ST Regina's was a small neighborhood church in the Rhawnhurst section of the city, a mostly residential area in the northeast. The area was bordered by Pennypack Creek to the north, and Roosevelt Boulevard to the east.

The church, a freestanding structure set back from the street, had a central tower with a domed cupola, topped by a gilded cross. The chain that ran between two posts, blocking entrance to the parking lot at the church's north side, had been cut to allow the investigators in. On the way up to the scene Jessica learned St Regina's had only been closed for two years.

In front of the church was a rusted lamppost. It was marked with an X.

Even though the hour was late, there was a small crowd of people gathering across the street. News stories of the murders happening in churches were breaking wider and wider, and now that there were three sector cars and four PPD departmental sedans in and around this small neighborhood church, the word had spread.

There was also a team from one of the TV stations.

When Jessica arrived, coffee in hand, she saw Byrne talking to Maria Caruso across the street from the church. Maria looked pale and drawn.

This was understandable, seeing as it was the middle of the night. Maria Caruso would be lead detective on this case.

'Hey,' Jessica said.

'Sorry to get you up and out,' Byrne said. 'I figured you wanted to be called.'

'No problem,' Jessica said, only half-meaning it. She gestured to the activity around them. 'I take it we have another victim.'

'Yes,' Maria said. 'Unfortunately we do.'

'In the basement?'

Maria nodded. 'Male white, sixties, DOA.'

'ME notified?'

'On the way.'

Jessica looked at the front of the church. It was another old neighborhood parish, a church with the capacity for maybe 200 people. 'How did they gain entry?'

'There's a back door to the priest's house. Broken window.'

'Any blood?'

Maria shook her head. 'None visible.'

Jessica looked at Maria. This was only her third or fourth case as a lead homicide detective, and by far the highest profile. Jessica wondered how she was holding up. She recalled her own experience as a lead detective early on. You work with other, more seasoned detectives, telling them what to do, not to mention a coterie of professionals – CSU officers, EMS personnel, lab technicians – many of whom are older, and have a great deal more experience. The potential for second guessing yourself, and making the wrong call, was always on your mind.

'Is this our guy?' Jessica asked.

'This is our guy,' Maria said.

'Is the victim holding a missal?' Byrne asked.

Maria swallowed hard. 'He is.'

The investigator from the medical examiner's office arrived with his photographer in tow. They signed the crime-scene log, entered the building. They emerged fifteen minutes later. The investigator briefed Maria Caruso, who made a few notes. They crossed the street to where Jessica and Byrne stood. It was Maria's show, and neither Jessica nor Byrne would make a move until she said so.

'Ready?' Detective Maria Caruso asked.

No one was.

No one wanted to be.

THEY PASSED THROUGH THE priest's house, a two-story brick structure attached to the church proper. It was spotless, save for years of dust, and the soot that shakes loose from constant road traffic passing by. The myriad footprints in the dust were made by investigators.

And the killer and victim, Jessica thought. She scanned the floor, but CSU had not flagged any area as evidence. No blood splatter, no shell casings.

Before the entrance to the main part of the church, there was a door on the left, leading to the basement. Maria directed Jessica and Byrne. This was the crime scene.

Jessica stood at the top of the stairs, began to descend.

The basement, she thought for the third time in the past few weeks. *You never get used to the basement.*

THIS TIME THE CELLAR was brightly lit, courtesy of the two field lighting units brought in by CSU. The lights were the only bright things in the space. Everything had a grim look of time and neglect. The concrete block walls were damp with condensation. There were small patches of ice.

'The victim is in the small room to the right, next to the oil furnace,' Maria said.

Jessica slipped on a pair of latex gloves, braced herself. She went in first. 'Oh, God,' she said before she could stop herself. Her stomach clenched.

On the floor, sitting against the wall, was the victim, a man in his sixties, perhaps his early-seventies. He was nude, and next to him sat a pile of neatly folded clothing. Next to the clothing was a pair of running shoes, with socks balled up inside. Next to all of this was a pair of wire-rimmed glasses.

Around him, on the floor, was a half-circle of small white stones.

There were no open wounds, no obvious signs of physical trauma, save for a thin trickle of blood running from the left corner of the man's mouth, which was slightly open. One thing struck Jessica immediately, something that did not make immediate sense. The man's throat bulged in an unnatural manner.

Jessica and Byrne did a quick look around the basement, which was three rooms; one large, two smaller. One small room held an oil furnace. The other small room had what looked to be a pile of vestments, mildewed and molded by time. In one corner leaned a pair of old wicker baskets, once used to make collections during mass, their tines thinned by mice and other vermin to use as nesting material.

The investigator from the medical examiner's office stood by. Maria asked him if he had forceps of any kind. He ran out to his car, returned with a bag of instruments.

As Byrne angled one of the field lights closer, focusing the light on the man's face, Maria put on a pair of latex gloves, knelt down. She gently prodded the area surrounding the man's jawline. It seemed unnaturally solid, even though rigor had not yet set in.

Maria took two fingers and tried to open the man's mouth. It opened with surprising ease. But even with the bright halogen lights, it was difficult to see down the victim's throat. Maria shone her Maglite inside, took the forceps and gently removed an object. It was a white stone, oval in shape, about three inches long. It was covered in saliva and blood. Maria turned it toward the light, and they all saw that there was something written on it. Although the writing was obscured, Jessica saw that whatever was written on the stone was not English.

Maria put the stone into an evidence bag, and looked back into the victim's mouth. There she saw two more stones of similar shape and size. Jessica had the sick feeling she knew what the cause of death had been. This man had swallowed – or, more likely, been forced to swallow – so many of these stones he had suffocated. The stones were almost identical to the ones on the floor, the half-circle that arced around the victim.

Maria handed the bag to a CSU officer. 'Once this is processed I want it sent over to documents, along with the missal that was in his hands.'

They would want Hell Rohmer to lay eyes on these things as soon as possible. There was no one better with the written word.

'Tell him I want to know what language is written on that stone, and what it means,' Maria added.

'Yes, ma'am.'

'And I want it last year.'

'You got it.'

TWENTY-SEVEN

THERE IS NO REST FOR THE RIGHTEOUS OR THE WICKED.

How could there be?

When the devil attempted to make his throne high above the clouds he was cast from heaven, only to find a more hospitable place to ply his craft. It was on that day the end was foretold.

They stand on the corner, two among the crowd, watching. The third church is now written. Pergamos.

'Do you know what his name means in Latin?' she asks. It is an old game, one of which neither of them has grown weary.

'Yes. It means "bearer of light."'

'Very good.'

An icy wind slices through the gathering on the corner. People stamp their feet, rub together their hands. They are cold, yet they cannot leave, cannot look away. Instead they stand and watch, transfixed by the spectacle. It is not often that evil walks into their lives in ordinary raiments.

She considers the road they are plotting, how long ago it had begun, how dark the nights. Beelzebub, Belial, Satan, Old Serpent. None of these names are accurate. There is only one name. That name is Man.

'Do you think light has been shed?' she asks.

'Yes, Mama.'

'Do you think they will follow?'

'I do.'

'*Why?*'

'*Because it is written in the stone.*'

She brims with pride. Another car arrives, more officials. Above them, in the early morning sky, a light struggles though the gray clouds, a light as silvery as Venus. Some call it the Morning Star. Some call it the Day Star.

Others call it by its ancient name, taken from the Latin lucem ferre.

Lucifer.

TWENTY-EIGHT

J ESSICA, BYRNE, AND MARIA CARUSO STOOD ON THE CORNER IN FRONT of the church. A crowd had already gathered on the other side of the street, despite the early hour. Jessica had asked Byrne to tell her what had happened the night before – the incident with DeRon Wilson that landed him on the news. Byrne promised to tell her the whole story, and added that he was scheduled to see the captain. There were many possible outcomes to that kind of meeting: nothing at all, suspension, even firing.

As Maria Caruso began to direct the neighborhood canvass, a young man walked out of the crowd. It was clear to Jessica he was crossing the street to talk to them. He looked familiar, but Jessica couldn't immediately place him.

Then she did. It was Father Michael Raphael. Today, instead of his cassock and collar, he wore a heavy parka and knit cap.

'Father,' Jessica said. 'What brings you down here?'

Raphael pointed across the street, at the TV cameras. 'I saw it on the early news. This is terrible.'

Jessica introduced the young priest to Maria Caruso. They shook hands.

'Is there any way I can be of assistance?' Raphael asked.

Jessica looked at Byrne, at Maria, back at the priest. 'Not really, Father,' she said. 'But thanks for asking.'

Raphael nodded, took a moment. Clearly there was something else on his mind. 'I've been thinking about your visit,' he said. 'May I speak freely?'

Jessica figured he was talking to her. 'Of course.'

'Detective Byrne asked about whether or not there was a formal ritual when a church was closed.'

'You're talking about deconsecration,' Byrne said.

'Yes. I did a little research.'

'What did you find?' Byrne asked.

'Nothing yet. Nothing formal anyway, at least as it applies to Catholics. The only real control the church has over what the sacred ground becomes is at the time of sale, I'm afraid. After that, with subsequent tenants, there really is not much the church can do.'

'So there is no rite?'

'Not that I could find,' Raphael said. 'But I found a few instances where churches – or at least sacred objects within the churches, like the altars – were destroyed to keep them from being desecrated.'

Raphael took a piece of paper from his pocket. 'This might help to explain things.' He handed the sheet to Jessica. 'It's from the code of canon law. The section on sacred places.'

Jessica unfolded the paper. She began to read. As she did, Father Michael Raphael quoted what was on the sheet, word for word.

'*Sacred places lose their dedication or blessing if they have been destroyed in large part, or have been turned over permanently to profane use by decree of the competent ordinary or in fact.*'

'So a church is deconsecrated by default,' Byrne said.

'Yes,' Raphael said. 'More or less.'

Jessica held up the paper. 'May I keep this?'

'By all means.'

The moment drew out. 'Is there something else?' Jessica asked.

Raphael pointed at the church. 'Would it be okay if I said a brief prayer?'

'Of course,' Jessica said. 'We'll take all the prayers we can get.'

Jessica lifted the crime-scene tape. As Father Raphael said his goodbyes, and ducked under the tape, Jessica got the attention of the uniformed officer guarding the church door. With a nod she told him that Father Raphael was allowed on the scene.

Jessica read the excerpt again.

Turned over permanently to profane use.

There could be no doubt about that, Jessica thought, considering what had been done in the three crime-scene churches.

'Detective?'

All three detectives looked up. It was one of the CSU officers. He was talking to Maria Caruso.

'I'll be back,' she said.

While Maria returned to the church, Jessica and Byrne walked over to his car, each lost in their own thoughts.

'*Seven churches*,' Byrne said, echoing the words the caller had spoken, words that began this dark odyssey, uttered what seemed like months ago.

'I don't want to think about that right now, Kevin.'

Byrne ran a finger over the small, *V*-shaped scar over his right eye. Jessica knew this meant the wheels were turning. It really was Byrne's only tell. To a great degree, Kevin Byrne was a cipher. Jessica had no idea what was coming, but she knew *something* was.

'I think we need a little spiritual guidance here,' Byrne finally said.

Jessica glanced at the steps leading to St Regina's. Father Raphael was no longer standing there. She scanned the crowd. He was gone.

'Do you want me to try and catch Father Raphael?'

'I'm not talking about the church,' Byrne said. He took his keys from his pocket, unlocked the passenger door on the Taurus, held it open for Jessica. 'I'm talking about something else.'

TWENTY-NINE

VILLA MARIA WAS A SPRAWLING COMPOUND, LOCATED IN A WOODED setting in Chester County. The building had at one time been a long-term care facility owned by the county for indigent patients, but purchased and refitted by the archdiocese in the late-1980s. In all, there were sixty-one retired priests at the facility.

From a distance it looked like a fading old resort, something you would find in the Poconos or Catskills. The only hint that it was not was the large statue of the Blessed Mother in front of the main entrance.

THE PRIEST SAT ALONE on the rear porch, a large fieldstone veranda overlooking the valley. The room looked like it had at one time been an open porch, but had been enclosed sometime in the seventies or eighties. There were two space heaters glowing in the corners.

The old man faced away from them. As Jessica and Byrne approached, Jessica was first struck by how small the man was. On the way up to Villa Maria, Byrne had told her stories about him, about how the priest had instilled fear and respect in not just the smaller kids in his parish, but the older boys as well.

'Only one ring at the first genuflection, Mr Byrne,' the old man in the wheelchair said.

Jessica and Byrne stopped in their tracks, looked at each other.

Father Thomas Leone had not turned around. There were no mirrors in the room. It was a bright winter day so there were no night-reflections to be found in the windows. Byrne had not called ahead to make any kind of appointment to see the man. They were not expected.

Was the old man prescient?

'How did you know it was me?' Byrne asked.

Leone dabbed at his lips, gently put the napkin back into his lap. His hands were gnarled with arthritis. 'I wish I could tell you that, at my age – as reward for more than sixty years in service of Our Lord – I have been imbued with the power of omniscience.' He lifted a thin arm, pointed out the window. 'The truth is, I saw you pull up in the parking lot.'

Byrne laughed, put his hand on the old man's shoulder, leaned in and kissed him on the cheek.

Jessica walked around the other side. Byrne introduced her.

This close, Jessica could see not only the ravages of time, but the ravages of disease. Leone unhooked the oxygen cannula and let it dangle over the side of the chair.

'Are you sure you should be doing that?' Byrne asked.

Leone shrugged. 'What are they going to do? Withhold my stewed tomatoes?'

The two men took a few minutes to catch up. Mostly they talked about who had died.

'Have they torn it down yet?' Leone asked.

'Not yet,' Byrne said. 'In a few days.'

Jessica knew they were talking about St Gedeon's, the church of Byrne's youth, the massive stone cathedral on Second Street.

Leone looked out over the grounds, which were still covered with a thin layer of snow. 'I married about five hundred couples at St Gedeon's,' he said. 'Baptized around a thousand babies.' He looked at Jessica, a twinkle in his eyes. 'Do you think those numbers add up?'

Jessica thought for a few moments, doing the math. 'Two babies each? Not for Italians and Irish,' she said with a smile. 'I think you must have missed a few.'

Leone smiled. 'It's possible.'

Byrne tucked the afghan back around the old man's thin legs as a draft skittered across the large porch. Leone put a hand on Byrne's hand.

'Do you still think about him, Kevin?'

Jessica looked at Byrne, found no answers there, then back at the old man. *Think about who?*

'Now and again,' Byrne said.

Father Leone took a few seconds, adrift in time. 'Do you remember how I found him?'

Jessica understood. They were talking about The Boy in the Red Coat.

'I do,' Byrne said. 'I remember as if it were yesterday.'

'Nothing seems like yesterday to me anymore.'

'It was Monday morning,' Byrne said. 'You called at 6:15.'

Leone looked surprised. 'Was it that early?'

'It was.'

'Were you awake?'

'I was doing my best,' Byrne said. 'I was on last out in those days. I was trying to *stay* awake.'

'You weren't down at Platt Bridge, were you?'

Jessica laughed. She had no idea that spot was so well-known. At one time some PPD officers on last out – the midnight to eight shift – would drive down to the area beneath Platt Bridge during the last hour or so of their tour and catch a nap. Jessica's father told a story of waking up in his squad car one morning with a dead squirrel under each windshield wiper. Nobody was more relentless with practical jokes than police.

'I know why you're here,' Leone said.

Byrne knelt down. 'We need help understanding this, Father.'

The old man nodded. 'Tell me how I can help.'

Byrne gave Father Leone the briefest details on what had been happening.

'These people are being found in closed churches?' Leone said.

'Yes.'

'The first body . . . where was it?'

'St Adelaide's.'

'Ugly place. Never liked it. Even when it was new.'

Jessica wanted to mention that St Adelaide's was built in 1853, but decided against it.

'I mean in the *church*, Mr Byrne,' Leone added. 'Where was the body found *in the church*?'

'In the basement. It was –'

'*Where* in the basement? In relation to the church proper. Was it directly beneath the altar? The vestibule? The sacristy?'

Byrne looked at Jessica. Jessica closed her eyes, relived the moment of descending the stairs. As a matter of procedure, one of the primary detectives always made a pencil sketch of the crime scene. It was rudimentary, but even in this digital age it was the most referred to document – besides the body chart – in the binder. Jessica had sketched the basement at St Adelaide's. She found it in her portfolio, took it out, showed it to Father Leone.

The old man studied it for a moment, his weary eyes suddenly flashing bright. 'This X . . . This is where the body was found?'

'Yes.'

He turned the sketch around four times. 'Which way is north?'

Jessica berated herself for not putting that on the drawing. In fact, she'd never put it on a crime-scene sketch. She would from now on. She turned the paper, showing Father Leone north.

'This is below the sacristy,' Leone said. 'What about St Damian's?'

Now it was Byrne's turn. He took out his drawing. The old man looked at it.

'You still can't draw, can you?'

Byrne reddened like a schoolboy. He tapped the N at the top of the sketch. 'At least I indicate north on my sketches.'

Byrne looked at Jessica, who stuck her tongue out.

'I was only in Damian's twice,' Leone said. He studied the sketch. 'But this is below the sacristy, too.' He handed the drawing back to Byrne, who filed it away. 'This was the baby?'

'Yes, Father.'

Leone made the sign of the cross. 'No need to see the third sketch.'

This was good, because they didn't have it. It was Maria Caruso's case.

'Look to the sacrarium,' Leone said.

Jessica glanced at Byrne, who nodded. Jessica wrote this down. The word was somewhat familiar, but she knew she would have to look it up, even if it was not going to mean anything in the end, even if it was just the rambling of an old man.

'Father, I hate to think that these killings are going to continue, but we have to be prepared for that,' Byrne said. 'If there is any way we can anticipate the killer's next move, we need to do everything in our power to be there first.'

'I understand,' Leone said.

'On the day the first body was discovered, at St Adelaide's, we received a telephone call,' Byrne said. 'A call relaying a rather cryptic message.'

'What was the message?'

'The caller said, *One God*, then *seven churches*.'

'Seven churches.'

'Do you have thoughts on this?' Byrne asked.

The old man thought for a few moments. 'I do.'

Father Leone pushed off the afghan, tried to rise to his feet. Byrne helped him.

'Whatever it is, I can get it for you, Father,' Byrne said.

Leone glared at Byrne, and for a moment Jessica saw the fire in his eyes, the look Byrne had described to her. 'I'm not dead *yet*.'

Byrne smiled, but still kept a light touch on the old man's arm. It took a minute, but eventually they made it over to the bookshelf. The bottom half was mostly popular fiction, brightly colored spines ripped and torn with use. The upper shelves were devoted to board games and jigsaw puzzles, haphazardly filed. On the right side of the bookcase were two shelves of leather-bound books. It was from this section Father Leone drew a volume, then slowly made his way back. He eased himself down into the chair, arranged the afghan over his legs.

'Seven churches,' Leone said. 'It's from the *Book of Revelation*.'

Jessica, who was anything but a biblical scholar, knew some of the major points of the Bible. *Genesis, Exodus*. Some of the *Psalms*. She had probably heard the least about *Revelation*, although the 666 number popped up from time to time in movies and fiction.

'This section is known by different names. The Seven Churches of Revelation, the Seven Churches of the Apocalypse, the Seven Churches of Asia – all the same.'

Leone flipped through the book slowly, continued.

'When Jesus appeared on the island of Patmos, in Greece, he gave John a mission to write down on a scroll what he saw and send it to the seven churches.'

'Were there specific churches named?' Byrne asked.

Father Leone looked up. 'Are you asking if the person you're looking for is targeting churches by name?'

'I suppose I am.'

'I would have to say no.' Leone riffled the volume, put the red ribbon between the pages. 'The meaning here is unclear. Christ was most likely referring to seven *communities*, not necessarily seven brick-and-mortar buildings.'

'Why these seven?'

'Christ believed these communities were failing in some way.'

Father Leone flipped a few more pages, found what he was looking for, put a finger between these pages. 'Let me think about this for a day. My mind isn't as sharp as it used to be.'

'Of course, Father,' Byrne said.

At this, the old man's eyes seemed to go distant again.

'Have they torn it down yet?' Leone asked again. He had clearly forgotten that he'd asked the question before.

Byrne had told Jessica on the way up that St Gedeon's was slated for demolition. It was on the list of closed churches they had gotten from the archdiocese. Jessica had never been inside, but she had been by it many times. It was an impressive structure with a high spire.

'Not yet, Father,' Byrne said. 'Not for a few days.'

'I want you to bring me a piece of it, okay?'

'Sure.'

'Nothing big. A small piece of stone.'

Byrne got down on one knee, brought himself face to face with the old man. 'How do we stop this, Father?'

The question brought the priest back to the moment.

'There have been three murders?' Leone asked.

'Yes. Three that we know of.'

At that moment there were investigators in four counties – city police, state police, county sheriffs – visiting all the closed churches on the list, methodically searching the premises.

'There will be four more,' Leone said.

The statement was uttered so calmly that a shiver plaited down Jessica's back. Was the old priest saying the killings could not be stopped?

'These churches,' Byrne said. 'Is there any way to know which one he'll pick next?'

'I don't know. But there is something you might find interesting, and perhaps most relevant to your case.'

'What would that be?'

Leone opened the book on his lap. 'There was a church, one of the seven, that waited patiently. A community that endured, if you will.'

'I don't understand, Father.'

Leone turned the book to face them. One page contained a large color-plate illustration of seven churches floating in a golden sky. Father Thomas Leone tapped the lower right-hand side of the illustration, and said, 'The sixth church of the Apocalypse is called Philadelphia.'

O VER THE NEXT SIX HOURS A TASK FORCE WAS ASSEMBLED AND coordinated at the Roundhouse. There had now been three murders – three bizarre murders, including the drowning of an infant – and it was no longer possible to keep a lid on the fact that there was a connection between them.

There was no talk among the detectives in the duty room of Byrne's appearance on the news the night before, but everyone knew he was set to meet with the captain. They all gave him space on this, knowing it could have been any of them. The video clip had already fallen off the news cycle, but there was little doubt it would resurface in the next day or so when there was a new witness or talking head to plaster across the screen.

Meanwhile, they all had a job to do.

ALTHOUGH THE CATHOLIC CHURCH was not the power it had once been in the city of Philadelphia, considering its large Italian and Irish population, it was still a mammoth financial and political force. There had no doubt been calls from the archdiocese to the mayor and district attorney.

The task force met at one end of the duty room. In attendance were Sergeant Dana Westbrook, along with Jessica, Byrne, Maria

Caruso, Josh Bontrager, Bobby Tate, and Dre Curtis. Bobby and Dre had fallen into a partnership a few years earlier when they worked a series of robbery homicides in West Philadelphia. Both were fashion plates, but with different styles. Bobby was all about Valentino and Armani, where Dre Curtis was old school. Every homicide unit has a lid man, and Dre Curtis seemed to have a hat for every occasion. On this day he was wearing a gray pork pie.

Before the meeting began Jessica and Byrne decided to hold off on what they had learned from Father Leone. At this point, it was still speculation.

THE THREE CHURCHES WERE marked on the large map with red push pins. The material they had gotten from the archdiocese was overwhelming. There were sixty-seven churches that had closed in the past fifty years. Of those, six had been razed, thirty-one had been repurposed, leaving thirty buildings standing vacant across four counties. Watching them all was going to be an enormous task, involving dozens of personnel, not to mention a lot of overtime money that simply wasn't there.

The third victim's name was Martin David Allsop. He had been fingerprinted at the morgue and, like Daniel Palumbo, had a criminal record. Twice convicted of gross sexual imposition on a minor, he had spent eighteen months in Curran-Fromhold on a three-year sentence. He had no family in Philadelphia. Until recently he worked as a salesman at the Best Buy on Roosevelt Boulevard.

When everyone was settled, Jessica took the lead.

'The first victim found was Daniel E. Palumbo, twenty-three, late of Latona Street in South Philly. As you all know, Daniel was once PPD. He was pronounced at St Adelaide's Church. Cause of death was ruled exasanguination, due to a sharp object – in this instance a sharpened barb on a length of barb wire – cutting the carotid artery.

'We have an eyewitness, Mara Reuben, whose mother lives across the street from St Adelaide's. On the day before we received a call, directing us to the location, Ms Reuben witnessed a man in a long coat and pointed hood exit the alley next to the crime-scene building, and make a mark on the lamppost directly across the sidewalk from the entrance.'

Jessica taped a pair of photographs onto the whiteboard, one of them a still picture from the pole camera on the corner; the other was a close-up photo of the X on the lamppost.

'This was taken from a pole cam, and seems to back up what Ms Reuben told us. The time code coincides with her recollection of events. Unfortunately, she could not give us a better description.

'A few days later we questioned one of Daniel Palumbo's known associates, one Thomas L. Boyce, who had one of the victim's old knapsacks with him. We found no solid leads in there. I then began a series of interviews at free clinics, which led me to the St Julius Clinic at Twelfth and Lehigh. One of the nurses there, a man named Ted Cochrane, remembered treating our second victim, Cecilia Rollins.'

Jessica had decided to let Byrne brief the task force on Cecilia Rollins. Her level of rage about the murdered baby was still on the red line.

Byrne stood up, consulted his notes. 'Although Daniel Palumbo's body was the first to be discovered, the medical examiner has ruled that Cecilia Rollins was the first to die. He puts the date of her death around February sixth. Her body was found in the basement of St Damian's.'

Jessica knew that *Byrne* knew he had to brief the team on how they got to St Damian's in the first place. He wasn't about to tell them that it came to him in one of his visions. The PPD brass, and even some of his fellow homicide detectives, were skeptical enough of Byrne's methods the way it was.

'After a search of St Adelaide's, a portion of an old prayer card was found in the bell tower, an item we believe was deliberately left by the killer. It was a funeral card from 1966, issued by St Damian's.

'The child's mother, Adria Rollins, nineteen, is severely mentally handicapped, and when I checked with DHS, they said they believed her great-grandfather – who signed forms claiming he was her grandfather – was competent enough as a guardian. When we went to question Adria, we found the old man deceased of natural causes, and

Adria alone. We believe the baby was abducted from their apartment.'

'Do we know anything about the baby's biological father?' Maria asked.

'We do not. Ms Rollins is currently in the pysch ward at Temple. We're awaiting word on whether or not she is well enough to be questioned. We checked the birth record, and the father is listed as unknown.'

Byrne turned his attention back to the photos on the board.

'Once again a mark was left on the lamppost in front of the church. As before, the premises yielded hundreds of partial fingerprints, which are still being processed. A search of the scene also yielded a candle-holder, the only candleholder still in the church that could not be matched to St Damian's.'

'And we think this was deliberately placed, too?' Bobby Tate asked.

'We do. There was an inscription on the bottom of the glass that revealed it was property of St Regina's, which turned out to be a closed church in Rhawnhurst. When we visited St Regina's, we discovered the body of Martin Allsop.' Byrne deferred to Maria Caruso. The Allsop case was hers.

'Allsop was sixty-nine, a resident of Torresdale,' Maria said. 'We ran his prints and found he had a rather lengthy record. He was a twice-convicted sex offender, and was on the city's watch list.'

'Any connection to the clinic?' Westbrook asked.

'None yet,' Maria said. 'At least, not according to the clinic. We haven't had the chance to question friends and family. If he had any friends.'

Byrne took the floor again. 'As to MO, Cecilia Rollins died as a result of drowning,' he said. 'Daniel Palumbo bled out, Martin Allsop died as a result of suffocation. Although he has not yet been autopsied, an X-ray revealed there are many more stones in his esophagus and stomach. One stone removed from his mouth at the scene had markings on it. The markings appear to be in a foreign language, one as yet unidentified. The lab has it now.'

While Maria Caruso took a call on her cell and stepped out of the duty room, Byrne flipped a few more pages on his pad, continued speaking.

'Our best guess is that the main suspect is male, white, somewhere around six feet tall, anywhere from twenty to fifty.'

'Great,' someone said.

'What about the marks on the lampposts?' Dre Curtis asked. 'Were they made in blood?'

'No. They are definitely not blood,' Jessica said. 'Preliminary reports reveal that the substance is a combination of a starchy compound, soil, with trace amounts of tannin.'

'Tannin,' Bontrager said. 'Are we talking tannin as in red wine?'

'We are,' Jessica said. 'But that's all we have so far. Some of the material is so old it has begun to break down. The lab is conducting more tests as we speak. They'll have more soon.'

Byrne continued. 'We ran this through ViCAP and, as you might imagine, the results were off the charts. Murder committed in the name of religion probably accounts for a third of the database.'

'What about trauma on the baby?' Dre Curtis asked.

Byrne shook his head. 'None. The ME ruled the baby drowned. There were marks on the baby's legs, but these were unrelated to the cause of death. There were no cuts or lacerations.

'CSU collected hair from all three scenes that shows promise. If the hair matches, and the owner is in CODIS, we'll have something.'

'Where *are* we on the DNA results?' Bontrager asked.

Everyone knew there was a backlog on DNA testing. The forensic lab had to process cases closest to the statute of limitations. Once in a while pressure was brought to bear to speed up the process. Jessica hoped this string of murders qualified.

All eyes turned to Dana Westbrook.

'I'll see what I can do,' Westbrook said. She stood up, took the floor. 'Something connects these victims. I want questions and answers.'

All five detectives looked at each other. Nobody wanted to raise their hand.

Westbrook continued. 'The victims lived in different neighborhoods, moved in different circles. As far as we know they never attended the churches in which their bodies were found.'

'Both Palumbo and Allsop did time,' Bobby Tate offered.

'At two different correctional facilities,' Westbrook replied.

'Jailhouse jaw,' Tate countered. 'It travels.'

'Possible,' Westbrook said. 'But that does not account for Cecilia Rollins. And why the baby? Why not the mother?'

'Revenge?' Bontrager asked.

'Not against the mother,' Jessica said. 'Adria is not functional. I can't imagine she had done something to someone so horrible that it would warrant the kidnapping and murder of her child.'

'What about the great-grandfather?'

'It's hard to make too many enemies at his age. And if he did, they would be too old to do any of this. I'm not seeing it.'

'Where was the baby born?' Westbrook asked.

Jessica checked her notes. 'Jefferson.'

'Maybe somebody put their eyes on the baby there,' Westbrook said. 'Any connection between Jefferson and the other two victims?'

Nobody knew. The appropriate detectives made the note.

'How is the killer picking the churches?' Westbrook asked. 'Why *closed* churches? I'm thinking this is significant.'

'The archdiocese has a website of all active parishes,' Byrne said. 'If you have a list from ten or twenty years ago, simple math would do it, a simple side by side comparison. Or maybe it's just by observation.'

'Might this be a vendetta against the Church?' Westbrook asked. It was almost rhetorical. It was on everyone's mind. Of course, if that were the case, there would be no predicting any pattern. There were churches all over the four counties. And there was no shortage of scandals involving the Catholic Church, some legitimate, some not. 'Or someone inside the Church,' she added.

This too was something no one wanted to think about, but neither could they rule it out.

'We find the motive on this one, we find our boy,' Westbrook said.

There was general agreement on this. It was not a case of finding a single gun to match ballistics. All three methods of murder – one victim bleeding out, one drowning, one suffocating – meant that it wasn't the means that tied the killings together, but the motive.

If they could find a connection between these three victims, they might find a common denominator, and their killer. Friends, families, lovers, co-workers, doctors, dentists, lawyers. Something tied these people together. They were being killed for who they were, and carefully deposited in Catholic churches.

Closed Catholic churches.

Westbrook continued. 'So this is where we are, folks. I want status reports from all of you every two hours. There've been three murders on our patch, and our psycho caller said "seven churches." I think we all know what that means. Like Kevin said, according to the archdiocese there are thirty empty churches scattered around four counties. Sixteen of them are in our jurisdiction, which makes them all our responsibility. State police and county sheriff's offices are coordinating surveillance in Montgomery, Chester, and Bucks. As for us, well, expect to do a lot of sitting, watching, and waiting.' She tapped the picture on the whiteboard, the photograph taken from the surveillance camera of the figure in the dark hood. 'Let's bring this fucker into our house for a nice long visit, shall we?'

The team stood up, gathered their materials. Before they could get their coats on, and get out the door, Maria Caruso came rushing in.

'We have prints,' she said.

At this, everyone in the room stopped doing whatever they were doing. They all looked at Maria.

'The prints were found on the inside back cover of the missal found at the Allsop scene,' she said. 'We got a hit from IAFIS.'

Maria read from the sheet. 'The prints belong to a man named Elijah Caleb Longstreet, white male, date of birth June twenty-fourth, 1951. Last known address is in a place called Cuzzart, West Virginia.'

'What's he in the system for?' Dre Curtis asked.

'It seems Mr Longstreet was involved in a number of assaults, one aggravated, did some state and county time in the seventies.'

'Is he still living there?' Westbrook asked.

'Hard to tell,' Maria said. 'I couldn't find any current records on him at all. No DMV, telephone, nothing.'

Dana Westbrook picked up the phone. 'I'll contact the West Virginia state police,' she said. 'See what I can find out.'

Jessica glanced at her watch. It seemed like she'd been up for days. She wanted a long, hot bath, but she was afraid she'd fall asleep in the tub and drown.

Westbrook looked at Jessica and Byrne. 'What are you waiting for?'

'What do you mean, Sarge?' Jessica asked.

Westbrook handed Jessica the sheet with Elijah Longstreet's last known address on it.

'Get down there.'

THIRTY-ONE

THEY SIT ATOP THE SMALL RIDGE OVERLOOKING THE VALLEY. THE AIR IS COLD, but the sun is bright and warm, painting the hills in lustrous hues of rust and gold.

'Tell me about how it looked then, Mama.'

She tells the story as she knows it, of when the house was built, of how fine and strong it had stood, how level and true the ridge, how plumb the jambs. She tells about how there had been neighbors who had helped, and how the woods then were neither ragged nor sparse nor timbered flat. She tells about how the water in the creek once ran pure and cold, and how, every April, if you squinted your eyes, and gave rise to the belief, the mountains seemed to blush yellow with flowers.

The house is fallen now, the old church stands empty, home to only pigeons and beetles and vermin. She tells about going there as a very young girl, when the service was full of majesty and mystery and solace. There was comfort in the Word, yes, there was.

But when the Preacher came to her that night it all changed.

She looks at the old stead, takes out what she needs, leaves it behind. It won't be long. She knows that she has a connection to the detective, one that transcends all the machines and test tubes and electronic equipment. One that lives in their two hearts.

'Are they coming?'

'Yes,' she says. 'Very soon.'

There is one God, she thinks, but He is many things to many people. Hers is the God of vengeance, and at his right hand sits the last saint.

There are four more churches to go.

THIRTY-TWO

The drive to West Virginia took just over five hours, but that was not according to Detective Jessica Balzano, who slept most of the way. When she awoke the car was stopped, parked on the side of a dirt road, with the strangest anomaly occurring. There was sunlight coming in the windows. Bright yellow sunlight. It was by no means warm, and there were patches of snow dotting the endless, rolling brown hills, but the sky was blue and the sun was dazzling.

Jessica glanced over at Byrne. He was staring out the window, lost in thought. When he noticed that Jessica was awake, he reached into the back seat, brought back a container of coffee.

Jessica sat up. 'Don't tell me I slept the whole time.'

'Purt near,' Byrne said with a smile.

'Wow. We *must* be in West Virginia.'

Jessica rubbed the sleep from her eyes. She brought down the visor, opened the lighted mirror. 'Oh, my God.' She snapped it shut, took the coffee from Byrne. 'Are you saying we stopped, you got out, bought coffee, got back in, and we drove some more without me waking up?'

'Actually we stopped *twice*.' He sipped his coffee. 'Last time was an hour ago. The coffee won't be hot, but it's strong and it's pretty good. Sweet rolls are in the back if you want one.'

Jessica opened the coffee, sipped. Byrne was right. It was forty-weight.

'You're going to love this,' Byrne said. He reached out, tapped a button on the navigation screen on the center console. Jessica put on her glasses, looked at the readout.

There were two lines. If they were in Philadelphia, or just about anywhere else, the entire screen would have been cross-hatched with streets, boulevards, expressways, turnpikes. Here, at the northeastern tip of West Virginia, there were two roads. One going north and south. One going east and west.

'Have you ever seen this screen so empty?' Byrne asked.

'Never.'

Driving around Philly, with its one hundred neighborhoods and thousands of streets, Jessica quite often needed to pull over, put on her reading glasses, and scan the screen. Out here, in the middle of nowhere, navigation was a lot easier.

'You said we stopped twice,' Jessica said.

'I stopped at the sheriff's office. There's only two deputies working. It's really more of an outpost.'

'They didn't see me sleeping in the car, did they? Please tell me they didn't see me sleeping in the car.'

'No. I parked a block away. The whole town was only five blocks long, so we were pretty much on the outskirts.'

'And you left me alone in the car? In the middle of such a hotbed of criminal activity?'

Byrne smiled. Jessica sipped her coffee again, then chugged half the lukewarm cup. She had to get it together. She rolled down her window, let some of the cold air in. 'What did we get from the sheriff's office?' she asked.

'Not much. The older of the two deputies was about twenty-five, and he said that the address we have used to belong to the Longstreet family, but no one has lived there for quite some time. He said our best bet was to see a woman named Ida-Rae Munson, who lives along here somewhere. He said if we couldn't find it to call him and he'd come out.' Byrne held up his cell phone. 'I tried. No signal yet.'

Jessica glanced out all four windows. There were rolling brown hills in all directions, but not a single dwelling of any kind.

'Did you get a map?'

'No,' Byrne said. He tapped the navigation screen again. 'This is about as detailed as it gets.'

Byrne pulled back onto the road. About a mile away they came to a long thicket on the right.

'Stop,' Jessica said.

Byrne stopped, backed up. There seemed to be an opening in the thicket, which led to a long hardpan lane that headed up to and over a ridge.

Jessica looked at Byrne. As he pulled in, scraping the sides of the sedan against the dried bushes, she finished her coffee, and willed herself awake.

There was no way of knowing what they were going to find over this ridge.

THE HOUSE SAT ATOP a low rise, at the end of a 200-foot driveway. The closer they got to the structure, the more Jessica began to wonder what kept it standing. It was a three-room shack, with a roof so patched and tar-papered it looked to be in danger of blowing off any second. The ridge of the roof was so bowed it looked ready to snap. There was a crumbling chimney to the left, one at the back. Smoke poured from the larger of the two. In the fields surrounding the shack were the rusted remnants of old trucks, stoves, car parts. A well pump stuck out of the ground at the end of a trampled trail through the weeds.

Jessica and Byrne got out of the car, walked to the house. The sun was still out, but a frigid breeze blew over the hill. They stepped cautiously onto the swayback porch. Jessica knocked. From inside they heard a dog bark. It was a high-pitched sound, which was good news. No one, outside of postal carriers, had more of a love/hate relationship with dogs than police officers. This did not sound like a big dog – Rottweiler, shepherd, or even an old redbone hound. This was a beagle at best.

The door opened, but there was no one there. Jessica looked down.

There, standing in front of them, was a boy of five. He had light blond hair shorn so close to his head that there were red, abraded patches on his scalp. He wore dirty jeans, at least two sizes too large. They were rolled up almost to his scabby knees. He was barefoot, even though the temperature had to be hovering around twenty degrees.

'Hi,' Jessica said.

Instead of answering, the boy barked. Loudly. At first, Jessica thought the boy might have yelled for an adult to come to the door, but when he did it a second time, there could be no doubt in her mind. The boy was imitating a dog. At least she *hoped* it was an imitation.

There was no dog. The sound they heard had been the boy.

'Is your mom or dad home?' Jessica asked.

The boy studied them for a moment, then turned and ran. He disappeared out the back door. A few seconds later they heard: 'Well, come if you're comin'. Stove's alight. Shake off the chill.'

Jessica and Byrne stepped inside. The main room was relatively uncluttered and organized, considering the home's exterior. To the right was a long table, along with a wood-burning stove. Next to that was a sewing machine.

As they stepped further into the room, Jessica saw the woman sitting in a rocking chair. She was somewhere between thirty and fifty, had graying hair pulled back into a ponytail, held an embroidery hoop in her hands. Her right foot was in a cast.

'Are you Ida-Rae Munson?' Jessica asked.

'I am in fact.'

Jessica produced her ID. 'My name is Jessica Balzano. I'm with the Philadelphia Police Department.'

'Phila*delphia*?'

Jessica heard a sound behind her. She turned to see the dog-boy crouched in the corner watching them, little terrier eyes studying them from the midday shadow. *When had he come back inside?* Jessica turned her attention back to the woman. 'We had quite a hard time finding your place.'

'House ain't moved in thirty years,' the woman said.

'I guess what I meant is that it's a bit sparsely populated in this area,' Jessica said, for some reason feeling the need to explain herself, and do so with proper grammar, which was far from one of her strengths.

The woman shrugged, ran a hand across her chin. 'There just ain't no more jobs, that's the simple answer. Not in the mines, not loggin', not pulpwoodin'. Nothin', nowhere. Everwho had some sense packed and gone.'

Jessica and Byrne just listened. Jessica figured *everwho* meant *whoever*.

The woman waved a hand absently at the area behind the house. 'We used to grow everything we needed, 'cept the ground got used up. All's we used to go into town for was boots and nails. Coffee, some. Still ain't no public water out here. When I heard y'all pull up I figured you was with the county, out to give me another shuffle.'

'We just need to ask you a few questions, if that's all right?' Jessica said.

'I ain't expected. Ask what y'got.'

Jessica took out her notebook and pen. 'Ma'am, do you know a man named Elijah Longstreet?'

The woman recoiled as if she had bitten into spoiled fruit. '*Elijah*?'

'Yes, ma'am. Do you know him?'

The woman looked out the window, and back again. In this light Jessica could see the woman had once been pretty. She had high cheekbones, silver-blue eyes.

'Weren't none of them Longstreets no good,' she said. 'They say we're kin way back, imagine. But I don't believe it. Not a word.'

The woman rocked back and forth.

'Ma'am? Elijah Longstreet?' Byrne asked. 'Do you know where we could find him?'

The woman snorted. 'I'd look to Hell. Shouldn't take too long.'

Jessica and Byrne exchanged a glance.

'Are you saying Mr Longstreet is deceased?' Byrne asked.

'God-fearin' people get *deceased*. Elijah Longstreet just *dead*.'

'Do you know what happened?'

The woman looked at Byrne as if she were talking to a mule. 'He died. That's what bein' dead *means*.'

Byrne took a deep breath. 'Ma'am, what I'm asking is, do you know *how* he died?'

'They say it was the lung got him, but it was the drink. It was always the drink with them Longstreets.'

'How long ago did he pass?'

The woman looked skyward, perhaps doing the math. 'Gotta be twenty year now. More, some.'

Twenty years, Jessica thought. Then why was his fingerprint in a missal found in the hands of a dead man in Philadelphia this week?

'Do you know if Mr Longstreet ever got up to Philadelphia?' she asked.

'Don't know nothing about Elijah Longstreet's comin' or goin'.'

Jessica took out a photograph of a cleaned-up edition of the *My Missal* found in Martin Allsop's hands. 'Do you recognize this book?'

The woman squinted at the picture, focused. 'Oh, Lord. Haven't seen one of them in years.'

'Do you own one of these?' Jessica asked.

'No,' she said. 'That's a book for children.'

At the mention of the word *children*, Jessica looked around the room. Somehow the barking boy had moved again without her seeing it. She wondered where he was. *Had they locked the car?*

A knot in one of the logs in the stove popped. Jessica nearly jumped at the sound.

'Elijah had a girl called Ruby,' the woman said, resuming her rocking. Perhaps this was her storytelling mode. 'Red-headed one. Funny girl. Touched some say. Too quiet, y'ask.'

'Ma'am?'

'Word was she had a devil-child.'

Jessica looked at Byrne, back at the woman.

'Lots of stories come out 'round that girl,' the woman continued. 'I know she took up with that preacher.'

'What preacher would that be?'

The woman laughed. 'You got a nickel? You do, I'll give ya five preachers and change. Ain't never been a shortage a preachers in West Virginia.' She tapped the photograph of the book, handed it back to

Jessica 'He used to hand them missals out like candy. Used to hand out a lot more than that, if you was young and fair.'

'Do you recall the man's name?'

She shook her head. 'Don't know nothin' 'bout his name. But I know that Longstreet young 'un Ruby run off slap-quick with him and his church caravan.' She rocked back and forth, just once, stopped. 'And her boy like to be the devil.'

'Not sure what you mean by that.'

The woman reached down next to her, picked up a rusted coffee can, spit into it. Jessica did her best not to look at Byrne.

'Said the boy was a bad seed. Said the father had the devil in him and the boy come out evil.'

Jessica put her notebook away. Even if she found something useful in this woman's words, she was pretty sure she didn't want to read her notes on the subject, or make it part of the permanent case file. What she *was* sure of was that she was good for about two more seconds of being in this house.

'Where would we find this Ruby Longstreet?' Byrne asked.

Another shrug, another spit. 'Longstreet name's tainted. She woulda changed it anyways, even if she ain't got married. I know I woulda.'

'Are you saying there are no longer any of the Longstreets living around here?'

'*Long* gone from here. Anyone with sense long gone from here. Her momma is up to the state nursing home in Weirton. Their house, what's left of it, is five mile up the road. More, a piece.'

'We went by there, but we didn't see anything,' Byrne said.

'Oh, it's still there. You gotta ride that ridge for a spell. Pon m'onor it's there. Nothin' but spiders and whistle pigs though.'

At first Jessica didn't know what the woman had said. Then she worked it out. *Pon m'onor* was *upon my honor*. She thanked the woman for her time. The woman didn't get up, didn't show them to the door.

Jessica took out a card, put it on the wooden table by the front window. She wasn't even sure this woman had a phone. 'If you can think of anything that might help us locate Ruby Longstreet, please give us a call.'

No response. Just the creak of the rocking chair.

As they reached the car, Jessica had the feeling they were being observed. After a few steps she turned.

The boy was sitting on the roof, watching them.

JESSICA AND BYRNE HEADED south. They didn't talk. The encounter with Ida-Rae Munson and the barking boy had pretty much taken the words right out of them. When they reached the five-mile mark, they came to the overgrown drive that led back toward what they assumed was the Longstreet property. Jessica stopped the car.

'You sure you want to do this?' she asked.

'Well, we're here, right?' Byrne asked. 'I mean, what would a trip to West Virginia be without a visit to the famous Longstreet Estate?'

Jessica wasn't finding the humor.

'It would be like visiting Asheville and not going to Biltmore,' Byrne added.

Against her better judgment, Jessica turned into the drive. She said a silent prayer that they would not encounter any more barking boys.

THEY RODE THE OVERGROWN lane back over the rise, more than a half-mile, and saw what was once a home. Two buildings, flattened by time and weather, sat next to a frozen pond. Behind it a dry gully ran down the hill.

In the pond were the remnants of an old pickup truck's fender and wheel well. As Jessica and Byrne got out, and moved closer, Jessica saw that the buildings had been burned, but, apparently, when they had fallen into the pond, the fire halted. Half-walls and a charred ridge pole stuck out of the ice. Tar-paper spread across an overgrown field. Emerging from the ground behind the house were a half-dozen crosses, simple monuments of twined-together two by fours.

'Well, our friend Ida-Rae was right,' Jessica said, as brightly as possible. 'Nothing to see here. Nope. Nary a thing. Let's go.'

Instead of responding, Byrne walked toward the pile of charred rubble. Jessica recognized the set of her partner's shoulders, his gait. She knew they were not going to leave any time soon.

Jessica followed, watching the ground for all manner of danger – snakes, rats, and especially old boards with big rusty nails sticking out of them. Once, when she was seven years old, she and her cousin Angela snuck onto a construction site in South Philly, and Jessica stepped on a board, putting a sixteen-penny nail through her right foot. Besides the excruciating pain, she'd had to get a tetanus shot, which was almost worse. Since then it had become a bona fide phobia. She could square off in the ring with big nineteen-year-old girls named Valentine, run after crazy men with butcher knives, but she was scared shitless of stepping on an old rusty nail sticking out of a board.

And snakes. She was not a snake person.

'I can't believe a whole family lived in a place this small,' Jessica said. While the rowhouses in cities like Boston, Baltimore, and Philadelphia were notoriously small, at least they could grow vertically. This had been a three- or four-room shack, one-story tall. Jessica looked to her right and saw an old metal bed frame grown over by weeds. She wondered how many people had slept in it.

She was just about to ask Byrne what she could do to help move this investigation along, when she heard a noise to her right. An animal sound. She turned and saw, on a ridge about fifty feet away, two black dogs.

Big black dogs.

'Kevin,' Jessica whispered.

'I see them.'

Both detectives slowly unsnapped their holsters, drew their weapons, held them at their sides. Jessica looked back at the car. It was at least thirty yards away. They would never make it, even at a dead run.

The dogs did not have their heads lowered, nor were they growling. But then again, neither Jessica nor Byrne had moved.

'What you want to do?' Jessica asked.

'Just stay as still as possible. Don't make eye contact.'

The dogs milled back and forth on the ridge, circling each other, nuzzling, sniffing the air. It looked as if they might be protecting something, but were unsure that Jessica and Byrne posed any threat. Jessica noticed they were well-fed, heavily muscled. After a few minutes they turned and loped down the other side of the hill.

Jessica and Byrne stood still for a full minute. Had the dogs left? There was no way of knowing, and Jessica would be damned if she was going to go to the top of the ridge and take a peek.

'Partner?' she said.

'Yeah?'

'I love the hell out of you, you know that, right?'

'I do,' Byrne said. 'And it means the world to me.'

'But if you don't mind, could you do me a favor?'

'I will surely entertain the notion.'

'Could we maybe get the *fuck* out of here?'

'I think we're okay,' Byrne said. 'I think they left.'

Jessica wanted to believe he was right. She wasn't so sure.

For the moment her thoughts returned to the case, and to Ida-Rae Munson's words:

Word was she had a devil-child.

In the context of the horrors they had seen in the desecrated churches, the words certainly took on a new meaning. She just didn't know what that meaning might be. Either way, it was time for some old school, shoe leather police work. She just didn't want to do it here.

'I think we should go back to the town,' Jessica said. 'Maybe there's some forwarding address for this Ruby Longstreet, some attorney who handled the property. I want to see the records of this place.'

Byrne reached into his coat pocket, gave Jessica the deputy's card. 'Nice kid. Believe me, he'll fall all over himself to help you.'

'What do you mean?'

'I'll wait here.'

Jessica looked at her partner. 'You're going to stay *here*.'

'Yeah.'

'In the middle of nowhere.'

'Yeah,' Byrne said. 'You might want to fix your hair.'

Jessica did a quick comb-through with her fingers. 'Better?'

'Better.'

'You sure you want to do this?'

Byrne just nodded.

Jessica backed her way to the car, listening for the sound of eight heavy paws loping up the hill. She heard nothing. She opened the driver's door.

'Kevin?'

Byrne looked over.

'The dogs?'

Byrne raised a hand, waved. He'd heard her.

THIRTY-THREE

BYRNE WALKED TO THE TOP OF THE HILL, WEAPON IN HAND. There was a tree line about a hundred yards away. There was no sign of the dogs.

He holstered, walked back down, stood at the base of the foundation where the old shack had stood, listened to the silence. He had grown up in the city, had spent most of his life in one. The mind-numbing quiet of a place like this was profound.

His mind was not quiet for long.

Who are you, Ruby Longstreet?

Byrne crouched down near the footer, an old track-style foundation made of packed earth and stones. He picked up one of the white stones and knew where he had seen one like it before. It was in the victim's mouth at St Regina's. He rolled the smooth rock in his hand, felt the malign presence of this place, a history that was fearsome and dark.

Who are you, Ruby Longstreet?

Byrne glanced skyward. The air was cold, but the sun warmed his face. He stood, walked around the frozen pond and saw, just at the bottom of the rise, the handful of homemade crosses, a half-dozen in all. This was the family plot. He wondered if Elijah Longstreet was buried beneath his feet.

Byrne looked at the edge of the overgrown area, saw an old realtor sign, rusted and battered by time and weather. He turned it over. There, painted on the back, was a telling legend.

Longstreets rot in hell

Ida-Rae Munson had not been kidding. The Longstreets were not the most popular family in these parts.

But he had known that. It didn't take an Ida-Rae, or a county zoning archive, or even God to tell him that. He knew it as soon as they turned onto the property. He felt it.

The father had the devil in him and the boy came out evil.

In his mind Byrne saw the end. He closed his eyes, and for the first time in more than two decades invited the darkness in.

Inside the darkness were two graves.

And although he could not see names on the headstones, he could see the date of death. It was less than a week away.

THIRTY-FOUR

S HANE ADAMS COULDN'T GET ONTO THE GROUNDS AT THE ROUND-house unobserved, but here it was different. Here, behind the apartment building in which Kevin Byrne lived, he was shielded from the street. Unfortunately, the Dumpster in the alley behind the building was full, and looked to contain trash from six different rowhouses, and one low-rise four-suiter. He'd never be able to pick through it, find what belonged to Byrne, and spirit it away. Not in broad daylight.

He left the alley, rounded the corner onto Third Street. The street was lined with parked cars. He found the one he was looking for, stepped into an alcove, checked his notes. It was Kevin Byrne's personal car. Shane looked up and down the street. If he approached the car, he could be seen by any one of a dozen vantage points. He took out one of his cell phones – specifically an old flip phone he'd had for years, one that was no longer connected to any service, and therefore was never in any danger of ringing at an inopportune time – and put it to his ear. He sauntered up the street, talking aloud into the phone, meandering in that aimless way people do when they're on the phone in a public place.

He leaned against the wall across the sidewalk from Byrne's car. He could see a few things on the dashboard. Nothing of much interest. He leaned forward, saw two large boxes in the back seat; one with a top, one without. The open box seemed to be full of papers.

Shane pretended to be on his cell phone as he leaned against the car, and covertly took as many pictures as he could of the back seat and front seat.

He then raced back to his own car, checked all the mirrors. The big cop was nowhere to be seen. Shane scrolled through the photos. Crap, except for the news clippings on top of the papers in the open box. One of the headlines read:

WHO IS THE BOY IN THE RED COAT?

By the time he got back to the station Shane found that he couldn't get the headline out of his mind. He sat down at a computer terminal, looked up the story.

There was a ton of information. Not nearly as much as there was for Philadelphia's most famous mystery – The Boy in the Box, a four- or five-year-old victim found in a box in the Fox Chase section of the city in 1957, still unsolved – but there was at least three months of data.

The Boy in the Red Coat case was not ruled a homicide, so the investigation went to divisional detectives at the time, who interviewed people in the neighborhood, trying to determine the boy's identity. They spoke to hundreds of people in the neighborhood, as well as everyone in the church's parish. The boy's picture went out nationally and internationally, but no one came forward.

So why were the papers in the back seat of Detective Byrne's car? Was he reopening a twenty-year-old case? Did it have something to do with the spate of murders happening in churches now?

Maybe there was something in his trash after all.

Maybe Shane would go back tonight.

THIRTY-FIVE

IN THE DREAM SHE CAN'T MOVE. SHE CAN SEE, BUT SHE CANNOT MOVE her arms and legs. She is in a big, drafty room. From somewhere in the distance she can hear chanting. Latin chanting. She looks up to see a tall figure standing in shadows. In his hand is a ring of barb wire. In the other is a handful of white stones. She suddenly realizes she is sitting on the rim of an old aluminum tub filled with ice. She manages to fall over, onto her side. When she looks into the tub, there is a newborn baby frozen inside.

But it isn't Cecilia Rollins.

It is Sophie.

Jessica woke up drenched in sweat, disoriented, her heart pounding. She turned, found Vincent dead to the world, as usual. It was a good thing Philadelphia didn't get too many hurricanes. Vincent Balzano would sleep through them and wake up on a beach in South Carolina.

Jessica had managed to stay awake on the ride back from West Virginia, mostly because Byrne chose that time to tell her about his run in with DeRon Wilson. Byrne's temper was formidable, but in the time she had known him he had only managed to lose it completely a handful of times. He told her that the brass were mandating that he see a psychiatrist for an assessment before meeting with the captain about whether or not there would be any problems arising from the incident.

By the time they returned to the Roundhouse Jessica found that she was completely exhausted. She found herself home, fed, bathed, and in bed by 10 p.m.

Now she was wide awake.

She got up, checked on Sophie and Carlos. Both were out like broken lamps.

JESSICA OPENED THE CLOSET door. Staring back was a jumble of boxes and baskets, plastic storage containers, things she had promised herself she would go through one of these days, weeding out the junk. The problem was that she was a sentimental fool. When they moved back to South Philly a year ago she had thrown out ten or so Hefty bags full of things she had collected over the years, including two full legal-sized boxes of Christmas and greeting cards. She had kept one small carton of cards, an old gift box from Strawbridge's.

Jessica walked into the kitchen and sat down. She opened the white box. Inside was her first communion rosary, a white rosary in a small leather pouch. There were also a few dozen prayer cards, mostly from St Paul's.

The two cards in the box that meant the most to her were for her mother and brother. There had been ten years or so between their deaths, but the wounds were still fresh, still open. She stared at the cards for a while, remembering the two services. She was five when her mother was buried. The church was filled with family and friends. Half the PPD showed up, it seemed.

Her brother's service was different. He had been killed in Kuwait in 1991, and there were members of every branch of the military at St Paul's that day, everyone in the neighborhood who had ever served their country showed up – men, women, young, old, from WWI through Desert Storm. Some of the old boys wore their uniforms.

Jessica held onto the two cards, made herself a cup of chamomile, took it into the living room. She curled up on the one big comfy chair they had, pulled a throw over her legs. Sometimes it was good to hurt, she thought. When you stop hurting, you start to forget. And she never wanted that.

THIRTY-SIX

MICHELLE CALVIN TRIED TO REMEMBER THE LAST TIME SHE HAD been in a church. Was it her sister's wedding? No, she had been in a church since then, hadn't she? But when? She couldn't recall.

As a child growing up in Savannah, Georgia she had been dragged to mass every Sunday, forced to sit in that sweltering, airless church on Margery Street. When she finally ran away at seventeen, never to return, Sunday became a day to do nothing but recover from Saturday night.

And there had been some serious Saturday nights.

She remembered. The last time she'd set foot in a church had been four years earlier, at her grandmother's funeral. It was held at St Gregory's, and the turnout was sparse to say the least. Her grandmother didn't have many friends. Grandma Rita had been what people in her day called a loose woman – three husbands, more boyfriends than she could keep track of, a taste for Jack Daniel's and a somewhat less than puritanical view when it came to backseat sex.

In many ways, Michelle had turned out the same.

But that was another life.

Now that she was in real estate, now that she had a career with a capital C, it had all changed. Three years earlier, at the ripe old age of twenty-six, she had turned her life around. It had taken one too many scrapes with the law – including a brief stint in jail and two years of AA – but she had finally gotten her act together. She had nearly lost her only daughter in the process, but somehow convinced the court that she had put her wicked ways behind her, and retained custody.

This job – its stability, its respectability, its ticket to better things – meant everything to her. Michelle Calvin was on the rise. And the sky, as they say, was the limit.

Michelle thumbed the combination on the lock box, removed the keys inside, unlocked the side door. Ahead was a short hallway with two doors on the right. The building was old, and had that musty smell of disuse. She walked into the central space which, she imagined, was once the main room of the church.

She hadn't read up on the property, but she believed that this had one time been used as a chapel. When the old hospital next door was torn down they left this structure standing. Over the past few years it had been used for storage by the archdiocese, but no longer as a place of worship. The archdiocese sold the building to a company headquartered in Cincinnati, Ohio who were now looking to unload it.

Michelle checked her watch. The buyer she was supposed to meet was ten minutes late. She'd give it another ten, then make the call.

As she took out her BlackBerry, a noise came from just behind her. She spun around. The woman had walked into the building and crept up behind her without a sound.

'I'm sorry,' she said. 'I didn't mean to startle you.'

The woman was well-dressed and accessorized. This told Michelle she was probably a serious buyer. Very good news. 'Not at all,' Michelle said. 'I just didn't hear you come in.'

They shook hands, talked about the weather for a few moments.

'Have we met before?' Michelle asked. The woman looked vaguely familiar.

'I don't believe so.'

It would come to Michelle. For the moment she gestured to the space, which was lit only by the light coming through the tops of some high, dirty windows. The rest of the windows were boarded up. There were no fixtures in the main room. 'They're definitely ready to sell,' Michelle said. 'They've been sitting on this for quite some time.'

'This was a church,' the woman said. It was a statement, not a question.

'Yes,' Michelle said. 'I believe it was a chapel when the hospital used to be next door. I don't know if it was ever a regular church, a church where people came to mass on Sundays.'

Michelle wondered why she added that. It looked like the woman was going to buy, and if Michelle had learned anything from Ray Rudolph, who was her boss and mentor, it was that anything you said after a client said *yes* began to talk them out of the sale.

'Is there a basement?'

Michelle consulted the listing. 'Yes, there is,' she said. 'But I've never been inside before, so I'm not sure where the stairs are. You look around, I'll do a little exploring.'

Michelle walked to the far side of the main room, and there found a hallway. She walked down the corridor, and to the right discovered a small room that had probably been used as a kitchen at some point. She saw capped gas pipes coming up through the old tile floor. Beyond this room was another door. She opened it, and saw stairs leading downward. There was a light switch. She tried it, and was happy to see that the current owners had not yet turned off the juice. The listing said there was electricity, but you never knew.

'I found it,' Michelle said.

No response.

Michelle was just about to call out again when she turned to find the woman already standing next to her. Michelle tried to conceal her surprise.

'Would you like to see the basement?' she asked.

'Very much.'

Michelle silently prayed that the basement would be somewhat presentable, as in no broken water pipes, no homeless people, no rats.

They slowly descended the stairs, Michelle on point. The basement was the same size as the main room above, broken into two sections by a half-wall. There were no ground-floor windows, just a pair of bare bulbs in grimy porcelain sockets. In one corner was an old stained mattress.

While Michelle mentally prepared to close the deal, she suddenly felt a sharp pain on the left side of her back, just below her shoulder blade. It felt as if she had been stung by a bee. She turned around. The woman was holding a hypodermic.

Had this woman just stuck her with a needle?

Michelle Calvin did not have long to think about it. Her central nervous system answered the question for her. She felt it first in her legs, a deadness that seemed to rise up from the floor, claiming every part of her body.

'What . . . what did you *do* to me?'

The woman did not answer. Instead she stared straight ahead, past Michelle, at the smaller second room, bathed in darkness.

'There is someone who wants to meet you,' the woman said. 'He has waited a long time.'

Michelle Calvin slumped to the floor, her mind swirling red.

Then, blackness.

An icy draft. She was on a mattress. She opened her mouth to scream, but no sound emerged. In fact, Michelle Calvin could not tell if she had even opened her mouth.

Was this a dream?

No. Michelle knew it wasn't, the same way she knew it *was* a dream sometimes, a realm in which there was an otherness to her senses, along with the belief that it all could end by opening her eyes.

But Michelle Calvin's eyes were already open.

This was really happening.

'She was a princess, you know,' the woman said. 'She was branded a whore because she dressed in finery and painted her face and body.'

My God, Michelle thought. *No.*

The woman knelt beside the mattress. 'You made a promise,' she said. 'Like the others.'

What promise?

'You made a promise, and now he will take his due.'

The woman began to slowly undress Michelle. Michelle could do nothing to stop her. Piece by piece the woman removed her clothes, folding them neatly on the floor next to the mattress.

When the woman removed the last of Michelle's clothing she took a white cloth from her bag and put it over Michelle's eyes.

MICHELLE HEARD FOOTSTEPS. How much time had passed? She had no idea. She couldn't see, she couldn't move. She couldn't *fight*.

'Thyatira,' came a whisper. 'Jezebel.'

Seconds later Michelle felt the mattress sag. First one side, then the other. Someone was on the bedding with her. Someone was *kneeling* over her.

'If you let me keep my daughter I will do anything. I will even make a deal with the devil,' the voice whispered in her ear.

Michelle began to cry. Those were her words. She had gotten her wish and now she was going to pay for it.

'*Ego te absolvo,*' the whisperer said.

The moments of Michelle Calvin's life blistered through her mind – shadow-ridden images, long-forgotten voices, coils of memory unfurling at hellish speed.

'*A peccatis tuis.*'

Michelle felt a fingertip at the base of her throat. The touch was gentle, probing, almost sensual. Try as she wanted, Michelle could not recoil from its touch.

'*In nomine Patris.*'

The finger was replaced by something else. Something cold.

'*Et Filii.*'

In the last second of her life, in the hollow place between two breaths, Michelle Calvin knew what it was.

'*Et Spiritus Sancti.*'

B YRNE WALKED INTO THE OFFICE, A CONVERTED ROWHOUSE ON Thirteenth Street, at just before 10 a.m. The waiting room was standard issue – rugged loveseat and two chairs, all upholstered in a non-threatening navy blue fabric. Two cheap mall prints on the wall, also non-threatening. The woman behind the reception desk was mousy but efficient-looking, with dull brown hair, freshly scrubbed skin. She wore a twenty-year-old Timex. Her nametag identified her as Antonia.

Byrne put on his best new-patient, not in the least bit crazy smile. Antonia looked up, returned a half-smile of her own.

'Hi,' Byrne said.

'Hello.'

'I have a ten o'clock appointment with Dr Goodwin.'

'Okay.' She turned to her computer. 'And your name?'

And just how many people have a ten o'clock appointment with Dr Goodwin today? 'Byrne,' he said. 'Kevin Byrne.'

The woman typed for twenty seconds. Byrne couldn't imagine that the appointment calendar was ten folders deep on the computer, but he waited patiently.

'Here we are,' the woman said. 'Could you verify your full address and home phone number, please?'

Deep breath. *Calm, Kevin.* He gave her his street address, and home number, which really wasn't a phone at all, but rather a wire connected to an answering machine. He really didn't want to get calls on that line, and Antonia reinforced the notion.

'Could I get your *full* address, please?' she asked. 'Including the city and zip code?'

Ah, Byrne thought. This was a *test*. They were testing his patience – his anger threshold – in the outer office. The session had already begun!

'That would be Philadelphia, 19147.'

'Got it.'

'That's in Pennsylvania.'

The woman flicked him a chilly glance. 'I assumed the Pennsylvania part.'

Yet the 215 area code didn't clue you in to the Philadelphia part. 'Of course.'

'Well, then. Just have a seat. I'll let Dr Goodwin know you're here.'

'Thanks, Antonia.'

The woman bristled at the familiarity, but that was the effect Byrne was going for.

He picked one of the chairs, cruised the rack of magazines. *Harper's*, *Real Simple*, *Web MD*. All his favorites. Then again, keeping copies of *Guns and Ammo* probably wouldn't be prudent, considering the number of psycho cops that came through here.

After a surprisingly short period of time, Antonia came around her desk, opened the door to the inner office. 'You can go right in.'

DR SARAH GOODWIN was younger than Byrne expected. That was happening to him a lot lately. When you're in your twenties, all the people who matter – doctors, lawyers, judges – are older. You *want* them to be older. Once you hit forty and the great beyonds the paradigm began to shift.

Dr Goodwin was petite and graceful, with deep chestnut hair to her shoulders. She wore a smart black suit, white blouse.

They introduced themselves, shook hands. All very clinical and professional.

The inner office was small but comfortable, lacking any real warmth: *de rigueur* couch with roll arms, a pair of stern-looking chairs facing an uncluttered desk, a browning ficus in the corner. Byrne picked a chair. Dr Goodwin sat at the desk, turned the flat screen monitor to face her, out of Byrne's line of sight.

'So,' she said. 'How are you?'

'You mean today, or in general?'

'Let's start with today.'

'Today, not bad,' Byrne lied. 'I'd rather be at work, all things considered. No offense.'

'None taken.'

Byrne tried to settle in the chair. It was too small. 'I've done this before, by the way,' he said. 'Twice.'

'I know.'

Of course, Byrne thought. Medical records last forever.

'I'm not sure I got too much out of it either of those times,' he added.

'That's okay. We'll consider this a fresh start.'

Fair enough, Byrne thought. 'What would you like to talk about?'

Dr Goodwin leaned back in her chair. 'We can talk about anything you like.'

'Well, I'd like to make our sessions worthwhile, but we both know this is a mandate. So maybe we should talk about the things that put me in this chair to begin with.'

'Fine.'

Byrne searched for the right words, found them. 'Well, it seems there are some people in the department who think I have anger-management issues.'

'Do *you* think you have problems with anger?'

'Not at all. I get angry just fine. I think it comes naturally.'

Dr Goodwin smiled. She was used to this kind of sparring. 'Would you like to talk about the incident that precipitated this episode?'

Episode. 'Sure. What would you like to know?'

'Why not tell me how the day began?'

Byrne had to think about this. He knew, of course, that everything said in this room was confidential, but he also knew that this woman was going to make a recommendation to his bosses. He had to play this right. 'I can't really say too much about the case. It's an ongoing investigation.'

'I understand.'

Byrne suddenly realized he was trying to play this woman, who was a lot better at this stuff than he was. 'Okay. Confession time,' he said. 'The case involves the death of a child and I guess I do have issues when it comes to the murder of children.'

'This is understandable, detective,' Dr Goodwin said. 'In your line of work, it has to come up quite often.'

'It does. Too often, I'm sorry to say.'

Byrne went on to describe his day, about his phone call to Gabriel and how he came to be in the same hallway with DeRon Wilson.

'Did you feel threatened by Mr Wilson?'

'Not at that moment, no. But he has a history of violence.'

'How did you react?'

Byrne decided to say it out loud. 'I lost my temper. I accosted Mr Wilson, pinning him to the wall.'

'Did you draw your weapon?'

Byrne knew that *she* knew the answer to the question. 'Yes.'

'Even though Mr Wilson had not produced a weapon of his own.'

'Yes. I felt the situation had the potential to escalate. There were a lot of people in that hallway, and I didn't know what was coming.'

'But you do feel that you lost your temper? That you reacted out of anger?'

Fuck it, Byrne thought. *Bring it on, Sarah Goodwin, MD.*

'Yeah. I did. The man is a slaver, a drug dealer. He's done time for both. If, right now, someone was putting a bullet in his head, I'd have a nice dinner and sleep like a baby. Sorry, but true.'

'Never be sorry for your feelings.'

Dr Goodwin typed a few lines. Byrne was grateful for the pause. He wasn't sure he had a lot more to say on the subject.

'I understand that there have been a lot of retirements in the Homicide Unit of late,' she said. 'Has this had any effect on you that you're aware of?'

Byrne thought: This woman is *good*. 'I don't know. Maybe it has. I know I'm one of the older detectives still on the line.'

'Does that bother you?'

'Not really. See, I don't think of myself as a man my age. But now that I've passed my twenty-five, maybe I *am* looking for a reason to stay. Maybe that reason, for me, is a kid like Gabriel. I may never see him again. He may go right, he may go wrong. But I know he got dealt a shitty hand.'

And then it happened. Byrne told her everything about Gabriel. The *real* reasons. The who, the why, the when. The doctor wrote it all down.

'This is very commendable,' she said.

Byrne wasn't sure what it was. 'Can I ask you something?'

'Of course.'

'I know you can't tell me anything specific, or betray any confidences, but you see a lot of cops in here. What do they talk about? In general, I mean.'

'Well, like a lot of people, they talk about fear.'

Byrne nodded. 'I think just the opposite.'

'And what would that be?'

'I'm not afraid anymore.'

'Why not?'

'Because I think I am blessed,' Byrne said. 'By all rights, I shouldn't even be here. I've been shot twice. I've been stabbed. I've been punched more times than I can count, sometimes even for good reasons. I've been given last rites. Twice. And yet I'm here. I have a job I love, a partner I love – a woman in whose hands I place my life everyday without hesitation. I have a father – who probably needs your services more than I do – who is healthy. I have a daughter who is bright and smart and beautiful and in possession of the biggest and most generous heart of anyone I have ever met. Dr Goodwin, you are looking at a man who lives in a state of grace.'

'Do you believe in God, detective?'

'I believe in God.'

Dr Goodwin waited a few seconds, then typed the new information. When she was done she glanced at her watch. 'I'm afraid our time is up for today.'

'And I was just getting into it.'

'Isn't that the way?' she said with a smile. Her entire demeanor changed when she smiled. 'We need to see each other one more time before I submit my report. Would you like to make the appointment now?'

Byrne pointed to the outer office. 'You mean with my BFF Antonia out there?'

Another smile. 'You don't have to make the appointment now.'

Byrne thought about it. He really had no idea where the next few days would take him. 'Can I call tomorrow when I have my calendar in front of me?'

'Of course.'

BYRNE SAT IN HIS car, wondering how he had done with the shrink. He had wanted to talk to her about Father Leone, about the passing of an era, about the long winter in his soul. He decided to keep all of that for next time. It had probably been a mistake to open up about Gabriel, but there was nothing he could do about that now.

Maybe it was not a bad thing, Byrne thought as he pulled out into traffic. If something happened, at least someone would know the truth.

THIRTY-EIGHT

S ERGEANT MATEO FUENTES CONSIDERED THE AUDIO VISUAL Unit TO be his own private fiefdom, a place with its own rules, its own methods and procedures, its own language. In his mid-thirties, Mateo Fuentes was precise in his manner and speech and dress, and considered visits by investigators and brass alike to be a personal affront. Nobody knew more about electronic surveillance than Mateo Fuentes. His personal library on the subject filled an entire wall in the unit.

At just after noon Jessica and Byrne ventured into Mateo's lair. He greeted them with stiff formality, and got right down to business. They stepped into an editing bay where two laptops sat on a table.

'You see the most interesting things in the basement,' Mateo said.

Neither Jessica or Byrne had an argument for this. 'What do we have?' Jessica asked.

Mateo held up a disc. 'I got this from Detective Bontrager. He's on the street now, but he wanted you to see it.'

'What is it?'

'It's surveillance footage from the night before the St Adelaide's victim was found.'

Mateo was talking about Danny Palumbo.

'If you're talking about the pole-cam footage, we've seen it,' Byrne said.

'We are not,' Mateo said in his terse manner, apparently using the royal *we*. 'This is *new*.'

'Where did we get new footage?' Byrne asked.

'It seems Detective Caruso wielded her not inconsiderable charms on the owner of an auto-repair shop around the corner from St Adelaide's. He let her see some of his equipment, as it were.'

Mateo took the compact disc out of the paper sleeve and slipped it into the optical drive on one of the laptops. A few seconds later he cued up the video image.

'According to Detective Caruso, the auto-body shop has four video surveillance cameras on the property. One of them is on a light pole diagonally across the street from the PPD pole cam.'

'And this footage is from around ten o'clock on the night before Danny Palumbo's body was found?' Jessica asked.

'It is.' Mateo clicked on the image. It was grainy, and the light level was very low, but it looked usable. Mateo fast-forwarded through passing cars and people until he got to the mark he sought. He stopped the recording. 'Now, if you check the time code here, it coincides with the pole-cam recording.' Mateo opened a second laptop which displayed the footage taken by the police camera. 'I synched up the two recordings to be within just a fraction of a second of each other.'

Mateo started both recordings in slow motion. On the police-cam footage, with which Jessica and Byrne were familiar, they saw the hooded figure emerge from the alleyway, stand in front of St Adelaide's, and mark the X on the lamppost, before exiting frame right. In the other footage the figure was not visible but its shadow was. Mateo rewound both recordings and played them again. As Jessica watched, she kept looking at the time codes, something nagging at her.

After the third viewing she knew what it was.

'You know what's missing here?' Jessica asked.

'The woman you interviewed that day while I was in the bell tower,' Byrne said.

'Exactly.'

'Run it one more time,' Byrne asked. Mateo ran both recordings again. When the image of the hooded figure reached the front of St Adelaide's, Mateo stopped both recordings.

The area where Mara Reuben said she was standing, in front of her mother's house, was deserted. For her to have seen the figure in front of the church, she would've had to have been standing across the street, in front of that address, at that moment.

There was no one there.

'You want a copy of this?' Mateo asked.

'Absolutely,' Jessica said. 'It would –'

With a flick of the wrist Mateo produced a disc.

'You know me too well,' Jessica said. She kissed him on the top of his head.

Mateo lifted one corner of his mouth in an expression that, for anyone else, would be considered a smile. 'Be careful,' he said. 'Once you go AV you never go back.'

Jessica and Byrne thanked Mateo, walked up the steps, back to the homicide unit duty room.

JESSICA CHECKED HER NOTES, found Mara Reuben's phone number, dialed it. It was out of order. There was no such number.

'Let's take a ride,' Byrne said.

Fifteen minutes later they stood on the corner, across the street from St Adelaide's. They approached the house Mara Reuben said belonged to her mother. Byrne knocked on the door. An elderly black woman answered.

'Yes?' the woman asked. 'Are you selling something?'

'No, ma'am,' Byrne said. 'Do you know a woman named Mara Reuben?'

'Who?'

'Wrong address,' Byrne said. 'Sorry for the intrusion.'

The woman looked at both of them suspiciously, and shut the door. Jessica heard three separate deadbolts turn. They walked back to the car.

'She got my attention that day,' Jessica said. 'You were inside the church. She was standing right in front of that rowhouse and I thought she wanted to talk.'

'And nothing about her story sounded shaky?'

'Not a thing,' Jessica said. 'But now we know she lied about her phone number, and she lied about her mother's house. Not to mention being there in the first place.'

'Yep.'

'Makes you wonder what else she lied about.'

'Yes, detective. It does.'

They headed back to the Roundhouse in silence. The investigations that comprised the task force – including detectives, CSU officers and laboratory technicians, working around the clock – probably involved close to one hundred people. Jessica thought about how one deranged person, one person with a deep and disturbing pathology, could manage to stay one step ahead of the collective wisdom and experience of so many people.

In the parking lot at Eighth and Race Jessica's cell phone rang. It was Hell Rohmer.

'Hell, I'm going to put you on speaker,' Jessica said.

'Who am I on with?'

'Just me and Detective Byrne.'

'I have a break on that stone,' Hell said. 'The writing on it anyway.'

'What do we have?'

'Well it took awhile – long for me, anyway – but the writing is Greek. It's not particularly well written.'

'What do you mean?'

'Well, I don't mean contextually. It's only the one word, after all. What I mean is that, at this size, with the tool that was used, it's not all that clear.'

'Do we know what kind of tool?'

'Not exactly. If there was trace evidence left by the tool, it was washed away with blood and saliva. Firearms are getting it back in a minute.'

The Firearms Unit, also located at the lab, handled evidence related to tools and tool marks.

'Anyway, because the characters were so primitively cut into the stone, it seemed like it matched a number of different words.'

Hell stopped. Jessica figured he was going through his notes. When he didn't continue, she realized he just wanted some sort of overture to his findings.

'And what does the word say, Hell?' she asked.

'It's a name. *Ignatios.*'

'Could you spell that?' Jessica asked.

Hell did. 'It's Greek for Ignatius.'

'Do you know anything else about it?'

'Well, I can tell you that he was born in 1491 at the castle of Loyola, and died in Rome in 1556, and that –'

'No, Hell,' Jessica said. 'I'm asking if there is –'

'There is,' Hell said. 'It's not really a church, but rather a chapel. *Used* to be a chapel.'

'It's closed?'

'It is. A couple of years now. Ever since they tore that old hospital down.'

Jessica heard her phone beep.

'I just texted you the address.'

'Thanks.'

'You got it,' Hell replied. 'I hope the good guys get there first.'

The good guys did not.

THIRTY-NINE

Jessica and Byrne stood at the foot of the mattress. Next to them stood Maria Caruso and Josh Bontrager. The sight before them was horrific beyond imagining.

The dead woman was white, somewhere between twenty-five and thirty-five. She was naked, except for a cloth that covered her eyes.

The old mattress beneath her body was soaked with blood. The woman's throat had been slashed. No, *slashed* was too kind a word, Jessica thought. Her throat had been savaged. The action had left the muscles in the woman's face in a rictus of terror.

'Detectives?'

It was a CSU officer in the small room off the main section of the basement. The four detectives walked across the room. The first thing Jessica noticed as she got closer were the dozen or so small yellow cones on the floor, placed there by crime scene officers, noting where blood evidence had been dropped. The drops led to the old stone archway.

Jessica stepped in first. There was something on the floor. When she knelt down to get a closer look, she realized what it was. Bile rose in her throat.

It was the woman's tongue. The killer had cut out the woman's tongue, and pulled it from her throat.

Jessica looked overhead, and saw the rusted iron pipe coming through the floor. They were below the sacristy.

Look to the sacrarium.

WHILE THE CSU BEGAN to process the basement, Jessica walked the first floor, made some rough measurements. Josh Bontrager drew the sketch. He would be the lead investigator on this case.

Four churches. Four brutal murders. No suspects.

Jessica knew this case would be folded into the task force, just as she knew that status reports on these murders had already reached the inspector level, most likely the commissioner.

She also had the feeling that whatever overtime money was needed to put the rest of the shuttered churches in Philadelphia County under twenty-four-hour-a-day surveillance would now be appropriated.

By early-afternoon they learned that, unlike the other cases, they already had an ID on the victim. A car parked directly in front of the chapel was registered to a woman named Michelle A. Calvin. A PCIC check provided a photo ID, and showed that a few years earlier Michelle Calvin had been arrested in a prostitution sting, and as a result served four months in jail. The search also yielded the woman's current employer, Rudolph Realty. Josh Bontrager put in a call and spoke to the owner of the victim's firm, Raymond Rudolph, who agreed to come down to the crime scene to talk to investigators.

As Jessica and Byrne emerged from the church, they saw Rudolph standing next to one of the sector cars, talking to Bontrager. Rudolph was clearly shaken. In his late-thirties, standing five-eight or so, Rudolph was dressed conservatively in a black trench coat, white shirt, maroon club tie. He turned a BlackBerry over and over in his gloved hands.

Introductions were made.

'You were her boss?' Bontrager asked.

'Yes,' he said. 'I was.'

'Do you know what brought her here today?'

'She had an appointment with a buyer.'

'This property is for sale?'

Rudolph nodded. 'It's been on the market for a long time.'

'What do you know about the buyer?'

Rudolph reached into his pocket, brought out a printout of an email. 'Michelle was here to meet a woman named Mara Reuben.'

Jessica looked at Byrne. *Mara Reuben.* The woman Jessica had talked to across from St Adelaide's. The phantom who was not on the video recording.

'Did you ever meet this woman?' Bontrager asked.

'No,' Rudolph said. 'I'm afraid not.'

'Do you know if this woman ever called Ms Calvin, ever left a voicemail?'

'I don't know, but I can check.'

'We'd appreciate that,' Bontrager said. 'Also, do you know if the woman ever visited your office? If, perhaps, someone else there has ever met her?'

'I don't believe so. Again, I'll ask. But keep in mind we're a small office. There are only five of us.' The expression on Rudolph's face said that it suddenly occurred to him that there were now only four.

'Can you think of anyone who might have had a problem with Ms Calvin?' Bontrager asked. 'Any deal that might have turned sour?'

Jessica knew that Josh knew that this murder was part of an ongoing ritual, not a personal vendetta, but it was a question that had to be asked.

Rudolph shook his head. 'Not really.'

They gave the man a moment to clarify his answer. He did not.

'Is that a *no* or a *maybe*?' Bontrager asked.

The man looked up, clearly conflicted about something. 'Look, it's not really my business what a person does, or what they used to do. I know Michelle had some . . . difficulties in life before she came to work for us. But she was bright and smart and, by all accounts, had turned her life around. I was happy to work with her, and happy to have known her. God judges, detective. Not man.'

Rudolph began to mist up. He turned away. Bontrager gave him time.

Jessica figured the man was talking about Michelle Calvin's arrest and conviction for prostitution, but maybe there was more to it than that. Maybe there was much more.

BECAUSE OF THE EVER-WIDENING scope of these related murders, everything was passing through the commanders of the various units. On scene now was the day work commander of the Crime Scene Unit. Sergeant Terry O'Neal was a veteran in his fifties, a jovial father of six, but heart-attack serious about his job. He had worked as a patrol officer when Byrne was coming up, and the two men had a long relationship.

Jessica overheard bits of their conversation.

'Every inch, Terry. Every fucking inch,' Byrne said, *sotto voce*. 'I'll pay for the overtime myself.'

'You got it.'

'There is something in this building that is going to lead us to the next scene, and I want to find it before he gets to the next church.'

And the next body, Jessica thought.

She took out her iPhone, opened a browser. On a hunch she did a search for names of people in the Bible. Before long she was rewarded. Of all the women in the Bible, there was one named Mara, and one man named Reuben. She called Byrne and Bontrager over. 'Look.'

The two men looked at the screen.

'In Hebrew, Mara translates as *sad*, and Reuben means *vision of the son*,' Jessica said. She put her phone away. 'I think I'm going to get together with a sketch artist today.'

'Good idea,' Bontrager said.

TWENTY MINUTES LATER, AS the investigators began the process of collating the details of a new homicide, Jessica looked out the window of the chapel, saw Byrne talking to a paramedic, a woman in a blue windbreaker. Jessica soon recognized her as one of the paramedics who treated Danny Palumbo.

Jessica observed the woman's body language and noticed that

there were private signals happening between her and Byrne. She couldn't see the woman's face, which would have helped, but it looked like there was something between the two of them that transcended the job.

Something intimate.

FORTY

S HANE WATCHED THE POLICE ACTIVITY FROM THE COFFEE SHOP ACROSS the street. There were a half-dozen sector cars ringing the old church, a gathering of rubberneckers. Shane hadn't gotten the details over police radio – you rarely did, you were lucky to get the nature of the complaint and an address – but he knew this had to be the discovery of another body. You didn't call out the cavalry over some kid breaking and entering for a place to hit the pipe.

But more important than the sector cars was the Ford Taurus that had arrived, and was now parked fewer than fifty feet away from where Shane stood. A PPD detective car parked outside the crime scene tape. A car that had brought detectives Byrne and Balzano.

Their presence here told him pretty much all he needed to know.

Cyn was on assignment up in Cheltenham, some kind of water main break. That was okay. This one Shane wanted all to himself. He had become so prolific at one-man-banding a story that he would defy any field reporter, anywhere in the world, to tell the difference with an on-air piece. He could even edit on the fly on his Mac Book Pro if he needed to.

This was the kind of investigative piece that would land him in Anderson Cooper's chair.

As a pair of CSU vans arrived at the scene, and the patrol officers in the street made the gathering crowd part for them, Shane saw his opportunity. He put up the collar on his coat, exited the coffee shop.

When he got near the car he dropped his shoulder bag – ostensibly by accident, if anyone was watching – and put the small magnetic tracking device inside the right rear fender. He stood up, dusted off his pants, glanced around. No one had seen him.

Perfect.

The car was, of course, a departmental car, and didn't belong to either Jessica Balzano or Kevin Byrne, but Shane knew that detectives tended to sign out the same cars over and over again. This allowed them to keep some of their personal gear in the trunks. The tracking unit was a little pricey, and Shane had already lost one, but the monthly fee for tracking via GPS was only $19.95. As long as his laptop could get a satellite signal, he could track the device anywhere in the world.

Shane had gotten shut out of the story featuring Byrne doing his Hulk act on that punk dealer, and it wasn't going to happen again. True, he'd gotten the exclusive with the kid's cell-phone footage, but he could have had crystal clear video if he'd been a little better at his surveillance technique.

He now had his DV camera with him, battery charged, with a second fully charged backup battery in the trunk.

When this story broke big – and he had the feeling that was going to happen very soon – he would be there.

FORTY-ONE

FROM THE VESTIBULE AT ST IGNATIUS'S JESSICA AND BYRNE WATCHED the crime-scene officers establish a search grid. A half-dozen technicians would spend the rest of the day and night collecting any and all potential evidence – hair, fiber, fingerprints, fluids. It was an exasperatingly slow and exacting process.

Byrne walked over to where Jessica stood.

'If they don't come up with something I'm going to rip this place apart with my bare hands,' he said. 'It's here.'

Before Jessica could respond her phone rang. She answered. It was Dana Westbrook.

'What's up, Sarge?'

'Well, first things first,' Westbrook said. 'We ran the name Mara Reuben and came up empty.'

This was no surprise.

'Where are you on the canvass?' Westbrook continued.

'We're just going to start,' Jessica said. 'CSU is here, and I just wrapped up with the sketch artist.'

A sketch of the woman Jessica had talked to across from St Adelaide's, the woman who called herself 'Mara Reuben,' would soon be circulated. Jessica had given a highly detailed description of the woman, but was now all but certain her beautiful silver hair was a wig.

'I'm going to send some other detectives down there for the neighborhood interviews,' Westbrook said.

'Why?' Jessica asked. 'What's going on?'

'We've got DNA results back.'

'Are you saying we have a hit?'

'We do.'

BY THE TIME THEY arrived at the Roundhouse a half-dozen task-force detectives had assembled in the duty room. There was more than a little electricity in the room.

Dana Westbrook spoke first.

'Folks, we have a serious break. We have DNA results from the first three scenes,' she said. 'As you know, there were hair samples found on all three sites, follicles stuck between the pages of missals. According to the lab, there was enough mitochondrial DNA present to make a match.'

Although Jessica was far from an expert on forensic hair analysis, it had come up often enough for her to have a basic understanding of what the lab could and could not do with a hair sample. If samples were matched with DNA analysis, it was better than a fingerprint.

'All three were between pages?' Byrne asked.

'Yes,' Westbrook said. 'In *Revelation*. Dead solid on all three. We ran them through CODIS and every bell, whistle, and alarm went off.'

The Combined DNA Index System was a database maintained by the FBI that matched profiles of unknown perpetrators against a state's database of convicted offenders.

'So we have a suspect?' Byrne asked.

Westbrook nodded. But there did not seem to be any glee in her face, or the expected – and well-earned – smug satisfaction all cops get from the *gotcha* phase of a homicide investigation.

'I'm not seeing happiness here, Sarge,' Maria Caruso said. 'Why are we not happy?'

Westbrook handed the report to Byrne. Jessica, Josh Bontrager, and Maria Caruso crowded around.

The DNA sample found on three separate crime scenes – three separate *homicide* scenes – belonged to a man named Roland Hannah, a self-styled evangelist preacher who had once terrorized the city with his vigilante murders. Both Jessica and Byrne had worked a collateral case, which took investigators up the Schuylkill River.

But that wasn't the amazing part.

The amazing part was that Roland Hannah had been an inmate in the State Correctional Facility at Graterford for the past five years.

THREE

THE LAST SAINT

'Who is worthy to open the book,
and to loose the seals thereof?'

– Revelation, 5:2

THE CHURCH IS LONG-SHADOWED, DARK AGAIN. THE TIME IS NEAR.

At four o'clock you hear the huge door open behind you, and see the failing daylight spill down the long aisle. Heavy footfalls approach, hard-soled shoes on worn tile. Oddly, you notice the sound of one tile, rattling loosely in its grout. You were always one for detail.

You glance toward the aisle, just as the shadow falls, just as it did thirty years ago this day. Now, as then, you find that you are holding your breath.

Thirty years ago you drew your weapon, and turned toward the light.

This time, all you have is your faith.

FORTY-TWO

Detectives Jessica Balzano and Kevin Byrne sat in a department-issue Taurus on the rise overlooking Graterford State Correctional Facility.

In her years on the Philadelphia Police force Jessica had only been here a handful of times. The realm of correctional facilities – their inner workings, their politics, the very world they occupied – was beyond the experience of most city detectives. The majority of a homicide detective's work took place at a different part of the continuum which began the moment one person lifted his or her hand in anger at another, and ended when a convicted suspect was led from a courtroom in shackles.

The Pennsylvania State Correctional Institution at Graterford was located in Skippack Township, Montgomery County, about thirty miles west of the city of Philadelphia. Built in 1929, it was Pennsylvania's largest maximum-security prison, housing more than 3,500 inmates. In addition to its five major cell blocks, and small mental-health unit, the facility was surrounded by 1,700 acres of farmland.

There were nine manned towers sticking out above its high walls, ringed with concertina wire.

Overcrowding was a problem in many US prisons, and in the Commonwealth of Pennsylvania it was no different. The prison population was currently at over 50,000 inmates, occupying space meant for just over 43,000.

In 2010 an inmate serving a ten-year sentence was released and went on to murder a Philadelphia police officer. A moratorium on paroles was instituted and, although that had eased, overcrowding was still an issue.

The crumbling facility was due to be mothballed when two new prisons opened near Philadelphia. Meanwhile Graterford was bursting at the seams.

The process by which a city detective arranged an interview with an inmate incarcerated at Graterford was a fairly complicated one, a process which had been smoothed over by the captain of the Homicide Unit and the district attorney's office.

Roland Hannah had confessed to three homicides, but waived his right to allocution – the process by which an individual stands before the court and explains his actions. To this day the reasons for those crimes remained a mystery, but only in the legal sense. It was clear to everyone, especially police investigators, why Roland Hannah did what he did. As a result of his confession Hannah was spared the death penalty, and was sentenced to three life sentences, without the possibility of parole.

But all of that now had the potential to change. Jessica and Byrne had been briefed before visiting the prison that Hannah's lawyer had already petitioned the court for his client's release, pending a new trial, all on the basis that Hannah had been framed then, as he was now. The reason for his prior confession, it was now being alleged, was diminished capacity, and no small measure of police coercion.

There were many questions, not the least of which was who was bankrolling Roland Hannah's new lawyer, James H. Tolliver, one of the priciest defense attorneys in Philadelphia.

THEY MET JAMES TOLLIVER just outside the meeting room. He was about fifty, well-tanned and well-dressed. He carried an expensive charcoal gray overcoat over one arm, and held a black leather Ferragamo briefcase.

Just where *was* Roland Hannah getting the funds? Jessica wondered.

While it was true that many lawyers at white-shoe firms did *pro bono* work, this case didn't seem to line up, politically speaking. Unless, of course, the ultimate strategy was that an overzealous police department and district attorney's office had railroaded Roland Hannah's conviction to close out a terrible run of unsolved murders.

They all introduced themselves. Polite, but stone cold.

'Against my advice, Reverend Hannah has requested that I not be present in the room when you speak with him.'

Good, Jessica thought.

'But rest assured that I will be listening to everything said in that room, detectives,' Tolliver added. 'If I feel you are moving into an area I think it unwise for my client to enter, I will be inside in a flash and this interview will be over.'

THE ROOM WAS PAINTED an institutional green. It measured ten by fifteen feet. There were three small barred windows, set high on the wall, letting in enough light to see what sort of day it was outside, but not allowing inmates to see much else.

At the center of the room was a table bolted to the floor. On one side was a dented metal chair, also secured. The other side held a pair of folding chairs that did not look much more comfortable.

At just after 2 p.m. the door opened, and the prisoner was led in. Both his feet and his hands were shackled.

Jessica had not seen Roland Hannah in years, their last meeting occuring at the hearing during which he confessed to murder. In the intervening years his hair, which he now wore nearly to his shoulders, had turned a fog white. He had lost weight, and the orange jumpsuit hung loosely on what had already been a slender frame. His face looked as if it were carved from alabaster.

The corrections officer sat Roland Hannah down on the metal chair. He took the cuffs from his hands then stood behind the prisoner, looking to Jessica and Byrne for his cue. Jessica nodded and the officer left the room, shutting and bolting the door behind him.

The fresh silence was deep and protracted. For almost a full minute no one spoke. It was Roland Hannah who broke the calm.

'Good afternoon, detectives,' he said. 'It has been a while. I hope you are well.'

In addition to his orange jumpsuit the man wore dark amber-tinted aviator glasses.

Roland Hannah was blind.

Jessica wondered how much Hannah had been told. She knew that he had met, at great length, with his lawyer, so she had to assume he knew everything – details of the current spate of murders, as well as the church connection.

'Mr Hannah,' Jessica said.

She saw the reaction on his face, the small tic of displeasure. He said nothing. Roland Hannah, at the time of the murders that put him in SCI Graterford, was an ordained minister. There was no way Jessica was going to call him *Reverend* Hannah. Not unless she needed to. Not unless there was fruit to be picked from this encounter.

'I would say "It's nice to see you again," but I am not a fan of irony,' Roland said.

'Do you know why we're here?' Byrne asked.

Roland Hannah remained silent for a few moments. It was impossible to read his expression behind the tinted glasses. 'Have you both come to accept Jesus Christ as your personal savior?'

'Why do you ask that?' Jessica asked.

'Well, I like to think of myself as one of His more evangelical minions, but this seems like quite an effort on your part. If you wanted to be baptized there are plenty of churches you could have gone to.'

'I've been baptized, Mr Hannah,' Jessica said.

'Praise His name. What is your chosen path?'

Jessica had the feeling he would try to engage her in this discussion. As little as she wanted to accommodate him, she knew it was necessary. 'I'm Catholic.'

Roland nodded. He turned his face to the meager gray light sifting through the high windows, then back toward Jessica and Byrne. 'I have a special affinity for the Catholics, you know.'

'Is that right?' Jessica asked.

'Yes, ma'am,' Roland said. 'From the time I was twelve or thirteen I had the notion I was going to become a Catholic priest. Mama was a Baptist, of course, but every chance I got I would sneak off to a Catholic mass. Took to hanging around the rectories, helping out at the CYO functions, generally being a nuisance. Even made myself a Roman collar once out of my mama's sewing basket.'

Jessica wasn't interested in the man's story, but she wanted to keep him talking. 'So, what happened?'

'Well, they told me I was too old to be an altar boy, and too young for the seminary, not to mention my lack of formal education. So, when tragedy touched my life, I chose another path. I was ordained a Pentecostal minister when I was just fifteen.'

'This was here in Philadelphia?' Jessica asked, although she already knew the answer.

'No, ma'am. I went back down to Appalachia, where I'm from.'

Roland took a moment, continued. 'My first ministry was in Kentucky. I was raised there, and my bishop felt I had a deeper under-standing of the people. I got a small roadside church in Letcher County.'

Roland Hannah shifted his weight in the chair. The shackles on his feet made a clinking sound that echoed off the old stone walls.

'You have to understand that these people are very poor,' he said. 'Their land — their very lives — had been raped by the coal compa-nies, the logging companies, the government. First they took the trees, then the coal, then the mountaintops themselves. These folks are skeptical of any organization, be it religious or secular.

'I did the best I could with what I had, which was very little. It is impossible to feed hungry children with just the Word. In time I became much more than just a minister to them.'

I'll bet, Jessica thought. She recalled Ida-Rae Munson's words:

He used to hand them missals out like candy. Used to hand out a lot more than that, if you was young and fair.

Roland leaned forward, continued. 'There was a woman of sixty who came to me one Sunday. She'd had a child at fifty-three, born out of wedlock, and believed the boy to be possessed by demons. And by this I do not mean the boy was violent or out of control in any earthly ways. She believed the boy was the devil *himself.*'

Both Jessica and Byrne remained silent.

'I observed the boy for three days in his home, and was both astounded and horrified by what I saw. I brought it to my bishop, who counseled prayer for the boy, but nothing more.'

'What did you do?' Jessica asked.

Roland leaned back, shifted his weight again. 'I returned to my ministry and told the woman there was nothing to be done. She fell to her knees and begged me to come back to her home one last time. She said that things had gotten worse.

'Of course I went. Once there, I found the child in swaddling, even though he was seven years old. The room was lit with oil lamps, and smelled of dead flowers and sulfur. She handed me the boy, and directed my hand to feel beneath the boy's thick, curly hair. I did as she asked.'

Jessica saw Roland run his hand along the scarred metal table top, perhaps searching for some sense memory. His fingers found the deep ruts in the surface.

'Do you know what I felt?' Roland asked.

'No,' Jessica said.

'Horns, detective. The boy had two small horns growing from his head.'

Roland Hannah bowed his head for a moment, mouthed what looked to be a silent prayer. When he finished he retuned to his tale.

'I performed the ritual, against the counsel of my bishop. It was a long, draining process, one that threatened my faith, as well as my life. But I believe something entered me that day, detective, something that exited that boy, who was just fine when I left him.' Roland Hannah knitted his fingers. 'Word spread over the county of this divine event. News was made in heaven, as they say. And even though I was just a boy myself, people knew I was possessed of the fire of the Spirit. The Holy Thunder Caravan was born that day.'

The room fell quiet for nearly a full minute. Jessica finally broke the silence.

'That's a very interesting story, Roland.'

'Praise Jesus.'

'*Very* interesting. But I'd like to talk about a different time in your life, if you don't mind.'

'Not at all,' Roland said. 'As you might imagine, I have nothing *but* time.'

'Let's talk about that tragedy to which you alluded before. Let's talk about the day your stepsister Charlotte and her friend Annemarie were murdered.'

The word *murdered* hovered in the air. Jessica remembered the case well. The two girls were brutally killed in Fairmount Park. Years later a great cop named Walter Brigham was destroyed by the investigation.

'Charlotte,' Roland said softly. 'If it's all the same to you, ma'am, I won't be talking about her.'

Jessica thought she detected a slight waver in the man's voice. It was maddening that she could not read his eyes, but it seemed she was rattling him. 'What *would* you like to discuss?' Jessica asked.

Roland Hannah smiled. 'You asked to see *me*, detective.'

Jessica shuffled a few papers, purely for Roland Hannah's benefit. 'Fair enough.' She pushed back her chair. The screech of metal on concrete was like a shout in the confined space. 'Let's talk about what happened five years ago, then. Let's talk about a string of very nasty murders in Philadelphia.'

Roland Hannah said nothing. His smile slowly disappeared.

'Let's start with a man named Edgar Luna, a man named Basil Spencer, and a man named Joseph Barber,' Jessica said. Edgar Luna, Basil Spencer, and Joseph Barber were three of Hannah's victims.

The blind man was silent for a long time. Outside a gust of wintry wind rattled a loose pane of glass. Finally, calmly, Roland Hannah spoke.

'I did not commit those vigilante murders of pedophiles years ago. I was framed for them, as I am being framed now.' He gestured to the room around them, a room he could not see. 'I am a blind man in prison. How could I be doing any of this?'

Jessica and Byrne both knew how this would play in court. It was not good for them.

'Then why did you confess?' Jessica asked.

'I was under a great deal of stress. I wanted it to be over. As you might imagine, I was traumatized over my affliction.'

Roland Hannah meant his blinding at the hands of another madman. Years after Charlotte's death Hannah had haunted the dark alleys of Philadelphia, looking for the man who had killed his stepsister. In the end, investigators believed Hannah thought himself an avenging angel, murdering anyone and everyone who was even suspected of pedophilia.

'I wonder if she still holds the rose,' Roland said.

'Excuse me?'

'Tell me about these killings.'

Jessica glanced at Byrne, and back at the prisoner. She knew Roland Hannah was trying to bait her, and she wasn't going to bite. As calmly as she could, she said: 'They are murders, not killings, Mr Hannah. Cold-blooded, pre-meditated murders.'

Roland Hannah nodded gravely, as if saddened by the news of violence. Jessica knew him to be a man without conscience, a killer who preyed on criminals, acting as judge, jury, and executioner.

When Hannah had confessed to three murders, investigators went to the burial sites. They found the bodies. As a matter of routine they collected hair and fiber evidence, as well as fingerprint and blood evidence, even though this material was never going to be used in court. With the possibility of a new trial on the horizon, the lab was now attempting to match forensic evidence found at those scenes with material collected at the current crime sites.

'From what I understand, the people being killed in your city – under your watch, I might add – are not the most savory characters,' Roland said. 'The people killed five years ago were just the same. Children of disobedience. Have you not considered that whoever committed those murders, framing me then, is doing the same thing now? Ridding the world of further sinners?'

'A baby was killed,' Jessica said. 'Are you saying she was a sinner?'

'Perhaps she had not yet been baptized.'

Jessica wanted to jump across the table. She calmed herself. For a few long moments she stared at Roland Hannah. All she saw was her own reflection in the dark lenses that masked his eyes.

'There is a lot of evil in the world, detective,' Roland added.

Spoken by a true expert, Jessica thought. 'Evil is pretty much my business, Roland.'

'As a man of the cloth, it is mine, too,' he countered. 'You may not know it, but I am pastor to many in here.'

'So, what are you saying? That this phantom killer is God's swift sword?'

No response.

'Do you want to tell me how you knew where those bodies were buried five years ago?' Jessica asked.

At this the door slammed open and James Tolliver entered.

'My client agreed to this interview as a courtesy to the district attorney of Philadelphia,' Tolliver said. 'Reverend Hannah felt it was his civic duty. Having done this duty, this interview is now over.'

A few moments later, without another word, a corrections officer entered the room, helped Roland Hannah to his feet, and the man was led from the room.

When he was gone Tolliver turned his attention back to Jessica and Byrne.

'I expect my client to be released into the custody of the Philadelphia County Sheriff later today. He will be held under house arrest, and undergo a psychiatric evaluation. If deemed competent, he will stand trial for the crimes he allegedly committed five years ago.'

'And the current crimes?' Byrne asked.

'I'm sorry,' Tolliver said. 'Have I missed something? Has my client been charged with new crimes?'

Byrne stepped forward. 'I know you don't come cheap, Mr Tolliver.'

Tolliver smiled as he buttoned his expensive coat. 'It's all relative, detective. I've never known a homicide cop to refuse overtime.'

'Roland Hannah doesn't have a penny.'

The lawyer said nothing.

'So who's paying you?' Byrne asked.

The lawyer smiled. 'There are two reasons I won't be answering that question.'

'And they are?'

'The first reason is that it is none of your business who is paying for my services. If, indeed, I am not here *pro bono*.'

'And the second reason?'

Tolliver opened the door, turned, and said, 'Now that you know the first, does it really matter?'

*

THE CORRECTIONS OFFICER BROUGHT out the box of personal effects. Until Roland Hannah was released, these materials were considered property of the Commonwealth, and therefore Jessica had jurisdiction, and the right, to examine them.

These were the things Roland Hannah had in his possession when he was arrested.

While Byrne made phone calls, alerting the bosses to what transpired, Jessica signed for the box, then took it to a small room next to the warden's office. There wasn't much to look through: dirty comb, a pair of used bus tickets, a battered wallet, a small wooden crucifix. Jessica opened the wallet. Inside was sixteen dollars, along with a page torn from the Bible. The 23rd Psalm.

Jessica opened the center of the wallet, lifted up the flap. Inside was a faded color photograph of a slender young girl, perhaps twelve or so. Behind the girl was a large truck. All Jessica could see was the beginning of the words painted on the side of the van, which looked to be HOLY and CARA. The girl held a flower in her hand.

Jessica flipped over the picture. On the back was a hand-written message.

DEAR MOMMA,
I'VE SEED SO MANY THINGS. THE OHIO RIVER IS BIG. I KNOW DADDY DIED OF HIS LUNGS, BUT HE WERENT GOING TO HURT ME. NOT REALLY. I KNOW THAT. I AM HAPPY NOW WITH THE PREACHER. I HAVE THE SPIRIT IN ME, AND I HOPE EVERYONE IS DOING GAYLY. LOVE ALL WAYS,
    RUBY LONGSTREET

I wonder if she still holds the rose, Roland Hannah had said.

He was talking about the girl in the photograph. Ruby. This was the red-haired girl Ida-Rae Munson had spoken of, the one who had taken up with a preacher.

A preacher named Roland Hannah.

She had a devil-child.

FORTY-THREE

B YRNE PARKED HIS CAR IN FRONT OF ST GEDEON'S. THE POSTERS announcing the upcoming demolition were affixed to the building itself, on the light poles, on the chain link fence that cordoned off the site. The building would be torn down in two days.

The knowledge filled Byrne with a deep sorrow. This had been the church of his youth. So much so that, in the neighborhood, they never called it St Gedeon's. It was just *church*. Byrne had been baptized here, confirmed here, had made his first holy communion here.

He remembered Father Leone standing on the steps on Sunday mornings, on the hottest days of August and the frigid days of February, saying goodbye to his flock, as well as noticing – and cataloguing – who didn't come to mass.

Byrne also remembered the call he had gotten that morning, the day Father Leone discovered The Boy in the Red Coat sitting in the last pew.

BYRNE HALF-RAN TO THE front doors of Villa Maria. The wind was bitterly cold and he had not brought a hat or a scarf or gloves with him.

As soon as the automatic doors opened he was greeted by the

institutional smells of disinfectant and cafeteria foods – most notably, creamed corn and applesauce. He was also welcomed by a blast of warm, humid air.

He walked to the front desk, blowing into his hands. The woman standing guard was not the same one he and Jessica had talked to. This woman was older. She had a round, pleasant face, bright henna-treated hair. Her plastic nametag read SANDI.

'Still cold out there?' she asked.

'Brutal.'

'How can I help you?'

'I'm here to see Father Leone. He's in 303.'

The woman just stared at him. She said nothing.

'Father Leone?' Byrne repeated. 'Father *Thomas* Leone?'

Still nothing, but now the woman began to worry the edge of the envelope in her hands.

'Old guy?' Byrne continued. 'Kind of a Spencer Tracy meets Dracula?'

'Are you a member of his family?'

Odd question, Byrne thought. But one fraught with peril. 'No,' he said. 'Just a friend.'

'Father Leone passed away last night.'

The words hit Byrne like a roundhouse punch. Yes, the man was in his nineties, in frail health, took a dozen medications a day, and was plugged into an oxygen tank. Still, Byrne was surprised. Father Leone was supposed to live forever. All priests were.

'I was just here. He seemed . . .' *Old and frail*, if the truth be told. But Byrne said it anyway. 'He seemed fine.'

'It happened during the night. I came on at six, and he had already passed,' the woman said. 'As to cause, I'm afraid I don't know. He didn't have any living brothers or sisters, so I don't think anyone is going to order an autopsy.'

Byrne suddenly felt hollowed out, as if his entire childhood had been torn away and discarded. The memories of his time at St Gedeon's came flooding back, the good and the bad, all of it shadowed by the recent, indelible image of Father Thomas Leone's slight shoulders in that cheap cardigan.

'If you want, you can call the morgue,' the woman said, taking a pen out of a cup on the desk, grabbing a scratch pad. 'The medical examiner's office is there, and when his body is transferred later today you could probably –'

'I'm a police officer,' Byrne said with a little more vitriol than he intended. He instantly regretted it. He backed off on his tone. 'I'm a city detective.'

The woman stopped writing on the pad. 'Your name wouldn't be Byrne, would it?'

'It would.'

'Detective Kevin Byrne?'

'Yes.' Byrne had no idea why she was asking. All he wanted to do was run as fast as he could out of this place of sickness, old age, and crippling illness, to put miles between himself and these thoughts of slow, lingering death.

'He left a package for you.'

'Father Leone did?'

'Yes,' she said. 'It was on his nightstand. It was addressed to you.'

'Do you have it?'

'I'm sorry,' the woman said. 'One of the volunteers here had an appointment near the Roundhouse. I sent it along with her. I didn't know you were coming.'

'Do you know what is in the package?'

Now the woman looked offended. She took a half-step back, started to cross her arms, stopped. She smoothed the front of her colorful floral smock, looked Byrne straight in the eyes. 'No,' she said. 'I didn't open it. It wasn't addressed to *me*.'

'I'm sorry,' Byrne said. 'That was rude of me.'

The woman's expression softened.

'Did you say he has not yet been transferred?'

'Not yet.'

'Would it be okay if I saw him?' Byrne asked. 'Just to . . .'

For some reason, the words *say goodbye* could not come out. It had been a long time since emotion stole his ability to speak.

'Sure,' Sandi said, picking up a phone. 'I'll have an attendant bring you down.'

'Thanks,' Byrne said. 'I won't be long.'

'You take your time. You just take your time.'

THE ROOM WAS ON the ground floor, near the back. Byrne walked in, closed the door behind him. The walls were bare, with a simple wooden crucifix over the bed.

The body beneath the sheet looked so small. How was this possible? Father Thomas Angelo Leone was a man who put the fear and grace of God into hundreds, if not thousands, of South Philly kids, a man who not only taught you to fight your battles inside the ring – with rules – but sometimes slipped on the 16-ounce gloves himself. Byrne recalled that there were a couple of pictures in the priest's house at St Gedeon's of 'Battling' Tommy Leone in his late-teens, clad in just-pressed satin trunks, sleek and muscular, the way only young men can be, giving his best John Garfield to the lens.

Now he was a small body under a sheet that had been washed so many times it was almost translucent. Byrne wondered if it had originally been blue or green. There was no way to tell.

Byrne steeled himself, took a deep breath, pulled back the sheet. It was an action he had performed many times in his career in homicide, but this was different. This was personal.

He looked down. Father Leone's old and weather-worn face was at peace, he thought.

Byrne closed his eyes for a moment, remembered his first confession. It had not occurred to him at the time – or to any of them for that matter, any of the rough-and-tumble kids in his class – that Father Leone knew them all by their voices, would forever know them by their sins.

Byrne opened his eyes, wondered what Father Leone's sins were, if the old man had gotten his last rites.

He took the old man's hand and –

– *saw the darkness rise up in front of him, a tidal wave of blackness so large it dwarfed the city of his birth, a wave given rise by* –

– The Boy in the Red Coat.

Byrne shook off the feeling, bent over, kissed the old man gently on his forehead. He covered the body, stepped into the hallway, closed the door. He put his hand on the glass pane. 'Rest well, Father,' he said. 'Rest well.'

By the time Byrne stepped back outside the temperature had dropped another few degrees. He looked up. Overhead, dark clouds gathered. That was okay with Byrne. The sun shouldn't shine on a day such as this.

IN THE PARKING LOT Byrne called in, got an update. The Crime Scene Unit had scoured every inch of St Ignatius's, checking for loose stones, unscrewing switch plates, overturning tiles. Bontrager said the team had found nothing that might point to the next crime scene, the next victim.

It had to be there, Byrne thought. He was sure of it.

He stood in the cold of the parking lot, letting the frigid air numb the grief he felt over the death of his old friend. It was still hard to believe.

What was in the package Father Leone had left him?

Byrne was just about to head back to the Roundhouse when his cell phone beeped. He took it out. It was an SMS message.

The message took a few moments to download, but when it did Byrne had to look twice to make sure he was seeing it right.

The text line read:

HOW U LIK ME NOW???!!!

Beneath the subject line was a photograph, a picture of a young boy tied to a chair. The boy's eyes were wide with fear. It was someone Byrne knew.

The message was from DeRon Wilson.

The boy in the chair was Gabriel Hightower.

FORTY-FOUR

J ESSICA KNEW SHE WOULD BE PULLING A DOUBLE TOUR, AND SINCE SHE didn't have time for even a power nap, she decided the next best thing was a workout.

By the time she gloved up she had put in thirty hard minutes on the treadmill and weights. She would be doing two rounds of sparring with her pal Valentine Rhames, who had consented to come in after her classes at Temple. Or kindergarten. Or whatever the hell it was she did during the day. As Jessica stepped into the ring she noticed that the skin of the young woman across from her was bone dry.

Oh, the arrogance of youth, Jessica thought.

The thought of youth brought Jessica's mind to Cecilia Rollins, and everything that the little girl would never know. She would never know her first kiss. She would never know her first heartbreak.

The fact that Roland Hannah would be walking out of Graterford any minute – granted, in the custody of a county detective – made Jessica even angrier.

The sound of the bell brought her back. Jessica moved to center ring, dropped her left shoulder. The feint drew the kid in, seeing the opportunity to launch a lead right hand. Jessica was perfectly positioned. She shifted her weight and threw a monstrous left hook. When she made contact she knew. It was like when baseball players catch the ball on the sweet spot. They don't even have to watch it go sailing over the fence. They *knew*.

Valentine Rhames dropped to the canvas.

Down. And. Out.

'Jesus Christ, Jess,' Joe Hand said, stepping into the ring. 'It's supposed to be a workout.'

Jessica walked to a neutral corner. A minute later Valentine's trainer had the girl seated on the stool, headgear off. Valentine was sweating, puffing hard, but fine.

Jessica bounced across the ring, looked into the young woman's dazed eyes, bumped gloves and said, 'Thanks for the workout, ma'am.'

Philadelphia, Jessica thought as she pulled off the gloves and headed for the shower, *don't fuck with me tonight*.

She stood at the counter at Starbucks, fixing her coffee, her mind a deadfall of thoughts about the case. It was one of the reasons she did not see the person who came up next to her. This was not good. She was distracted.

'All the best-looking women read the *Daily News*.'

She turned to the voice. It was a young man, twenties, well dressed, nice looking. He was pointing at Jessica's folded copy of the *News* on the counter.

'Oh, I don't read it,' Jessica said. 'I just use it to sneak my handguns onto the bus. Easier than using the *Inquirer*.'

The young man laughed. He put his coffee down, took off the lid, added two sugars. 'I have a little bit of a problem. Would it be terribly rude of me to ask your advice on something?'

'Not terribly,' Jessica said. 'Only somewhat.'

Another smile. 'Okay. Well. It's my daughter's birthday today. I have to get her something, and I'm totally clueless.' He took out his wallet, removed a picture. It was a photograph of a girl of about eight standing in front of Sacred Heart of Jesus school.

'She goes to Sacred Heart?' Jessica asked.

'Yes. It's the school over on –'

'Moyamensing. I know where it is.'

The young man looked at the photograph for a few more moments, put it away. 'Anyway, I've got to get her something. Any idea what she might like? Since the divorce she's been living with her mother and I'm a bit out of the loop.'

Jessica glanced at her watch. 'You know, I'd love to stay and chat, but I've got about ten minutes to get to Eighth and Race.'

'I could give you a ride, if you like.'

Jessica turned to face him fully. 'Could you now?'

He smiled, pointed to a car parked at a meter a few doors down the street. 'I'd be happy to. My car is right there. We could talk on the way.'

Jessica put the lid back on her coffee. 'You know, I usually don't ride with strange men, but I think I'll take you up on that offer.'

'I'm really not that strange,' he said. 'Promise.'

'I just need to hit the ATM next door. I'll be right back.'

'I'll be right here.'

Jessica hesitated. 'Damn.'

'What is it?'

'I was going to get a scone, but I forgot.' She fished around her jeans pocket. 'Could you get one for me?'

The young man held up a hand. 'I would be happy to. My treat.'

'You're a doll.'

Jessica grabbed her coffee and her copy of the *Daily News*. She walked out of the Starbucks, made a right turn, skirting pedestrian traffic. By the time she reached the ATM machine she had the knife in her hand.

FORTY-FIVE

Sʜᴀɴᴇ Aᴅᴀᴍs sᴛᴏᴏᴅ ᴏɴ ᴛʜᴇ sɪᴅᴇᴡᴀʟᴋ, ʜᴀɴᴅs ᴏɴ ʜɪs ʜɪᴘs. Hɪs right front tire was flat. Nᴏᴛ low, *flat*. Even from a few feet away he could see the neat slice in the side.

On the way to examine the tire situation a little more closely he looked at the windshield. Underneath one of the wipers was what appeared to be a business card. Shane picked it up, looked at it. The front of the card read:

Dᴇᴛᴇᴄᴛɪᴠᴇ Jᴇssɪᴄᴀ Bᴀʟᴢᴀɴᴏ
Pʜɪʟᴀᴅᴇʟᴘʜɪᴀ Pᴏʟɪᴄᴇ Dᴇᴘᴀʀᴛᴍᴇɴᴛ, Hᴏᴍɪᴄɪᴅᴇ Dɪᴠɪsɪᴏɴ

He flipped the card over. There was a message written on the back in blue ink:

Shane: Your meter's expired. I called PPA. Don't worry, the ticket should't be more than $40. Enjoy the scone! P.S.: She might like a subscription to Muse.

Shane Adams looked both ways, up and down Walnut Street. Jessica Balzano was, of course, gone. He was just about to walk around his car to the trunk, and his spare, when he sensed a presence to his left.

He spun around. There, standing at the back of his car, was a Philadelphia Parking Authority officer.

Jessica Balzano wasn't kidding. In addition to the flat tire, he was getting a ticket.

Fucking *bitch*.

FORTY-SIX

WHEN JESSICA ARRIVED AT THE ROUNDHOUSE THE DESK OFFICER pointed to a woman standing on the other side of the lobby holding a large white envelope in her hands. The woman, Jessica was told, had asked for Kevin, who no one, including Jessica, seemed to be able to reach. The duty officer said she told the woman that she could just leave the package, that it would be safe, but the woman was adamant, and insisted on waiting for Kevin.

Jessica crossed the room, introduced herself.

'I'm Detective Byrne's partner. How can I help you?'

The woman was clearly distraught about something. 'They said he wasn't here.'

'No,' Jessica said. 'He's on assignment. But maybe I can help you.'

The woman turned the nine by twelve envelope over in her hands. She remained silent.

'If you have something for Detective Byrne, I'd be happy to pass it along to him.'

'Well, I guess it would be okay to give it to you.'

Jessica took the envelope from the woman, glanced at it. It was addressed to Detective Kevin Byrne in a very shaky hand. The logo in the upper left hand corner was familiar. It belonged to Villa Maria.

'I don't understand,' Jessica said. 'Who is this from exactly?'

'I'm so sorry.'

This was getting stranger by the second, Jessica thought. 'I'm afraid I don't know what you mean. Sorry about what?'

'About Father Leone.'

'What about him?'

The woman started to tear up. 'He passed away. I thought you knew.'

Jessica felt the air leave the room. The sweet old man she had just met, the man who had occupied such an important part of Kevin Byrne's past, was now gone. 'May I ask what happened?'

The woman reached into her tote bag, brought out a lace hand-kerchief. She dabbed her eyes. 'He passed away in the night. He wanted Detective Byrne to have whatever is in the envelope. I mean, I know he was old, and in poor health, but it's still a shock to me. Especially after Detective Byrne's visit. I've never seen Father Leone so happy, so energized. Whatever Detective Byrne said to him meant a lot.'

ON THE WAY UPSTAIRS Jessica tried calling Byrne again. She got his voicemail. Sometimes it was absolutely infuriating the way he would turn off his phone when he was on duty. She texted him a *call me immediately* message, then paged him for good measure.

Jessica sat at her desk, still reeling from the encounter in the lobby. Sometimes it seemed like she was constantly surrounded by death. She sifted through her message slips. Nothing pressing. Before she could return a call her cell phone rang in her hand. It was Maria Caruso.

'Hi, Maria.'

'Looks like we'll be working together tonight.'

'You talked to the boss?'

'Yeah. Dana said Kevin called in sick. I'll lay it out when I see you. We're on surveillance duty.'

Sick? Jessica didn't buy it. Something was up. She decided to try Byrne again as soon as she hung up with Maria. 'Where are you?'

Maria told her.

'I'll be there in twenty minutes.'

*

THEIR FIRST ASSIGNMENT WAS staking out St Barnabas's, a closed church in North Philly. The building had a recessed central pavilion flanked by a pair of tall, arched windows. It was a smaller version of St Augustine's, the historic church designed by Nicholas Fagan.

When Jessica and Maria arrived they parked on Fourth Street, did a quick visual inspection of the exterior and the grounds. The doors were locked and chained, the windows intact. By the time they returned to the car, and settled in, it was dark.

THE TEMPTATION DURING A stakeout, especially at night, was to drink a gallon of coffee, but that always meant being near a bathroom. It was one thing for male detectives, quite another for females. For now Jessica and Maria set up with high-sugar treats, small binoculars, and plenty of time.

Josh Bontrager, Dre Curtis, and Bobby Tate were all within a seven block radius, along with another dozen detectives from both the Fugitive and Special Investigation Unit squads. All sector cars, city-wide, were on alert to double up their patrols in and around the closed churches.

'YOU GUYS HAVE BEEN partners a long time,' Maria said. 'You and Kevin.'

Although homicides were assigned to a single detective, and there were no departmental rules that said you had to work with a specific partner – or any partner at all, Jessica could name a half-dozen detectives who were so ornery or sloppy in their work habits that they worked mostly alone – most detectives found another one in the unit and gravitated toward that person.

'Yeah,' Jessica said. 'About seven years now.'

As soon as she said *seven years* it hit her that time was really passing. Her first case was the Rosary Killer, and now she was on another case to which the underpinnings and tenets of the Catholic Church were undeniably connected.

'I never really thought I would get here,' Maria said.

'You mean the Homicide Unit?'

'Yeah. The clock never stops, does it?'

Jessica thought back to her first harrowing days in the unit. If it hadn't been for Byrne she probably wouldn't have lasted six months. Who was she kidding? More like six *weeks*. 'No,' she said. 'It really doesn't.'

'I worked a case, three months ago. The kid on that playground in Point Breeze.'

Jessica knew the case. A nine-year-old boy was the victim of a drive by shooting. 'I remember,' she said. 'That was a bad one.'

'*Oh*, yeah. I had to do the notification. It was my first. I was a total wreck.'

Jessica recalled her first notification as a homicide detective. The victim's name was Tessa Ann Wells. 'I'm sure you did just fine.'

'I don't know about that. The mother went absolutely crazy. I mean, it's understandable and everything – she'd just lost her boy. But I kept thinking that if I had worded it a little differently, or taken another approach, maybe it would have gone a little better.'

'There are only so many words,' Jessica said. 'All you can do is be there for them.'

Maria looked out the window for a few moments. 'I wasn't there when they arrested the kid who did the shooting. Fugitive squad took him down.' Maria toyed with the string that hung from her hoodie. 'I heard they had to draw their weapons. Not sure how I would have handled that.'

Jessica thought about the times she had pointed her weapon at another human being. Most people – with the aid of more than fifty years of television police shows – thought the process was easy, or at least not that difficult. Many believed a police officer could wound or kill a person, then go out to dinner, take a shower, watch a little TV, then hit the sack. Nothing could be further from the truth. It was life-changing. She'd known officers – stable, psychologically sound, family men – who never came back after firing their weapons.

'You make the call, and remember your training,' Jessica said. 'It's all you can do.'

As soon as the words left her mouth Jessica realized what she sounded like. She sounded like the grizzled old veteran giving words of advice to the fresh young rookie.

When the hell had that happened?

AT TEN O'CLOCK THEY rotated to the third church on their list, St Simeon's on Germantown Avenue. A large gothic brownstone with a soaring spire, St Simeon's had been closed for five years. According to their information, the building had recently been sold to a developer from San Diego.

A number of streetlights were out on this stretch of Germantown, which provided the detectives with a small amount of cover. Jessica and Maria parked a half-block away from the church, cocooned in shadow. From their vantage point they could see the south side and rear of the building.

Since the widespread media coverage of the murders had begun, the AV Unit had installed, or was in the process of installing, new pole cameras near the closed churches. It was a slow and expensive undertaking.

Because of his prowess with all things AV, Sergeant Mateo Fuentes was heading up the task force within the task force. He and two other officers from AV were dedicated to monitoring these cameras. They had a dozen in place, with more than a dozen to go. Teams were going to work all night.

TEN MINUTES AFTER THE detectives set up position a car pulled to the curb a half-block behind them. Inside a figure settled in, and watched the watchers.

FORTY-SEVEN

THE EGG'S NEST WAS A COP BAR IN THE NORTHEAST, LOCATED ON Roosevelt Boulevard and Revere Street. The crowd was sparse, mostly married cops and state troopers with their girlfriends, eyes flicking to the front door every time it opened.

Byrne took a high-top at the back, ordered a double Bushmills straight. He thought about what brought him to this place, and what he was about to do.

At ten o'clock Vincent Balzano walked in wearing a leather jacket, black T shirt, jeans, motorcycle boots. He shared a few pleasantries and laughs with the cops at the bar. Vincent then leaned in and gave his order to the barmaid, made his way back.

'Thanks for coming, Vince.'

'Any time, brother.'

The waitress brought Vincent's beer, and a second Bushmills for Byrne. The two men clinked glasses.

'*Sláinte*,' Byrne said.

'Better days,' Vincent said. He sipped from his beer, put it down, interlaced his fingers. 'How can I help?'

Byrne glanced around at the other patrons. They were mostly cops, but even so he had to be careful with what he had to say. 'You know a dealer named DeRon Wilson?'

'*Know* him? We've been trying to bury that motherfucker for five years.'

'You heard about my little problem on the news?'

'I did.'

Byrne told him the specifics, including the detail that it was Wilson he had braced.

'I had no idea it was him,' Vincent said. 'Sorry to hear you're jammed up over that piece of shit.'

'Thanks.'

'What do you need?'

Byrne lowered his voice. 'I need to find him.'

Vincent Balzano was a veteran detective, not only of the streets, but specifically North Philadelphia. If you were a narcotics cop, there were few places in the country tougher to work.

'I'm not going to ask you why, but I need to know what I'm calling in,' Vincent said.

'I understand.'

Byrne told Vincent about Gabriel Hightower. He showed him the picture on his cell phone.

Vincent took a few seconds to rein back his anger. He drained his beer. 'I know all of his KAs, but I don't think they're going to give him up,' he said. 'He's got a few stash houses, though. Let me make a call.'

Vincent took his cell from his jeans, stepped out of the bar. Five minutes later he was back. He didn't sit down. 'Nobody's saying where DeRon is holed up, but I reached out to a detective in North. He said he thinks DeRon has been staying with his girlfriend. He's got triplets with her.'

'*Jesus*. There's three more of him?'

Vincent laughed. 'I think they're girls. Word is this girlfriend lives in Juniata Park, but nobody knows exactly where. The good news is that DeRon's brother Carter is going to make a drop tonight.'

'Do we know where?'

'I'm waiting on that text right now.'

'And this Carter is going to give his brother up?'

'Carter likes to pose, but he's no hardass,' Vincent said. 'If we find him, I'll turn him.'

Byrne downed his shot, looked over both shoulders. Even though there was no one in earshot, he still lowered his voice. 'You might need to go off the reservation here, Vince.'

'How far off?'

'Like, maybe, Cleveland.'

Vincent's phone buzzed. He checked the text, zipped his jacket, grabbed his car keys, and said, 'I've always liked Cleveland this time of year. Let's do this thing.'

FORTY-EIGHT

S HANE ADAMS SAT WATCHING THE TWO WOMEN IN THE CAR, HIS heart racing.

He had changed the tire in short order – he had learned to change a tire as a boy out of necessity, his mother didn't know a lug wrench from a pipe wrench – and was back on the road in fifteen minutes.

He had to hand it to Detective Balzano. She was sharp. He should have known that he was getting played. He had spent only an hour or so going through the trash behind their rowhouse in South Philly. He knew that both Jessica and her husband Vincent were cops, which meant that there were probably a half-dozen weapons in the house, and he didn't fancy getting shot to death in a pile of garbage.

He did learn a few things from Jessica Balzano's trash. He learned that Jessica's daughter went to Sacred Heart of Jesus, and he had hoped this might be a point of entry for him. He'd found the picture of an eight year old in someone's trash a year earlier, having no idea if or how he was going to use it. He'd then found a picture of Sacred Heart online and, with a little bit of effort, was able to PhotoShop the girl in front of it. It was a passable ruse behind the scuffed plastic laminate in his wallet.

Or maybe not. It seemed the detective had made him from the start.

She would not give him the slip again.

SHANE HAD BEEN DOING things like this – shadowing cops, politicians, judges – his entire career. Although it wasn't technically illegal, he was walking the thin line between journalism – or at least what passed for journalism these days – and interfering with a criminal investigation.

But, as the saying went, it was easier to get forgiveness than it was to get permission.

The streets around this part of North Philly were mostly empty at this hour. The occasional car passed by. Each time Shane lowered himself slightly in the seat. Just because the two detectives in the car a block ahead of him were facing the other way didn't mean they couldn't see what was happening around the area. Shane Adams was pretty good at covert surveillance, but cops, especially homicide cops, were experts.

St Simeon's. He looked it up on his smart phone, but couldn't find much information about it, except that it had been closed for a long time.

Shane lifted the opera glasses, scanned the area. Nothing moving. The two detectives were just sitting, watching the church. It was mind-numbingly boring work, but he knew they were watching the church because they thought something might happen there. The very idea was intoxicating.

Shane Adams was actually at a crime scene *before the fact.*

He could barely breathe. In fact, he had left the station so quickly, following the two detectives, he had forgotten to stop for food. And he had most definitely forgotten to take a leak. Ten cups of coffee without a pit stop.

He checked the immediate area. He saw no one. He eased open his door, ran around the back of his car, then a few feet into an alleyway between a burned-out rowhouse and a closed rib shack. He unzipped, and relieved himself.

Before emerging from the alley he looked both ways. No traffic. The two detectives were still silhouetted in their car up the street. In his earpiece he heard no new police-scanner activity.

He crouched low, circled his car, slipped inside. Nothing like the pause that refreshes, he thought. He felt a million percent better.

Except that he was starving. He reached over, opened the glove compartment. There he found a half-dozen unpaid tickets, the car's owner's manual, a pair of nail clippers. Clippers were an essential part of the reporter's tool kit. If you gripped a microphone on camera, your nails mattered. Shane was hoping for a stale protein bar, a half-eaten bag of pork rinds, something.

Maybe in the backseat, he thought. Sometimes he left half-eaten Subway sandwiches when a story called. He got up on his knees, spun around.

And came face to face with a killer.

'Shane Adams reporting,' the killer said with a smile.

Shane felt a pinprick on the side of his neck. It felt exactly like the time he had been hit with a pellet from a BB gun when he was six years old. But this was no BB. Within seconds he felt his legs fail him, then his arms.

As the warmth spread over him, through him, he felt the waters of the Ohio River, heard his mother's voice calling him to supper. But it wasn't his mother's stern voice, it was the darkness itself beckoning with a final call:

'It seems you have one more story to tell.'

FORTY-NINE

THE BUILDING WAS A TWENTY-FOUR-STORY HIGH-RISE NEAR THE corner of Fourth and Washington. It was one of the few remaining old high-rise buildings in the area. It had recently been converted into a senior living facility. On the way over, Vincent explained to Byrne that one of DeRon Wilson's dodges was to use the place as a stash house. He said Wilson's grandmother had passed away in 2009, but Wilson kept the place.

At nine o'clock Carter Wilson left the building, and headed down Fourth Street to his car. He rounded the corner and was just about to open the door when two men walked up behind him. Instinctively Carter's hand went to the 9mm pistol in his belt.

Vincent Balzano stopped him.

WHERE DERON WILSON WAS small and wiry, Carter Wilson was of average height, but flabby. Too much junk food, too much sampling of the product. Vincent easily pushed the man to the top of the dead-end alley.

'You know who I am?' Vincent asked.

Nothing. Just Carter Wilson's version of a jailhouse stare.

'Coulda *swore* I asked you a question,' Vincent added.

'I know who you are.'

'Good,' Vincent said. 'That saves me a lot of time.'

Carter nodded in Byrne's direction. 'Who's that?'

'Him? He's the angel of fucking death, Carter. Believe me, you don't want to deal with him.'

Carter continued to stare at Byrne.

'Time to look at me,' Vincent said.

Carter took a half-second too long to follow directions. Vincent turned Carter roughly around, slammed him into the wall. He emptied the man's pockets, put the contents onto the top of a fifty-gallon drum, one of three in the alley: a few dollars, some loose change, car keys, an empty condom wrapper, a cell phone, and a disposable lighter.

'Put your hands down and turn around,' Vincent said.

Carter slowly did as he was told.

'Where are you coming from?' Vincent asked.

'The store.'

'Oh yeah? Which store is that?'

'I don't know, man.'

'You don't *know*? You were just there, how could you not know? Are you talking about that Rite-Aid on the corner?'

'Yeah, yeah. That's the one'

'There's no Rite-Aid up there.'

Carter shook his head. 'Man. Why you *playin'* me like this?'

Vincent smiled. 'I'm not playing, Carter. Truth is, we have somewhere to be. Do you know where we're going?'

Carter remained silent.

'That was a question,' Vincent said.

'How would I know where y'all going?'

'We're going to see your brother.'

Carter pulled a face, like he'd never heard the word before. 'My *brother*?'

'Yeah. Your real brother, not your play brother, or your cousin-brother. The one called DeRon. We can't seem to locate him.'

'Did you try his house?'

'Damn,' Vincent said. He looked over at Byrne, and back. 'Why didn't *I* think of that? Yeah. We tried his house, Carter. We also hit all his spots, all his corners, so we're pretty sure the word is out that we want to have a little chat with him. That's why we came to you, my man.'

Stone cold silence.

'Okay. Look. I'm not going to insult your intelligence – such as it is – by asking you the question again.'

Vincent reached into his jacket pocket with one leather-gloved hand and pulled out a neatly wrapped package, a clear plastic baggie of what looked like two ounces of cocaine. He handed it to Carter, who took it.

'What's this?'

'It's yours,' Vincent said. 'I just found it on you when I patted you down.'

Everything seemed to hit Carter all at once. Instead of flailing, railing, or running, he seemed to implode. He just stood there, wide-eyed and shocked. Vincent took the package back.

'That ain't *mine*, man!'

'Of course it is. Got your prints all over it. And with your record, I'm pretty sure you're looking at federal time.'

Vincent tossed Byrne the keys to Carter's car. Byrne opened the trunk, found a zippered canvas pouch, opened it. Inside was what looked like thirty or forty thousand dollars.

'Oh, Carter, Carter,' Vincent said. 'We add that money into the mix and you are looking at a deep, dark hole.'

Carter started to vibrate. Byrne had seen it many times. It was the involuntary muscle reflex that always preceded supersonic felony flight. Carter was getting ready for liftoff.

Vincent casually pulled back the hem of his leather jacket. There in a holster was a massive .45 auto. 'Feel free to run.'

'Why, man? Why you doin' this?'

'Because I need your brother, and I need him now.'

'I don't –'

'Done fucking with you.' Vincent pulled his weapon, cocked the hammer, put it to Carter's right kneecap. 'You've now got ten seconds.'

'Elbow,' Byrne said.

Vincent looked over. 'Elbow?'

'Yeah,' Byrne said. 'If you shoot them in the elbow, they can still walk. Hurts like a motherfucker, but we won't have to carry him down to the river.'

'*The river?*' Carter yelled

'Good point,' Vincent said. He turned back to Carter. 'You now have *two* seconds.'

'Wait!' Carted said. 'I page him. Then he texts me back with the place I gotta go.'

Vincent took a moment, then picked up the disposable cell phone. 'This is the phone he texts you on?'

'Yeah.'

'And he doesn't call, or leave a voicemail?'

'No,' Carter said. 'He don't want his voice on nothin'.'

'Who else has this number?'

'Nobody. Just DeRon.'

'Page him.' Hands shaking, Carter did as he was told. Twenty seconds later, as promised, a text message came across the screen. It was an address.

'See how easy that was?' Vincent asked.

Carter said nothing.

Vincent tossed the cell phone to Byrne. Carter opened his mouth to protest, but thought better of it.

'We can't have you tipping your brother now, can we?' Vincent said.

'I ain't gonna call him.'

'Promise?'

'Yeah.'

Vincent laughed. He turned the man around, muscled him over to the open trunk.

'Get in,' Vincent said.

'What the *fuck*, man? I *tole* you where he is.'

'I know,' Vincent said. 'And on behalf of the entire PPD let me say that we really appreciate your cooperation. Now get in the fucking trunk.'

Reluctantly, Carter got in the trunk. Before Vincent slammed it shut, he took the baggie out of his pocket. 'I'll just put this in the back seat.'

'You can't leave that out like that!' Carter yelled. 'What if the cops come by?'

'If they do you can make them some pancakes,' Vincent said. 'It's Bisquick, asshole.'

Vincent slammed the trunk lid, threw Carter's keys into a sewer.

Ten seconds later the two detectives headed to North Philly.

FIFTY

THE VOICE ON THE HANDSET BELONGED TO JOSH BONTRAGER. WHEN Jessica heard it she nearly jumped.

'Jess,' Bontrager said. 'Please tell me you're on radio.'

Jessica keyed her handset. 'I'm here,' she said. 'What is it, Josh?'

'I've got Mateo on my cell. He's monitoring the camera behind St Simeon's.'

Jessica glanced over at Maria Caruso. They had been lulled into that torpor that happens when you stare at something so long you no longer see it. It was a common – and dangerous – malady that occurred on long stakeouts.

'What about it?' Jessica asked.

'He's got activity behind your church.'

This got Jessica's undivided attention. She took her phone from her pocket, put it on silent. If there was something coming down, it would be better to do this off police band. 'Have him call me.'

A few seconds later Jessica's phone vibrated. 'What do we have, Mateo?'

'I'm not sure,' he said. 'I've got a shadow on the wall behind the north side of the church. Someone just walked up that alley and stopped.'

'Shadow?' Jessica asked. 'As in one person?'

'Yes,' Mateo said. 'Can you see any of the north side?'

'No,' she said. 'I'm out of position.'

'Hang on,' Mateo said. 'I have more movement. Whoever it is is heading for the north side entrance to the church. I'm going to lose him in a few seconds.'

'Is Sergeant Westbrook there?' Jessica asked.

'I'm here,' Westbrook said. Mateo had the phone on speaker.

'Do you want us to check it out?' Jessica asked.

'Yes,' Westbrook said. 'I'm sending backup. Stay on radio.'

Jessica kept her cell on silent, stuffed it in her jeans pocket. She and Maria got out of the car, circled back to the trunk. Jessica opened it, and both women slipped on Kevlar vests. Simultaneously they unsnapped their holsters, checked the action on their Glock 17s, reholstered.

Jessica looked both ways, up and down the street. There was an older compact car parked a half block away, but she saw no one in it.

She glanced at her watch. It was 10.20.

Detectives Jessica Balzano and Maria Caruso crossed the street, and headed to the alleyway behind St Simeon's.

FIFTY-ONE

W HEN BYRNE ARRIVED AT THE ADDRESS HE HAD GOTTEN ON CARTER'S cell phone, he realized he had not formulated a plan on what he would do when he found DeRon Wilson.

His prayer was that nothing had happened to Gabriel. Byrne knew that, if not for his own involvement with the boy, none of this would be happening. *No*, he amended. If it wasn't for Kevin Byrne's *temper*, none of this would be happening. He knew it as he was walking down that hallway that night, knew it when Wilson gave him that defiant look – a look he had seen a million times before on the job – knew it when he stupidly drew his weapon. Granted, he didn't expect it to be splashed all over the nightly news, but that was no excuse.

He had dealt with the DeRon Wilsons of the world for more than twenty-five years. Why did he lose it so completely this time?

Vincent had wanted to come with him, to see this thing through to the end, but Byrne had cut him loose. He had no idea how bad this would get, and there was a good chance things were about to escalate. Vincent Balzano had done him a solid, and Byrne didn't want to thank him by putting Vincent's career in jeopardy. There would come a moment – there always did in police work – when Byrne would be there for him.

Before he could enter the building he felt a phone vibrate, a call coming in. Byrne fished the phone out of his pocket. It was not his own cell phone, but rather the cell phone he had gotten from Carter Wilson.

Who else has this number?

Nobody. Just DeRon.

Byrne checked the screen. It was a voicemail. He hit the appropriate buttons.

After a few seconds, the message played. The whispering voice made Kevin Byrne's blood run cold.

'*One God, detective,*' the disembodied voice on the other end of the line said. '*Seven churches.*'

A second later he got a text on the same phone. It read:

IF YOU ENTER THE BUILDING THE BOY WILL DIE.

For a few seconds Byrne could not move. He drew his weapon, glanced around, overhead. He could be observed from a hundred different vantage points.

He put the phone in his pocket, turned on his heels, and ran.

FIFTY-TWO

WHEN JESSICA AND MARIA ROUNDED THE CORNER, INTO THE alleyway behind St Simeon's, they saw no one. Weapons drawn, they found a door into the church, the glass in it broken, slightly ajar. Jessica kicked open the door.

The nave of the church was empty. It looked to have been recently cleaned. All the pews were gone, the altar had been dismantled, even the confessionals removed.

Jessica and Maria made their way slowly across the empty space. They passed through the church and found a doorway leading to stairs.

They still-hunted down the steps into the basement, their weapons over their Maglites, one tread at a time. If the killer was waiting for them, he would see the light. It was extremely risky, but there was no choice. The basement was pitch black.

'Listen,' Jessica whispered. The two detectives stopped, held their breath.

It was the sound of water dripping.

When they reached the bottom of the stairs, there was a large empty room in front of them. Jessica scanned the walls to the right. There was only one other doorway. If there was a body in this basement, it would be in that room.

'Jess,' Maria said. She pointed to the floor. There in the dust were smudged footprints, as well as two long lines which appeared to have been made by someone or something being dragged.

Sirens rose in the distance. Jessica and Maria could not wait. They walked quickly over to the far wall. There was no choice but to announce themselves.

'Philadelphia Police!' Jessica yelled. The sound of her voice echoed off the stone. No reply. They inched closer and closer to the opening, weapons and flashlights held high, leveled.

When they got to the opening Jessica paused. She took a deep breath, exhaled. Her breath was silvery and vaporous in front of her.

The basement, she thought.

She spun into the doorway. In the other room she saw a body hanging from an I-beam in the center of the ceiling. The victim was a light-skinned black male. He was nude, awash with blood. On the floor beneath him, as with the other victims, was a pile of clothes. But what made this sight horrifying beyond Jessica's grasp was what else lay on the floor beneath the victim.

Hands. The killer had cut off the victim's hands. It wasn't dripping water they had heard. It was dripping blood.

The two detectives stepped fully into the room, turned 360°. The room was clear.

Outside, they heard the sector cars arrive.

'Set up a perimeter,' Jessica said. 'And get me two patrol officers down here.'

Without a word, Maria Caruso holstered her weapon and ran out of the room. As Jessica heard her footsteps heading up the steps, she walked forward. She put on a latex glove, gently lifted the victim's chin and shone her light in his face.

'Oh my God.'

The hanging man was DeRon Wilson, the drug dealer with whom Byrne had his run in. Jessica's phone vibrated in her pocket. She answered. It was Mateo Fuentes.

'What's up Mateo?'

'Talk to me, detective.'

'What do you mean?'

'Do you have the suspect?'

'No,' Jessica said. 'We're just setting up a perimeter. We couldn't have missed him by much.'

'Did Detective Byrne get a good look at him?'

At first, Jessica thought she'd heard wrong. She had not. 'What do you mean?'

'Who are you partnered with?'

'Detective Caruso,' Jessica said. 'Why?'

'I thought you were out with Kevin.'

'Why would you think that?'

Another long pause. *Way* too long.

'Mateo.'

'Because I'm looking at footage from a minute ago. Footage taken from the north side of St Simeon's.'

'What about it?'

'It's Detective Byrne,' Mateo said. 'And he's running away from the church.'

Byrne stood in his apartment. He knew it might be the last time he saw any of these things. He knew it was possible that this would be the last night of his life.

He had walked into so many apartments and houses in his time in homicide, places to which the victims had every intention of returning – five minutes, five hours, five days later.

The way victims left things always got to him. The bathrobe on the back of the chair, the steak defrosting in the sink, the unfolded laundry in the basket, the bookmarked book.

How would they look at his place? he wondered. Would it be Jessica? In so many ways, he hoped it would. She would understand.

The seven churches of Asia, all in Turkey. It was no coincidence.

He remembered hearing the story as if it were yesterday.

We were stationed in Incirlik, part of the 628th Airlift Support. This was between the wars, so things weren't too crazy, right?

Now, what you have to remember is that the antiquities black market is off the charts in Turkey, or at least it was back then. There's Persian, Roman, Greek antiquities. Stuff from the Crusades. If you want it, and you have the green, someone will find it for you.

So we get a little R & R, and my best buddy in the unit wants to take a ride to this place called Pasli. Four of us head out, taking the Persian Road south, then off road for hours. Up and down these dirt roads. Nothing. It's almost sundown now, and we're not going to find it. We see this old guy walking up one of the back roads. Had to be ninety and change.

My buddy talks a little Turkish to him, and the guy points at his feet. My buddy says something about shoes, getting him new shoes, but the guy shakes his head. He points at his feet again. This goes on for awhile, back and forth. Dead end.

On the way back to the Jeep my buddy stops, jumps up and down a few times. He suddenly realizes what the old man was saying. The place we were looking for was right under us. The ground was hollow.

We make our way down this cliff, and come upon this old door. Thick old door bolted right into the rock. For the rest of the night my buddies try to shoulder the thing open. No luck. I didn't want anything to do with it, but you know how it is. You get enough booze in you and you'll do anything.

Just before dawn, with my buddies passed out, I thought I'd give it a shot. I go down there, and I just touch the door, and it opens. All I did was touch it.

Inside was this big room, carved right out of the mountain. I run my flashlight around, and I see what I figure is dust. Big balls of dust. Or maybe it was rocks. But it wasn't. You know what it was? It was skeletons, man. Little *skeletons. A whole room full of them. They were all placed neatly, side by side.*

At that moment something happened inside me, Kevin. I think I actually heard my heart change. I fell to my knees, and I tried to cry, but nothing came out. Believe me, it came out later. Almost every day since. But then, in the middle of this night, I had to ask myself why. I don't mean why they did it, whoever did it. I mean, why did the door open for me?

One hundred dead children. God doesn't put that in front of you for no reason, does He? No way.

I came back stateside, bummed around for two years, drank too much. I knew I wasn't smart enough to become a doctor or a lawyer or anything. So I decided to become a cop. How else could I do good, man?

How else could I do good?

*

MARCUS HAINES HAD LOOKED at Byrne that night, asking the question.

How else could I do good?

A few days later Marcus Haines stepped in front of another door. Byrne remembered the burst of automatic-weapon fire, recalled the red mist that was the back of Marcus Haines's head.

This time the door wasn't in Turkey but rather a North Philly hellhole, a place where children were made slaves to a drug called crack cocaine. Marcus Haines had finally found the door where the souls of another hundred children lay, and had taken a bullet meant for Kevin Byrne.

How do you repay a debt like that?

Byrne picked up the picture of Marcus, then took Gabriel's school photograph out of his pocket. He held them side by side. Marcus looked so much like Gabriel, the son he never lived to know. Byrne recalled that night with Tanya Wilkins, how he had hit her. She had been pregnant with Gabriel at that moment. He hadn't known then.

Byrne took out his cell, made the call. The woman answered in two rings.

'Do you know who this is?' Byrne asked.

'Yes,' she said. 'We've been expecting your call.'

'We?'

'My son and I.'

Byrne said nothing.

'God chooses us for a reason,' the woman said. 'Are you ready?'

'I'm ready.'

There was a moment of silence. Then, 'Do you know what you must do?'

'I do.'

'It has all led to this moment. Do you feel the weight of providence?'

More than you know, Byrne thought. 'Yes. But there's something I need first.'

'I am listening.'

Byrne told her what he needed. The woman agreed to get it for him.

'Do you want to know where we will be?' she asked.

'I know where you'll be. I just don't know how long it will take me to get there.'

'We are patient.'

'Expect me.'

Byrne clicked off, sent Jessica a text message. He put his cell phone on his dining-room table, next to his service weapon and his badge.

How else could I do good, man?

Kevin Byrne knew.

FIFTY-FOUR

J ESSICA COULD NOT FIND BYRNE. SHE TRIED EVERY CELL, LANDLINE, pager number, text. Nothing. She had not told Maria of Mateo's call – indeed, Jessica had asked Mateo to keep it to himself as long as he could. She couldn't ask him to lie or erase the footage of Kevin, but Mateo was a stand up cop, and agreed to follow her lead on this. He promised not to say anything. For the moment.

St Simeon's was now crowded with personnel. Jessica had seen the look on Dana Westbrook's face when she pulled up, and it wasn't good. Their killer had committed a crime, right under the noses of two detectives, and this would not play out well with the media.

Jessica decided to worry about the wrath of her boss later. Her immediate concern was Kevin Byrne.

What had he been doing at the church?

Jessica walked out of St Simeon's. Her phone rang. It was Maria. 'Yeah, Maria.'

'I'm checking the cars on the street. There's a compact car about a half-block from your location.'

Jessica recalled the car from when she entered the church. 'What about it?'

'It looks like we've got a second victim.'

'There's a *body* in that car?'

'Yeah.'

'He's DOA?'

'Oh, he is definitely DOA. There's something on the seat next to him you should see, though.'

Jessica jogged down the alley, turned the corner. She saw Maria a half-block away, standing near the car. She walked the remaining distance, thinking there was no need to run. A DOA tended to stay dead.

When she arrived she looked in the driver's window. The victim was a white male, late-twenties, early-thirties. His head was back on the headrest. A thin trickle of vomit leaked from the corners of his mouth. Jessica shone her Maglite into the car.

'Ah, Christ,' she said.

'What? You know him?'

'His name is Shane Adams. He's a reporter. He tried to shadow me earlier today.'

Jessica ran her Maglite around the inside of the car. The backseat was full of junk, the kind of stuff you'd have if you lived half your life inside your car – extra clothing, fast-food trash, Handi-Wipes.

'You are not going to believe this,' Maria said. With her gloved hands she took a digital video camera out of the front seat and put it on top of the car. 'This was playing when I walked up to the car.' She hit a button, turned the LCD screen to face them.

At first the image was out of focus. Soon it became clear. It was the image of a cross. It was hard to tell on the small screen what the cross was made of, but the closer Jessica looked at it, the more she realized it was made of glass.

'Is that a window?' Jessica asked.

'I'm pretty sure it is,' Maria said. She froze the image, pointed at the screen. 'It looks like this is tinted glass, doesn't it?'

The two detectives looked at each other at the same moment, understanding flowing between them.

'Stained glass,' they said in unison.

'Keep playing it,' Jessica said.

Maria hit the button. The video continued. The stained-glass image of the cruciform began to lose focus again, and Jessica soon realized what was happening. There was an image behind the glass that was starting to come in to focus. A few seconds later she saw what it was, and her heart skipped a beat. There, on the other side of the cross, was a person, perfectly framed, as if on the cross.

There could be no doubt. The person was Kevin Byrne.

Jessica ran back down the street, up the alley. She looked at the side window next to the door that gave entry into the church. There was a cross in the stained glass. It was identical to the crucifix in the video.

The killer had just shot this footage.

FIFTY-FIVE

J ESSICA PACED THE SIDEWALK IN FRONT OF THE CHURCH. THERE WERE police cars everywhere. Dana Westbrook had said that she wanted her back at the Roundhouse on the double.

'Are you okay?' Maria asked.

'I've had better days.' Although Jessica knew she was expected at Eighth and Race any minute, she knew she wouldn't rest until Kevin Byrne was in her sight. 'What I think we should do is –'

The envelope, Jessica thought. *The envelope the woman had dropped off for Byrne.*

The envelope from Father Leone.

Jessica reached into the car, retrieved the envelope from the back seat, tore it open. In it were pages from the Bible, along with other pages, handwritten on old, yellow-edged typing paper.

These were messages from Father Leone. Messages from beyond the grave.

As Jessica's eyes scanned the pages, things began to make a clear, horrifying sense. It was about the seven churches of the Apocalypse:

Unto the angel of the church of Ephesus . . . thou has left thy first love . . .

Cecilia Rollins, Jessica thought.

Unto the angel of the church of Smyrna . . . ye shall have tribulation ten days . . .

Danny Palumbo was in that basement ten days.

To the angel of the church of Pergamos . . . give him a white stone, and in the stone a new name written . . .

Martin Allsop. The white stones. The name of the next crime scene written on a stone.

Unto the angel of the church in Thyatira . . . Jezebel . . . I will cast her into a bed . . .

Michelle Calvin was found on that bloody mattress.

Unto the angel of the church of Sardis . . . I will come unto thee as a thief . . .

DeRon Wilson had his hands cut off.

Jessica found that her own hands were shaking as she looked at the last two entries. The final two churches were Philadelphia and Laodicea.

Her eyes roamed the page, looking for a clue, a thought, a line that might help her penetrate the mind of a killer.

UNTO THE ANGEL OF the church of the Laodiceans . . . I counsel thee to buy of me gold tried in the fire . . . and white raiment . . .

To the angel of the church in Philadelphia . . . he that hath the key of David . . . but do lie . . .

The final page was a single piece of old onion-skin typing paper. On it was a hand-scrawled note from Father Leone, perhaps the last thing he ever wrote. To Jessica, it was just as cryptic as the pages of *Revelation*. It read:

IT WAS A VESTMENT, KEVIN. THE FIRE OF THE HOLY SPIRIT.

What did he mean by this? What vestment?

Jessica considered calling Byrne again, but she knew she would get his voicemail. She looked at her key ring.

'I'll be back,' Jessica said.

'Where are you going?' Maria asked.

'I'm going to Kevin's house.'

'I'm coming with you.'

Jessica glanced at the swarm of PPD personnel descending upon St Simeon's. They had both given their statements, and neither of them were going to be the lead investigator on the case.

'Let's go,' Jessica said.

FIFTY-SIX

Jessica and Maria parked on Third Street, around the corner from Byrne's second-floor apartment. Jessica did not see her partner's car, but that was not unusual. Sometimes he was forced to park more than a block away.

Within a minute they were in front of Byrne's door. Jessica knocked, listened. Silence. She knocked again. They heard no movement within.

Jessica took out the key, gently slid it into the lock, turned it. She opened the door an inch. 'Kevin?'

No answer.

The apartment was dark. The only light was from the green digital clock on the kitchen stove. Jessica flipped the switch, and three lamps came on. The apartment was exactly the way she had seen it the last time she had been there.

'Kevin?'

Nothing. She edged over to the bedroom. Empty. The bathroom was empty, too.

'Jessica,' Maria said.

Jessica crossed the apartment. Maria was standing at the dining-room table. There, neatly arrayed, were three things Kevin Byrne never left home without. His weapon, his shield, and his cell phone. Next to Byrne's phone was a blue flip phone Jessica had not seen before.

She picked up the blue flip phone, navigated the menu.

There were two text messages: One was the address of St Simeon's. The second message made her blood run cold.

IF YOU ENTER THE BUILDING THE BOY WILL DIE.

What boy?

Jessica then picked up Byrne's cell phone. She knew she was invading his privacy, but she had no choice. She checked his voicemail messages, and she was right. Eighty percent of the messages were from her. Then she saw an SMS message with a photo attached.

The subject read: *how u lik me now???!!!*

The accompanying picture was of a young black boy tied to a chair. Jessica looked closely at the boy's face. She knew who it had to be. Gabriel Hightower.

She looked at the last number Byrne had dialed. She wasn't familiar with it. Or was she?

'Do me a favor,' Jessica said.

'Sure,' Maria replied.

'Could you run down to the car and get my portfolio?' Jessica handed the keys to Maria, who was out the door in a flash.

Jessica launched the browser on her phone and did a reverse lookup on the second-to-last number Byrne had called. It was an all-night pharmacy around the corner. She did the same thing for the last number, but hit a dead end. There was no listing.

Maria returned with Jessica's portfolio. Jessica opened it, pulled out the contents. She soon found the item she was looking for. It was a photocopy of a piece of paper they had found in Danny Palumbo's backpack.

Jessica put the paper down on the table, with the maddening feeling that what she was looking for was right in front of her but she could not see it. None of the numbers lined up.

She closed her eyes for a moment, recalled going into Danny's room at Loretta Palumbo's rowhouse. The answer was there. Why couldn't she see it? She recalled the neatly made bed, the empty closet, the magazines arrayed on the shelves, the acrostic number puzzles of which Danny Palumbo was a fan.

Jessica opened her eyes, glanced back at Danny's handwritten square of numbers, looked diagonally, and saw it. It was the same number as Byrne's last phone call. Danny Palumbo had this phone number in his possession.

Jessica looked again at the picture of Gabriel Hightower, and the last piece of the puzzle snapped into place. She crossed the room, found the box containing the framed photograph. She held up the picture of Byrne with Marcus Haines next to the picture of Gabriel Hightower. There could be no mistake.

Gabriel Hightower was Marcus's son. Marcus had taken a bullet meant for Byrne. That's why Byrne was doing all of this.

Jessica put the photograph down. She had no choice. With a trembling hand she picked up Byrne's phone, hit redial, calling the last number Byrne had dialed.

In a moment the phone was answered.

'You've reached the voicemail of Dr Sarah Goodwin . . .'

FIFTY-SEVEN

THE BRIDGEVIEW MOTEL WAS LOCATED JUST A MILE OR SO FROM Philadelphia International Airport, the city's main airport, located in the southwest part of the city. Just a few blocks from both the Delaware River and I-95, the motel was used by the business traveler who wanted two or three hours' sleep between flights, but wanted to avoid the exorbitant rates charged by the big chain hotels.

It was also used by both the city police and county sheriff's department to hold prisoners en route to other locations.

Byrne parked at the far end of the rear parking lot, farthest away from the light. The room in which he was interested was number 209, the nearest room on the end. The curtains were closed, the lights were on.

He got out of the car, crossed the lot, knocked on the door. A few seconds later he saw the curtains part, then heard the chain being moved. The door opened.

'Kevin,' the man said.

'What's up, Tony?'

Anthony Colasanto was a veteran detective, a few years older than Byrne. He had come up in three of the South Philly districts, had spent time in Major Crimes, and now was assigned, through the DA's office, to various details, including protection details.

'What brings you out here?' Colasanto asked.

'Restless night,' Byrne said. 'Plus, you know this was originally my case.'

Colasanto nodded. 'Sure. Of course. Come on in.'

He opened the door wide. Byrne stepped through. Colasanto gave another visual sweep of the parking lot, the surrounding area, then closed, locked, and chained the door.

Byrne took in the room. A queen-sized bed in the center. Beyond that, a small round table, one chair. To the left was a dresser and desk. Atop the dresser was an old 23-inch portable showing the news. Colasanto had a game of solitaire in the works on the table.

Byrne held up the cardboard carry tray he had gotten from Starbucks, containing a pair of large coffees.

'Thought you could use some real coffee.'

'You are a fucking mensch,' Colasanto said. 'Or whatever the Irish call a mensch.'

'I think we call it a mensch, too.'

Byrne took one of the cups from the tray, put it on the table. Next to the cup he placed a handful of creamers, sugar packets, Equal packets, and stirrers. 'I didn't know how you take it,' he said.

'Like my women,' Colasanto replied.

Colasanto opened the coffee, took a small sip. Byrne had waited in the parking lot long enough for the coffee to cool down to a drinkable temperature. Colasanto raised the cup. 'Thanks, buddy.'

Byrne took his coffee, pulled the other chair up to the table. The two men caught up – who retired, who had what ailment, who got divorced.

'Saw that fucking video,' Colasanto said. 'Did I hear this right? That POS in the tape got killed in North Philly tonight?'

'Yeah,' Byrne said. 'Shame.'

'Guess he won't be pressing charges.'

'Not unless there's a DA in hell.'

'I know a few who belong there.'

Byrne laughed. 'When's your relief coming?'

Colasanto looked at his watch. 'Not until seven tomorrow morning.'

Byrne nodded toward the adjoining room, which had its door half open. The room was dark. 'How is it going?'

'Easy tour, Kev,' he said. 'I mean, what's he going to do, right?' Colasanto drained his coffee.

'Do you know the details?'

'Not all of them.'

Byrne told the story from the beginning. He knew he needed a little time. About ten minutes into his routine he saw Colasanto's lids start to droop. Three minutes later the man was out cold. Before he could sag to the floor, Byrne got up, caught the man mid-slide. Byrne then picked him up, put him on the bed. Anthony Colasanto was not a big man, and Byrne handled him with ease.

Byrne took out the small plastic trash bag in his pocket, bagged everything in the room he had touched – the coffee cups, lids, tray, creamers. Unless a federal team did a million-dollar sweep of the room, he had never been here.

He moved over to the windows, parted the curtains an inch or so. The parking lot was exactly the same as it had been when he'd left it.

He stepped into the second bedroom.

'Detective Byrne,' Roland Hannah said. 'It's nice to see you again. If you'll pardon.'

'Not a big fan of irony either, Roland.'

'No. I imagine not.'

'Are you ready?'

Roland Hannah didn't respond. Byrne flipped on the light. Hannah was sitting in a chair at the foot of the bed. He was fully dressed. He was not wearing his amber aviator sunglasses.

'I hope you didn't hurt him,' Roland said.

'He was a police officer,' Byrne replied. 'I don't hurt cops.'

'Just criminals?'

'And those who would have me believe they are not.'

Byrne looked out the back window of the motel room. The lot behind the motel was empty.

'Why have you come for me?' Roland asked.

Byrne said nothing.

Before they left, Byrne took Anthony Colasanto's cell phone and two-way radio, then cut the motel room's phone line. It wouldn't prevent Colasanto from putting the word out when he woke up, but it would slow him down a little. If Byrne knew anything about the pills he had dissolved into Colasanto's coffee – and over the years Kevin Byrne had become quite the expert on sleeping pills – they had a few hours. Which was more than enough time.

Byrne led Roland Hannah to the door. There, he turned and did a quick sweep of the room. He had taken care of everything. He opened the door, checked the sidewalk and parking lot again. Silent and still. He walked the blind man over to his car, unlocked the back door. Roland Hannah slid in.

Byrne handcuffed Hannah to the door handle of the back seat.

Two minutes later, they drove into the night.

FIFTY-EIGHT

BY THE TIME JESSICA AND MARIA REACHED THE ROWHOUSE WHERE Sarah Goodwin kept her private office, there were a half-dozen sector cars in front of the building. The street was blocked off at both ends, and a SWAT team was in the process of deploying on nearby rooftops and fire escapes.

Josh Bontrager, Jessica, and Maria would breach the entrance, accompanied by two SWAT officers. The entry would be a no-knock, hard entry. This was a suspect in multiple murders.

As they prepared for the breach, the three detectives secured their Kevlar vests. Jessica silently berated herself for not putting it together before. Danny Palumbo, Adria Rollins, Michelle Calvin, and Martin Allsop were all prime candidates to have been analyzed by a psychiatrist before court proceedings. Sarah Goodwin did consulting work for both the county and city law enforcement agencies. Jessica knew that Byrne had seen her professionally, and it was very likely he had opened up about Gabriel and DeRon Wilson, knowing – or at least believing at the time – it was all confidential.

Jessica also knew that the video camera they had found in the reporter's car was either on its way to or had already arrived at the crime lab. Maria had tried to delay it as long as possible, but there was only so much she could do. Any second now the criminalists would place Byrne at the scene at St Simeon's, and questions would start to be asked.

As Jessica approached the door she scanned the area. She did not see Dana Westbrook on scene. This was a good thing. Jessica had a lot of explaining to do to her boss, and she was not prepared to do any of it yet.

The SWAT officer with the ram took up position on the small porch. He looked to his two fellow officers. The other two SWAT officers carried AR-15 assault weapons. On a silent three, the ram hit the door, blasting it almost off its hinges.

'Philadelphia Police!' one of the SWAT officers yelled. The two men rolled into the front room. One of them flipped on the light. After a few seconds:

'Front room clear!'

The two officers methodically went room to room in the rowhouse, and ultimately found no one. The only space left to clear was a closet in the main office.

Her weapon aimed low, Jessica positioned herself to the left of the closet door. She was flanked on her right by one of the SWAT officers. The officer raised his weapon, pointed it at the closet. He made eye contact with Jessica. The second SWAT officer pulled open the door.

The dead body in the closet was that of a white woman in her forties. She wore a lab coat over a dark blue pantsuit, no shoes. There were no visible wounds on her face or hands, no blood, no apparent trauma. Heart racing, Jessica knelt down, put two fingers to the woman's neck, found no pulse. Before she stood up Jessica noticed the edge of a plastic nametag peeking out from behind the lapel of the lab coat. Although she should have put on a latex glove, she had no time. She gently turned over the lapel. The nametag clipped to the dead woman's coat read: SARAH GOODWIN, MD.

'*Shit!*' Jessica yelled.

As the SWAT officers and detectives stood down, Jessica began to pace the small office. This did not make sense. Worse than that, she knew how it was going to look for Byrne. Sarah Goodwin was his psychiatrist, and now she was dead.

'Jess.'

It was Maria Caruso calling her from the waiting room. Jessica walked out there. Maria was looking at a framed photograph on the wall. In the picture two women sat on the edge of the desk in the main office. The caption read: *Dr Sarah Goodwin and her assistant Antonia Block open a new office.*

Jessica looked at Dr Goodwin, then the other woman in the picture. She knew her, but not as Antonia Block. Jessica recognized the woman in the photograph as Mara Reuben, the woman she had interviewed across the street from the St Adelaide's scene.

She was looking into the face of a murderer.

Jessica pulled the piece of paper out of her pocket, the one she had kept from the envelope Father Leone had sent Byrne. She looked at the hand-scrawled note.

IT WAS A VESTMENT, KEVIN. THE FIRE OF THE HOLY SPIRIT.

Jessica knew where Byrne was.

FIFTY-NINE

HE IS MUCH BIGGER THAN SHE IMAGINED. OR MAYBE SHE JUST SEES
him that way. She thinks it must have been this way for the Apostles as well.

*They are sitting in a circle surrounded by seven candles. Ruby, the boy,
the detective. There is one empty chair.*

'What should I call you?' the detective asks.

'Ruby,' she says. 'I want you to call me Ruby. Will you do that?'

'Yes.'

'It's been so long since anyone has called me that.'

'Your father was Elijah Longstreet?'

'Daddy.'

'You are also Mara Reuben?'

'Yes.'

'And also Antonia.'

Ruby smiles. 'Antonia Block.'

The detective nods. 'From Antonius Block. In The Seventh Seal.'

*'My little conceit,' she says. 'I was afraid you would see through that
when you came to Dr Goodwin's office.'*

'The last name wasn't on your nametag.'

'Of course.'

*When she had gotten the job as the medical assistant she didn't know
much about the computer system. It didn't take long to learn. Forging the
prescriptions from Dr Goodwin was much easier. Eventually Dr Goodwin*

allowed her to call the pharmacies using the office code. This night, when the detective needed the sleeping pills, it was effortless.

'These people,' the detective says. 'The victims. You knew their psychiatric histories.'

'Yes.'

'Why did you select them?'

There were many answers to this. 'We selected them because they all made a deal with the devil.'

The detective looks at his hands for a moment, then back at Ruby. His eyes are cold jade stones in the candlelight. 'And you collected what the devil was owed.'

'Yes. It was the only way to rid my son of the demons he has carried all these years.'

Night after night, after Ruby prayed, she had read the transcripts of Dr Goodwin's consultations with her patients. She had been privy to all their thoughts, their desires, their shame, their guilt. She had seen inside their souls, all of them children of disobedience. The young girl had asked the devil to stop the abuse she was suffering at the hands of the building's superintendent, the coupling that had produced the baby. Ruby had visited the building earlier in the day and granted Adria's wish. Edward Turchek would no longer abuse anyone.

Ruby did not hurt Adria Rollins.

The young man who was a police officer, the one called Daniel, had told Dr Goodwin that he would do anything if his HIV did not become full-blown AIDS. It did not. He paid.

The old pedophile said he would do anything to not have to go back to prison. He got probation. He, too, paid.

'Why DeRon Wilson?' the detective asks.

'Who?'

'The man at St Simeon's. The man who took Gabriel.'

'A thief is a thief,' Ruby says. 'He made his deal the moment he held out his hand for golden coins. When you told Dr Goodwin about your relationship to the boy, and why you were trying to save him, we knew you would do anything for him.'

The detective glances at the young boy, and back to her. 'So, this has all been about the preacher?'

'Yes.'

'All of this was designed to get him out of prison?'

'Not all of it.'

The detective glances around the vast expanse of the basement room. *'And there are just two churches left?'*

'Yes. Just two.'

'Will we be going somewhere?'

'No,' Ruby says. *'This church merged with another years ago. It must all end in this place, at this time.'*

Ruby considers the detective for a few moments. She has seen his face over the years, in her mind, in her prayers. The face of St Michael the Archangel. There is no doubting his strength.

'You are the last of your kind,' she says. *'You are the last saint.'*

The man shakes his head. *'No.'*

Ruby stands, listens to the ancient stone walls. Something is happening. She feels a stirring within. *'You have brought him here?'*

'Yes,' the detective says. *'He's in the next room.'*

'My son is here, too. It is time they met as men. A boy should know his father, don't you think?'

The detective says nothing.

Ruby smoothes her hair, then instantly berates herself for this small weakness. It has been so many years since she has seen the Preacher. The last time was when he was standing on that carrousel.

Frailty, thy name is woman.

'Please bring him to me,' she says.

The detective stands, crosses the room, opens the door, and steps into the darkness.

SIXTY

BYRNE LIFTED ROLAND HANNAH TO HIS FEET. HE WALKED HIM ACROSS the large basement room, toward the candlelight. Hannah's hands were bound behind him, his mouth gagged.

When they reached the circle of light Byrne uncuffed the man's hands, sat him on the old wooden chair. He removed the gag from Hannah's mouth, sat down next to him. Byrne looked at Gabriel. The boy was crying.

While he was gone the woman removed her dark coat. Dressed in a flowing white gown, she now sat next to Gabriel. Around her waist was a corded white belt. In her lap were a pair of golden knives with razor-sharp edges.

I counsel thee to buy of me gold tried in the fire . . . and white raiment.

Roland Hannah cocked his head, as if he'd suddenly heard something.

'Ruby,' he said.

Mary Longstreet blushed. 'Preacher,' she replied. 'How did you know it was me?'

Roland Hannah smiled. His teeth were small and yellowed. 'A flower does not lose its bouquet, does it?'

'Only when it dies, I reckon.'

'Even then it lingers.'

Mary Longstreet reddened even more deeply. She remained silent.

'You have become a woman,' Roland said.

'A long time ago.'

'How long has it been?'

Mary Longstreet looked at the floor for a moment. 'A spell, Preacher.'

Byrne noticed a slight change in the woman's accent. The West Virginia had begun to creep back into her voice.

'And your boy?' Roland asked.

'The devil is still inside him.'

Roland Hannah said nothing. Without the dark amber glasses, the man's eye sockets were deep, scabrous holes in the candlelight.

They sat, the four of them, in a circle. Every so often Byrne would glance at Gabriel. The boy looked small, and terribly frightened. His hands were shaking.

Mary Longstreet gestured to a room off the large space that was the basement of the cathedral. 'That room yonder,' she said to Byrne. 'It must happen there.'

'Beneath the sacrarium,' Byrne said.

'Yes, sir.'

The sacrarium, Byrne now knew, was the sink in which all consecrated items had to be washed. What flowed from these sinks could not be treated as other waste waters. The marks on the lampposts were made from the earth beneath the churches, washed by decades and centuries of Christ's blood and flesh.

Mary Longstreet stood, put both knives through the corded belt. Byrne saw that one of the knives sliced through the thin white fabric. A blood rosette bloomed. She had cut herself. She didn't seem to feel it.

As she crossed behind Roland Hannah, Byrne noticed that she now had something else in her hand. At first, in the dim light, he didn't know what it was. Soon he was able to focus. It was an antique hairbrush.

'Remember how I used to brush your hair, Preacher?' she asked.

To Byrne there was no question that this woman standing in front of him – a woman who had killed at least five people, a woman who now had a pair of razor-sharp daggers within reach – was regressing before his eyes. Her body language had become more adolescent, her voice had risen a half-octave. Her accent was becoming more Appalachian with every word. She pronounced the word *hair* as *har*. She was returning to the age she was when she met Roland Hannah for the first time.

'I do, Mary Elizabeth,' Roland said. 'You still have your mammaw's brush?'

Mary Elizabeth, Byrne thought. Not *Ruby*. Hannah was trying to manipulate her.

'Yes, Preacher. Save for my boy, it's all I have left. Ever what I've done, I've done for him.'

She began to slowly brush Roland Hannah's hair.

'Your hair's gone right gray, Preacher. White, some.'

Roland Hannah smiled. 'I wouldn't know.'

Byrne looked at the brush, and understood. Mary Longstreet had kept it all these years. It was from this brush she'd gotten Roland Hannah's hair, evidence she used as bookmarks in the missals. Evidence she used to get him out of prison, and into this chair.

'It's still pretty, Preacher. Y'all had the prettiest hair. For a boy.'

She continued to brush Roland Hannah's hair in long, careful strokes. Byrne made eye contact with Gabriel, who seemed to be edging off his chair. Byrne saw the boy look into the darkness of the basement, toward the stairs. He was getting ready to run. When Gabriel looked back at Byrne, Byrne shook his head. It was too risky. Mary Longstreet was just a few feet away, and the knives were very sharp. He'd never make it.

Still, Gabriel got ever closer to the edge of his seat.

When Mary Longstreet finished brushing Roland Hannah's hair, she placed the hairbrush on her chair, then drew one of the knives from her waistband, the dagger tipped with blood. One by one she extinguished the candles. When she had snuffed all but two, she positioned herself behind Gabriel.

'Ruby?' Byrne asked.

'Yes, sir?'

'I want you to do something for me.'

'All right,' she said. 'If I can.'

Byrne glanced at Roland Hannah, then back at the woman. 'I want you to take me instead.'

She looked at Byrne with curiosity. 'You? The devil's not in you.'

In that moment Byrne felt the weight of his own sins, just as he knew that it didn't matter anymore. None of it – the job, the visions, the anguish over the city he loved, the sadness that in all that time he had not made a difference. The only person in this room who mattered was Gabriel.

'You don't know the things I've done,' Byrne said.

The woman stared at Byrne for a long moment. She lay the dagger gently on Roland Hannah's right shoulder. 'Don't you understand, detective?'

'Understand what?'

'The Preacher is Philadelphia,' she said. 'He's the sixth church of the Apocalypse.'

Byrne saw the candlelight dance on the keened edge of the blade. He had to keep her talking. 'I do understand. But what of the *last* church?'

Mary Longstreet's eyes softened, and Byrne knew. *She* was the last church. When Roland Hannah was dead she would take her own life.

'I can't let you do this,' Byrne said.

Whatever softness had come to Mary Longstreet was instantly replaced by a red rage.

'*You* have no say in the matter, sir.' In an instant she stepped behind Gabriel, put the blade to his throat. 'Maybe the *boy* is Philadelphia. Maybe *this* is how it will be.'

'Don't,' Byrne said.

She flipped the knife, reversing it in her grip. It seemed to be a long-practiced, expert move. She touched it to the boy's forehead. 'I will write upon him the name of my God, and the name of the city of my God, which is new Jerusalem.'

For a moment Mary Longstreet's words echoed off the stone basement walls, unanswered. Then:

'He that hath an ear, let him hear what the Spirit saith.'

Mary Longstreet's eyes flashed at the sound of the voice. It was Roland Hannah's.

'You! You don't talk, Preacher,' she said. 'You don't talk at *all*.'

'We can be together again, Mary Elizabeth,' Roland said. 'Don't you see? We can leave this wretched place.'

'No, sir.'

'We can found a new church. A church of our own. Together.'

Byrne saw Mary Longstreet's eyes lose focus. For a moment it seemed she couldn't hear or see anything, that her vacant stare was cast inward, at a place back in time.

'You can be my eyes,' Roland said.

Roland Hannah stood up, took a hesitating step forward, his hands stretched in front of him. Mary Longstreet didn't move, didn't try to stop him.

'You've always been special to me, Mary Elizabeth. You know that. Ever since I set eyes on you that first time in Brandonville. Remember?'

Mary Longstreet's hands began to tremble. Byrne saw the tip of the blade pierce the skin on Gabriel's forehead. A trickle of blood ran down the boy's face in a twisted rivulet.

Byrne knew he had to act. He stood up, slowly walked across the circle. He held out his hand. 'Ruby?'

The woman said nothing.

'I will kill the Preacher for you.'

'That is a task for my son,' she said. 'He has waited a long time.' She put the blade to Gabriel's throat. 'I'd thank you kindly to sit down now, sir.'

As Byrne took a step back he noticed movement in the vastness of the basement, shadows growing on the candlelit walls.

Jessica and Maria Caruso were in the room, guns drawn. Byrne saw other figures in the darkness. There had to be a dozen officers.

Mary Longstreet saw them, too.

In one fluid motion Byrne spun and knocked the knife from Mary Longstreet's hand. Just as quickly she drew the other dagger. She danced to her left with blinding speed and drew the blade across Roland Hannah's throat. Hannah's body jerked and thrashed, spastic in its death throes. He put his hands to his throat, but he couldn't stanch the bleeding. As blood spurted across the circle, extinguishing one of the remaining candles, Mary Longstreet flung herself at Gabriel.

Byrne dove in front of the boy. The dagger entered the right side of Byrne's stomach, slashing clean through. The pain was white fire.

But it didn't stop Byrne. He reached for the hand that held the weapon and tried to turn the woman around.

In the madness of the moment Byrne saw Jessica run toward them. Hands slicked with blood, Byrne lost his grip on the woman. Mary Longstreet pivoted, regained her footing, and slashed wildly at Jessica. As Byrne fell to the floor he saw the wound open in Jessica's shoulder, above her Kevlar vest.

No, Byrne thought.

No.

Then, as blackness descended, and the last of his will fell away, a hellish fury came to the cathedral basement. Gunfire roared. The smell of cordite and blood filled the air.

For Kevin Byrne it all faded to a distant past, a time when he was just a young boy, and these walls held more mysteries than answers.

SIXTY-ONE

J ESSICA COULDN'T HEAR. THE GUNFIRE HAD STOLEN ALL SOUND. SHE was on her back, saw feet moving around her, heard muffled shouts and commands. She looked to her right and saw the body of Roland Hannah, his throat savaged. There could be no question. He was dead.

Jessica tried to sit up but the pain was too great. She saw Gabriel on his side, just a few feet away, his face streaked with blood. She did not know where the woman was. But right now neither of them were her priority. In the fog and confusion she found Byrne. He too was covered in blood, but not moving.

Jessica gathered all her energy and crawled across the cold stone floor.

With the last of her strength she reached Byrne, put two fingers to his neck. There was a pulse, but it was faint. She saw steam rising from his open wound, felt the life force leaving his body. She held him close.

In the distance she heard the sirens.

'Hold on, partner,' she whispered. 'Hold on.'

Jessica closed her eyes, waiting, and in that moment heard the heartbeat of angels.

SIXTY-TWO

WHEN CHRIST APPEARED ON PATMOS, AN ISLAND OFF THE COAST OF Greece, he sent his disciple John to visit the seven churches in Asia, and said:

'Write on a scroll what you see and send it to the seven churches: to Ephesus, and to Smyrna, and to Pergamos, and to Thyatira, and to Sardis, and to Philadelphia, and to Laodicea.'

Seven churches. She is the last.

Ruby sits in the final pew at St Gedeon's, the same place her boy sat so many years ago. In her hand is a birth certificate, dotted with blood and tears. Now they would know his name.

Gedeon Mark Longstreet.

He would no longer be The Boy in the Red Coat. He would no longer be a cipher. When he died that day, in that clinic in Doylestown, she had spirited his small body away, and come to Philadelphia. She brought him to this church, the namesake of his patron saint.

She sat in the dark that night, sewing together the coat made from the Preacher's vestment, the item Carson Tatum had gotten for her, vowing to one day return. She had specifically asked for the red vestment, the fire of the Holy Spirit.

Her lifeblood spreads on her white raiment. In the gloom of this final dusk she sees the men, guns raised, slowly approaching. They will never reach her. She glances down, at the bullet wound in her chest.

It is time.

Mary Elizabeth Longstreet closes her eyes and, like her son surely had so many years earlier, feels a peace blossom within her, and thus blessed, steps into the beyond.

REVELATION

'Forgive, and you will be forgiven.'

– LUKE, 6:37

As you remember it, the rehabilitation process was slow and painful. Jessica Balzano was out of the hospital in five days. She fully recovered – with the help of a great deal of physical therapy – and was back on the job in three weeks.

Kevin Byrne's recovery took a little longer. The doctors said that it might be better if he retired, all things considered. There was a great deal of speculation about this throughout the unit, and the department as a whole, but one day in late-summer Kevin Byrne showed up for day work – a bag of TastyKakes in tow – and within two hours was out on a new assignment with Jessica.

They said his injury caused him to be a little more reflective, to take a little more time before approaching a door.

You never noticed it.

The body of Mary Elizabeth Longstreet was cremated and interred on a shelf in the medical examiner's office. There was no family to contact. There was no service. Mary Elizabeth had legally changed her name to Antonia Block in 2003, and gotten the job at Dr Sarah Goodwin's office three years later. In her small apartment in South Philadelphia investigators found dozens of bound volumes of patient histories and transcripts. The histories of six patients had been highlighted.

One of Dr Goodwin's patients, a man who had been to prison twice for armed robbery, was targeted by Mary Longstreet. He was replaced in her mad scheme by DeRon Wilson, a crime of opportunity.

Investigators also found a great many other things. In Mary Longstreet's closets were full sets of clothing, outfits for a boy of ten, twelve, fifteen, as well as one for a fully grown adult. Each was a black suit, white shirt, and black tie. None had ever been worn.

In the closet they also found a long coat with a pointed hood, a coat investigators determined Mary Longstreet herself wore in the surveillance video taken at St Adelaide's.

In a deposition, the county detective tasked with guarding Roland Hannah – one Anthony James Colasanto – stated that he had mixed up his medications that night, and as a result had fallen asleep. He figured that while he was passed out Mary Longstreet kidnapped his prisoner and took Roland Hannah to St Gedeon's. Detective Kevin Byrne had nothing to add. No one in the Philadelphia District Attorney's office pursued the matter any further.

They say Kevin Byrne was for a long time obsessed with the evidence collected from St Ignatius's, the former chapel in which Michelle Calvin had been found brutally murdered, her body posed on a bloodied mattress. They say Byrne pored over the evidence for weeks, looking for a clue he was certain would be there, a clue designed to lead investigators to the final church. One day he found it. It was on the mattress tag:

UNDER PENALTY OF LAW THIS TAG NOT TO BE REMOVED EXCEPT BY CONSUMER

All but six of the letters had been carefully painted out with Michelle Calvin's blood, leaving a single word.

GEDEON

Father Thomas Leone was buried in Holy Cross cemetery in Lansdowne. At the request of Kevin Byrne, the priest's headstone was crafted from one of the keystones of St Gedeon's Church, which was demolished a few weeks after the cases were closed.

The final police report, the summary of events that told the official story of what happened during that terrible rampage thirty years ago, contained a detail that changed your life forever. According to ballistics, the bullet that killed Mary Elizabeth Longstreet came from your weapon.

As you consider this ancient history, which is still such a fresh wound in your heart, a long shadow falls across the aisle. You turn, and see him for the first time in thirty years.

Gabriel Hightower has grown to be a big man, now just over forty. His recovery was swift, but then again he had only been eleven years old the night of that tragedy. The only reminder of it, at least on the outside, was a small, crescent-shaped scar on his forehead.

With the help of counseling Gabriel returned to school, and graduated at the top of his class. He went on to study architecture at Penn State.

No one knew whose money helped pay for the schooling. There was an unconfirmed rumor that it was money taken from DeRon Wilson's brother Carter on the night Wilson died.

Gabriel graduated with honors, and got a job with a prestigious architectural firm in Center City. He is now married with two teen-aged sons of his own, Francis and Kevin.

'Detective Caruso,' he says.

As he takes you in his arms, you realize no one has called you *detective* in almost thirty years. For the past three decades it has been simply Maria.

You sit in silence for a few moments, letting the years catch up. Gabriel Hightower is in his prime. You are a late-middle-aged woman. For some reason his kind eyes don't find you that way. Before speaking, he reaches into his pocket, takes out something, hands it to you. It is a small, beautifully folded origami swan.

'This is for me?' You have been collecting swans for years – ceramics, paintings, charms.

'Yes,' he says.

'How did you know?'

Gabriel Hightower grins. It is a heart-rending smile, sad and warm at the same time. 'Your necklace,' he says. 'I saw it that night.'

You hold the swan, take a moment, wonder how to begin. You have waited thirty years.

It is time.

'I got the call at just after six that night,' you say. 'We were to stake out three churches, the last one being St Simeon's. It was so cold. Do you remember how cold it was that night?'

He smiles, nods, waits.

As the church once again falls silent you take Gabriel's hand.

And tell your story.

ACKNOWLEDGEMENTS

With deepest gratitude to:

Meg Ruley, Peggy Gordijn, Jane Berkey, and everyone at the Jane Rotrosen Agency;

Kate Elton, Georgina Hawtrey-Woore, Susan Sandon and the team at Random House UK;

Dominic Montanari, Kathleen Franco MD, Sergeant Joanne Beres, Rick Jackson, Brian Zoldessy, Ramon Alvarez, Robert Kaminski, and Lou Baldwin;

Mike Driscoll, Pat Ghegan, Dominic Aspite, and the rest of the Philly crew;

The city and people of Philadelphia. While the places of worship mentioned in this book are based in fact, their names, locations, and dark secrets revealed within, are fiction.